# *Hazel*

## JULIE HEARN

### OXFORD
UNIVERSITY PRESS

# OXFORD
### UNIVERSITY PRESS

Great Clarendon Street, Oxford OX2 6DP

Oxford University Press is a department of the University of Oxford.
It furthers the University's objective of excellence in research, scholarship,
and education by publishing worldwide in

Oxford   New York

Auckland   Cape Town   Dar es Salaam   Hong Kong   Karachi
Kuala Lumpur   Madrid   Melbourne   Mexico City   Nairobi
New Delhi   Shanghai   Taipei   Toronto

With offices in

Argentina   Austria   Brazil   Chile   Czech Republic   France   Greece
Guatemala   Hungary   Italy   Japan   Poland   Portugal   Singapore
South Korea   Switzerland   Thailand   Turkey   Ukraine   Vietnam

Oxford is a registered trade mark of Oxford University Press
in the UK and in certain other countries

British Library Cataloguing in Publication Data

Data available

ISBN: 978-0-19-279214-3

1 3 5 7 9 10 8 6 4 2

Typeset in Meridien by TnQ Books and Journals Pvt. Ltd.,
Chennai, India

Printed in Great Britain by Cox & Wyman Ltd, Reading, Berkshire

For Phil, who went with me to the island, and for Debbie and Si who were already there.

'When we are born, we cry that we are come
To this great stage of fools'

*King Lear*

'One han' can't clap'
*No man is an island, no man can stand alone.*

Antiguan proverb

# CHAPTER 1

'*Hey . . . Are you crazy or what? Come back!*'
'*What's she doing? What in the Devil's name is that woman playing at?*'

'*She must have taken leave of her senses . . .*'

'*Oh no . . . Oh, Cyril, I daren't watch . . .*'

'*It's heading straight for her!*'

'*She's not budging. I can't believe she's . . . Oooof! Keep your eyes closed, old thing. Lean on me, that's right, but whatever you do DON'T LOOK! Ladies . . . all of you . . . Little girl, avert your eyes.*'

Hazel Louise Mull-Dare, being very nearly thirteen years old, objected to anyone calling her a little girl. Under less shocking circumstances she would have fixed the man on her right—the Cyril one—with the evil eye. She might even have told him, in her iciest tones, not to be so rude. But it would be insensitive, she knew, to make an issue out of her relative grown-upness when someone had just been trampled by a horse. And trampled so badly, by the look of it, that she probably wasn't going to see the sun go down, never mind her own next birthday.

'*Oh, Cyril! What's happening? Is it . . . ghastly?*'

Hazel continued to stare at the woman lying out on the turf like a big, broken doll. It was ghastly, all right, and had

1

happened so *fast*. Too fast for her to make any sense of it until her pulse, and her thoughts, stopped racing.

*Serves her right*, was her eventual response followed, a bit later, by *poor thing*.

'She's not dead is she, Cyril?'

Hazel had never seen a dead body before, or anyone's blood but her own. It was . . . it was . . .

She raised herself up, on the tips of her new shoes, swaying with the effort to see.

The man on her left caught hold of her arm. Had the Cyril-person been so presumptuous Hazel would have stamped on his toes. Hard. But the man on her left was her father so it was all right.

'You're not going to faint, are you, pet?'

Hazel shook her head and settled back on her heels, only faintly ashamed of her desire to know precisely where the woman had been kicked, and if there were any bits of brain on her clothes.

Her own wits were recovering nicely—enough to re-call, in some detail, precisely what had happened: she had nipped under the rail; a thin woman in a dark coat which had flapped as she strode out onto the course; then the horses had come—thundering round the curve one . . . two . . . three . . . And the woman in the coat could have got out of their way; could have ducked back under the rail, no harm done. But no. As calm as you like she had faced what was coming, one arm raised as if the thor-oughbred galloping straight at her was a bus that would stop, or a donkey plodding wearily down a beach.

And in that tiny space of time—shorter than it would take to clear a throat, pick up a cup, or stroke a cat from head to tail—Hazel had known for certain that this woman was in total command of what she was doing. That, for her, this was not a sudden act of madness but a moment of perfect glory.

*Her own fault, then. Definitely her own stupid fault.*

People behind began pushing and jostling, pressing Hazel's tummy up against the rail.

'Hey!' her father shouted back at them. 'Steady on.'

Then the crush eased as some of the people pushed all the way forward and ran, shouting, onto the course. None of them bothered to look right before they ran, or to listen out for the drumming of hooves. *Stupid twits*, Hazel thought. *Serve them right if a big old straggler came charging round that corner RIGHT NOW.*

'It may not be as awful as it looks, pet,' her father said. 'I think he's coming round.'

He was talking about the jockey, Hazel realized. The one whose horse had reared up and sent the woman flying with one brutal clobber of its hooves. The jockey had fallen, too, but more neatly than the woman, as if he had rehearsed it.

'You're right,' she heard the man called Cyril say. 'That's one lucky chappie out there. And that horse of his knew what to do: get up, avoid the bodies, and keep right on running. Could be it was lamed, though. You reckon they'll have to shoot it?'

Hazel's father said he didn't know. He squeezed Hazel's arm, in case the thought of a horse being shot was Too Much For Her Delicate Senses.

'Bad luck if they do,' said Cyril. 'Which one was it, by the way? I missed the colours in all the kerfuffle.'

3

Hazel's father said it had been the King's horse, Anmer, that had struck the woman, and thrown its rider to the ground. He sounded mournful, as if Anmer had been human, and a personal friend.

'Really?' Cyril whistled through his teeth. 'The *King's* horse. Bad luck . . . '

They were talking over Hazel's hat. It was a very pretty hat, with pink roses on the brim, but having it leaned over was making Hazel feel more like a garden hedge than a young lady.

She stood up on tiptoe again, partly to make herself less hedge-like, but mostly to keep up with what was going on.

People were swarming all over the course. Swarming and yelling and hiding the woman's body from view. Most of them looked, to Hazel, like ordinary spectators—from the lower classes, most of them, and with no clear idea at all of what to do for the best. Then two men appeared, carrying a stretcher. Just the one stretcher though, for just the one victim.

*Where's hers?* Hazel wondered, as the injured jockey got borne away.

The crowd around the woman had shifted, to let the stretcher-bearers through. They re-formed immediately, into a gawping huddle, but not before Hazel had noticed that the only people attending to the woman's injuries were policemen.

'Hello . . . what's happening now?' said one of the voices above her hat.

And there, no more than a couple of yards away, was a man going berserk. 'Are you satisfied?' he was bellowing, right into the face of a woman standing next to him. 'Are

4

you?' And then he raised what looked like a truncheon and began striking the woman's shoulders . . . her arms . . . her neck . . . the top of her head . . .

Hazel felt a thrill in her stomach which went away once she realized that the weapon being used was only a rolled-up newspaper. Such fury though! The man's face was puce with it, and he was spitting for King and Country.

'How far do you think this will get you, eh?' he roared, bashing the woman with the day's headlines again . . . and again . . . and again. 'You and your lot? What possible good will it do your cause, you ignorant . . . misguided . . . *invert!*'

Cyril's lady friend squeaked, just above Hazel's ear. She had opened her eyes, finally, but was clutching her Cyril as if the whole world had gone barmy and she herself might be trampled on, hit, or called a nasty name any moment now.

Hazel waited, with growing interest, for someone to confront the furious man and make him stop. But nobody moved a muscle, unless it was to get a better view. The woman being attacked seemed almost resigned to it. Perhaps, Hazel thought, she was the man's wife, although that didn't really excuse him from lashing out at her in a public place, particularly when everyone watching had witnessed enough horror for one day. And what was the thing he had called her? She was sure she had heard it correctly, but it wasn't a word she recognized. Not as an insult, anyway.

The woman raised her elbows, to protect her eyes.

And although being swiped with a rolled-up news-paper was nowhere near as dangerous as being kicked by a fast-moving animal, it seemed to Hazel the more uncomfortable thing for people to have to watch—perhaps because it was lasting longer and because this man, unlike the King's horse, could have controlled himself.

Suddenly, as suddenly as he had started, the man ran out of steam. 'Go on,' he spat, lowering the newspaper and jerking his thumb towards the nearest exit. 'Clear off. You're not wanted here.'

The woman's hair was all messed up, whacked loose from its pins by a flurry of blows. Her face was chalky-white but oddly defiant as she scanned the faces of those closest to her in the crowd.

For a split second she looked straight at Hazel. And only then did she falter, her face flushing and her shoulders sagging as she admitted some private defeat and bent to pick up . . . what? Hazel couldn't see. But whatever it was got bundled away under the woman's coat before she began moving—scurrying—away through the crowd with her head down and pins poking like thorns through the disorder of her hair.

'Good riddance,' Hazel's father muttered.

'What?'

Hazel looked up so fast that her hat slid off her head, tightening the ribbon at her throat. It wasn't like her father to be churlish, particularly towards women. It would have been more in his nature, surely, to have leapt to this one's defence.

'What do you mean, Daddy?' she said. 'Who is that woman? Do we know her?'

'Never mind,' her father replied, in a tone Hazel recognized as the one that Brooked No Argument. 'And put that hat on properly, pet. You don't want to catch the sun.'

The Cyril person and his lady friend were dithering over whether to get the next train back to London or wait for further announcements about the race.

'D'you think they'll write the whole thing off?' Cyril wondered. 'Out of respect?' It wasn't clear to Hazel whether he meant for the fallen horse, the injured jockey, or the trampled woman.

Hazel's father said he very much doubted it. He was looking glum, and so was Cyril, which Hazel took for a sure sign that the horses they'd backed had run about as fast and as well as clowns in baggy trousers.

'Come along, pet,' her father said. 'No point hanging around. Let's find the Old Girl and go home.'

By Old Girl he meant their motor car—his pride and joy. Most people, when he said this, assumed he was talking about his wife. Only Hazel understood that 'Old Girl', with its clear intimations of something homely and reliable, in no way described her mother.

She looked back at the course. The trampled woman had been taken away and there was nothing more to see.

The Cyril person tipped his hat as Hazel and her father took their leave. His lady friend was still all of a dither, but remembered her manners enough to smile and say: 'Goodbye, little child. I do *hope* you won't have bad dreams tonight.'

The look she got in return could have wilted a flower.

The Old Girl was hot to the touch and smelt of baking leather. For a while, as he followed the signs out of Epsom, Hazel's father was very quiet.

'Daddy—was it the King's horse you had your money on?' Hazel asked him. 'Did you change your mind, at the last minute?' He was always doing that—getting a sudden hunch, just before the race began, and betting accordingly. Sometimes he told Hazel he'd done it and sometimes he didn't. Sometimes he cheered the right horse on, and sometimes he yelled for the one he'd changed his mind about, depending which one was in the lead. It meant that Hazel was never quite sure if they were on a winning streak or not. Most of the time, she couldn't help thinking, they weren't.

'Never mind,' she said, when her question went unanswered. 'Some you win, some you lose. It's all even-stevens in the end.'

He smiled, then, but winced, too, as if her words (which were originally his) had hurt as well as cheered him.

Then: 'Best we say nothing to mother,' he said. 'About what happened back there.'

Hazel was waving, majestically, at two small boys standing up ahead on a garden gate.

'Why not?' she wanted to know.

Her father parped the horn, to amuse the small boys as the Old Girl slid past in a cloud of peppery dust.

'It might worry her,' he said. 'And then *you* wouldn't be allowed to go gallivanting around the countryside with me any more. In fact, best say nothing at all about where we've been today. We'll pretend we went to the zoo. Minty sweet?'

Hazel put the humbug in her mouth. She knew full well, and wanted to say, that reports of people getting trampled and attacked at the Epsom Derby would barely

8

register with her mother—although she would certainly be upset about the injured horse. But she wasn't supposed to talk while sucking a sweet, in case it fell down her gullet and choked her to death. And it would be bad manners, she knew, to crunch.

By the time the sweet was finished her father was humming the 'Bees-Wax Rag' and parping the horn to the beat (*dum dah, dum dah, dummitty dum de dum dah PARP! Dum PARP dah, dum PARP dah* . . . ). The horn was meant to sound like a trumpet and Hazel was supposed to giggle. She was in no mood, though, to play that old game, and her father's own heart wasn't in it either, she could tell.

'You'll have to say,' she said. 'About the zoo.'

'I will,' he replied. 'Don't worry, pet. I know it's a lie, but it's only a little one, and she probably won't even ask.'

'I hope not,' Hazel fretted, for she hated lies, even little ones, and dreaded the thought of being put on the spot.

'That woman,' she said, changing the subject, 'the one the King's horse banged into. Do you think she's dead?'

Her father sighed. Then he took a hand off the Old Girl's wheel and patted Hazel's arm.

'Try not to think about it,' he told her. 'What's done is done.'

Hazel looked out of the window, at hedges and trees, and at the smaller roads, winding off and away—*there and gone, there and gone, there and gone*. The Old Girl was picking up speed now that they were through the little villages and onto the London road. If someone were to step out in front of *them* right now it would be a terrible thing. A

9

dreadful, messy thing. Would that person bounce off the bonnet, Hazel wondered, or go under the wheels and end up like pastry—rolled flat?

'I believe,' she said, 'that she did it on purpose, that woman. I believe she *threw* herself to her doom.'

'Nonsense!'

Alarmed by the harshness of her father's tone, Hazel swivelled round to look at him. His profile was as stern as a Roman emperor's and both his hands were clenched tightly round the steering wheel as if to stop it spinning like a firework.

'Most likely,' he added, in a more normal voice, 'she thought it was safe to cross. An unfortunate accident, that's all it was, pet. A tragic miscalculation. So no more gloomy supposings; and definitely not a word to your mother about where we've been. All right? That's the ticket. Another mint?'

He went back to humming his dance tune, only less merrily and without parping the horn.

Hazel closed her eyes. The mint she hadn't wanted rasped against the inside of her mouth as she bullied it with her tongue and resisted the urge to crunch. She was right about the trampled woman. She knew she was. Not about her being dead, necessarily, but about it having been deliberate. Wilful.

In her mind she saw, again, the kick and the fall. The woman had resembled an ungainly bird, flying through the air like that with her black coat billowing. A stoned crow. A smashed rook. A blackbird hit by a pea-shooter. Just like all of those, except for a sudden flash of colours— green, mauve, and white—beneath the dark coat.

10

It was odd, Hazel thought, that the woman had worn a heavy coat on such a beautiful summer's day. Perhaps she had been ill with influenza, and feeling shivery. Perhaps she had believed the afternoon would turn chilly. And yet . . . the other woman—the one who'd been bashed with a newspaper and called a . . . what was it again?—*she* had been wearing a coat too. A big winter coat, all buttoned up. And whatever it was she had retrieved from the ground had been concealed, deliberately, beneath it.

*There is more to know,* Hazel told herself, swallowing the sucked-small sweet. *Much more.* And as her father revved the Old Girl's engine, approaching the home straight, she determined to find out what.

Even if it did prove Too Much For Her Delicate Senses.

# CHAPTER 2

## The Times
### *Thursday June 5<sup>th</sup> 1913*

# A MEMORABLE DERBY

The desperate act of a woman who rushed from the rails on to the course as the horses swept round Tattenham Corner, apparently from some mad notion that she could spoil the race, will impress the general public even more, perhaps, than the disqualification of the winner. She did not interfere with the race, but she very nearly killed a jockey as well as herself, and she brought down a valuable horse. She seems to have run right in front of Anmer which Herbert Jones was riding for the King. It was impossible to avoid her . . .

*T*/*hump!*
     Hazel lowered the newspaper and held her breath. She had never been forbidden, exactly, to enter her father's study, or to read *The Times*. But she knew it would look bad if she was caught.
*Thump! Thump!*
It was Florence sweeping the stairs. Florence was all

12

right, and probably wouldn't tell. Only, she might mention it to Mrs Sawyer, the housekeeper, who was a bitter old fright and probably would.

Quickly, in case the door should suddenly open, Hazel read on:

Some of the spectators close to the woman supposed that she was under the impression that the horses had all gone by and that she was merely attempting to cross the course. The evidence, however, is strong that her action was deliberate and that it was planned and executed in the supposed interests of the suffragist movement. Whether she intended to commit suicide, or was simply reckless, it is hard to surmise . . .

'Are you there, sir? May I come in?'
*Oh . . . fiddle!*
Quickly, Hazel skimmed a few more lines:

. . . She is said to be a person well known in the suffragist movement, to have had a card of a suffragist association upon her and to have had the so-called 'Suffragist Colours' tied round her waist . . .

'Sorry, sir, I'll . . . Oh! Miss Hazel, it's you. You frightened me half to death.'

Annoyed, Hazel folded her father's copy of *The Times* and put it back on his desk. *Alive, then. The trampled woman was still alive. And it had been deliberate. She'd been right about that.*

'I needed something,' she said, her face turning very

pink. It wasn't a lie, for she had needed something—information. All the same, it was agony to say it.

She expected Florence to go. To say that she would come back later. It was rotten luck to have been caught red-handed but inevitable, really, given the number of servants in the house and the way they constantly milled around with their dustpans and fly swats and the stuff they used to clean the carpets when one of the dogs had a mishap.

Florence, however, showed no signs of leaving. Instead, she put down her dustpan and began flicking a feather duster at things.

'No school today, miss?' she asked, brightly.

'No,' said Hazel. 'I am indisposed.'

It wasn't The Done Thing to mention bodily functions—particularly those of a feminine nature—to servants. But Hazel didn't care, for she had only told the truth.

*Serves you right for asking,* she thought, as Florence flicked faster, to cover her embarrassment. And really, it was ridiculous—wasn't it?—that feminine things were never to be discussed, not even discreetly between two grown girls, when there were dogs in this house mating with chair legs, displaying their under parts, and leaving evidence of their own bodily functions on every stair and landing.

Florence began dusting a framed photograph of Hazel's mother. It was already clean enough to glint but Florence dusted it anyway, her eyes fixed, devotedly, on the face behind the glass. Hazel was familiar with this look of adoration. It softened her father's features every night at dinner. And she had seen it all her life in the rheumy eyes of assorted greyhounds, spaniels, and mongrels whenever

14

they heard a latch click and her mother's voice calling out their names.

It was a peculiar look, Hazel decided. Hungry, almost. She could forgive it in her father, and dumb animals couldn't help themselves, but this girl, presumably, had a mother of her own to dote upon, so should leave other people's alone.

'Florence,' she said. 'Do you know what a suffragist is?'

Florence stopped what she was doing and stared at Hazel in surprise. Not devotion. Just surprise.

'A suffering what, miss?'

'A suff-ra-gist,' Hazel repeated, patiently. 'They are . . . special people, I believe. Women.'

'Do you mean them doolally women, miss? The ones what want the vote?'

Hazel shrugged. Maybe she did. Maybe she didn't. She knew what The Vote was though, for her father had one which he had used, a few years back, to try and keep Mr Asquith from becoming the Prime Minister and sending the country to Rack and Ruin.

Florence lifted an ebony statuette and gave the desk beneath it a cursory tickle with the duster. 'Careful,' said Hazel, automatically, for the black statuette, of an ancient goddess called Isis, was both lovely and rare, and one of her father's most treasured possessions.

'You don't want to be bothering about them kinds of women, miss,' Florence said, replacing the ebony Isis just so. 'They're as mad as March hares, according to Cook. She says there's one in particular tore up all the orchids in Kew Gardens the other week. Imagine that! Ripped them clean out their tubs in great big handfuls she did,

15

shouting "Votes For Women!" all the while. And there's been windows smashed and all sorts. And what for? Let the men run the country, is what Cook says. We womenfolk have other cats to skin . . . '

She sniffed derisively, tickled a brass letter rack, and looked around for something else to clean.

Hazel watched, uncertain how to proceed with this interesting conversation. It was doubtful that Florence had ever been to school. Almost certainly she wouldn't be able to read *The Times*. And yet she clearly knew plenty—far more than Hazel, anyway—about the ways of the world.

'I would be interested to meet a suffragist,' she said. 'Do you know where I might find one?'

Florence looked alarmed. 'Goodness, no, Miss Hazel,' she exclaimed. 'What a question! You'll find none in this household, that's for certain. Your father wouldn't tolerate it and nor would Mrs Sawyer.'

*What about my mother?* Hazel wondered, although she knew, well enough, that her mother wouldn't really care if a servant broke a few windows on her afternoons off, so long as she didn't kick the animals or turn pale at the sight of their excrement.

Florence was cleaning one of the glass-fronted bookcases, standing on tiptoe to sweep the feather duster in wide, ponderous arcs. To Hazel, she looked like a hefty fairy waving a wand. *Clap hands if you believe in fairies! Clap hands, children. Everyone clap your hands together, or poor Tinkerbell will die!* Hazel had been deliberately sitting on her hands at performances of *Peter Pan* since she was five years old, so there was nothing whimsical about her image of Florence as a domestic sprite. And instead of

16

smiling to herself she scowled, for there were dictionaries in that bookcase she had planned to consult after finishing the article in *The Times*.

'Just one more question,' she said to Florence's broad, pinafored back. 'If a man calls a woman an "invert" what does he mean by it?'

Was it her imagination or did Florence's spine stiffen?

'You've got me there, miss,' Florence replied. 'I can't answer that one. Now . . . where's that pan and brush? If you'll excuse me I'll need to sweep, in a moment, where your feet are.'

Hazel looked down at her feet in their soft white shoes. They were very small feet, taking up the tiniest fraction of space on the vast expanse of carpet. From her feet she looked at *The Times*, which Florence had re-folded, and then up at the row of leather-bound dictionaries locked away behind tickled-clean glass.

*There is more to know. Much more.*

'I have things to do as well,' she said, huffily. 'So I'd better go and make a start.'

Nothing.

She had nothing whatsoever to be getting on with. Oh, there was a piano to be played, a handkerchief to be embroidered, and a book about a phoenix and a carpet to start reading. There was a rocking horse she could thrash, while pretending to win the Derby, or a collection of seashells to sort through. But none of those things interested her anywhere near as much as staying right here in her father's study, learning all that *The Times* and the dictionaries could tell her about the doolally women who wanted The Vote.

'Haven't you forgotten something, miss?'

Pausing in the doorway, Hazel turned.

'Whatever it was,' said Florence, 'that you needed.'

Hazel flinched.

'I will come back later,' she snapped.

Up the stairs she went, watching carefully where she trod. Up the stairs to her pink and white bedroom with its view across Kensington's rooftops blocked, for the time being, by the leaves of a giant magnolia. One of the maids had been in to straighten and tidy. The rose-coloured bedspread was stretched, tight as skin, over her mattress. A window had been opened, but only a notch, and her silver-backed hairbrush retrieved from a drawer and displayed, like a hint, dead centre of the dressing table.

Over in one corner stood a doll's house, its brick-painted front shut tight and fastened with a big hook and eye. It was a long time since Hazel had played with it; so long that she could no longer remember whether the mother doll was in bed with a headache or down in the kitchen frying miniature eggs in a tiny pan. The father doll, she knew, would be sitting alone in the drawing room. And the little girl doll was hiding in a cupboard.

Sometimes, when she woke in the night, there was moonlight glinting on the doll's house windows and she imagined all the little people inside shaking their tiny fists and shouting: 'Play with me! Play with me!'

It was the same with the larger dolls. And the teddies. And the wooden animals in the ark. She remembered all their names—even the ark's two ladybirds, though barely bigger than full stops, had been given names once upon a time—but the idea of *playing* with them no longer appealed. And when she thought about them, or caught sight of some of them, propped awkwardly on a shelf, she felt irritated and strangely sad.

Only the rocking horse attracted her still because, if she closed her eyes and held tightly to the reins, it was almost like riding a real one. And she could ride it, and ride it, and fancy herself galloping far away . . . to the desert sands of Arabia, or a tropical jungle. Anywhere, really, where she wouldn't have to eat horrendous things like rice pudding and boiled greens, or embroider stupid bluebirds on ridiculous handkerchiefs which no one ever blew their noses on because of the bumpy stitches.

The rocking horse was called Spearmint. There it was—Spearmint—branded on his neck in black and gold. He'd been named by Hazel's father after the winner of the 1906 Epsom Derby. Hazel would have preferred something else—a name that didn't make her think of Zulus and humbugs—but hadn't been given the choice.

It was warm in the room, despite the opened window. And the light shining in through the magnolia leaves had a bilious tinge. What with the roses on her wallpaper— blowsy pink things, as big as babies' faces—and the knots of silk flowers decorating the headboard of her bed, it was like being in a conservatory. Or the hothouse at Kew Gardens.

*Now there was a good idea for a game.*

Her winter coat was in the wardrobe, stinking of moth-balls. It wasn't black, nor did it reach her ankles, but she put it on all the same and buttoned it up to her neck.

How odd it felt to be wearing such a thing on an otherwise ordinary morning in June. Odd and somehow . . . disobedient.

19

Looking at herself in her full-length mirror Hazel experienced a rush of warmth that had nothing to do with the mugginess of the day or the weight of her coat. *Is this how they feel?* she wondered. Her hair looked wrong though. She couldn't help the colour any more than she could help the freckles that went with it, but the long looseness of it was childish. She needed hairpins. Her mother would have some, but she didn't want to be caught, twice in one day, rummaging among her parents' things.

Lifting the hair in both hands, Hazel twisted it into a loose bun and tied it with a ribbon—a dark ribbon; nothing frivolous. That was better, although it still needed a few pins to keep the bun in place and complete the . . . aha! Spillikins. There was a box of ivory spillikins among the games on her toy shelf. They would do the job—for now.

And her silk scarf. The green one. Where was it? Shame she didn't have a mauve one, or a white one either, but she could always make do with hair ribbons, to get the colours right.

Dressing up had never been so much fun.

Downstairs a latch clicked and the dogs began to bark. *'Pipkin, my darling boy . . . Hello, Rascal. How's my naughty Rascal then? Dottie—where are you? Where's my precious little sweetheart? I'm home!'*

Luncheon would be served soon, on the strike of midday, and it would be Cause For Concern, Hazel knew, were she to appear for it dressed for frost and with spillikins in her hair. She had five minutes, at the most, to play her game. Seven, perhaps eight, before Florence or one of the other maids came tapping at her door.

*Snip* went her nail scissors—such a little sound, but so satisfying. *Snip, snip, snip . . .*

How must that suffragist have felt—the one Florence had spoken of—as she decapitated all those valuable orchids at Kew Gardens? Would she have winced, a tiny bit, or simply felt triumphant? Hazel couldn't remember whose idea it had been to twine artificial flowers through the rungs of her bedstead, to make the headboard look like a garden trellis. Not hers, certainly. And not Mrs Sawyer's, or Florence's either, for they called such arrangements dust traps. Anyway, she had never cared for them. And although there were no orchids tied to her headboard there were enough artificial roses and violets and pansies, and enough stupid white things which may or may not have been daisies, to make lopping their heads off a most satisfying act.

*Snip . . . snip . . .*

There would be salad for lunch, as the day was so warm. A salad of greens. And fresh fruit for dessert, with ice cream if she was lucky and blancmange if she was not.

What would a suffragist eat for lunch?

Anything she wanted.

A banquet . . . a sandwich . . . or nothing at all.

*Snip . . .*

The trampled woman was still alive. She had done a doolally thing, rushing out like that in front of the King's horse, but she had done it bravely, and knowingly, so that more people would understand about The Vote. About how important it was for women to have it as well as men.

Hazel had never really thought about The Vote before. Certainly she hadn't consciously suffered from not having

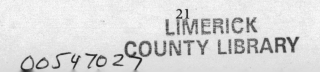

one of her own to look forward to. All she knew—and she knew it right to her bones—was that it must be amazing to feel so strongly, so . . . *passionately* . . . about a thing that you would risk your very life for it.

Later, after lunch, she would make believe that Spearmint was running in the Derby and that she was a bold suffragist making a grab for his bridle.

Downstairs the dogs had settled, in a devoted heap, at their mistress's feet. The maid who brought the salad in avoided their tails with practised ease as she set down her tray and straightened up.

'Should I let Miss Hazel know, ma'am, that luncheon is served?' she asked.

'Oh—is Hazel at home?' replied Mrs Mull-Dare. 'Then, yes, do by all means, although I have only an hour to spare so she may prefer a tray upstairs. Or out on the lawn perhaps. And could you bring a bowl of water for the dogs? Poor Dot-Dots is gasping, aren't you, my poppet? I must see about getting her groomed, for she is far too uncomfortable, with all that hair, and Rascal and Diggy Bert *will* insist on chasing her, despite the heat . . . '

Dottie the too-hairy mongrel understood not a word of this but wagged her tail anyway, relieved to be taking a much-needed break from the attentions of two frisky males.

'*Votes for Women!*' whispered Hazel, slicing through the stem of a perfect white rose.

# CHAPTER 3

The following morning, although still indisposed, Hazel was anxious to get back to school. Not because she expected to learn any more about the suffragists in that dreary place—she was just fed up with being at home.

The Kensington School for the Daughters of Gentlemen was less than four streets and a few minutes walk away. Hazel would have liked to go there and back alone, dawdling or skipping as she chose, but had never been allowed to. Her mother would have let her, but her father had always said no, it wasn't The Done Thing for a respectable young girl to be out in the streets by herself. Only on the rare occasions when another gentleman's daughter came back with Hazel for tea were the two girls permitted to walk from the school to Hazel's home without a chaperone, but only if they moved quickly (*no running*) and did not call in at the sweet shop (*too vulgar*) or veer off into the Gardens (*too dangerous*).

On most mornings, at precisely five to nine, one of the servants would stop sweeping, cooking, or swabbing a dog stain long enough to take Hazel to her lessons, and another would meet her, outside the school, on the dot of two p.m. But if he wasn't needed urgently, at his office in the City, Mr Mull-Dare liked to accompany his daughter himself.

Since the spring, it seemed to Hazel, the City's need for her father had not exactly been vital. Indeed, he had been at home so much recently that her mother had suggested he start walking the dogs—an idea he had greeted with barely-concealed horror and a string of lame excuses.

It was a huge relief to Hazel that her mother had not insisted. For Heaven forbid that any of her walks to and from the Kensington School for the Daughters of Gentlemen should be intruded upon by half a dozen badly-behaved animals, criss-crossing leashes as they lunged at lampposts, sniffed each other's bottoms, or tried to drag her father into the road.

As it was, if she absolutely *had* to be chaperoned, she preferred her father's company above anybody else's. He was nearly always cheerful, for a start, in a proud and affectionate way that didn't quite match the blind adoration he showed towards her mother, but was good enough. And being with him could be fun. Being with him turned the things that were vulgar or dangerous for young ladies to do alone into perfectly normal and acceptable activities. Either they nipped into the sweet shop for a little bag of something, or went the long way round the edge of Kensington Gardens, to inspect blossom, autumn leaves, or the frozen cobwebs that Hazel, as a much younger child, had secretly enjoyed swiping and wrecking, with her mittened fists.

On this day though—Friday, 6 June, 1913—Mr Mull-Dare seemed distracted and they didn't veer off anywhere.

'Not today, pet,' he said, as they passed the sweet shop

by. And although the Gardens looked inviting, he made no move towards them.

Hazel wondered, briefly, whether he was cross with her. Had Mrs Sawyer been telling tales, about her being in his study? Or had one of the maids, puzzled by yesterday's severe pruning of the flowers on her bedstead, had words?

But, no. Whatever was troubling her father had nothing to do with her, Hazel decided. For if it had, he would have confronted her by now and they would have Thrashed It Out Between Them. He would have forgiven her, as he always did, and then let the matter drop.

Gently, even though they were not about to cross a road, Hazel took her father's hand. Without a word he squeezed her fingers and she sensed, through her skin, that he felt comforted, a bit.

'So—what delights do the Whiney Gumms have in store for you this morning?'

Hazel giggled.

The Whiney Gumms . . . It was a perfect description of the middle-aged Gumm sisters who ran the Kensington School for the Daughters of Gentlemen between them. For they did whine. A lot. Particularly Miss Amelia.

In the right kind of mood, Hazel's father did a wonderful impersonation of Miss Amelia Gumm—the younger one who had fluttery hands, and eyes that blinked so fast, when she was anxious, that it looked as if she was flirting with a sailor or trying desperately hard not to cry. He was in no mood this morning, though, to mimic anyone, which was a shame. He could have been an actor, Hazel believed, if he hadn't been a gentleman.

25

'Shakespeare,' she told him, wrinkling her nose. 'We're doing Shakespeare today.'

'Are you, by Jove? Excellent. Jolly good . . . '

He didn't ask which play, or whether she understood it. Nor did he ruffle her hair and say, 'See you at two, my bibbetty-boo,' as he usually did. She considered asking what was wrong . . . imagined her mouth opening and the words *What's the matter, Daddy?* coming out. But, then, he might not like being questioned, like . . . like a criminal or something. He might go all huffy and then she would feel awful.

''Bye, Daddy,' she said, letting go of his hand and hurrying up the steps to her school.

'Goodbye, pet,' he replied.

Miss Eunice and Miss Amelia Gumm were hovering in the hallway, for they made a point of answering the door themselves to welcome each of their pupils in. On Mondays and Wednesdays they trilled their greetings in French, raising their voices to such a pitch, if a parent remained in earshot, that their '*bonjours*' echoed, desperately, halfway down the street.

Today being a Friday they made do with patting Hazel's cheek, sticking her hat on a peg, and then hustling her towards the Yellow Room where nine other girls, ten copies of *King Lear*, and an atmosphere of deep despondency were waiting.

Hazel took her place at the table. It was a round table, like the one King Arthur was said to have favoured when he met his knights to discuss business, and wars. According to the Whiney Gumms, sitting in a circle with no one at the top or the bottom, made everyone feel equal, whatever their status in life.

26

Since none of the girls had a status in life yet, apart from being gentlemen's daughters, Hazel had never quite seen the point. Also the Whineys, unlike King Arthur, never sat, only stood at the blackboard, or strode around quoting things, so what did it matter if the table was round, square, or that five-sided shape whose name everyone had clean forgotten because geometry had only been taught for half an hour some time back in April?

Resigned to Shakespeare, and a dreary few hours, Hazel sat. The Whineys were still out in the hall, awaiting a late arrival, so she looked around the circle of faces and said: 'I saw a woman kicked in the head on Wednesday. At the Epsom Derby. There was blood everywhere. It was gruesome.'

Some of the other girls gasped.

'Do . . . do you mean kicked by another *person*?' stammered Millicent, whose father was In Chemicals. 'By a *man*?'

'No, silly,' said Gloria whose father was In Mining. 'By a horse. It was in all of the newspapers. She was a suffragette, like Emmeline and Christabel Pankhurst. And Ma says . . . '

'Suffra-*gist*,' Hazel interrupted. 'She was a suffra-*gist*.'

'Same darn thing,' drawled Gloria. 'My ma says that if she dies it will be a triumph for the Pankhursts, because then they'll have a martyr for their cause. And in any case, the poor thing's bound to be a vegetable, if she survives, so she might just as well croak. The sooner the better, Ma says, before the public loses interest.'

Hazel looked at Gloria with the beginnings of respect. She was the newest among them, having recently come from a school somewhere else, and with her plump chest

27

and knowing eyes seemed a great deal older. Older, certainly, than timid little Evelyn, whose father was In Docks and Harbours, and older, by far, than cry-baby Verity whose father was In Property.

Gloria spoke with an interesting accent because her mother was from New York. And rumour had it that her Knightsbridge home had real diamonds set into the lavatory seats.

'Do you know what an "invert" is?' Hazel asked her.

Gloria raised her eyebrows. Then in strode Miss Amelia.

'To work, young ladies, to work!' she twittered. 'Act one, scene two of *King Lear*. Who wishes to read aloud? Octavia? Marvellous—off you trot!'

Octavia's father wasn't In anything. Out of all the girls' fathers he was the only one whose wealth and title went back over ten generations. 'Old Money' Hazel's father called it (somewhat enviously, Hazel always thought). And although it didn't matter two hoots to Hazel, or to the other girls, whether their money was old, young, or just coming into its prime, Hazel couldn't help suspecting that it meant rather a lot to the Whineys. And that if the table in the Yellow Room had been shaped like a plank instead of a hoop, Octavia de Willoughby would have been placed, with all due reverence, at the head of it.

She read very nicely though, Octavia did. Much better than anyone else. Perhaps, Hazel thought, it came naturally, this clear, confident way of speaking, when you were the only girl in the room whose ancestors had eaten dinner with Henry the Eighth and had their portraits done by Holbein.

*'Thou, Nature, art my goddess; to thy law my services are bound. Wherefore should I stand in the plague of custom . . .'*

But what did it mean? What did it all *mean*; particularly that bit about standing in a plague of custom? King Lear had banished his daughter, Cordelia, from his kingdom because she didn't love him enough—or so he thought. Hazel had gathered that much last week, from Miss Amelia's reading of the first scene. But the way Shakespeare put things . . . it made her feel like a baby again; a little baby listening to grown-up conversations which she could neither grasp nor follow.

Hazel yawned, Verity slumped, and most of the others were gazing dismally at custard-coloured walls as Octavia stumbled over an unfamiliar word.

*'Lag of a brother? Why b-bas—bast—'*

'Bastard,' Gloria cut in, smoothly. 'B-a-s-t-a-r-d, bastard. It means illegitimate. A brat born out of wedlock.'

For a moment there was shocked silence. Then Verity tittered and all eyes turned, anxiously, to Miss Amelia. Hazel found she was holding her breath.

Sure enough, Miss Amelia's face and throat were livid, and her eyes blinking rapidly as she stared in disgust and disbelief at the back of Gloria Gilbert's head. Then: 'We will have our walk now, young ladies,' she said, her voice unnaturally high. 'Before it thunders. Because yes . . . I do believe the barometer tells of rain, and it would be bad bananas, wouldn't it, to get caught in a shower later? Bring your sketchbooks and follow me. Quick sticks!'

With little sighs and mutters, the girls abandoned *King Lear* and pushed back their chairs.

Hats. They needed their hats—those annoying cartwheels of straw that most of them, given the chance, would have sent spinning into the Round Pond in Kensington Gardens to float, until they rotted, among water lilies and weed and the wreckage of toy boats.

*'So much nicer, girls, to be out in the fresh air. So good for the constitution.'*

While hats were being crammed reluctantly on, and ribbons tied under chins, the door to the Green Room flew open and there stood Miss Eunice, puzzled by this sudden change to the morning's timetable. Behind her, the school's younger pupils—around a dozen girls, aged eight to eleven—looked up from perfecting their handwriting.

'Sketching!' Miss Amelia twittered. 'We are going to put the finishing touches to our "Landscapes in June". I'll fill you in later, dear heart. Not to worry.'

Miss Eunice frowned. She was twice the size of her sister—so big she filled the doorway—and her voice, when she raised it, was as gruff as a man's. She was about to raise it now but then thought better of it. 'Take a jar,' she said. 'And the net. And bring me back a dragonfly for my nature table—two if you can get 'em.'

'Oh, absolutely . . . a *splendid* idea. Hazel—you may fetch a jar. I'll dig out the net. Into line, the rest of you. Quick sticks. Double up.'

The specimen jars were kept in a cupboard, next to the hall stand. Hazel chose a biggish one, with holes in the lid, so that the dragonflies, if they got any, would be able to breathe—at least until they died from hunger, or exhaustion, or from whatever else eventually did for all living things that ended up on Miss Eunice's nature table being studied.

Closing the cupboard, Hazel accidentally knocked against the hall stand, dislodging the day's post—two letters and a small packet—which had arrived earlier and been set aside unopened.

One of the letters slipped right off the stand and landed at her feet. She picked it up and put it back with the rest of the post. *'Miss A. Gumm and Miss E. Potter,'* said the writing on the envelope.

*How very peculiar . . .*

The other girls had formed a short line, in pairs as required. Usually Hazel doubled with Millicent, or with Jennifer whose father was In Steel. But today those two were together, leaving only Gloria by herself, at the end of the line, looking dreadfully bored and way too grown-up to be chivvied into a hat and herded out for a constitutional by one of the Whineys.

Hazel was pleased. She had yet to double up with Gloria, or to know her even a little, and it would be much easier to talk if they were bringing up the rear.

*'All set, girls? Off we trot!'*

The barometer had surely lied. There wasn't a cloud in the sky, or the tiniest hint of rain, as the ten girls, in their hated hats, and the one Whiney, brandishing a pole with a net the size of an ogre's sock trailing from it, filed out of the school, down the steps and then left towards Kensington Gardens.

'She's nuts,' said Gloria, as they all crossed over a road. 'She's completely off her rocker.'

'Who is?' Hazel replied. 'Miss Amelia?'

'Sure. All that fuss about *King Lear*. She skipped some choice words herself, last week, when she read us the first scene. Didn't you notice?'

Hazel had to admit that she hadn't.

'Well, she skipped "womb" and "whore" and "amorous". No wonder it made no damned sense. I've looked ahead and she's got "bosom" and "lust" and "brothel" to come. And plenty more "bastards" as well. I'm sure looking forward to seeing how she gets past all of those . . . '

Hazel was impressed.

'Would you like to come for tea at my house, Gloria?' she asked. 'Next Friday perhaps? On my birthday?'

'Sure.'

'Maybe your mother—your ma—would tell you more about the suffragis—suffra*gettes*—and then you could tell me. I'd really like to meet a suffragette, wouldn't you?'

'Sure. I guess.'

They crossed another road. In the distance Hazel could see the balloon woman, sitting in her usual place, at the entrance to the Gardens. The balloons—red, yellow, orange, and green—were tugging gently at their strings, their colours lollipop-bright in the sunshine and looking fit to melt.

Further along, on the other side of the road, stood Hazel's home.

She intended pointing it out in a minute, to her new friend Gloria. It was on the tip of her tongue to say 'See that house over there? The one with the blue door? That's where I live.' And then: 'My father is In Sugar,' she planned to add, with a certain amount of pride. 'Cane sugar, from the Caribbean.'

Of her mother and the dogs she would say nothing at all, unless specifically asked.

A small boy, denied a balloon, began wailing up at his nanny.

A sudden breeze lifted the rims of the girls' straw hats. A few leaves, and a scrunch of paper, came bowling towards them, pattering along the pavement like strange, hurrying feet.

'Oh, I say,' cried Miss Amelia, as her specimen net flapped in her face.

And 'Look! Look!' cried most of the girls and 'Whaaa?' went the angry, and now extremely puzzled, little boy as several balloons blew free from the balloon woman's grasp and went floating and bumping away.

'See that house . . . ' Hazel began telling Gloria. And then stopped.

Not because Gloria wasn't listening—although she wasn't. And not because Miss Amelia was hurrying them all towards the Gardens, '*Quick sticks, girls*', before the sun went in—although she was.

But because when the front door to her house flew open, and Mrs Sawyer came running out—Mrs Sawyer the housekeeper, who never, ever ran anywhere—she knew straight away that something had happened.

Something terrible.

And so convinced was she about this that the chill that ran through her had nothing to do with the unexpected breeze, and the fear that gripped her stomach seemed perfectly . . . horribly . . . in time and tune with a sudden, resounding, bang.

# CHAPTER 4

The sun didn't go in. The breeze dwindled away to nothing, leaving the sky cloudless and the morning as hot as before.

Miss Amelia was perspiring—inevitably, perhaps, given the way she had gone leaping after a red balloon and caught it, smartly, in her net. If it hadn't gone and burst like that she would have returned it to the balloon woman and basked in the recognition of a job well done. A small but definite achievement.

There were thin shreds of scarlet rubber caught in the net, like the entrails of a particularly exotic specimen. She would pick them out when they reached the Round Pond, while the girls completed their sketches.

It was *very* hot. Usually this particular path was crowded with perambulators and strolling nannies. Right now it was deserted. Miss Amelia found she preferred it this way, for the sight of so many babies upset her. Such helpless, dear little beings. And the knowledge that she would probably never marry, now, and have one of her own . . . well, sometimes it flailed at her heart.

'*Hey-ho, girls. Nearly there.*'

She stood aside, to count her pupils as they passed. God forbid she should lose one. And were their hats on

34

correctly? For no daughter of a gentleman could afford to blight her complexion with sunburn or a freckle.

'*Two, four, six . . .*'

Hazel Mull-Dare, of course, was already freckled, poor child. It went with having her type of red hair—the ginger kind. Quite clearly she favoured her father, in the looks department. For although the mother was a red-head too (or had been, in her youth) she was rumoured, also, to have been a great beauty.

'*Eight . . . Oh!*'

The girls at the front stopped walking. Jennifer and Marjorie (father In Tinned Goods) began wafting their sketchbooks in front of their faces. It was too hot to walk. It was too hot to *breathe*. And why the sudden exclamation from Miss Amelia? Had someone dared to take her hat off? Was it Gloria?

'Hazel, dear,' Miss Amelia twittered. 'Are you quite all right?'

Hazel swallowed and nodded.

'Are you sure? Not feeling . . . um . . . grim biscuits in the tummy area, or anything?'

Hazel shook her head.

'Well . . . let Gloria carry the jar, dear, and sing out if you need me.'

Gloria took the specimen jar by its string handle, and on they all went towards the Round Pond. 'My ma won't be happy if I turn brown,' Gloria drawled, clasping the jar to her chest, so that her fingers were out of the sun. 'There's to be a house party at Henley-upon-Thames this weekend and I've to look suitably pale and interesting for it.' She said nothing at all about how deathly pale, and extremely uninteresting, Hazel had suddenly become.

*It's kind of her not to question me*, thought Hazel, mistaking indifference for tact.

No one—not Miss Amelia, not Gloria, or any of the other girls—appeared to have noticed Mrs Sawyer go rushing into the street. They had been too busy squinting up at the sky, and making little grabs at the escaping balloons. Only Hazel, it seemed, had seen the housekeeper pause, one hand clutching the railings, the other clamped to her mouth (*to stifle what? A sob? A scream?*) and then continue to run, in jerky skirt-hampered strides, along the pavement and up the steps of the house two doors along.

The house where a doctor lived.

The Mull-Dares' own front door had been left wide open—unthinkable under ordinary circumstances. You could see a tall spray of lilies in a vase on the hall table, and the silver tray where visitors left their calling cards. You could see the dogs' leads hanging on their own individual hooks, each one a different length and colour. It was like looking at a person with their mouth wide open and seeing their tonsils and their tongue and bits of food between their teeth. Hazel could have gone there. She could have crossed over the road, and been home in a matter of seconds . . . past the lilies, the silver tray, the dangling leads . . . right into the thick of whatever it was that had happened.

To her father.

To her mother.

To Florence, or one of the other servants.

To a dog.

*Please let it be a dog. Let it be Diggy Bert choking on a slipper.*
*Or Pipkin or Dottie, having some kind of fit. And if it has to*
*be a person, then let it be a servant. And if it isn't a servant*
*then . . . then . . . Oh, just let it be a dog, please . . . only a dog.*

And because she so wanted to believe that it *was* only
a dog; and because Mrs Sawyer hadn't seen her watching;
and because Miss Amelia had just burst a balloon, with
a sudden resounding bang, and all the other girls were
giggling behind their hands, as if everything was normal,
she had turned away from that open door and fallen
back into line with Gloria.

Normal.

That was the ticket.

Everything right as rain and on an even keel. All good
bananas and cheerful biscuits. If she kept telling herself,
over and over again, that nothing too terrible had happened at home then surely . . . maybe . . .

*See you at two, my bibbetty-boo.*

Only that's not what he had said.

The Round Pond was glinting, like gun metal, in the
heat. On Saturdays, Sundays, and public holidays it was
fringed, all around, with fathers and sons sailing model
boats. Once Hazel's father, lacking both a son and a boat,
had taken a banknote from his pocket, folded it into a
floatable shape and set it on the water.

It had been a gusty autumn day. A Saturday. And
proper little boats were bisecting the pond as swiftly and
neatly as knives through pie. The man next to Hazel's
father had been down on one knee, his son leaning companionably against his shoulder as they prepared to launch
a magnificent model yacht.

'I'll bet you a shilling ours reaches the bank over there in . . . oh . . . less than a minute,' Hazel's father had said gaily to the man. 'In fact, let's make proper sport of it. Another shilling—no, half a crown—on it beating yours. Deal?'

Hazel had looked at the model yacht, its sails fat with fresh air as it left the bank. It was like a swan: regal and lovely and in no apparent hurry. Then she had looked at her father's banknote, bobbing and spinning and skittering away like a crazy pup let off the lead.

'Deal,' the man next to them had said.

'*Hazel . . . Hey, Hazel!* Wake up. Did you bring an eraser? My pond looks like a damned soup dish . . . and how the hell can I finish off my cloud when there isn't one there any more?'

The other girls were grumbling too. About having to draw standing up, because sitting down might mark their frocks. About the annoying shadows being cast on their sketchbooks by the brims of their hats. But most of all about the impossibility of completing their 'Landscapes in June' when the people they'd been drawing were not in evidence today and everything from the look of the sky to the colour of the pond had changed.

And nobody had brought a rubber. Only pencils from the art cupboard which went from sharp to blunt annoyingly fast and, as Gloria pointed out, were no darn good for shading.

Miss Amelia had no sympathy.

'Invent, young ladies. Invent!' she twittered. 'See the cloud in your mind's eye. Remember the child throwing stones at the water . . . the angle of his little arm, the play of light on his face. Picture the nanny asleep on the bench. Conjure nymphs if you will . . . or Neptune rising from the Pond with eels in his beard . . . Anything! Draw anything! Let your imaginations roam freely, girls, since there is so little, today, to observe . . . '

'Nuts . . . ' muttered Gloria, rubbing at her cloud with the pad of her thumb. 'That woman is totally insane. And I'd better not have caught the sun. I've a Peer of the Realm interested in me—I have, you know. He'll be at the party this weekend and I tell you what, Hazel, he's quite a catch. Imagine! I could end up a peeress if I play my cards right. Ma says they wear ermine and velvet at coronations and have coronets embroidered on their sheets. Ma says . . . '

Hazel took up her pencil and frowned at her own 'Landscape in June'. So far the various lines and smudges on the page could just as easily be a 'Seascape in November' or a 'Mountain Range in March'. Not that she cared.

She needed something, though, to focus her mind. To stop her thoughts from skittering back along the Garden paths to that wide open door.

Her father's face, as his banknote picked up speed— caught by the wind at just the right angle—had been a lot more animated than it was when they looked for catkins, or simply walked. And she had been proud to be with him, sharing his excitement, even though it had nothing to do with her and all she could do was watch.

Which coat had he been wearing? His brown checked one? Yes. With a scarf the colour of conkers.

It was hard to draw a person next to a pond without getting the proportions all wrong. And she had no colours, either, to fill in the browns of her father's coat and scarf, or the foxy-red of his hair. His pose, though—she could try and capture that. The way he had leaned forward, punching the air with his fist.

'Go on *Moneyspinner*!' he had shouted, his feet slipping a little on the Pond's edge. 'Go on there! You can do it!'

Moving her pencil, just for a moment, Hazel drew a tiny shape in the lower segment of her pond. *Moneyspinner* . . . How she had giggled over that! Such a perfect name, just like 'Whiney Gumms'. Quickly she drew a slightly bigger shape, lagging behind in the pond: the model yacht, whose name she never knew since its owners had been too timid to cheer it on.

'Two more minutes, girls,' cried Miss Amelia, from wherever she had gone to stalk dragonflies.

Hazel's pencil flew back to the shape of her father. He had taken his hat off, ready to throw it high in the air, in triumph. She sketched in his hair, all windblown and tufty, and made little marks on his face for freckles. It was difficult—impossible—to capture him precisely, although she could see his face, in vivid detail, in her mind's eye.

He had been laughing—crowing almost—as the distance between *Moneyspinner* and the splendid yacht stayed roughly the same. Laughing and cheering even though the yacht was cutting a smooth straight course through the water while the folded banknote was whirling, precariously, over each little ripple and being tipped almost flat by the wind.

Other men and their sons had stopped sailing their own boats to watch. They hadn't entered into the spirit of

40

the race, though. Not properly. Beside Hazel's gleeful flame-haired father they had seemed a dull lot.

'Right, young ladies. Time to go.'

Gloria gave a wicked chuckle.

'Hazel,' she whispered, nudging at Hazel's drawing arm. 'Look at this.'

'Careful. Don't jog me. I'll look when I've finished mine.'

It seemed important, suddenly, to finish. To make this portrait of her father as true to life as possible. The proportions were wildly inaccurate—he looked more like a giant next to a puddle than a person next to a pond. But that didn't matter. Getting his face right did. And she hadn't done his feet yet, or the fingers around the hat.

'Ready, girls? Sketchbook away, Miss Mull-Dare. You too, Miss Gilbert. Quick sticks.'

None of the other girls had needed telling twice. They were already back in line, wilting miserably beneath their hats and desperate for drinks of water.

Miss Amelia, marching briskly, was almost back among them. Her net was over her right shoulder, at an acute, triumphant angle, and in the jar swinging from her left hand something glimmered.

'I'm not finished yet,' Hazel said, trying not to botch the shape of her father's left foot.

'Well, never mind, dear. Come along now. I have my specimens and everyone else is waiting. Gloria—do as I ask, please, and close your book. *Oh . . . I . . . say!*'

Hazel was about to pencil in her father's smile. It was the last thing. After that the likeness would be complete, and as good as she could get it.

But the girls standing directly behind her: what were they laughing at? Jane (father In Textiles) and Phyllis (father In Publishing) were giggling helplessly. And stupid little Verity was making a noise like a kitten down a well. And the other girls—the ones further along the line— were calling out: *'What?' 'What is it?' 'What's happened?'*

Miss Amelia, on the other hand, had gone very, very quiet.

And Gloria?

Irritated, Hazel stopped what she was doing and looked. Gloria had stopped drawing, too, and was holding her sketch at arm's length. Her expression could not have been more innocent, as she appraised what she had done, but it was immediately clear to Hazel that the only reason her 'Landscape in June' was being held aloft was so that everyone could see it.

'Hmmm.' Gloria raised her sketch a little higher. 'I think it needs a bit more shading. On the bosoms. What do *you* think, Hazel?'

*'Close the book. Close that book immediately, you . . . you vulgar, disgraceful girl!'*

Hazel had never heard Miss Amelia Gumm so angry. Hysterical, yes. Angry, no. She was half tempted to turn round, to see how fast her teacher was blinking, and what colour her throat had gone, but Gloria's 'Landscape in June' was marginally more interesting.

'Golly,' she said. And then: 'I don't know. About the shading.'

Gloria, it seemed, had taken Miss Amelia's advice to 'Invent! Invent!' completely to heart. Only her imagination hadn't so much roamed free as run riot. Neptune

42

was there—at least Hazel assumed, from the eels, that the male figure was Neptune—and so was a nymph, a very *naked* nymph. But it wasn't just the bosoms on the nymph that were rude (although they were a lot bigger and bouncier than the ones you saw on statues, or in paintings) it was the way the two figures were posed.

'Golly . . . ' Hazel murmured again, for it was the same position her mother's dogs got into sometimes. The mating one. Only whereas Dottie, from what Hazel had seen, was never all that happy about having Rascal or Diggy Bert in such close proximity, Gloria's nymph was clearly ecstatic.

There were make-believe clouds in the drawing, too, and the suggestion of a pond. Gloria had even sketched a couple of dragonflies—or were they midges?—hovering above Neptune's naked buttocks. It was in portraiture, however, that she clearly excelled, for the nymph's face, with its googly eyes, thin nose, and hair scraped back in a straggly bun, was the absolute spit of Miss Amelia.

*Goodness me*, Hazel thought, her fears about home diminishing a little as she responded to this delicious piece of wickedness.

'Is she "amorous" enough, do you think?' Gloria wondered. 'My "whore" with the big "bosoms" and a look of "lust" in her . . . '

'NOW!' cried Miss Amelia. 'Close that sketchbook NOW!'

'But, Miss Gumm,' Gloria protested, her voice as loud and sweet as a chorister's. 'I'm only quoting Shakespeare . . . '

'Be . . . *QUIET*!'

And, with a whistle and a whoomph, the specimen net crashed down.

Hazel jumped, her sketchbook tumbling from her hands at the exact same moment Gloria's did. Behind her, the other girls fell silent—cut off mid-giggle as Miss Amelia jerked the pole and Gloria staggered backwards, her head enmeshed, her fingers scrabbling, frantically, at the net's heavy metal rim.

Slowly, Hazel bent down to retrieve the sketchbooks. Hers and Gloria's. She hadn't finished her father's face. There was an empty gap where his mouth needed to be. Her book had fallen shut and it bothered her, as she picked it up, that her father's image was somewhere in there, leaning over the pond, unable to smile.

Gloria's book had landed splayed open, with Neptune and the nymph still very much on display. The page had loosened, though, and came away completely when Hazel tried to tuck it back.

'Tear it up.' Miss Amelia's voice was somewhere between a hiss and a growl; no trace of a twitter now.

'Pardon?'

'Tear it up. Right now. Immediately.'

Hazel looked at Miss Amelia and was reminded of volcanoes. There were pictures of volcanoes, at various stages of activity, in the school's geography books. Miss Amelia was looking dormant, after her huge outburst, but the tone of her voice, and the fiery red of her face, were clear warnings that she could explode again at any moment.

The specimen jar had been set on the ground. But the net remained taut in Miss Amelia's grip; and Gloria's head was still in it.

Slowly, Hazel began to rip. From the top to the bottom of the sketch she went, neatly separating Neptune from his nymph, then diagonally across both pieces, and diagonally again. After that it got difficult, particularly with her own sketchbook tucked, awkwardly, under one armpit.

'Smaller! Smaller!' shrieked Miss Amelia. 'And hurry up!'

The girls in line were all watching Hazel's hands as if looking anywhere else had been forbidden, on pain of death. Stupid little Verity had begun to cry.

As quickly as she could, Hazel continued ripping. She couldn't hold on to all the torn up bits of paper, but Miss Amelia said nothing as they fluttered away . . . Neptune's left ear . . . a trident prong . . . part of a cloud . . .

In the end Hazel let all the pieces go. If Miss Amelia wasn't bothered about leaving litter in Kensington Gardens then neither was she.

'Now pick up the jar and get into line.'

The paralysing intensity of the girls' stares and the tone of Miss Amelia's voice were making Hazel feel as if *she* was the one who had drawn a rude thing in her sketchbook. It was grossly unfair, being picked on like this, but it seemed safer to do as she was told. Back in line, all by herself, she watched some scraps of Gloria's sketch go floating away on the pond, like bread for the ducks.

*Moneyspinner* had sunk. Just a yard or so from victory it had completely disappeared—pulled under by a current, or defeated by the wind. 'Oh well,' her father had said. 'That's life . . . '

'Right,' Miss Amelia snapped. 'Forward march. Gloria? Stand up this instant.'

45

Hazel, like Verity and the others, had been avoiding looking at Gloria. But now she couldn't resist it.

*What if she didn't move?*

Gloria didn't look dead, for she wasn't lying down, only sprawled on the ground in a semi-sitting position, with her hands gone limp by her sides and her head flopped forward, inside the net, as if she was examining her knees.

Hazel couldn't tell if Gloria's eyes were open or shut, for they were concealed beneath the netting and by the crumpled brim of her hat. But there was certainly no blood anywhere, which was a hopeful sign—wasn't it?

'Get up, I said. *Come along.* I can tell you're only shamming, you horrible child.'

Hazel adjusted her grip on the specimen jar. It felt heavier than before which was odd considering how weightless a couple of dragonflies were.

*If something's happened to Gloria,* she told herself, *if she's fainted—or worse—then everything will be all right when I get home. That's the bet. That's the deal. But if . . .*

'My father will take you to court for this.'

Gloria's voice wasn't quite as hysterical as Miss Amelia's but it was close.

'He'll sue your ass off. You wait and see. Then the judge will send you to prison, or straight to a loony bin you . . . you . . . *crackpot.*'

'Stand up, Gloria,' Miss Amelia repeated. 'Or do I have to drag you?' She sounded perfectly calm, but Hazel wasn't fooled. Inside, the woman was molten. Perhaps Gloria sensed this too, for she said nothing more, only drew a shaky breath and staggered to her feet. There were grass

46

stains on her dress, Hazel noticed, and her hands were grazed and dirty.

Miss Amelia adjusted the angle of the pole, as Gloria rose, so that the net stayed firmly in place.

'Now walk,' she commanded. 'And the rest of you— fall in behind.' And she swivelled the net, like a fisher-woman landing a mermaid, forcing Gloria to sidestep, clumsily, right to the front of the line.

'Go on,' she yelled, tapping the rim of the net against the width of Gloria's shoulders. 'Keep moving.'

'Ouch!' hollered Gloria, dramatically, and Hazel winced. Surely Miss Amelia didn't intend that one of her pupils should walk all the way back to the Kensington School for the Daughters of Gentlemen trapped in a net, with her hat squashed down over her eyes?

But Miss Amelia did.

'You wait,' Gloria warned, lurching blindly along at the end of the pole. 'You just wait, that's all.'

'Quiet!' was all Miss Amelia would say, manipulating the pole for left, right, or straight ahead, oblivious (or so it seemed) to the shocked and curious stares of occasional passers-by.

Back through the gates of Kensington Gardens they all trooped, and onto the street. The balloon woman had gone. The front door to Hazel's house had been closed. It was one o'clock in the afternoon and very, very quiet.

'Let me out!' hollered Gloria. 'I'm warning you.'

'Not a chance,' crowed Miss Amelia. 'Keep walking.'

The other girls were drooping and stumbling, but the school's steps were in sight and it was almost time to go home.

*Please be there*, Hazel begged, in her head. *At two on the dot. Just be there.*

The specimen jar banged against her left leg. She held it further away, trying not to jolt or worry the two insects fluttering uselessly inside. Her sketchbook slipped a little, under her right arm, but she nudged it up again and pressed it tight against her heart.

# Chapter 5

'You go,' Mrs Sawyer told Florence. 'But don't say anything. Not a word. It's not your place to decide how much to tell her.'

Florence had been crying. Her face was all blotchy. 'Can't somebody else go?' she pleaded, twisting her hands in her apron. 'Me nerves are shredded. That poor, poor . . . '

'Pull yourself together,' Mrs Sawyer snapped. 'And do as you're told. Miss Mull-Dare will be out in less than five minutes and we don't want her walking home alone.'

'It wouldn't hurt her,' Florence mumbled, half to herself. 'For once.'

Mrs Sawyer gripped the edge of the kitchen table. Across the room, Cook was chopping onions for a pie, her eyes streaming. Mrs Mull-Dare's luncheon tray had been brought back down, untouched. Only the dogs were eating and drinking as usual, although the hairy one—Dottie—had only just stopped whining, and the rest kept sniffing along the strip of light at the bottom of the study door, their ears pricked and their tails raised.

How much did those animals understand, Mrs Sawyer wondered? More than they were given credit for, probably. It was Dottie, after all, who had raised the alarm, howling

49

outside the study like the Hound of the Baskervilles and scratching at the paintwork.

'We've had one dreadful accident already today,' she reminded Florence in hushed tones, 'And we'll not risk another by allowing that child to roam the streets unaccompanied. So look sharp and get yourself to the school.'

Still grumbling under her breath, Florence left the room. It crossed Mrs Sawyer's mind to call her back and tear her off a strip for insolence, but the moment passed and she let her go. They had all suffered a shock. A dreadful shock. It wouldn't hurt to make allowances until things returned to normal. She said as much to Cook who looked up from her pile of onions and shook her head.

'Normal?' she cried, scrabbling for a handkerchief to wipe her runny eyes. 'Things'll never be the same in this house, Mrs Sawyer, after what he did. Never. There'll be consequences. Reaper-cush-uns. You mark my words.'

At the Kensington School for the Daughters of Gentlemen the older girls had done no more than pick at their lunches which, as a result of being served late, had been as cold as cat food anyway. Gloria, her face mutinous, sat very still and ate nothing at all. Every now and then, though, she raised a hand to her throat and rubbed it. Hard.

After a while Hazel put down her own knife and fork and leaned across the table. 'It's all right,' she whispered to Gloria. 'She hasn't left any marks. You'll still be pale and interesting for your party.'

Gloria scowled. 'My voice box is swelling,' she hissed. 'I can feel it.'

50

Chastened, Hazel lowered her eyes.

Miss Amelia, having released Gloria from the net and banged a gong for lunch, had disappeared upstairs without a word, leaving Miss Eunice to supervise the meal. And if Miss Eunice noticed Gloria's apparent problem with her throat, or was surprised by the general air of shock in the room, she didn't show it.

'Manners, Miss Mull-Dare,' she boomed, when Hazel started whispering across the table. And then, as the hall clock struck two: 'School dismissed.'

Gloria and the other girls moved fast, scraping back their chairs and heading for their hats as if the first one out of the house might win something. Miss Eunice left the room quickly too, her big feet making the floorboards twinge as she plodded towards the stairs. Hazel, left alone, felt peace and quiet settle all around her like snow.

A fly had landed on one of the plates and was circumnavigating a cold potato. Any minute now the Whineys' ancient housekeeper would come in to clear the table and be surprised and cross to find Hazel still there.

Nevertheless, Hazel stayed where she was, her insides all jumpy, her eyes following the skittery movements of the fly.

*If it reaches that piece of carrot my father will be out there, waiting for me. But if it doesn't . . .*

The fly, as if reading her mind, crawled obligingly onto the carrot but the jumpy feeling in the pit of Hazel's stomach remained exactly the same.

*If it stays on the carrot for more than fifteen seconds . . .*

But her heart wasn't in it. She was putting things off, that was all; pretending to herself that the actions of a stupid fly could somehow change what was already done.

She stood up. The fly rose from the plate. The hall clock ticked away another minute.

Her hat looked forlorn, hanging all by itself. She lifted it from its peg and took as long as she could adjusting the fit of it and tying the ribbon beneath her chin.

*By the time I undo this ribbon,* she told herself. *I will know.*

The door to the Green Room had been left wide open. Against the far wall stood Miss Eunice's nature table and Hazel couldn't help but notice that the badger's skull and the crumbly robin's nest had been moved to make space for Miss Amelia's specimen jar. Fleetingly, it crossed her mind to go in there and set those dragonflies free. To open the window and shake out the jar so that those poor insects—should they still be alive—could flutter out across the streets of Kensington and back to the Round Pond.

But she had enough, already, to worry about and no longer saw any point, or comfort, in betting the lives of any-one or anything against her father's. She simply allowed herself one final surge of hope for him as she tugged open the Whineys' front door.

Florence was standing alone on the pavement, looking fretfully up at the school.

'Where's father?' Hazel cried out then, all hope receding as she hurried down the steps. 'What's happened to him?'

Florence's expression went from anxious to panic-stricken to unreadable in less than a blink. 'He couldn't make it, miss,' she said, carefully. 'So Mrs Sawyer sent me instead.'

Hazel wasn't having that. Tempted though she was to run straight back into the Whineys' house and hide away in their art cupboard, with her fingers stuffed in her ears, she wasn't about to be fobbed off. Not by Florence. Not by anyone.

'Something *has* happened to him,' she insisted, her eyes fixed on the maid's face—on the blotched cheeks and the pink-rimmed eyes. 'Tell me the truth. Is he . . . dead?'

The word 'dead' was bitter in her mouth, like sherbet. She had never realized before how close it sounded to 'dad'.

Florence's heavy work-chapped hands came down upon her shoulders and rested there gently like an auntie's or a vicar's. 'No,' Hazel heard her say. 'No, miss . . . He's . . . there's been a . . . a bit of an accident . . . but he's not dead. Nobody's dead. Now, don't ask me anything else, please. I've said more than I should already and Mrs Sawyer'll swing for . . . be right angry with me, if she finds out.'

Hazel nodded. And although a hundred questions were forming in her head—*Did he fall? Trip over a dog? Choke on a humbug? . . . Has he cut himself? Or broken a bone . . . Is he still able to walk? Talk? See? Smile?*—she didn't want to voice them. Not yet. Not straightaway. It was enough, for the moment, to know that her father was alive.

Enormous Relief was a strange thing, she realized. It really did wash through you, but any inclination to dance for joy—or to speak and move normally, even—was hampered by a draining-away sensation that left you as mute as a jelly and every bit as wobbly. She was glad when

Florence took hold of her arm as they crossed over the road and turned her in the direction of home.

'Cook was wondering about your birthday cake,' Florence managed to say, as they passed the sweet shop. 'She thought you might like something different this year. A big round one perhaps, with your name on it. Or she thinks she could manage a flower-shape, with the right kind of cutters.'

Flower-shapes? Cutters?

*Whatever has happened*, Hazel told herself, *it can't be that awful or Cook wouldn't be thinking about cakes. And Florence wouldn't be wittering on about them either, unless it's to distract me. To fob me off.*

'I don't want to talk about food,' she said. 'I don't want to talk about anything. I just want to get home.'

'Of course,' Florence answered, humbly. 'Of course you do. I'm sorry.'

Hazel's birthday cakes had always been shaped like numbers, to match her age. Enormous great numbers, larded with icing and candied flowers, and far too big, really, for her needs. When she had first reached double figures there had been so much cake left over, going stale, that she and her father had fed large chunks of the '0' to some ducks on the Round Pond.

'Perhaps you should have had a party this year, pet,' her father had said, peeling off a strip of icing and eating it himself, so it wouldn't gum up a hapless mallard's beak. 'For all your friends from school.'

'No,' Hazel had shuddered. 'No I shouldn't.'

And he had smiled, reassuringly, and patted her arm, to show that he hadn't meant it; that he had only been teasing.

Parties or no parties, she had always had a cake. Mrs Sawyer approved of the ritual and no one had ever opposed it. The number thirteen was unlucky, though. Hazel knew that, and wasn't at all surprised by Cook's reluctance to bake a one and a three at the same time and arrange them side by side on a silver board. Her father would never bet on anything on the thirteenth day of the month, and would check a horse's stall number as a matter of course. There were thirteen at the Last Supper and thirteen witches in a coven.

Not for the first time Hazel wondered how many other girls in England—or even the *world*—were turning thirteen on June 13th. And in 1913 to boot. And this year, to top it all, June 13th fell on a Friday—so how horribly unlucky was that?

*So unlucky, maybe, that bad things were happening a week early? With worse still to come?*

They were home.

'Where is he then?' Hazel demanded as they entered the hall. 'Where's my father? Is he in his study? Can he walk?'

The bigger dogs came lolloping and buffeting their way down the stairs, heading straight for her. Diggy Bert reached her first and licked her hand. Dottie sniffed at her shoes and let out a sigh like a grieving person. They didn't usually greet her like this. Mostly, they left her alone.

Mrs Mull-Dare's hat was on the hall table—thrown there in a hurry, by the look of it. Hazel stared at its trailing ribbons and felt her stomach tighten.

'Your mother's in her parlour, miss.' Florence was backing hastily away, towards the passage that led out of the hall and down to the kitchen. 'I'd go straight up if I were you.'

Reluctantly, Hazel climbed the stairs, the dogs slobbering at her heels. Passing her father's study she paused. *Was* he in there? Sitting quietly, perhaps, with a bandaged foot, gazing at his ebony statue of Isis, and the picture of his wife? Nursing a glass of brandy along with a snapped wrist? Trying to read the sports page in *The Times* even though he'd clonked his head and was seeing a trillion stars?

She didn't knock, just tried the door. It was locked.

On she went, to the next landing. The door to her mother's parlour was wedged wide open for the convenience of the dogs so she went straight in.

'What's happened to him?' she cried. 'Where is he? And why is his study locked?'

Her mother's face was as pale as the lilies in the hall and as unreadable as Florence's had been. For some reason Hazel's thoughts flew to Miss Amelia . . . to her blinking eyes and mottled throat . . . and she couldn't help but wish that the people closest to her were as open with their feelings, and as easy to see through, as that old Whiney Gumm.

'Well?' she demanded. 'Tell me!'

Her father would have scolded her for speaking sharply to her mother. It would have saddened him. But her father wasn't here. Not in this room; not downstairs in his study; not anywhere in the whole house, she was sure of that by now.

Her mother shooed Pipkin from the settee, and took both Hazel's hands in her own. 'Sit down, pet,' she said.

Hazel sat. It was the shifting of the dog, more than the taking of her hands, which prepared her for the worst. She had her mother's complete attention, for once, and it felt as strange, and as dizzying, as Enormous Relief had just a short while ago.

As usual, she couldn't look for long at her mother's face without feeling a puzzling mixture of love, exasperation, and resentment. Instead, she found herself staring down at the carpet (at the swirly brown pattern chosen specifically to camouflage dog stains) as she listened to what she was being told.

'Your father has had to go away for a while. He's been working too hard. *Much* too hard. And worrying a lot. About money, mostly. The sugar business is in a bad way, you know—well, you probably don't know, but it is. And he's been losing more than usual on the horses. Anyway, it has all made him rather poorly. The worrying, I mean. And this morning he . . . it all became too much. So he has gone to a place in the country; a rest home recommended by Doctor Collins where he can . . . well, where he can rest for a while. Until he feels more like himself.'

Hazel absorbed the information slowly, turning each word over in her head. Then: 'Why is his study door locked?' she asked.

Her mother flinched. 'Is it locked?' she replied, her voice so light and vague that her mind could easily have been elsewhere. Only the flinch, and the tightening of her fingers gave her away. 'Well . . . I don't know. Perhaps Mrs Sawyer thought it best to keep it locked while he's away . . . to keep the dogs out,' she added, as if Dottie, Rascal, and the others had developed uncontrollable urges to read *The Times* or smoke cigars and would stand on their hind legs and paw that study door open, given half a chance and a quiet moment.

Hazel thought about Doctor Collins. It was his house she had seen Mrs Sawyer running to.

'*More like himself.*' What did that mean exactly? How unlike his real self had her father become, then, before going away to this rest home?

'Florence said there had been an accident,' she said, not caring very much if it got Florence into trouble. 'What kind of an accident?'

Her mother withdrew both her hands then, and bent to smooth the hair from Dottie's eyes. Hazel, her own eyes still fixed on the carpet, clenched her fists in her lap and waited.

'Your father has had a breakdown,' her mother said, eventually. 'Do you know what that means?'

'Yes thank you,' Hazel replied.

In her mind's eye an image appeared of her father, dancing like a puppet on long, strong strings . . . dancing and twitching and trying to smile while bits of his body—fingernails, toes, kneecaps—broke off. Clunk went a broken-down foot, and clank went his broken-down right hand, while his freckles broke down one by one and blew away in all directions, like the torn-up scraps of Gloria's sketch.

'But he will be all right,' her mother added, gently. 'So long as he rests, and does what the nurses say, he will be back home with us again in no time.'

'When can we visit him? Can we go tomorrow?'

Her mother, she knew, couldn't drive the Old Girl, but

they could hire a chauffeur for the day. Or go by train. She would take her father a bag of sweets—humbugs, his favourites, and wine gums to make him think of Miss Amelia and laugh. She would tell him she had a new friend called Gloria who was exceptionally good at drawing.

'He's not allowed visitors,' Mrs Mull-Dare said. 'Doctor Collins says not. It would only exhaust him. He needs absolute peace and quiet, you see, but it won't be for long. Not long . . . '

Hazel looked up from the carpet. Her mother was gazing out of the window. She wasn't crying or anything, but the way her voice had faltered, and then stopped altogether, suggested to Hazel that she might be about to start. Dottie and Pipkin had snuggled so close she looked as if she was wearing them, like dirty furs, *If she cries*, Hazel thought, *those dogs will want to comfort her whereas I will want, more than anything, to go straight up to my room.*

'Is there . . . anything else you want to ask, pet?'

She was hoping there wouldn't be, Hazel could tell.

'He'll be home for my birthday, won't he,' she said, making sure to sound confident and to keep the question mark out of her voice.

Mrs Mull-Dare turned, finally, and looked her daughter full in the face.

'We can hope so,' she said gently. 'But I wouldn't bet on it.'

# CHAPTER 6

It was a dreadful weekend. Utterly miserable. Meals were served punctually, the sun rose and set, but Hazel felt her father's absence so keenly that, had she known precisely where to find him she would have walked there. Barefoot. In the dark. Across stones.

'I know where he is,' she said to Florence on Saturday morning. 'Now how do you pronounce the name of the place again? The place in the country where the rest home is?'

It was mostly true, about knowing where he'd gone, but her voice sounded squeaky and false, and Florence was not to be hoodwinked.

'Excuse me, miss,' she said, squeezing past Hazel on the stairs. 'I've the beds to do.'

Hazel followed her up the stairs and down the landing.

'I know everything . . . mostly . . . ' she faltered, standing first on one leg and then the other, outside her parents' room. 'My mother told me.'

Florence, who had her back to the open door, jumped visibly. But, for once, she didn't say anything about leaping out of her skin, or being frightened half to death.

'Then you need ask me no more questions, need you, miss,' was all she said. 'Nor anyone else in this house who gets paid to do a good job and mind their own business.'

She had pulled back the covers on the double bed and was making a big show of plumping up the pillows. But the bed, Hazel noticed, hadn't been slept in. Not even on one side. 'All right. I'm sorry,' she murmured, turning quickly away before the sight of her father's dressing gown, hanging forlornly from the bedpost, could reduce her to tears.

Mrs Mull-Dare had gone out and was not expected back until suppertime. Hazel assumed she had gone to work, and thought nothing of it. Ever since she could remember, her mother had busied herself, most days, at the home for stray dogs in Battersea. People thought she was wonderful, dedicating so much of her time to the welfare of lost and starving animals. They didn't seem to realize, as Hazel did, that there was very little sacrifice involved.

'Doesn't she worry about getting bitten?' the girls at school would ask. 'And how can she bear the *smell*?'

'No' and 'Easily' were the honest answers to such questions.

If Hazel's mother had to go to parties—which she occasionally did, if they were to do with the family being In Sugar—she could look beautiful, without even trying. But small talk bored her rigid and she made no secret of the fact that, in her opinion, even the daftest and most flatulent of hounds was better company, of an evening, than most of the human beings she encountered socially.

As a small child, Hazel had been thrilled by her father's tale of how he had gone to Battersea Dogs' Home to look for his sister Alison's greyhound, and fallen madly in love

61

with the red-haired young woman who wrote his details in a ledger. ('*My mother!*' she would squeal, even when the story was no longer new. '*That's right,*' he would reply, his face all bright and soppy. '*Your mother.*')

Three times, Mr Mull-Dare told Hazel, he had spelt out his surname, while the red-haired girl apologized for being a slow writer. She had only recently learned her letters, she'd told him, and capital D, P, and B and the little line that split certain names muddled her.

'Please don't worry,' he had said to her. 'It's not a proper name anyway. Mull-Dare. It used to be Moulder but one of my ancestors changed it. My family is In Sugar, you see. And it doesn't look good, does it, having "mould" in your surname when you're trying to sell something so pure and so sweet.'

He had never told anyone this before, he said to Hazel. But somehow he had known within minutes . . . seconds even . . . that one day this lovely young woman would share his name and that it wouldn't matter tuppence to her if it was Mull-Dare, Moulder, or Pestilent-Rot; just as it wouldn't matter, either, how ill-bred and worthless his rat-scally ancestors had been before one of them won the deeds to a sugar plantation in a game of poker.

('*What's poker?*' Hazel had asked in alarm, when the story was first told, for she was picturing wild and danger-ous men taking stabs at one another with irons from the fire. '*A grand game of cards,*' her father had replied, '*which I'll teach you one day, when you're older.*')

His sister Alison's greyhound had been found that same afternoon, locked accidentally in an outhouse and none the worse for it. Still, he had gone back to the dogs' home every day for three months, pretending the search was still on.

The red-haired young woman (*'Red hair like YOU, Daddy,'* Hazel would remind him, *'and like ME.'*) . . . the red-haired young woman became Mrs Mull-Dare before the year was out. And she never knew, because Hazel's father never told her, that the hound her sister-in-law fed chocolate to, until it died of digestive disorders a month before the wedding, was the same one that had been lost.

'Your sister shouldn't keep greyhounds if all she does is lose them and feed them the wrong things,' was all she ever said to her husband on the matter. 'You showed more concern for that missing pet of hers than she ever did. It's one of the reasons why I'm marrying you. The main reason, actually . . . '

At this point in the story Hazel aged . . . six? . . . seven? . . . she can't remember . . . would stuff her hands against her mouth to stifle the giggles.

'Let's tell her! Let's tell her!' she would whisper, gleefully.

'Shhhh. No!' her father would reply, putting a finger to his lips and pretending to be scared. 'She would order Mrs Sawyer to cut out my lying tongue and feed it to the pups. She would make me live in a kennel, without any straw! She would take away my best suits and make me an itchy coat—a tartan one, in red and brown . . . '

By now his eyes would be rolling in mock terror and Hazel's ribs would be aching with laughter. For her mother, at around this time, had bought herself a sewing machine and started making preposterous little coats to keep Rascal and Diggy Bert—both puppies then—warm in the winter.

63

'But . . . if she asks me, then what will I do? What will I say?'
Even as a very little girl, Hazel would not, could not, answer
a direct question with a lie.

'She never will, pet,' her father had soothed. 'I'd bet all
the sugar in the world—a whole mountain of sugar—that
she will never even dream of asking. Trust me.'

For years, it seemed, Hazel had been able to keep her
father's confidence; delighting in the knowledge that both
she and he could take or leave the dogs her mother doted
upon, and wouldn't be *too* horribly upset if they all died
of distemper. It wasn't like lying, this withholding of a
fact. It was their secret, this silent antipathy towards the
animals. A bond that made it easier for Hazel not to mind
too much when she was in bed with the measles, or a very
bad cold, and her mother was miles away in Battersea,
calming a stray and making sure it ate.

Anyway . . . the day after her father broke down, her
mother went out as usual. And although she *was* back in
time for supper, as promised, there was something about
her; an air of such weariness as she picked up her knife and
fork, that Hazel was immediately suspicious. Only people,
Hazel knew, exhausted her mother so utterly and turned
her face the colour of ash. People and long journeys.

'You've been to visit him, haven't you,' she said straight
away. 'You've been to that rest home. Without me.'

Mrs Mull-Dare continued to chew, very slowly, on a
mouthful of cheese soufflé.

*Swallow it*, Hazel willed her, bitterly. *It's soufflé, not grit*.

They were sitting at each end of the long mahogany
dining table—Mrs Mull-Dare at the head of it, in her
husband's usual place, with Hazel opposite. It meant that

64

the empty space, with no cutlery, glass, or mat set out, was on the side where Hazel normally sat. This layout had been Mrs Sawyer's idea. It was supposed to make Mr Mull-Dare's absence seem less raw and obvious. To Hazel it felt more as if he had been obliterated. For good.

Mrs Mull-Dare put down her knife and fork.

'I left very early,' she said. 'You were still asleep.'

It sounded lame. It *was* lame.

'You . . . you told me,' Hazel spluttered, 'that he wasn't *allowed* visitors. You *LIED*.' She was glad she hadn't started eating yet, for she would have choked. Glad, also, that there were no servants in the room to see her cry.

'Don't cry. Really. Don't.'

Through her anger, and her tears, Hazel saw that her mother was sitting ramrod straight and clutching the edge of the table so hard that her knuckles had gone white.

A nudging at her shins made her jump. It was Dottie, trying to lick her hand.

'I should have gone as well,' she cried, shunting Dottie off her with a movement of her leg that wasn't *quite* a kick. 'You should have woken me up. Now he'll think I don't care and that I didn't want to see him. Just because . . . because . . . *you didn't want me with you*.'

The injustice of it . . . of knowing that she had been left behind, to worry and wonder . . . was monstrous, and more than she could bear.

'You don't understand,' Mrs Mull-Dare said, softly. 'He's not himself. It would have been . . . '

'LIAR. You're a rotten, bitchy liar.' And Hazel was up, across the room, and out of the door before another word could be said. She didn't care who heard her as she went stomping up the stairs, sobs heaving in her throat, and if Dottie, or one of the servants, had dared to follow she would have lashed out for sure, with her feet *and* her fists.

Slamming her bedroom door took some of the heat out of her, but not all. Crying steadily she whirled to face the room, hating every inch of it. Those dolls—she felt like throttling one. Her white muslin dress, freshly ironed and laid out for Sunday—she wanted to rip all its frills off with her two bare hands. Even the rocking horse infuriated her. Given a whip, she would have thrashed the paint off it.

*Liar, liar. Rotten bitchy liar.*

Her father would have been shocked—mortified.

*But he's not here, is he. Nor is he himself.*

It was airless in her bedroom for the window had been closed to keep out the midges that swarmed up through the trees at dusk. Hazel wasn't supposed to open windows, in case she cut herself or fell out, but she went over anyway, undid the catch, and pushed until the big glass pane was wedged tight in the branches of the magnolia, and she could breathe.

It was almost nine, but still light. Leaning her elbows on the sill and cupping her chin in her hands Hazel stared up through clumps of leaves and felt her pulse and her heartbeat slow down. It was a long time since she had thrown a tantrum like that. Redheads were volatile, everyone said so, but still . . . it was neither ladylike, nor The Done Thing, to call one's own mother a liar and a bitch and then go storming off.

She wondered, vaguely, what the consequences would be but decided that, for the moment anyway, it didn't matter and she didn't care. She was all cried out, and no longer in the mood for a fight. And although the tears were still wet on her face, and her breath all juddery, there was a peacefulness to this quietening-down process that she vaguely remembered from being little. The calm after the storm.

She didn't know how long she stood there; only that the stars had come out and that seeing them twinkling away between the branches of the tree had made her think of Gloria—or, rather, of the lavatory seats in Gloria's house which were said to be set with diamonds.

*They must be worth a fortune, those diamonds. What if one came off and stuck to you without you knowing? Would they call you a thief and send you to prison? Would Gloria's father sue your ass off?*

Her head was nodding, between her cupped hands. She could barely keep her eyes open. Her nightdress was on her pillow, in a quilted bag shaped like a water lily. Too tired to bother with it she stripped to her petticoat and slid under the covers.

She must have fallen immediately and soundly asleep, for the click of the window being shut woke her up with a jerk that jarred her spine. And in the few moments that it took for her to remember where she was, and why she had her petticoat on, somebody stepped across to her bed and sat on it.

*Daddy?*

But the person sitting on the mattress was too light a presence to be her father.

She kept her eyes scrunched shut. It seemed the safest bet.

'A girl from your school was here.'

Opening only one eye, Hazel peered warily at her mother's shape.

'She left you a letter. I'll put it here, on your bedside table, shall I, so you can read it in the morning?'

'All right.'

Hazel's voice was small. The voice of a four year old.

She waited for her mother to say something else, but she didn't. Nor did she leave. She just sat where she was, on the edge of the bed, not touching Hazel but not reproaching her either.

Was she waiting for an apology?

*Well, she can wait a long time then. She can wait until winter comes and the leaves fall off the trees. She can wait until the dogs starve and the servants give up on us and go and work for someone else.*

*She can wait until my father comes home; or until my rocking horse kicks up his hooves and neighs.*

'Florence said she sounded American, and looked eighteen years old at least. Is she really still at school?'

Cautiously, Hazel shifted her head on the pillow. So Gloria hadn't gone to a party in Henley-on-Thames after all. She was still here, in London.

'Yes,' she said.

'And is she your friend?'

'Yes.'

Her mother patted the bedclothes, just missing Hazel's shoulder. 'I'm glad you've got a friend,' she said. 'Someone to talk to. Someone your age. It might help . . . take your mind off things.'

*Things? Things? My broken down father and me not being allowed to see him are 'things' now, are they?*

Hazel opened her mouth, in the dark, and then closed it again. To mention her father now would be like pressing a new bruise. And what would it gain her? Not much, she was certain. Not for the moment.

And Gloria . . . Gloria had been here. Of all the things she could have done with her time, now that she hadn't gone to Henley-on-Thames, to dance with a Peer of the Realm, Gloria had chosen—had wanted—to see Hazel.

'Her name is Gloria,' she said, shyly. And she found herself telling her mother what had happened that morning, beside the Round Pond. 'Gloria drew a picture with Miss Amelia in it,' she said. 'The picture made Miss Amelia look . . . foolish . . . so Miss Amelia whacked her specimen net down over Gloria's head and trapped her. Poor Gloria had to walk all the way back to school like that, with people staring.'

Recounting the story was oddly soothing for it made the incident in the dining room, between herself and her mother, seem tame.

*I yelled at you—but Gloria drew a wicked picture, for everyone to see.*

*Miss Amelia erupted like a volcano—but you haven't even told me off.*

*Compared to Gloria and Miss Amelia, we are considerate human beings. We are being kind to one another.*

'When I was a very little girl,' Mrs Mull-Dare said, 'some woman—a stranger—hooked her umbrella under my collar, lifted me up, and dumped me in a puddle.'

'Why?' Hazel was falling asleep again. She could feel herself going, lulled by her own story-telling and by her mother's apparent forgiveness.

'She thought I had lice, and that she might catch them.'

'How mean.' Hazel yawned, and snuggled deeper beneath her covers. 'And did you?'

'Did I what?'

No answer.

'Did I what, pet?'

'Umm . . . have lice.'

'No I didn't. Sadly, I was used to being treated badly by people who didn't care about me. Now, had my mother been alive *she* would have acted, always, with my very best interests at heart.'

'Always?' Hazel dared to mumble. 'Are you sure?'

'Absolutely certain. She could have swung me over the rooftops, on the end of a fishing line, and it would have been all right.'

Hazel wriggled, uncomfortably. 'That's silly,' she said. 'That could never happen. You're just making things up now.'

'Well . . . yes, I am. But I'm trying to make a point, which is that when a mother acts in a way that seems shocking or mean it may be that she is trying to protect you. To spare you from something—some sight or situation—that you're not quite old enough . . . quite ready . . . to deal with.'

Hazel swallowed, glad of the dark so that she could pretend, without too much trouble, to have drifted back to sleep.

*She's waiting for an apology after all*, said a little voice in her head. *So go on.*

*Not on your Nelly*, she answered it back.

And after a while, just when the silence had grown as

hot and as heavy as an extra blanket, her mother got up and left the room, closing the door behind her. And Hazel lay very still, for a long time, feeling guilty and angry in turns and wishing with all her might that she could wake up somewhere else. That she could *be* someone else. Just for a while.

Gloria. She would quite like to be Gloria for a bit; if only to see what it was like to have a big chest, an American Ma, and the nerve to draw people mating.

The letter . . . what was in the letter that Gloria had left for her? What was so urgent that it couldn't wait until Monday morning?

Her fingers tingled to open that letter, but it was too dark, now, to see anything properly.

Tomorrow.

She would read her friend's letter tomorrow. It was something to look forward to. The one and only thing.

# CHAPTER 7

*Dear Hazel,*
*This is just to let you know that I will not be at school next*
*week, or ever again. You can probably guess why. That crazy*
*Gumm woman is in for it. My father says he'll see her in court.*
*She is HISTORY and so is that dumb school.*

> *Yours in haste,*
> *Gloria*

*P.S. I am DEFINITELY coming to your birthday party*
*next Friday. I wouldn't miss it for the world. Will all the other*
*girls be there? Octavia and Verity and so on? I do hope so!!!*

Hazel read her letter five times, and then three times more
after breakfast. Then she went in search of Florence.

'I wonder,' she said, 'how my new friend Gloria found
out where I live, for I certainly didn't tell her.'

Florence was down on her knees in the drawing room,
swabbing a particularly valuable Persian rug. 'That
wretched Rascal,' she grumbled, wrinkling her nose as
she wrung out the cloth. 'That tiresome mutt. He must
have got in while I was opening the shutters. Either that

or someone left the door open . . . Your friend, miss? You mean the American girl? Well, I wouldn't know, I'm sure. She put us all in a bit of a flutter, she did, calling so late without an invitation. And so soon after . . . and with a young man in tow as well. I told Mrs Sawyer he was probably the young lady's brother, or a cousin. A relative of some description anyway, I said. Was I right?'

'I don't know,' Hazel said. 'I mean, yes. Probably.' And she left the drawing room, to look for her mother.

Mrs Mull-Dare was writing a letter. She had ink on her fingers and was looking fraught. 'There's so much to do . . . ' she said, turning from her bureau as Hazel appeared. 'I'm not sure where to start.' The dogs were shifting restlessly at her feet. They had clearly not been walked.

'He's not going to be at home for my birthday is he?'

'No, pet. It's not looking likely.'

'Or for Royal Ascot, even.'

'No, probably not.'

'But he'll definitely be all right in the long run? Right as rain? Promise?'

'I'm sure he will. Yes, I'm certain he will. You're not to worry.'

'Well then . . . ' Hazel paused, then continued in a rush: 'I'd like a party, please. On my birthday. For *all* the girls in my class. A proper supper party, nothing babyish. I'll tell Mrs Sawyer, shall I, that she's to start planning it? And I'll do the invitations myself as there's no time, now, to get any printed.'

She waited.

For a second or two her mother looked baffled.

Then: 'A party?' she said. 'You want a *party*?'

'Yes.'

'But . . .'

Whether she had intended to say, 'But you *hate* parties. Ever since you were little you've hated them,' or 'But how can you even think about a party when your father has had a breakdown?' Hazel would never know, for she paused, then sighed, and then said, 'Of course . . . of course you can have a party.'

'Thank you,' Hazel said. And she left the room quickly, before her mother could change her mind, or say anything else at all.

*Things To Do For My Birthday Party:*

1. *Invitations (smart ones) for: Gloria, Millicent, Jennifer, Marjorie, Verity, Phyllis, Octavia, Evelyn, and Jane. MAKE SURE GLORIA'S GETS DELIVERED STRAIGHT AWAY.*
2. *Supper menu: a salmon thing, cold chicken and sausages, fried potatoes, ice cream (pineapple, chocolate, strawberry and peach), a fruit punch in a big glass bowl (NOT the pudding basin). My cake.*
3. *Games*

Hazel stopped writing then, took a very deep breath, and chewed the end of her pencil. She hadn't had a birthday party since she was seven and had steadfastly refused to attend anybody else's. Parties made her anxious—at least, they used to—and her father had decided that, as

74

they were clearly Far Too Much For Her Delicate Senses, they were best avoided altogether.

Games. Did girls of her age still play party games? Somehow she couldn't imagine Gloria pinning the tail on a donkey or being thrilled by a round of musical chairs. Evelyn had had a conjurer at her last party and Octavia's guests had played croquet on the lawn. Listening to Millicent and the others talking, animatedly, about these events she had felt a moment's regret for having missed them. Only a moment's though, and then the feeling had passed.

Did the girls at school know how she felt about their parties? She had always tried to sound wretchedly sorry about missing them, but was so bad at fibbing that they had surely guessed. Luckily, Octavia, Jennifer, Phyllis, and Jane always celebrated their birthdays during the holidays when it was possible to write and say she would be away at the seaside, or visiting her aunt Alison in Scotland. Sometimes she was actually doing these things, so didn't have to lie (although fibbing on paper, she'd discovered, was a lot easier than doing it to someone's face). During term time her father always came to her rescue, arranging outings and treats to coincide with people's celebrations so that she could say, in all honesty, that other plans had been made.

If pressed, Hazel could not have told precisely why she hated parties. It wasn't as if anything truly terrible had ever happened to her at one. Thinking back, she supposed there were lots of little reasons rather than one big one: the behaviour of the other girls, for a start, always so different, socially, to what it was at school . . . flouncier, somehow, and oddly cruel. And then there was the pressure to join in with everything—the mirth, the eating, the wretched games—when it was all such a whirl and she rarely felt like whirling.

Parties had made her feel lonely, she decided. More lonely than when she was actually alone. And because it was awful to feel like that, when you were very little, she was glad that her father had stepped in and made it all right for her not to take part. On her own birthdays, in recent years, he had taken her for tea at the Ritz Hotel. Just the two of them.

Games . . .

She couldn't remember ever having won a single one. More often than not she had been the first one left standing, at musical chairs . . . the first to blink, or wobble, when she was supposed to be a statue . . . the first to be found in hide-and-seek.

*Maybe I just hate losing*, she thought. *Like father, and that rat-scally Moulder who won us our sugar plantation. Maybe that's something I've got from my ancestors, like freckles.*

No games then. Not at this, her first birthday party in ages, and her first grown-up party ever.

She crossed out the word 'Games'. Gloria, she knew, liked to dance. Well, there were some records downstairs which they could play on her father's gramophone. Not boring old waltzes either, but Ragtime which was much more up to the moment. Better still, perhaps they could hire a band. The dining room was big enough.

### 3. *Entertainment: music and dancing.*

There.

Mrs Sawyer was neither impressed nor enthusiastic.

76

'A birthday party?' she said, when Hazel cornered her with her list of demands. 'On Friday? Here? Are you quite sure, Miss Mull-Dare, that it's what you actually want? And that your mother has agreed? It seems a bit . . . '

Her voice trailed away to nothing.

'A bit what?' Hazel snapped. 'A bit *what*?'

'Never mind. If Mrs Mull-Dare has said you may have a party then a party you had better have. Nothing stronger than lemonade in the punch, mind, and if that American young lady is to be asked she's not to smoke cigarettes. Not in this house.'

Hazel was amazed.

'Why would she?' she said. 'What makes you say such a thing?'

Mrs Sawyer sniffed.

'Well, it wasn't peppermints I smelt on her breath when she called here yesterday evening, that much I *can* be sure of. As for the young gentleman driving the car . . . if he was her brother then I'm the King of Spain's daughter. Still . . . far be it from me, Miss Mull-Dare, to tell you who to invite and who to steer well clear of. Although I'm not sure your dear father would approve of such a . . . '

Again, her voice petered out.

'The cake,' she said, briskly. 'We must decide about your cake. I'll talk to Cook.' And away she went, before Hazel could ask about the salmon thing, or the right kind of bowl for punch, or the possibility of fitting ten girls and a Ragtime band in the dining room, with enough space left for dancing.

And . . . oh!

Back in her bedroom she picked up her pencil and wrote a fourth, and very important, reminder on her list:

4. *NO DOGS to be seen or heard under any circumstances. Rascal and Diggy-Bert, in particular, to be shut away or taken out.*

She paused, tapped her pencil against her teeth, and added:

5. *Mother not to appear unless she wears something clean and pins up her hair. Mother not to talk about the dogs, or about being a vegetarian. Mother not to try and make any of my friends become vegetarians.*

Had it been her fifth or her sixth birthday party at which her young guests had been offered dishes of semolina because jelly, so her mother had blithely informed them all, was made from the boiled-up skins and hoofs of poor helpless creatures? And how old had she been the year of Jennifer's fancy dress event, when the others had gone as fairies or princesses while she had been buttoned into something brown, with her mother's powder puff stitched to her bottom?

Reaching for a rubber, she glowered at number five before rubbing it out.

Peter Rabbit indeed . . . How the fairies had laughed, tossing their curls and pointing their wands like little daggers. How the princesses had teased her ('*Hop, hop to the tea table, baby rabbit . . .* ') And who was it—she had never known—who had put raisins under her chair, like droppings?

'*Mother not to appear under any circumstances,*' she wrote.

In a drawer she found a pack of white cards; very grown-up but perhaps just a little too plain for what was, after all, a celebration. Reaching for her coloured pencils she began drawing borders—swirls and stripes, like streamers, and small circles which she could have turned into balloons but chose not to. Without really thinking, she used shades of purple and green.

### *Please come to my party on Friday June 13th*

Just forming the words 'Friday June 13th' felt a lot like tempting fate. It looked wrong, as well, in coloured pencil. Childish. *Purple ink,* she decided. *That's what I need. Purple ink against the white background will match the border and look very smart.*

Her mother had coloured inks in her bureau. They had been a present, last Christmas, from Aunt Alison, along with a special pen and a selection of nibs. 'For calligraphy, my dear,' Aunt Alison had cooed. Those inks, Hazel knew, were still sealed in their box and the pen had never been used.

Well, she would use them now.

The parlour was deserted—no mother and no dogs. They would be out walking, Hazel guessed, so would be gone a long time, particularly if Diggy Bert had slipped his lead and begun chasing cars.

She knew she ought to wait, really, for permission to use the calligraphy set. But having started her invitations she wanted them finished. Only then, with each girl's name clearly printed, and the date, time, and place inked in, would she feel that this party was definite, with no going back.

The bureau was closed but not locked. Where would the calligraphy set be?

The top drawer slid open easily. There were dried pig's

ears in it, for the dogs to nibble on, and a stack of calling cards, still loosely wrapped in cellophane:

## *Mrs Ivy Mull-Dare*

Hazel's mother never paid calls on anyone, unless they had lost a dog, but the cards were nicely printed, in a flowing calligraphy script, so Hazel slid one out to copy from.

One of the pig's ears got caught, as she pushed the drawer shut. The slight cracking sound it made, and the grease it left on her fingers as she prodded it back, sent a shudder right through her. It was a mystery to her, and always would be, how a vegetarian could even look at such gruesome objects, never mind feed them as treats to her pets.

The bottom drawer was full of stuff to do with the Battersea Dogs' Home. Letters, mostly, from people who had found their missing darlings there and just wanted to say that Hazel's mother was a saint, an angel, a diamond . . . Hazel picked up a photograph of a poodle wearing a polka dot bow round the ridiculous fluff on its head. *'Maybelline just wants to say thank you, thank you, thank you from the bottom of her doggy heart!'*

Yee-uck!

There was a bundle of letters, tied with ribbon. Love letters, probably, from her father. Personal, sacred things. Hazel's fingers fluttered over them and she felt her face growing hot, even though she had no intention of untying the ribbon and peeping.

The calligraphy set was at the very back of the drawer. Hazel pulled it out. It hadn't been used, but the box was open and there was a sheet of paper inside which looked as if it had been crumpled into a ball and then smoothed flat again. The paper was yellow and clearly a lot older than the calligraphy set. Hazel recognized the handwriting at once as her aunt Alison's.

# THINGS TO REMEMBER

1. Do not speak to one in an inferior position in life to yourself as though they were dogs. Neither gush at them nor be too familiar.

2. Do not use a knife when eating rissoles.

3. When two ladies, slightly acquainted, meet, the one of the highest rank or greatest age bows first.

4. Never read what you would blush to say out loud.

5. Avoid the words 'chap' and 'toff'.

6. Sitting should be done with the backbone at right angles to the thigh bones and the feet uncrossed and resting on the ground.

7. In making a call, the visitor does not send in her card if her acquaintance should be at home but leaves it on departure or if the friend is out. A married woman leaves two of her husband's cards with one of her own. Of the two, one is meant for the lady called upon, the other for her husband. Should the lady called

*upon be unmarried or a widow the caller leaves
only one of her husband's cards.*

Hazel couldn't help smiling. Her aunt Alison was a very bossy person. 'Formidable', father called her. She had married well (Uncle Douglas was a Scottish laird) and lived in a castle with stags' heads on the walls and a loch on all sides, like a gigantic looking glass. Aunt Alison had one child, John, who was a bit older than Hazel and away at school somewhere in the north. Hazel was very fond of John. He had the Mull-Dare freckles, for a start, along with the thick orangey hair, so looked exactly like a brother of hers might have done, had she had one. He was gentle, too—almost too gentle, for a boy, Hazel sometimes thought, since he was nervous of the bats that bumped and squealed around the turrets of his home, and positively terrified of mice.

Carefully, she folded Aunt Alison's list, slipped it under the poodle picture, and closed the drawer. She had the calligraphy set and that was all she had come in here to look for. There was no reason for her to lower the bureau's flap, to see what else she might find. No reason, and no excuse under the sun.

The flap's hinges squeaked a warning:

*Curiosity killed the cat . . .*

The letter Mrs Mull-Dare had been writing earlier was propped, unfolded and unfinished, against a blotter. The handwriting was so terrible it looked as if an insect had paddled in ink and then gone for a stroll across the page.

With some difficulty Hazel read:

*Dear Alison,*

*You will have got the telegram by now* ('received' Hazel corrected automatically) *telling you the news about your brother Maurice. I saw him yesterday and he is as well as can be expected under the sircomestances* ('circumstances', mother . . .). *He appears full of remorse and has given me his word that he will not try again. I beleeve* ('tssk') *he means it but the doctor says it is early days and he must rest and be watched.*

*He is very very worried about money. I do not know how much he lost at the Epsum Derby but it was a lot. Hazel is all right at the school because he has already paid the fees for all of next year. That at least is one worry off his mind.*

*This is a difficult time here, of course. Hazel will finish school soon for all of July and Orgust* ('tsssk') *and I want to ask if you and Douglas would mind if she—*

And that was all there was.

*If she what?*

It was easy enough to guess. And, really, if her father wasn't coming home soon she would much rather be in Scotland than in London. If cousin John was at home they would go fishing, and for picnics beside the loch, and Uncle Douglas would take them into Glasgow to buy treacle toffee and the boiled sweets that were called 'Granny Sookers' because when you sucked them they were so sour that your face went like an old granny's.

83

Aunt Alison would go on a lot, asking irritating questions about what, precisely, Hazel was being taught at the Kensington School for the Daughters of Gentlemen, and whether her mother had any plans, yet, for introducing her to eligible young men. But that was all right. She could cope with that. Just.

She glanced, once again, at the unfinished letter. *He has given me his word that he will not try again*.

Try what again? Betting on horses, probably.

*I don't know how much he lost at the Epsum Derby, but it was a lot.*

Hazel felt her face heating up again. She herself had never been asked about that day at Epsom, much to her relief. So . . . if father had confessed to losing a lot of money there, had he also told about the suffragette being trampled by the King's horse?

It would be better, Hazel reckoned, if her mother knew about that, then she could at least tell Aunt Alison precisely why the race had ended badly. Still, it wasn't something Hazel wanted to talk to her mother about. Her father might have lost his bet anyway, with no interference from anyone. And what the suffragette had done seemed too important somehow, too . . . *noble*, to be belittled by Mrs Mull-Dare's annoyance or (and this seemed far more likely) by her total lack of interest. She herself began to wonder, for the first time in days, how the injured woman was doing, and whether she was up and about yet, planning more actions.

Then she closed the bureau and left the room, to finish her invitations.

# CHAPTER 8

B y Monday morning nearly every girl at the Kensington School for the Daughters of Gentlemen knew that Hazel Mull-Dare's father had tried to hang himself. They knew, but had promised their parents they would say nothing about it; not to each other, not to their teachers, and certainly not a word to poor Hazel herself.

Miss Amelia and Miss Eunice knew as well, and it made Miss Eunice growl and Miss Amelia twitter to think that the scandal might reach the newspapers and damage the good name of their school. However, as Miss Eunice was swift to point out, the school's reputation could already be in jeopardy thanks to Miss Amelia's somewhat heavy-handed response to Gloria Gilbert's 'Landscape in June'.

'If only you hadn't *prodded* the brat,' she grumbled. 'At least not in the neck where any marks were bound to show.'

'Dear heart, don't,' Miss Amelia begged. 'I cannot bear to be reminded. But her *neck*? No, no, dear, I netted her very carefully—*very* carefully indeed—so you need have no fear on that score. Really, none at all. And Miss Gilbert, if she has any sense, will refrain from mentioning a single word about it. After all, that sketch of hers was quite obscene . . . ' She paused, shuddering at the memory . . . 'so lewd and so revolting that any right-thinking person would have to agree that she brought that punishment upon herself.'

'Upon her own head,' muttered Miss Eunice. 'Quite literally.'

Gloria's absence quickly became the subject of whispered conjecture among the older girls, while Miss Amelia was at a cupboard, rummaging. It was a relief, for most of them, to have something they could gossip about openly, for the taboo subject of Hazel Mull-Dare's father was so tantalizing they were tingling with the awful thrill of it and having trouble keeping quiet.

'*Perhaps Gloria is indisposed.*'

'*No. She was indisposed six days ago. Nobody's indisposed that often.*'

'*Some people are. My cousin Daphne is.*'

'*It'll be because of what happened at the Round Pond, don't you think?*'

'*Heavens, what if she was badly hurt? What if her neck . . .*' Jennifer had been going to say '*swelled up so badly that she couldn't breathe*' but bit the words back just in time. Ashamed, she glanced across at Hazel Mull-Dare to see if she'd noticed.

Hazel hadn't. 'Gloria won't be back at all, not ever,' she informed everyone, grandly. 'She came round to my house on Saturday to tell me so. But she'll be at my birthday party. Definitely.'

Millicent, Evelyn, Phyllis, and Jane nudged one another under the table. The others blinked and looked embarrassed. Hazel Mull-Dare hadn't had a party in *ages*. And to have one now . . . well, it seemed a little odd, under the circumstances. Not hard-faced necessarily, but definitely Not The Done Thing.

Only Octavia de Willoughby seemed unamazed, but then Octavia de Willoughby came from a family in which recollections of fabulous parties had become inextricably mixed, like the threads of a grand tapestry, with tales of great-great-great-uncle so-and-so losing a duel, or a broken hearted ancestor throwing herself in a lake.

'Right then, girls. *King Lear*. Act one, scene two. Quick sticks! We didn't get very far on Friday, did we? Octavia, dear heart—perhaps you would like to continue from where you left off.'

Miss Amelia was doling out the books as if they were sweets, or playing cards—*one for you, one for you*. She looked strangely pleased with herself, Hazel thought, but it could just be she was glad that Gloria Gilbert wasn't there. Perhaps she hadn't been told, yet, that Gloria's father was going to sue her ass off. Perhaps she believed she was safe.

Hazel hadn't given much thought, over the past couple of days, to the fate of the school should Miss Amelia be sent to prison. She had been too busy planning her party. Thinking about it now, though, she began to feel alarmed. Her father, according to the letter in her mother's bureau, had paid a year's fees in advance for Hazel to continue her studies here with the Gumms. It was one less worry, her mother had told Aunt Alison. One less thing for him to fret about.

*That crazy Gumm woman is in for it.*

*She is history and so is that damned school.*

Would her father lose his money if the school closed? Hopefully, Hazel told herself, it wouldn't come to that.

The other girls had opened their *King Lear*s and were staring, dismally, at Act one, scene two. Quickly, Hazel reached for her own copy and found the right page.

'Just skip over the white bits, girls,' said Miss Amelia, gaily. 'One has to remember that dear Shakespeare was writing for a very *different* and considerably less *refined* audience than ourselves. We may be privileged, in these enlightened times, to study the great man's work but that doesn't mean we have to be subjected to certain— ahem—terms.'

Bending her head, so that her hair curtained the book, Hazel flipped through the whole play. On almost every page a word—in some cases several words—had been covered by a sliver of white paper, cut carefully to size and glued into place.

The other girls were looking mystified. But then, they didn't know, as Gloria had, and as Hazel did, about the bosoms and 'lust' and 'brothel'. And all those 'bastards'. And 'womb'.

*'Kent banish'd thus! And France in choler parted!*
*And the King gone tonight . . . '*

It must have taken Miss Amelia a very long time, Hazel mused, to blot out all the rude words in all of the books. It must have taken her a whole morning at least, the silly old bat . . .

Imagining her teacher bent over a pile of *King Lear*s, pouncing on certain phrases with her splinters of sticky paper, made Hazel want to giggle. Would her father be amused as well, if she got the chance to tell him? She wasn't sure that he would, not even once he got better. He might, she realized, actually agree with Miss Amelia that the blotted-out words would have been too much for the girls' Delicate Senses.

That night, over supper, she asked her mother about hiring a ragtime band to play at her party. The answer was a very definite no. They couldn't afford it.

In all her years on earth, Hazel had never had to consider how much something cost. Everything she had ever wanted, along with quite a few things she hadn't (new hats, piano lessons, tickets for *Peter Pan*) had simply appeared. Good things, it seemed, would always flow her way just as water flowed from taps and sugar flowed from her grandfather's mills, far away in the Caribbean. Even losing on the horses hadn't seemed like anything much to worry about. Until now.

'Records, then,' she said, quickly. 'I'll play records on the gramophone instead.'

Mrs Mull-Dare winced.

'It won't cost anything,' Hazel added. 'Not a penny.'

Mrs Mull-Dare flapped her fingers and shook her head, as if Hazel had misunderstood something—some vital fact about the gramophone that had nothing to do with money.

'I'm sure father would allow it,' Hazel said. 'I'm absolutely certain he would. And anyway it's not as if he has to know about it, is it? It's not as if he's bothered, right now, about the gramophone, or me, or my birthday, or you or . . . or about *any*thing . . . is it?'

She was pushing her luck, she knew she was, speaking like that, even if it was the truth. Her mother was bound to declare the gramophone out of bounds now, to teach her some respect, and might even call the party off altogether.

Holding her breath, as she waited to see what would happen, Hazel was aware that, should her celebration get cancelled, she wouldn't be too upset. For now that the invitations were out, and everyone had accepted, she was beginning to get scared. Really, she had only planned the thing to please Gloria. And to take her mind off her father's breakdown, of course.

'All right, pet,' her mother said. 'All right. Just be careful not to scratch any of Daddy's records, and make sure—absolutely sure—that they go back in the correct sleeves. You know how particular he is.'

'Thank you,' Hazel mumbled. And for a while she wasn't certain who she hated the most: her mother, for being so reasonable while failing to understand a single solitary thing, or herself for being the sort of daughter who would wheedle and coax, and speak unkindly about her father to get her own way.

*But Gloria is bound to be impressed*, she reassured herself, hurrying upstairs to her own room. *For father has the very latest Ragtime records and has shown me all of the steps. I know how to dance the Turkey Trot, the Grizzly Bear, and the Bunny Hug. I can teach all of my friends.*

*I can teach Gloria.*

Friday June 13th dawned chilly and wet which Cook said was only to be expected given the dire nature of the date. She had put her sharpest knives to the back of the drawer (*'Nobody's chopping anything today. We'd lose our fingers for sure'*) and was standing well back from the kettle as it boiled and spat on the range.

'This house,' snapped Mrs Sawyer, 'is up to the rafters in ill-luck. I very much doubt, Cook, that there can be any more in the offing whatever the day, the year, or the age of our young lady.'

Quick as a blink, Cook touched a wooden chopping board.

'Hush, Mrs Sawyer, do,' she whispered. 'You're tempting the fates.'

'Oh—piffle.' Mrs Sawyer couldn't be doing with the fates. Not today. Not with an important legal gentleman due at eleven, to discuss the family's financial situation with poor Mrs Mull-Dare. Not with Lady Mac (Miss Alison, as she used to be) arriving any day. And not, on top of everything else, with all those girls from the Kensington School for the Daughters of Gentlemen expected at seven o'clock prompt, for Miss Hazel's birthday party.

'Has the salmon arrived?' she asked.

'It has,' said Cook. 'And it's a whopper.'

'Good. And Miss Mull-Dare wants the big crystal bowl for her lemonade punch, and the silver ladle for serving. The bowl will probably need a good clean out with bicarbonate of soda. Get Florence to do it.'

Cook shuddered, her fingers moving back towards the wooden chopping board.

'If she drops it,' Mrs Sawyer snapped, 'it will be for no other reason than she's all thumbs. *And* it will come out of her pay at the end of the month.'

'If there *is* any pay at the end of the month,' Cook muttered into the kettle's steam. 'For any of us.'

Florence didn't drop the bowl. The important legal gentleman came and went discreetly, and the morning passed without mishap. Hazel, home from school by 2.15, spent the rest of the afternoon in her bedroom agonizing over what to wear for her party and what to do with her hair.

'You can't go wrong with your white muslin, miss,' said Florence, having come up just before five to find the bed heaped with discarded frocks, skirts, and blouses and Hazel herself hopping anxiously around in front of a mirror in nothing but a petticoat and her new charm bracelet. 'Your white muslin and the pink sash.'

'I've gone off pink,' Hazel fretted. 'Pink is for little girls, and it clashes with my hair. I wish I had a purple sash or, better still, a purple and green one.'

Florence threw her a worried look. 'Why those colours in particular, miss?' she said. 'If you don't mind me asking.'

Hazel twisted her hair on top of her head. It was no good. Loose and wavy it looked stupid and childish. Bunched in a floppy topknot it resembled nothing so much as Pipkin's rear end.

'Because I think purple and green would suit me better,' she said, watching in the mirror for Florence's reaction. Florence relaxed, visibly. 'And because,' she added, sweetly, 'they are the suffragette colours and I happen to admire the suffragettes. I think they're wonderful.'

Straightaway, Florence looked anxious again; then cross as well as she locked eyes with Hazel in the mirror and realized she was being observed. Turning away she began picking clothes off the bed, tutting over a creased skirt and frowning at a knotted sash as if they could, and should, oblige her by un-creasing and un-knotting without any help from anybody.

'Fat lot to admire, miss,' she couldn't help saying, keeping her back to the mirror while she gave a blouse a good shake and hustled it onto a hanger. 'A *fat* lot to admire, I'd say, when it puts you into an early grave.'

'What . . . what do you mean?' Hazel kept her voice neutral.

'That woman at the Derby, miss. The one what threw herself in front of the King's horse. She died. The funeral's tomorrow. There's to be a big fuss by all accounts—not that *she'll* know much about it, will she, lying cold as a stone with her head kicked in. Oh . . . I'm sorry, Miss Hazel, I shouldn't . . . Now—this white silk is pretty, and perfectly suitable for the evening. Why don't you pop it on and I'll help you with your hair? I think if we pin it more towards the back, and maybe find a flower—a *fresh* flower . . . a rose, perhaps—to hide the pins, it will do very well.'

Without a word, Hazel got herself into the white silk dress. It didn't need a sash.

'Lovely!' declared Florence. 'Now, let's see about that hair.'

There was no avoiding the mirror for hair-brushing but Florence focused so resolutely on the brush, her own hands, and the back of Hazel's head that even accidental eye contact was avoided. She hummed for a while as well, to discourage further conversation about suffragettes, and when that became oppressive, and a little too obvious, she began to talk about the party.

'The table looks lovely, miss,' she said. 'And Cook's iced the cake. I think you'll like it. It's lovely . . . '

Hazel sat very still and let Florence ramble on. *I didn't*

*know that dead suffragette*, she was thinking to herself. *I don't even know her name. And yet . . .*

Amazingly, she found she was having to fight back tears.

*It's because I'm anxious*, she told herself, swallowing hard and biting her bottom lip. *About my party. In case my friends don't . . . in case Gloria doesn't . . . enjoy it.*

But it wasn't just the party making her feel so weepy. In her mind—her memory—the Epsom Derby niggled and nagged because it was the last outing she had shared with her father; the last outing, and the most likely cause of his breakdown. In her mind all the little things about that day—her father's silence in the car; the way he had tried so hard to be jolly, after losing all his money; the bone-white of his knuckles as he held tight to the Old Girl's steering wheel—had grown bigger since his breakdown. Larger and larger these small memories had loomed until they seemed far more important than anything else that had happened that day.

And now the suffragette was dead. Cold as a stone, like Florence had said. And memories of Derby Day were re-shuffling once more, the big things growing smaller again, and the small things growing big. And all Hazel knew, or sensed, was that she was mourning an unknown woman as if she'd been a relative, while the father she adored had become remote to her. A stranger.

'There . . . How's that, miss?'

Hazel blinked a few times, then looked at herself in the mirror.

'Oh,' she said, 'I look . . . '

'Lovely,' Florence declared. 'You look absolutely lovely. Quite the young lady.'

Turning sideways, Hazel gazed, bashfully, at her profile. She certainly looked different. Pretty, almost.

'You're good with hair, Florence,' she said, with a watery smile. 'Thank you.'

'You're welcome, miss. Now, I'll go and see about a rose from the garden, shall I? To pin on the side? A not-quite open one it will have to be, so as the petals don't drop.'

'Not pink though,' Hazel told her, quickly. 'I don't want pink.'

'Right you are.' And Florence set off for the garden, giving silent thanks, as she went, that no rose she'd ever clapped eyes on had been purple or green.

# CHAPTER 9

**W**here is she?
*Where's Gloria?*
*Why isn't she here yet?*

It was almost seven thirty. The fried potatoes, Hazel knew, would be about to go in the pan, and at least two stomachs in the room had rumbled.

'Are we waiting for Gloria?' said Phyllis. 'Is she definitely coming?'

'Perhaps her neck is still bad,' suggested Evelyn. 'Perhaps it's . . . ow! Jennifer? Don't *pinch* me. What did you pinch me for?'

Hazel stood up and walked across to the big bay window. They were downstairs, in the main sitting room, and she was being reminded, with every minute that passed, how much she hated parties.

Behind her, the girls from her class smoothed their pretty frocks, patted their hair, and made exaggerated faces at one another.

*Is Hazel all right?*
*Are we going to sit here all night or what?*

Along with the looks, a kind of shiver passed among them, for they were all wondering—they couldn't help it—if this was the room Mr Mull-Dare had tried to hang himself in.

Hazel assumed that they were bored. At school it didn't matter. At school it was the Whiney Gumms' job to capture their attention and keep it. Here and now it was her responsibility and she hadn't a clue how best to amuse and entertain so many girls. The dancing was for after supper and she hadn't planned anything for before. Why hadn't she? This was awful.

*And where was Gloria?*

A trickle of cold sweat ran down her back as she scanned the empty street.

'That suffragette died,' she said, for the want of something interesting to say. 'Her funeral is tomorrow. My father and I were right there when she got kicked in the head by the King's horse. I told you, didn't I? My father lost a lot of money at that race but it doesn't matter much. You win some, you lose some, father says. It's all even-stevens in the end.'

Sensing the glances zipping to and fro, she swung round. Wide-eyed, each girl returned her gaze, their faces cleaned as if by a flannel of any snide or knowing look that might have given them away.

Millicent, Verity, and Evelyn, however, weren't quite quick enough.

Hazel leaned back against the windowsill. She could feel her hair starting to slip from its pins. Florence hadn't been all that good with it after all. The sill felt hard against her spine, as if it might dent and spoil her dress.

'My father—' she started to say. And then the doorbell rang.

'That'll be Gloria.' The relief in Jennifer's voice was so obvious that anyone would think they'd been chained to their chairs for the past hour, and that only Gloria had the power to set them free. 'That'll be Gloria, at long last.'

And the other girls began to chatter and stir, like birds, leaving Hazel to take a very deep breath and pull herself together. She heard the front door close, then a voice— a hearty male voice—saying, 'Ooops . . . sorry, old thing. Nearly dropped it!'

*Daddy?*

The others hadn't noticed. They were too busy chatting, getting into the party spirit now that everyone was here and they could relax.

Hazel couldn't move. She could barely breathe. Was it really him; recovered enough to come all the way home and take her to the Ritz? Was that why Evelyn and the others had been acting so strangely? Because it was a surprise and they all knew?

Then the sitting room door swung open and in barged a stranger: a slim fair-haired young man carrying something heavy in both arms; something big and square, wrapped up in silver paper, which he deposited on the floor, in the middle of the room, with a loud triumphant 'Ooof!'

'Where's the birthday girl, then?' he said, straightening up. He was rather good-looking, Hazel supposed, even though something about his face made her think of ferrets. Certainly he glowed with confidence, seeming certain of a welcome and his right to be in the room. But he was too cheaply dressed to be a gentleman (Mrs Sawyer would have called him vulgar) and Hazel hadn't the faintest idea who he was.

'It's me, Hazel Louise Mull-Dare,' she said, her pulse

thrumming from surprise and disappointment. 'And you are . . . ?'

'This is Valentine—Val for short. I needed him to carry the present. He's a poppet. Can he stay?'

Everyone, including the young man, swivelled round at the sound of Gloria Gilbert's voice. Hazel, aware that she was blushing, now that Gloria was finally here, said, 'Of course,' very quickly, and then, to the young man: 'I hope you like sausages.'

'I like everything,' Val-for-short told her, with a sly wink. 'Absolutely everything.'

Jennifer and Marjorie began tittering behind their hands.

*What?* Hazel thought, although she suspected it had something to do with her saying sausages.

Gloria was giggling, too, but not unkindly and, mercifully, not at Hazel.

'You are so WICKED,' she chortled, giving Val a little push. 'A bad, bad boy.'

'*Moi?*' he replied, striking an injured pose. 'Surely not?'

And was it Hazel's imagination or was he deliberately looking down at Gloria's chest? There was certainly enough of it on display, for her blouse was very thin. She remembered what Florence had said about a young man waiting in a car, when Gloria called last Saturday, and wondered if this was the one. She was sorry he wasn't her father, come to take her to the Ritz, but at least Gloria was here and that, she was a little ashamed to discover, made her almost as happy as seeing her father would have done.

'Hazel?' said Gloria. 'Hey, Hazel. Are you going to open

your present now? Because if you are, it's right over there, not hidden away down my front.'

Hazel jumped. She was blushing for England now, her face clashing violently with the roots of her pinned-up hair. And Val was smirking—smirking, and staring so intimately at her, through narrowed blue eyes, that it seemed he could see right through to her personal thoughts and feelings.

Quickly, she hurried to where her present had been deposited, knelt down in front of it and began tearing away silver paper. There were more wrappings underneath and then some kind of box.

'You have to press that catch and lift the lid back,' Gloria told her.

Hazel did as she was told. The other girls craned their necks to see.

'Oh, my,' breathed Jennifer. 'What are you going to do with *that*?'

Hazel touched her present lightly, with the fingers of one hand. It was what her mother did, she realized, when greeting a new dog.

'She'll *type* on it, of course,' said Gloria.

'What?' Jane sounded shocked. 'Like an *office* worker?'

'Sure.' Gloria leaned over Hazel's shoulder and began plink-plonking the keys with letters on them. 'It was Ma's idea. Ma says it never hurts a girl to prepare herself for the world of work. We won't all marry rich men, you know. There ain't enough to go around. Not titled ones, anyway.'

'But . . . ' Whatever Jennifer had been going to say, she quickly changed her mind.

'I'll *never* have to earn a living,' said Octavia, complacently. 'Whether I marry or not.'

Gloria pressed a few typewriter keys down slowly, one after the other. 'T-W-I-T,' she spelt, so that Hazel could see. 'Well, lucky for you, Miss Moneybags de Willoughby,' she scoffed. 'Some of us might not have it so easy. *Some* of us might end up as old spinsters, with no family fortune to fall back on and no one giving a damn.'

Hazel winced. So far she had been only puzzled, and somewhat intrigued, by this strange gift. So far she had quite liked the idea of learning to use it; of making words from her own head appear on a page, each one perfectly printed and neatly spaced.

Now, though, that quiet pleasure was being spoiled. *She means me, doesn't she?* she thought, anxiously. The word 'spinster' made her think of girls in fairytales, locked up in towers and told to spin flax into gold. She had no opinion one way or the other about remaining one herself—marriage still seemed as distant and as foreign to her as her grandfather's sugar plantation—but what exactly had Gloria meant about having no family fortune to fall back on? *Does she know?* she worried silently. *About father losing all that money at the Derby?*

'It could happen to *any* of us,' Gloria said then, giving Hazel's arm a friendly squeeze. 'We should *all* learn to type in case we end up alone. And to drive. And to cook, too, although, hell—I'd probably set a boiled egg alight!'

She laughed gaily and Hazel smiled. It was all right. Gloria and her ma, they were just being practical. If it had been Jennifer's birthday, or Phyllis's, they would have got this typewriter instead.

'It's a wonderful present,' she said. 'Thank you.'

Gloria gave her arm another squeeze and then kissed her, ripely, on the cheek.

'You're welcome, honey,' she said.

Supper was served, as planned, upstairs in the dining room, but not before Mrs Sawyer had drawn Hazel to one side, and made it clear that the presence of an uninvited male guest was Not The Done Thing at all and that, under ordinary circumstances, he would have been out on his ear.

'You mean if my father had been here?' Hazel had replied quietly, as all of her guests, including Val, took seats at the table.

Mrs Sawyer had winced, at that, and said nothing more; only fixed young Valentine with an icy stare as if daring him, on pain of a whipping, to take liberties with the young ladies or walk out with the family silver.

'If that boy's gentry,' she fretted, a few minutes later, to Cook, 'then I'm the Duchess of York. You should see his jacket. It isn't even lined. And that American girl's no better than she ought to be either, striding in here like she owns the place, and an hour late to boot. Mrs Mull-Dare will hear of this, as soon as she gets home.'

Cook was making final adjustments to the birthday cake—a vast sponge, shaped and iced to resemble a gramophone record. It was all done, apart from the hole in the centre, and this she was creating, very, very carefully, with the point of a large knitting needle.

She didn't answer Mrs Sawyer, or even look up. So far today she, and everyone else coming into her kitchen, had got away without injuring themselves or breaking the best china. There were still four hours to go before

Friday 13th became Saturday 14th and she, for one, was not about to drop her guard or get distracted from the delicate task in hand.

'Mind you don't stab yourself,' said Mrs Sawyer, sarcastically.

Back upstairs, Hazel was beginning, at last, to enjoy herself. She was at the head of the table, which made her feel special, and Gloria, although not next to her as she'd hoped, wasn't far away.

'Excellent scoff,' said Val, pushing back his empty plate. 'Shall I do the honours with the punch? No need to call a servant for a few little refills, eh? Hazel? More for you, old thing? Millicent? Verity?'

By the time ice cream was served Hazel couldn't understand why she had ever hated parties. All these girls—her friends—were having a wonderful time. Even stupid Verity was chatting away, nineteen to the dozen. And Val was being the perfect gentleman, seeing to the drinks. Only Gloria appeared subdued, all of a sudden, and for some reason kept putting down her cutlery to adjust the velvet choker she was wearing round her neck.

Hazel had noticed the choker earlier. It was navy blue, with a cameo pinned to it, and so wide it was just an inch or so short of being a scarf. She had assumed it was the latest fashion.

'Are you all right, Gloria?' she said.

Gloria sighed.

'Not really,' she replied, loudly enough for everyone to hear. 'I'm having difficulty swallowing, if you must know. I just didn't want to make a fuss.'

Immediately everyone quietened down.

'Is it your neck?' said Hazel. 'Is your choker too tight?'

'Oh dear . . . ' Gloria's right hand went fluttering to her throat. 'Oh dear, Hazel . . . I really *didn't* want to make a big deal of this. Not under the circumstances . . . with it being your birthday and all. However, since you ask . . . ' And she reached behind her neck and ripped the velvet away.

All the girls, including Hazel, gasped. Val shook his head in disgust. 'That teacher of yours should be locked up,' he said. 'Before she kills someone.'

Gloria gave a tiny cry.

'Does it still look bad?' she said, her voice quavering. 'Oh dear . . . '

'Bad?' Val thumped the table with his fist. 'It looks positively *awful*, doesn't it, girls? Only a criminal or a lunatic would inflict an injury like that upon another human being, don't you agree?'

Nobody spoke. All eyes except Hazel's were on the remains of the ice cream, melting in pretty colours at the bottom of china dishes, or on the sideboard where the cut-glass punch bowl reflected the light so beautifully.

'Miss Amelia must have netted you ever so hard,' Hazel said, eventually. 'I didn't think she had, Gloria. Not *that* hard. Not hard enough to leave such dreadful marks.'

'Well she did,' snapped Gloria. 'Clearly.'

'Y-yes.' Hazel wasn't used to being snapped at. 'I can *see* she did . . . I'm sorry. I didn't mean . . . '

Val chinked a spoon against the side of his glass and held up a hand, for silence.

'Go on, Glor,' he said. 'Say your piece.'

Gloria cleared her throat.

'The thing is, girls,' she said . . . 'Oh dear, it hurts to *speak* even . . . The thing is, Val's right. Your Miss Gumm is a dangerous woman. As mad as a bony mule. She could quite easily kill somebody one day—she could have killed *me*.'

Hazel looked, again, at the purple-blue bruises blooming like pansies on her friend's neck. From what she could recall, the rim of the specimen net had been lower down, circling the top of Gloria's shoulders.

'My father's pressing charges,' Gloria continued. 'He has photographed these injuries of mine and is taking Miss Crazy to court. There's bound to be a fuss, because of my ma being an heiress, and In Society and all. It'll be in all the papers. Old Gumm Boots will be ruined and serve her right.'

She paused, then, and looked around the table. The daughters of gentlemen stared back, appalled. Evelyn had the hiccups.

'Anyway . . . ' Gloria took a small sip of her punch, swallowed carefully, and carried on: 'I've been thinking. If Miss Gumm spills the beans about that sketch I drew the judge might be shocked. He might be so shocked he'll let her walk free from court. And that wouldn't be right, would it? In fact it would be a total travesty of justice.'

'*Hic!*' went Evelyn while the others all nodded and murmured that yes . . . yes, of course . . . a complete and total thingummy of justice. Absolutely.

'And so,' Gloria said, 'I want you all to promise, *on your mothers' lives*, that you won't tell. That if anyone ever asks—a policeman, a reporter, your folks, anyone at all—you'll say there was nothing whatsoever about that sketch of mine for old Gummy to get in a lather over. If it's her word against ours they'll believe us for sure, what with her being bonkers and all. You can say I drew Neptune, if you like, and a nymph, because they're classical, but *don't*, whatever you do, let on that they were *in flagrante delicto* . . . '

Jane, Millicent, Phyllis, Marjorie, Evelyn, and Verity looked puzzled. Jennifer blushed and Octavia sniffed, disdainfully. Evelyn was still hiccupping.

'What's inflagrantaydelectoe?' asked Hazel.

Val leant back in his chair, the better to enjoy everyone's faces. 'A bit of how's your father,' he said, knowingly. 'A roll in the hay. Making the beast with two backs.'

Only Jennifer looked away.

'Oh, for goodness' sake,' he chortled at the others. 'Putting you-know-what you-know-where. Playing hide the sausage. Now do you get it?'

Some of them did get it, and some of them didn't. All of them, though, had a very strong feeling that this was not a suitable subject for Valentine to be pursuing with the daughters of gentlemen. Not at the dinner table, and certainly not upon first acquaintance. Phyllis and Verity wanted to go home. Evelyn continued to hiccup. Amazingly, given the amount of gin Val had added to the lemonade punch, none of them felt sick. Yet.

Hazel, who had drunk the most, was surprised but not the slightest bit embarrassed to learn so many new expressions for mating. One of them—how's your father—had startled her, momentarily, but then Val wasn't to know, surely, about her own father breaking down and being sent to a rest home. At the Kensington School for the Daughters of Gentlemen, girls' fathers very often went away, for weeks at a time, on business. And nobody had asked, yet, about hers, for which she was deeply grateful.

Light-headed, but alert, she looked again at Gloria's throat.

'I don't see that it matters,' she said, slowly. 'About your drawing. Because if Miss Amelia did *that* to you there's really no excuse. I'm sure she'll be punished for hurting you, Gloria, whatever you drew. So why do we have to lie?'

Slowly, Gloria dipped a finger into her bowl of melting ice cream. She didn't look at Hazel as she raised the finger to her mouth and licked it clean.

'Because I've asked you to,' she said. 'All right?'

'No.' The word was out before Hazel could think twice. 'I don't think it is all right. Not really.'

'Now look here, Hazel.' Val leant abruptly across the table, no sign of a twinkle now in his eyes. 'It's all very well being a goody two-shoes, in fact it's really rather sweet. But you know as well as I do, that Glor was only having a bit of fun with that sketch. She's a fun-loving girl, our Glor, but a prissy old judge mightn't see it that way. And imagine the scandal if it got into the papers? Poor Glor's ma and pa would have a fit. And Glor's chances of getting hitched to a Peer of the Realm would . . . '

'That's enough, Val, thank you.' Gloria shot him a look— a very brief look, but chillier, by far, than the contents of his pudding dish. Then she turned sideways, cold-shouldering Hazel as she appealed to the others: 'Girls . . . Verity,

Millicent, Octavia. You've got little sisters at that school. You wouldn't want Miss Gumm whacking them over the head with that great big net of hers now, would you?

'No.'

'No.'

And, 'Of course not.'

'Well then . . . will you promise? To keep quiet about the silly little drawing, so that old Gumm Boots gets her just deserts?'

They promised.

'Evelyn?'

'I . . . *hic* . . . promise.'

'Jane? . . . thank you, honey . . . Phyllis? Marjorie? . . . Excellent . . . Jennifer?'

'I promise.'

Gloria picked up the velvet choker and lifted it to her neck. 'We're like the suffragettes,' she said. 'Bound together for a common cause. And you are all fine friends—the best a gal could wish for. Drat this fastening . . . Hazel, would you mind?'

'Me? . . . Oh. Of course.' Standing up made Hazel reel. The floor seemed to tilt, like the deck of a ship, then everything righted itself and she hurried round to help Gloria re-fasten her choker.

'Just hold my hair out of the way,' Gloria ordered her. 'So it doesn't get caught up.'

Obediently, Hazel lifted the weight of Gloria's hair from the back of her neck. It was softer than her own hair and a much safer colour. Holding it felt odd—wrong, somehow—and she had to concentrate hard to keep from stroking it. Gloria's fingers, so close to her own, were

108

fiddling with the choker's hook and eye. Flustered, Hazel raised the hair higher, so their skins wouldn't touch. She was sure, if she'd been Gloria, she could have fastened that choker by now. And Val was watching—leering—again in that intimate, knowing way.

'So,' Gloria said. 'That just leaves you, Hazel. The odd one out. Everyone else has promised to keep quiet for me, honey. Won't you?'

Hazel gripped the two handfuls of hair so hard that, had it been Gloria's wrists in her hands she would have hurt them. Not trusting herself to speak she simply shook her head. And although Gloria didn't see her do it, she could tell from Val's face that Hazel Mull-Dare was not going to change her mind. Even more infuriating, one or two of the other girls were swapping uncomfortable looks, as if this one act of dissent was giving them second thoughts as well.

'Right then!' Gloria jerked her neck forward and to one side, making Hazel flinch as she dropped the hair. 'I heard there's to be dancing. If so, the servants really ought to come and clear the table, don't you think? It's getting late.'

'Maybe no one will ask,' Hazel said, quickly. 'About the drawing, I mean. They might not, Gloria. And then none of us will have to lie about it.'

'Forget it,' Gloria answered, her voice all bright and brittle as if she couldn't care less any more. 'Let's have some fun. Let's dance.'

# CHAPTER 10

And so they danced. Once the table had been cleared and pushed back out of the way, they danced like crazy things. Not the Turkey Trot though, or the Grizzly Bear, or even the Bunny Hug.

'A bit old-fashioned, isn't he, your papa?' said Val, flipping rapidly through Mr Mull-Dare's collection of gramophone records without picking out a single one. 'A bit behind the times.'

Hazel could have slapped him.

And then: 'This'll do,' he said. '*El Choclo*. Not the most up-to-date version but better than a slap in the face with a wet herring. Hey, Glor, they've got *El Choclo*.'

'Good,' said Gloria. 'Put it on. Can you tango, girls? No? *What* . . . none of you? Then Val and I will have to teach you, won't we? Put the record on, Val.'

Hazel held out her hand. 'I'll do it,' she said. She didn't want Val touching the gramophone. She didn't want him laying hands on any of her family's things. Didn't the other girls realize how rude he was being, making remarks like that about her father's records? They didn't seem to. They were too busy talking, and pairing up to dance.

Val shrugged and handed her *El Choclo*.

'Thank you,' said Hazel.

'Come along, girls,' Gloria called out. 'Quick sticks.'

The mimicry was perfect. Even Hazel smiled. 'My father and I, we call Miss Amelia and Miss Eunice the Whiney Gumms,' she heard herself saying, above the giggles of the others. 'Like wine gums, you see, only "whine" as in moan on and on all the time.'

'Really?' Gloria's voice was as sour as a Granny Sooker. 'Well, I'm surprised, Hazel Mull-Dare, that you would even *think* about calling your darling Miss Amelia rude names. Who'd have thought it, with you being so . . . passionate . . . about her. So ready to defend her, at all costs.'

Hazel began winding the gramophone, her face burning. 'It's not like that . . . ' she began. 'I'm not . . . ' but Gloria wasn't listening. She was ushering the other girls to the side of the room with instructions to look and learn.

'The tango is a real sassy dance,' she said. 'My ma learned it in New York and it's all the rage in Paris. We should have split skirts, to do it properly, and a lot more men, but I guess we can make do. Ready, Hazel?'

The needle dropped, *El Choclo* crackled and began. Gloria and Val met in the centre of the room. Woozy and miserable Hazel watched. She didn't recognize the sound pouring from the gramophone's horn and wasn't sure she liked it. The rhythm was odd, like horses going too suddenly from a trot to a gallop, and the way Gloria and Val had started moving—it was as if they were joined together, by sweat or by glue.

Cheek to cheek, body to body, they swept across the floor . . . then tore away, then clamped together, then tore away again. Gloria raised her right leg, laughed, wobbled

111

and cursed her un-split skirt as she attempted to clinch the leg around the top of Val's thighs. Val arched her backwards, raised her up and then sealed her close to his side as they swept, once again, across the floorboards.

Shiny-eyed, and deeply impressed, Jennifer and Millicent, Phyllis and Jane, Verity and Evelyn, Marjorie and Octavia watched from the edge of the room attempting, with gin-fuddled senses, to memorize each move . . . each twist . . . each grasp . . . each bend.

'Phew!' Gloria gasped as the music finished and the girls all clapped and cheered. 'I need another drink! Val? Do the honours.'

Val pulled a face. The punch bowl had been replenished with lemonade, ginger beer, and slivers of fruit, but the bottle in his own pocket was empty. 'Just weasel's pee from now on, I'm afraid,' he murmured, moving so fluidly towards the sideboard it was as if he was still dancing. At least three daughters of gentlemen watched him go, their eyes growing shinier as they imagined themselves moving with him, cheek to cheek, hip to hip.

Gloria picked up her empty glass and followed him.

'Psst—Val,' she hissed, as soon as they were out of earshot. 'I'm going to make Hazel Mull-Dare pay for crossing me. I don't know how yet, but I will.'

Valentine raised one eyebrow and topped up his glass.

'But your pa will still take the old biddy to court, right?' he whispered back. 'Now that he's got the "evidence"? Great bruises, by the way, Glor. Why, they're almost—'

Gloria pinched him, hard, through his cheap shirt.

'Shut up,' she hissed. 'I can't risk it. Not if Miss

Goody-Two-Shoes won't keep quiet about the drawing. What if it all came out in the press? What if one of the papers had a go at reproducing what I drew? She may have torn it up but she had a damned good look. No. Stories about me being attacked by a nutty teacher are one thing—any man would sympathize with that. But I'll never get to be a Peeress if there's a scandal about my drawing. I'll have to tell Pa to forget the whole thing. I'll tell him some tale . . . God how I hate, loathe, and detest Hazel Louise Mull-Dare . . . '

Val took her glass from her and half filled it.

'Shame to waste the "evidence" though,' he mused. 'Unless . . . ' But Gloria wasn't listening. She was scowling at the wall, her grudge against Miss Amelia Gumm paling to insignificance as she plotted a very different kind of revenge against that freckle-faced carroty-haired, prissy goody-two-shoes who had dared to throw a spanner in the works.

Val added a slice of lemon to the glass in his hand and swirled it, once, twice, three times while he weighed something up. He had had an idea. A rather spiffing one. But all things considered—his own interests in particular—he had decided to keep it entirely to himself.

'Your weasel's pee, old thing,' he said, offering Gloria the drink.

But she motioned both it and him away.

Undeterred he leaned in close: 'If you let me have the photographs,' he murmured into her hair, 'your father will have no evidence of the assault, and no case to take to court. And you'll know where they are should you ever change your mind. All right? All right, Glor?'

113

She nodded, irritably. 'Yes. Fine. All right. Come and fetch them tomorrow.'

'What time?' he said, trying not to sound too eager. 'It might take a while for me to get across town. It's that mad woman's funeral. The one who chucked herself at the King's horse.'

'Whenever you like. Early. I don't care . . . wait a minute, you mean the suffragette, don't you? Emily Wilding Whatsit. They're giving her a huge send-off, aren't they?'

'Yes. Nine. I'll come at nine if that's not too . . . '

'Fine . . . yes . . . shut up. I need to think . . . '

Val shrugged, raised his own glass, and drank a silent toast to his own cunning.

'Shall we dance?' he said.

But Gloria, her brain ticking over a plan of its own, had already turned away.

'Hazel?' she called out merrily. 'Let's you and me have the next tango. Don't worry about music, this is just to show the others.'

Confused, Hazel stepped away from the gramophone. 'What do I do?' she said, shyly. 'I've never . . . '

'Relax,' Gloria told her. 'I'll talk you through it, every step. Come on. I'll be the man.'

And whether it was the gin loosening her limbs, or just her own sense of rhythm kicking in, Hazel found, after just a few false moves, that she could do it. She could tango.

'You're a natural, honey,' crooned Gloria. 'Let's have the music again—come on, everyone, join in! There's plenty of room so long as we all dance in the same direction. Val—wind the gramophone.'

114

Hazel's hair had come loose from its pins and was trailing down her back. She felt for the white rose that Florence had fixed so carefully, but it was just a stalk. There were petals on her shoulders but no time to brush them away as the music began and Gloria pulled her close.

The others were useless, prancing like colts and tripping over their hems. But their clumsiness only made Hazel feel more accomplished . . . happier . . . exhilarated, even as Gloria, still being the man, pressed her close, twirled her away, and then pressed her close again.

Down the room they swept, trailing white petals. Gloria's cheek felt as soft as an apricot, and if her bruised neck was hurting she was being very brave. 'I'm sorry, Gloria,' Hazel said to her. 'I just wouldn't be able to lie. About the drawing. About anything. I can't do it. Not if I'm asked. I . . . '

'Hush,' breathed Gloria, against her jaw. 'It's all right.'

'Really? So we can still be friends?'

'Of course.'

Down in the kitchen Mrs Sawyer looked up at the clock and tutted. 'I'm not waiting a minute longer,' she declared. 'It's time she cut her cake. Those friends of hers are getting over-excited, shrieking like gypsies, and carrying on . . . '

'Ah, but it's good to hear a bit of laughter, don't you think so, Mrs Sawyer?' said Cook. 'A little bit of laughter to lighten the gloom.'

'Humph!'

Cook poured herself another cup of tea. An hour and a half, that's all that remained of this God-forsaken day. An hour and a half and so far, so good. 'Mrs Mull-Dare wants to take the cake up herself,' she reminded the housekeeper. 'With the candles all lit, and the plate spinning round like a turny-table.'

'Humph!' went Mrs Sawyer again, only louder this time. 'And how, might I ask, is that to be accomplished?'

'On the square tray, Mrs Sawyer, with an upturned saucer under the cake plate. You'll light the candles, just before Mrs Mull-Dare goes into the dining room, and then you'll give the plate a good old spin, like a merry-go-round. That way it'll look like a proper record being played on a grammy-phone while everyone sings "Happy Birthday".'

Mrs Sawyer shook her head and raised her eyes to the ceiling. A gramophone record indeed. A young girl's birthday cake, in her opinion, should be a nice flower shape and preferably pink. 'If you go and stand in the drawing room,' she said, 'it sounds like elephants up there having a stampede. If that's dancing, then I'm the Queen of the Nile.'

*'Stay there, darlings. Just for a moment. It's all right, Dottie, I'll only be a second.'*

Cook heaved herself from her chair and went to fetch the tray with the upturned saucer on it. 'The cake's ready for you, madam,' she said. 'Only there's an extra candle on it, if Miss Hazel doesn't mind. Fourteen—one for luck. Here we go now . . . onto the saucer . . . that's it . . . I'll give you the matches, shall I, Mrs Sawyer? Lovely . . . '

Left alone, Cook went back to her chair, sighing with relief as she sank against its springs. An hour and ten minutes until Saturday 14th. Touch wood—she tapped the arm of the chair—they were home and dry.

Exhausted, she allowed her body to sag and her eyes to close. If the young ladies wanted cocoa, she decided, Florence would have to see to it. But it was probably too warm tonight for cocoa and, anyway, they had the rest of that lovely lemonade punch to finish.

Upstairs, Mrs Sawyer struck a match.

'There!' Ivy Mull-Dare said, once the candles were all lit. 'Dottie—*down*—this isn't for you . . . Are you going to open the door for me, Mrs Sawyer?'

'I'm supposed to spin it first, ma'am—the cake, I mean, not the door. It's supposed to look like a record, going round and round on a grammy-phone.'

'Is it? Is it really? All right then—can you reach? Dottie—*sit*! All done, Mrs Sawyer? Good. In we go. *Dottie*, will you please get—'

*CRASH!!!!!*

# CHAPTER 11

'Miss Hazel, wake up. Wake up, miss. You're wanted.'

Hazel stirred. She was already semi-awake but opening her eyes had seemed like too big an effort so she had been lying there for ages, all twisted up in her pink silk coverlet, and trying not to think.

Her mouth tasted odd, as if she had eaten something rotten, and she would have given all the keys of her new typewriter for a long cold drink of water.

'It's your friend, miss. On the telephone.'

*Telephone?*

The telephone was all the way downstairs, in the passage leading to the kitchen. Mrs Sawyer used it to place orders with tradesmen, and said it was a boon. Hazel had never touched it and wasn't completely sure how it worked.

*Friend?*

'Which friend?' she croaked, for, really, it was a miracle she had any left after last night's fiasco with the dogs and the cake.

'The American, miss.'

Moving felt peculiar. Moving fast actually hurt. But Hazel got herself into her dressing gown and down to the telephone in under two minutes.

'Hello?' she said into the strange metal trumpet you used for speaking and listening. 'Gloria?'

Hearing Gloria's voice, coming back at her through the trumpet thing, was like pressing a seashell to her ear and finding it had a soul.

'Hazel!' Gloria called to her. 'Get dressed pronto. We're picking you up in an hour.'

'Oh!' Hazel felt her spirits rise. 'Where are we going? And who's "we"?'

'Gotta dash, honey.' Gloria's voice went quiet and then loud again, as if she had turned away for a moment. 'And anyway, it's a surprise. Trust me. You'll be amazed. Oh . . . and wear white. I am.'

The line went dead.

Turning round, Hazel caught Mrs Sawyer watching from the other end of the passage. 'I'm going out,' she called to her. 'With my friends.' It felt marvellous, saying that. Grown-up.

'Does your mother know?' Mrs Sawyer replied.

'She won't mind,' Hazel answered, honestly. 'I know she won't.' The words *But your father would* and '*I know*,' thrummed invisibly between them before Hazel hurried away, to dress herself in white.

The Gilberts' car arrived promptly. It was being driven by a uniformed chauffeur and Millicent and Verity were already in the back, pale-faced and quiet in spotless white frocks. Hazel was so disappointed to see them that she had trouble hiding it. Of all the girls she knew these two had always been the dullest, and she couldn't understand why Gloria had included them in this special surprise.

'Jump in, Hazel. We need to hurry. The roads are already jamming up.'

Swallowing her disappointment, Hazel clambered into the car. It was roomier than the Old Girl and seemed to purr as they left the kerb. 'Hello,' she said to Millicent and Verity. And then: 'I'm sorry about the dogs last night. They get over-excited sometimes and . . . well . . . you saw for yourselves what can happen. Dottie's always getting under people's feet. And Pipkin hates crashes and loud noises, so I'm afraid he just couldn't control himself.'

'That's all right,' Millicent said. 'Shame about the cake though.'

Verity nodded, and turned a little bit green. But then, it was Verity's slippered foot that had skidded in Pipkin's mess.

'There sure were a lot of hounds bounding around,' remarked Gloria, cheerfully. 'No wonder your ma tripped over one and dropped the cake. I'm surprised she didn't fall flat on her face and hurt herself. Have you always had dogs?'

'Always,' Hazel told her, mournfully. 'All my life.'

'But your ma's lovely though, isn't she? A real Bohemian. Not many women over forty can wear their hair loose like that without looking like witches. Is she arty?'

Hazel said she didn't think so, for she had never known her mother to paint anything, ever. 'But she was an artist's model when she was young,' she said. 'There are portraits of her—at least three, I think—in a private house near Oxford.'

'Oh, my. Have you seen them?'

Hazel had to admit that she hadn't. 'Where are we going?' she said, to change the subject. 'And why are there so many people around? What's happening?'

'You'll see,' said Gloria. 'Actually, I think we should walk from here; it'll be quicker. Simmonds can come back at four and take us for tea at Fortnum and Mason. Bring the newspaper when you collect us, Simmonds, please—the one I've left ready, in a bag beside the hallstand. There's information in it these girls need to know about.'

'Right you are, Miss Gilbert.' Simmonds brought the car to a smooth halt, then adjusted his cap before stepping smartly round to the passenger side and opening the door.

'Thank you, Simmonds,' said Gloria, as he reached into the car and helped her out. She said 'Simmonds' the same way she said 'honey' and seemed not to notice, or mind, when her chest brushed against his fingers.

Scrambling after her, Hazel took the chauffeur's outstretched hand. *This is exactly how life should be*, she thought happily to herself. *Being out with my friends . . . being helped from a car like a proper young lady*. 'Thank you, Simmonds,' she said, but it sounded silly coming from her, as if she was playing charades. 'You're welcome, little miss,' he replied, looking straight over her head towards something, or somebody, else.

The street was crowded with people, nudging their way along and craning their heads to look further down the road. In the distance, Hazel could see policemen. Lots of them.

'Where are we?' Millicent wanted to know.

'Two streets down from Victoria Station,' Gloria told her. 'We won't get any closer; it's not even worth trying.

121

Let's stay here, by the kerb. I don't think we'll have long to wait. I've brought flowers to throw. Here, Hazel—have some.'

Mystified, Hazel dipped into a paper bag and brought out a handful of petals. Rose petals, mostly, in hot shades of red. 'Ouch!' she yelped as a thorn jabbed her finger.

'Sorry,' said Gloria. 'I thought I'd got them all out.'

There were more people coming now, nudging in behind them and all along the pavement. A couple of women tutted because they couldn't get any further. 'I go all funny in a crush,' grumbled one of them. 'You know I do.' Her companion, who was dressed all in black, said she did know, but it was worth a little discomfort, surely, to be in the right place at the right time; bearing witness.

'They're expecting trouble, I reckon,' said a man off to Hazel's left. He meant the police.

Hazel peered down the road to where the uniformed men had braced themselves like bulldogs, shoulder to shoulder, against what was now a large surge of people on the pavement behind them. *Women*, Hazel realized. *It's mostly women down there*.

And then the penny dropped.

'Her name was Emily Wilding Davison,' Gloria was telling Millicent. 'They say she had a return ticket to Victoria Station in her coat pocket, so it can't have been suicide, but Ma says that's nothing to go on. Ma says you never can tell what a person will or won't do on a day they've decided is their last on this earth.'

'We're here for that suffragette, aren't we?' Hazel said, softly. 'The one I saw getting trampled. But what . . . '

'Something's going on,' Millicent interrupted, as a murmur rippled through the crowd and the wall of policemen braced itself and shuffled its boots.

*'She's here . . . '*

*'She's coming . . . '*

The petals in Hazel's hand had grown sticky, like sweets. Holding them loosely she leaned forward, along with everyone else, and wondered: *how is she coming, exactly?* For some reason she thought of Snow White, lying in a glass coffin for everyone to see. The suffragette, from what she remembered, had not been a pretty girl, like Snow White, and this was no fairy tale. Still, there needed to be something . . . some remarkable thing to bear witness to. The crowd was expecting it, she could tell.

And then *'Oh . . . '* went up the sigh, like a breeze through a crop, and then: silence.

The girl chosen to lead Emily Wilding Davison's funeral procession, and carry the standard of the Women's Social and Political Union, was very young. She was wearing a simple shift and, with her cropped hair and limpid features, had the look of a medieval saint. Behind her came twelve more young girls, all of them dressed in white. Some carried laurel wreaths, others held vast banners, the words 'Fight On' and 'God Will Give The Victory' stretched in silver thread across deep purple velvet.

Following on were older women; union members in white, with Madonna lilies, tall as sceptres, in their hands; others dressed in black and nursing great swags of irises.

The faces of all these women—young and old—were solemn but not wretched, and although most looked

123

straight ahead, some kept turning sideways to gaze, bold as brass, at other women in the crowd.

*Join us!* their eyes said. *Don't stay on the sidelines. Join us and fight for your rights!*

'Aren't you glad you came?'

The warmth of Gloria's breath in her ear made Hazel jump. She nodded, unable to speak.

The hearse was visible now and Hazel could see the suffragette's coffin, draped in brocade and heaped with wreaths. It seemed grimly significant that it was being drawn across London by horses—albeit slow-moving ones—and Hazel felt the connection, like a blow to her own body, as their hooves came clopping closer.

Verity and Millicent were throwing their rose petals—flinging them wildly and far too soon. Hazel got the feeling that they were about to cheer, like little children at a carnival, and could only hope to goodness that they wouldn't. The coffin was passing in front of her. *Goodbye*, she communed silently with the woman inside it. *You'd be amazed how many people are here. As many as were at the Epsom Derby, I should think. That's good, isn't it? For your cause, I mean.*

She didn't throw her petals. It didn't feel like the right thing to do. Instead she opened her hand and let them fall, like drops of blood upon the ground.

'How about three cheers for Herbert Jones?' bellowed a voice from the crowd—a man's voice, as crude as a burp. The walking women ignored him, although their eyes went flinty, and their fingers appeared to tighten around the stems of their flowers. It took a moment for Hazel to remember who Herbert Jones was.

'That jockey didn't die as well, did he?' she whispered to Gloria. 'The one who was riding the King's horse?'

'Nope,' Gloria replied. 'He's back in the saddle. Has been for days.'

Nobody else was yelling, and the Herbert Jones supporter did not heckle again. Hazel was glad there had been no real trouble. What if eggs and flour had been thrown? Or the coffin booed and spat upon by men who wanted The Vote kept all to themselves? She would have been mortified, she realized. She would have taken it personally.

The women passing now, behind the funeral bier, were wearing ordinary clothes. Some of them looked gaunt and seemed to be walking with difficulty. At first Hazel assumed they were ordinary spectators—people who had decided to leave early, so were tagging along behind the coffin—then she noticed yet another group, in scarlet and blue robes, following on behind and all at once the women dressed normally became the most intriguing. *They're the most important ones*, she guessed. *The true leaders*.

And then she saw her. The woman from the Epsom Derby; the one who had been shouted at, and whacked with a rolled-up newspaper. For a split second their eyes met, just as they had at the racecourse.

*I recognize you*, the woman's look said. *Or something in you . . . something bold*. And she turned her head, prolonging the eye contact as she passed Hazel by.

*Join us! Join us now!*

It was like being pulled by a rope. It was like having iron filings in your heart and a magnet in the road.

125

'Show's over,' Gloria said, grabbing hold of Hazel's arm; holding her back as she swayed to go. 'Let's find Simmonds. I'm gasping for tea, aren't you?'

The tea room at Fortnum & Mason seemed a tame place to be after that. But then anywhere would, thought Hazel, dizzily; anywhere at all. Gloria ordered China tea for four and then tugged the waiter's sleeve, forcing him to bend low over her chest while she whispered in his ear.

'Well!' she declared, as the waiter left the room. 'That sure was a great send-off, particularly for someone without a drop of royal blood in her veins. What did you think of it, Hazel? Didn't it make you want to become a suffragette immediately? It did me.'

Hazel looked at Gloria in surprise.

'Did it?' she said. 'Did it really?'

'Sure. Why not? It's about time we gals showed what we're made of.'

'*Sugar and spice and all things nice,*' piped up Verity. '*That's what . . .*'

'In fact,' Gloria interrupted, 'I think we ought to do an action. All four of us. Together.'

Hazel leaned across the table. She had thought it was all over; that the thrill of being among the suffragettes was going to have to fade as she and Gloria and Millicent and Verity sipped their tea at Fortnum & Mason and maybe ate scones.

'What,' she said, keeping her voice very low, 'were you thinking we might do?'

'Oh—I haven't decided yet,' Gloria replied. 'But it would have to be fairly dramatic, wouldn't it? Something . . . unusual. Something to show the world—or

126

the Women's Social and Political Union anyway—that the Kensington School for the Daughters of Gentlemen is *not* full of shrinking violets and mindless ninnies.'

'Nothing dangerous!' squeaked Verity.

'Or bad,' added Millicent.

'Of course not.' Gloria's voice was all sweetness. 'But it would need to be soon, don't you think, while the whole country is in mourning for Miss Davison and sympathetic to her—our—cause.'

Hazel could feel her heart bumping fast again, beneath her white dress. *The Women's Social and Political Union* . . . 'How do you know so much?' she asked Gloria. 'Did your ma tell you?'

'Nah.' Gloria reached into the bag she had brought from the car, produced a newspaper and shook it open.

'Listen and learn, girls,' she said, over the teacups and the sugar bowl. 'Listen and learn . . . '

Open-mouthed, and more admiring of Gloria than ever, Hazel listened. Her tea grew cold and she had to remember to blink, to breathe, even, as she hung on to every word being read to her.

'Is that true?' she kept saying. 'Is that really how it is?'

And while her mind was still absorbing the fact that, without The Vote, she herself was no better off than a slave or a bird in a cage, the tea-room door swung open and in came the waiter.

'Hurrah!' cheered Gloria, folding her copy of *The Suffragette* away and clapping her hands as the waiter lowered a birthday cake very carefully onto a trolley, struck a match and began lighting the candles.

They were green candles, Hazel noticed, and the icing sugar was white . . . pure white, dotted with candied violets. Green, white, and mauve . . . the suffragette colours. 'For me?' she managed to say. 'Is that really for me?'

'For you!' chuckled Gloria. 'To make up for the one that got spoiled. Happy birthday, Hazel; here's to you. Here's to *all* of us. To the KDG—The Kensington Daughters of Gentlemen—and to the fight for our right to vote. Clink on it, girls . . . '

*Chink* went Millicent's teacup against Verity's, and Hazel's against Gloria's and then *chink-clunk* chimed all four cups at once, sealing a pact there would be no turning back from.

And if the waiter sneered, as he pushed the trolley closer, Hazel failed to notice. Nor did it register, as she puffed out all her candles in one exuberant breath, that there were precisely thirteen of them—no extra one this time, for luck.

# CHAPTER 12

The atmosphere at home seemed strangely altered when Hazel finally got back. Not as much as when her father went away but enough to put her on her guard. There was a heady whiff of perfume in the hall, stronger, even, than the usual pong of wet dog and soiled carpets.

Lily-of-the-valley.

There was only one person Hazel knew of who wore that particular scent.

'Your aunt Alison is here, miss,' said Florence. 'She arrived just after you went out with your "friend".'

'Is my cousin John with her?' Hazel asked, hopefully.

'No, miss. It's just your aunt. You'll find her upstairs, in the parlour. Mrs Mull-Dare has only just got in herself, and is taking her bath. I must tell Cook you're back so she can make a start on dinner. We've been worried, miss, you've been gone that long. Where . . . ?'

'Thank you, Florence,' said Hazel, quickly.

The parlour door was wedged open, as usual, so Hazel, tiptoeing quietly up the stairs, saw her aunt before her aunt saw her.

*She looks sad*, Hazel thought to herself. *Sad and old*.

Rascal and Dottie, banished from the sofa to their rug

in front of the hearth, wagged their tails and raised their heads but didn't jump up to greet her. *You're not who we're waiting to see*, they seemed to be saying. *But you're better than this old bitch with her whiffy flower smell and pushy hands*.

Diggy Bert was beside the bureau, gnawing the remains of a pig's ear. Pipkin was nowhere to be seen but, being the smallest and the most nervous, was probably shivering behind the curtain.

'Hazel . . . my dear.' Aunt Alison's face changed—smiled—as Hazel entered the room. It wasn't spontaneous though; more as if she'd flicked a switch to brighten a room that would otherwise have stayed very dark.

'Hello, Aunt Alison.' Hazel went forward to kiss her aunt's cheek. 'I hope your journey down wasn't too tiring. Dinner won't be long. Shall I ring for more tea?'

All her life Hazel had known—sensed—the right way to talk to her aunt. Politely. Safely. With All Due Respect.

'I'm awash with tea, dear,' Aunt Alison replied. 'But do sit down—here, next to me—so we can have a little chat.'

Hazel sat. Aunt Alison had orangey Mull-Dare hair but had missed out on the freckles. She was as stiff as a corset and nowhere near as much fun as Hazel's father. Still, she was family and Hazel was fond of her, after a fashion.

'Have you been somewhere pleasant today, dear?'

'Yes. I have.'

Aunt Alison waited; expecting more. Hazel looked away. She could feel her face changing colour and blessed the sound of Diggy Bert's crunching, filling the awkward silence.

'So where exactly did you go?'

Hazel sighed.

'To Victoria Station,' she replied. 'To watch the funeral procession of Emily Wilding Davison.'

Aunt Alison drew a startled breath.

'There was no trouble,' Hazel added, quickly. 'No trouble at all, apart from one man shouting. My friends and I—we were perfectly safe. The police didn't blow their whistles once and nobody spat or even pushed. And we took tea afterwards at Fortnum and Mason.'

Diggy Bert had finished his pig's ear and was licking the carpet, his tongue rasping the fibres like a brush. Dottie and Rascal had fallen asleep, in a disconsolate huddle that occasionally twitched and broke wind. 'Your father,' said Aunt Alison, slowly, 'would not have approved. In fact, he would have forbidden it.'

Her use of the past tense struck Hazel, immediately, as a troubling thing. 'Have you seen my father?' she cried. 'Have you been to the rest home?'

Aunt Alison's face softened immediately. 'Not yet,' she said. 'I haven't seen him yet. But I understand he is making very good progress and taking a little soup.'

*Soup? A little soup? But father likes a hearty breakfast, with kidneys if mother isn't here to smell them, and a whole mountain of scrambled egg. He likes cake with icing sugar and lots of cream. He eats sweets all the time—wine gums and humbugs and mint imperials. He has the appetite of a lion, or the largest dog in the world. He must have broken down a very great deal if all he can manage now is a little bit of soup . . .*

'In the meantime,' Aunt Alison was saying, 'we need to be thinking, very, very hard, about how we conduct ourselves in his absence.'

131

Hazel had been around her aunt long enough, over the years, to be able to translate this sentence into much plainer sense:

*'We' means 'you'—i.e. 'You need to think . . . '*

*'Conduct' means 'Behaviour' and bad behaviour—the worst—includes going out, unchaperoned, in support of suffragettes.*

'Yes, Aunt,' she said. 'I understand. I'm sorry.'

'Good. There are testing times ahead for you and your mother, as I believe you understand. And given your reduced circumstances we cannot afford a scandal.'

Translation:

*'Testing times' means 'really, really difficult'.*

*'Reduced circumstances' means 'you have no fortune any more because your father lost it on a horse'.*

But a scandal? What did she mean by that, precisely?

'All right,' Hazel said.

'Good girl. Now, let's see about another pot of tea after all, shall we? Dear Ivy clearly needs at least an hour to transform herself from a dog's best friend to the lady of the house, and I do want to talk to you, at much greater length, about your future.'

Translation:

*Talk 'to' you means talk 'at' you. All you are required to do is agree with every word I say.*

By the time Hazel's mother joined them—her hair loose and damp and Pipkin clutched, like a hairy shield, in her arms—Hazel had been left in no doubt whatsoever about what was expected of her, during the testing times ahead.

Marriage.

A good one.

Preferably to a Peer of the Realm—a duke or an earl—although anyone with old money and a few acres of land would do. 'Marrying up', Aunt Alison called it.

'Like my mother,' Hazel had observed, mournfully.

'Well—not quite like her.' Her aunt's nose had wrinkled before she could stop it. 'You are, after all, a Mull-Dare, with an excellent pedigree.'

'But what about the rat-scally?'

'The who, dear?'

'My great-great-great-somebody-or-other. The one who won us our sugar plantation in a game of poker. The one called plain old Moulder.'

Aunt Alison had turned so pale that, had she inherited the freckles, they would have stood out twice as much as usual, like speckles on an egg.

'We don't mention that person,' she had said, her voice so low you would think the settee had ears, or the dogs might snitch to the servants. 'We particularly don't mention him to our prospective husbands. Ever.'

'What about after we're married? Can't we tell them then?'

'Absolutely, definitely not.'

'But what if they ask?'

'Then you lie, dear. You smile a pretty little smile and you lie through your teeth.'

There was fish for dinner, because Aunt Alison had insisted on it. Baked fish, boiled potatoes, and carrots. Hazel's mother, however, had a wedge of something made from squashed peas and porridge oats, and wouldn't even touch the sauce because the fish had been cooked in it.

'For goodness' sake,' sighed Aunt Alison. 'You do take things a bit far, Ivy. A fish, after all, is a cold-blooded thing. No sense, no feeling.'

'They have faces,' Hazel's mother answered quietly. 'That's reason enough for me.'

Hazel, still full of birthday cake, ate what she could and then set her knife and fork together, politely, on the plate.

'May I speak?' she asked.

'You may,' her aunt replied.

'I was wondering: shouldn't I love the person I marry? Shouldn't that be more important than whether he's got old money?'

Her mother looked bewildered, as if these questions were unexpected. Aunt Alison dabbed her mouth before saying:

'We're jumping the gun a little, dear, don't you think? You have another year at school before we need to start grooming you, seriously, for the joys and responsibilities of matrimony. I haven't told you this yet, but your uncle Douglas and I are quite prepared to invest whatever sum is necessary to bring you out into society, a few years from now. You'll be a perfect English rose by then, I hope—a prize to be treasured by the right kind of man.'

Translation:

*'Perfect English rose' means hair up, mouth shut, and freckles carefully blotted under at least three layers of powder.*

*'Right kind of man' means staggeringly rich, and very easily deceived.*

Hazel looked at her mother.

'Did you marry for money?' she asked. 'Or for love?'

'Well, really . . . ' Aunt Alison came dangerously close to spluttering cod onto the cloth. 'One of the first things you are going to have to learn, Hazel dear, is not to be so forthright. Men don't like it. It makes them uncomfortable.'

Hazel's mother, however, smiled across at Hazel as if her sister-in-law wasn't there.

'Love,' she said. 'Definitely love.'

'Well then . . . '

'Because your father loved me so much it seemed cruel to say no.'

Hazel felt her mouth lift. Her mother had gone back to cutting into her horrible porridgey rissole.

*Was that a joke, or what?*

Aunt Alison wasn't sure either, and so the meal ended in a polite and tentative silence.

```
The quick browN FOX jumped over the lazy
dog.
   Hazel Louise Mull-Dare
   This is my new typewriter. It is an
Underwood Number 5 from New York.
   ?.()25$
   It is splendid!!!
Today has been very unusual and has left
me with a lot to think about. My best
friend Gloria and I want to become suffra-
gettes (or suffragists, which means the
same). We decided this after watching the
funeral parade for Miss Emily Wilding
Davison, a famous suffragette who was
```

fatally injured at the Epsom Derby, right in front of my very eyes. My father saw it too (the fatal injury, not the parade).

After the parade Gloria and I went to Fortnum & Mason with two other girls and Gloria told us about how marriage is no better than prison for the female sex, even if there is wealth involved, and it will never be any better until women get the vote and can say how they think things should be in this land.

We are calling ourselves the KDG which stands for the Kensington Daughters of Gentlemen. Gloria is going to plan an action for us to do. It will not be dangerous, like Miss Davison stepping in front of the King's horse (which is what killed her) but it has got to be carried out soon while people are thinking harder about women's rights because of poor Miss Davison.

When I got home my aunt Alison was here and she spoke to me, at great length, about my future. It seems that when I get married I am expected to marry up, to bring extra wealth into the family, so she and my uncle Douglas are going to pay for me to learn more social graces so that I will be prettier and a better bet. It won't be for a while yet because I have another year at least to go at the Kensington School for the Daughters of

Gentlemen, but it is something I must
think about and do my best to get used to.

I dare not tell my aunt, or anyone
else in this household, about what Gloria
and I and the other two girls are
planning. My father, who is away at the
moment, would not approve at all. But I
am sure that if I do succeed in marrying
up one day he would not want me to feel
like a prisoner in my own house. So if
Gloria and I and the other two girls have
helped women get the vote by then he will
not have to fret and that can only be a
good thing.

P.S. I would hope to marry for love as
well as for money, as my mother did (I
think). And if my husband ever asked about
my ancestors I would tell him the honest
truth — that they were Moulders.


Hazel stopped typing and looked, approvingly, at the
words on the page. She had never kept a diary before.
She had been given them, yes, but had always felt con-
strained by the conventional prettiness of the covers (as if
whatever you wrote between them had to be equally
pretty and nice).

Typing was better. Typing was fun; like playing the
piano only with something to show for it afterwards.
And if you typed the day's events, you could keep going for as many pages as you wanted, or stop after just
one line.

There was something else too, Hazel realized. When you read back over what you had typed, it was like reading about somebody else—someone in a story. It was probably to do with the way the sentences looked, she decided. Like part of a book, or an article in *The Times*.

She read, again, the line about her father being away at the moment. Seeing it set down like that, as if it was not important, made the fact of it more bearable somehow. And the things she had typed, about becoming a suffragette before marrying up, seemed very wise to her and beyond reproach.

Carefully, she began turning the bits of the typewriter that wound the paper out. She was all thumbs to begin with; uncertain if she was doing it right and worried about scrunching the paper or—worse—seeing it disappear into the machine's innards, like a tasty meal.

When the page was free she slipped it into a drawer. There was ink on her thumbs where she had accidentally pressed against the typewriter ribbon. Soap and water and a brisk scrub with a nail brush got the worst of it off—enough, anyway, to stop the ink from marking whatever she touched. Still, both her thumbs remained clearly smudged.

They were the colour of pansies, those smudges. They looked as if they hurt. And had Hazel stopped to think about it she might have made a connection. The penny might have dropped. They were the exact colour, shape, and size, those smudges, as the bruises she had seen on Friday, on her best friend Gloria's neck.

# CHAPTER 13

The first official meeting of the KDG was held in the Mull-Dares' sitting room. Hazel had hoped it would be at Gloria's house, for she was longing to see the lavatory seats, but Gloria said Hazel's place would be safer.

'My ma will be having an "at home" on Monday,' she said, over the telephone, 'but I'm assuming yours will be out rescuing hounds.'

Hazel agreed that this would doubtless be the case. 'Although my aunt might be here,' she added, 'and my aunt, I have to tell you, does not approve of suffragettes. She said to me this morning that they are all bitter and twisted, with unreasonable grudges against men.'

'You haven't told her anything, I hope, about the KDG.'

'Not about us, no. Only that we went and watched Miss Davison's funeral parade. She hasn't asked about anything else.'

'All right. Good. Just keep your mouth buttoned, honey, or we'll never get anywhere, and I've had the most *amazing* idea for the most *brilliant* action. See you tomorrow. Tell the others.'

Monday afternoon was wet, blustery, and unseasonably cold.

'You'll be wanting cocoa, I expect,' sniffed Mrs Sawyer after lunch. 'You and your "friends".'

'I'll ring,' Hazel told her. 'If we need anything at all, Mrs Sawyer, I'll ring the bell. Where is my aunt, do you know?'

'Lady Mac,' said Mrs Sawyer, 'has gone shopping.'

'Oh, good. I mean—Aunt Alison loves shopping, doesn't she. When she's in London, that is. I expect she'll be ages and ages choosing new hats and gloves and things. I expect she told you she'd be gone until at least five o'clock, didn't she?'

Mrs Sawyer threw her a suspicious look. 'Something like that, miss, yes.'

*Phew!*

Verity and Millicent arrived first. They sat on the settee, almost shoulder to shoulder, and said polite little 'noes' to cocoa. Hazel couldn't imagine two more unlikely suffragettes. They looked about as militant as baby mice.

'I don't think I can belong to the KDG after all,' faltered Millicent after several minutes of difficult silence. 'I didn't dare tell Gloria over the telephone but I really don't think I can.'

'Me neither,' Verity said. 'I'd like to belong, I really would, but my parents would be *furious*; father in particular.'

Millicent nodded. 'Mine too. My daddy says Emily Wilding Davison was bonkers. I heard him telling mother that she set fire to pillar boxes outside the House of Commons and threw stones at a Baptist Minister because he looked like Lloyd George.'

'Who's Lloyd George?' chorused Verity and Hazel.

140

'I don't know,' Millicent admitted. 'Someone high up in the Government, I expect. Anyway, they should have thrown away the key, my daddy said. When they sent Miss Davison to prison.'

'Prison?' exclaimed Hazel. 'Miss Davison got sent to prison?'

'Well of course she did. The police and the courts aren't going to *thank* you, are they, Hazel, for setting fire to things and throwing stones at innocent people. Miss Davison went to prison and refused to eat when she got there. It's called going on hunger strike and suffragettes do it on principle. My daddy says good riddance. Let them starve themselves to death if that's what they want.'

Verity shuddered. 'I would hate to go to prison,' she murmured, her eyes filling with tears. 'I believe I would die of shame.'

'We might all go,' Millicent told her, bleakly. 'We might all get crammed in the same *cell* if Gloria's action is against the law.'

'I'm sure it won't be,' Hazel said, quickly. 'Let's wait and see shall we? Gloria will be here any minute. Shall I ring for tea and cake?'

Verity and Millicent shook their heads. They were too anxious to eat or drink, they said. Too knotted up over what they were going to say to Gloria Gilbert, to get themselves out of the KDG.

When Gloria finally joined them it felt, to Hazel, like the sun coming out.

'Holy mackerel, it's chilly out there!' She still had her jacket on as she bounced into a chair. 'Italy's going to be like an oven compared to this.'

Hazel was startled. 'You're going to Italy? When?'

'Mmm? Oh . . . '

A roll of the eyes, a flick of the hand, and Italy might have been of no more consequence, to Gloria Gilbert, than a trip to the sweet shop. 'Not for a while yet. Ma likes to go. Italian men are *so* dashing. And they sure know how to treat a lady. You should come with us, Hazel. It'd be fun. Right now, though, we've more important things to think about. I've the latest copy of *The Suffragette* here, and a pamphlet Christabel Pankhurst has written which I'm afraid will shock you all rather a lot.'

'What about your idea?' Verity dared to squeak. 'For an action? Because I've been thinking about it all night, Gloria, and I really don't think . . . '

'All in good time, honey. All in good time. Now—I'll bet the ring on this finger that none of you know what syphilis and gonorrhoea are. Am I right? Hazel? Verity?' She waggled the hand so that light caught the tiny pinprick of a sparkle set in a thin metal band on her right hand.

Hazel was still thinking about Italy. About how going to Italy with Gloria Gilbert would be like a dream come true. 'Is the first one somebody's name?' she guessed, not really paying attention. 'A girl's name?'

'Hah! You're thinking of Phyllis, aren't you? Nice try but wrong. Verity? Millicent?'

The two other girls shook their heads, baffled.

'Well, I'll tell you. They're diseases. Vile diseases that men catch through their thingybobs when they get *in flagrante delicto* with prostitutes. You all know what kind of women prostitutes are, don't you, girls?'

142

Of course they did, they said. Everyone knew *that*.

'Fallen women,' said Verity, mournfully. 'Poor, immoral creatures who will end up in Hell unless they repent, like Mary Magdalene did.'

'Yes. Well, the worst of it is, hundreds of thousands of men pass these diseases on to their wives. They do, Verity, it's the God's honest truth. Christabel Pankhurst has looked into it all very thoroughly. *Very* thoroughly. And she has the testimony of a doctor, as proof. Listen.'

Gloria picked up the pamphlet and started to read:

'"The infection of innocent wives in marriage is justly declared by a man doctor to be the crowning infamy of our social life . . . Seventy-five to eighty per cent of men (*that's a LOT of men, girls—most of 'em, in fact*) have, before marriage, been infected with one form or another of venereal disease (*that's syphilis, like I told you, or the other thing*). Thus, out of every four men only one can ever marry without risk to his bride."'

Gloria stopped reading and slowly lowered the pamphlet.

You could have heard a pin drop. You could have heard the cheap chip of glass, in the ring on Gloria's finger, fall from its setting onto the floor.

Hazel cleared her throat. *Only one out of four men had a healthy thingybob? Then that meant that she, Gloria, Verity, and Millicent had a very high chance indeed of marrying one who didn't and of catching one of these awful diseases themselves.*

'What . . . what happens to women who get infected?' she said. 'Does . . . does it hurt? How can you *tell*?'

Gloria consulted Christabel Pankhurst's pamphlet.

'Backache . . . hysteria . . . weakness and depression . . . loss of healthful beauty . . . '

'Oh dear!' interrupted Millicent. 'Oh dear, that's awful. I have an aunt in Wolverhampton with all of those complaints. Oh dear!'

'There you are then,' Gloria told her. 'No doubt your uncle is wholly to blame for sowing his wild oats. And it gets worse. Listen. Gonorrhoea can stop you having children, or more than one child anyway. And it gets passed to the kids, causing blindness, deafness, and all manner of defects. Shocking, ain't it? And yet men, who are the cause of all this, seem not to suffer much at all. I reckon their thingybobs should fall off, and I bet Miss Pankhurst does too, although she's far too polite to say so in print. All she says here in her pamphlet—and quite right too—is: "to discuss an evil and then to run away from it without suggesting how it may be cured is not the way of suffragettes".'

Hazel's heart was racing. *I am an only child*, she was thinking to herself. *But I don't have any defects, except freckles. And mother is a strong person—always busy—and beautiful too, everyone says so, even though she is past fifty now and her hair is turning grey. She surely doesn't have si-Phyllis, or the other thing, and neither does my father. And anyway, he loves my mother. He would never sow any wild oats.*

'Rich men are just as guilty as poor ones,' Gloria was saying. 'Of sexual vice, I mean. It's one of the reasons they don't want us women to have the Vote in case we decide to get rid of all the prostitutes and spoil their fun.'

Verity began to sniff. 'I shall never marry,' she whimpered. 'Never.'

'Me neither,' whispered Millicent.

'Now, now girls,' Gloria scolded. 'That's hardly fighting talk.'

Hazel swallowed, hard. For all her resistance to the idea of marrying up, and to being groomed for it, like a horse, she had not been able to stop herself, these past few days, imagining the sort of man who might, one day, be her husband. Kind. He would surely be kind. And funny—funny enough to make her laugh out loud.

She had even daydreamed about the home they would have together (no dogs; no curtains or bedspreads in pink; sausages and bacon for breakfast every day and *The Times* left in the parlour, where women, as well as men, would be able to read it) but had shied away from picturing the mating side of things.

Now here was Gloria talking about prostitution, and husbands with diseased thingybobs, as if they were as much a part of wedlock as a shared surname and golden rings. And by the sound of it they *were*. For Christabel Pankhurst had spoken to doctors, and got the facts. She had published these facts in a pamphlet for anyone to read. And as a leading suffragette, and an honourable person, she surely wouldn't lie, or even dream of frightening women and girls unnecessarily—would she?

'What can we do, Gloria?' Millicent's voice was timid but firm. 'What does Miss Pankhurst say we should do?'

Gloria had rolled the pamphlet up into a tight tube and fastened it with a rubber band. She didn't need to consult it again as she replied: 'Why, take action, of course. Direct, hard-hitting action in support of women's rights. We need power, girls. Power to change the laws that allow men to get away with disgusting and dangerous behaviour—preferably before we each get to marry one.'

'*Hear, hear.*' Verity's voice was tiny. A bird's trill. A bat's squeak. But it gave Hazel a warm feeling, in the pit of her stomach, to hear the words said and to know that however different she and Verity had always been they had found, after all these years, some common ground.

'What have you got planned, Gloria?' she asked, eagerly. 'For us? For the KDG? Can you tell us now?'

'Sure. But shuffle closer. You never know who might be listening outside a closed door.'

Obediently, all three girls left their seats to huddle on the carpet at Gloria's feet. Smiling, Gloria bent from her chair and began to whisper.

'Oh my,' murmured Millicent when the whispering stopped. 'Oh, Gloria, that's brilliant.'

'Isn't it,' Gloria agreed. 'Isn't it just.'

'And it's not against the law? Are you sure about that?'

'Positive. I got Val to check.'

'*Val?*' Hazel felt the shock of that all over her skin; crawling there with cold little legs. 'You've told *Val* about our action? But this is supposed to be a secret. Our secret. And . . . and . . . Val's a *boy*.'

'More of a man, actually, honey,' Gloria chuckled. 'If you get my drift.'

Hazel, blushing hotly, shook her head, ignoring the drift.

'I don't think you should have told him,' she said. 'It was wrong of you.'

Something hard—something more than annoyance— flickered in Gloria's eyes; only for an instant, though, and then she shrugged, leaned forward again and planted a kiss on top of Hazel's head.

'There,' she said. 'I'm sorry. I should have asked you first. Forgiven?'

Hazel couldn't look at her.

'Verity? Millicent?' Gloria coaxed. 'You've both met Val. He's a poppet—agreed?'

'Yes.'

'Oh *yes*.'

'Then it shouldn't surprise you that he supports women's rights and wants us to have the Vote. Or that he's tickled pink about this action of ours and wanted to help. I'm OK with it. Are you?'

'Yes, of course.'

'Yes, yes.'

'Good. Hazel? If you don't agree we'll have to call the whole thing off. No more KDG and no action. Val will be sorely hurt to hear you didn't trust him but I guess he'll understand. Some girls just don't like men, full stop. Don't like 'em and don't want to know 'em. Those Gumm sisters are like that, you can bet your life, but I must say I never suspected . . . '

'All right.'

'What's that, honey?'

'I said all right. I agree. It's fine for Val to know, and to have helped.'

'Are you sure?'

'Yes.'

It didn't feel like a lie. It felt like the truth because it was what she wanted to believe. For what, otherwise, was she to admit to? That she didn't trust Val an inch? That she didn't like men full stop? Or that she didn't like Val because he liked Gloria and Gloria liked him back?

She didn't want to think about questions like that.

'I say we set the date straightaway,' Gloria was saying. 'How about this Saturday afternoon? Two o'clock? Millicent, can you get what we need by then?'

Millicent nodded. 'I think so,' she said. 'Yes, I'm sure I can.'

'Just tell your pa it's for a school project. Tell him Miss Amelia Gumm believes young ladies should understand just enough about these things to be able to converse, over dinner, with important men of science.'

Millicent nodded. 'Yes. That's clever. He'll go along with that.'

'Then all we need do now is draw straws, to see who'll perform the actual deed. It's a pity we can't all do it, but there we are.'

Dipping into her handbag Gloria produced four drinking straws—three cut in half, and one just an inch or so long. 'Close your eyes,' she said. 'Then if I jumble the straws around in my hand, so just the top bits stick out, and you each take one in turn, leaving one for me, that'll be fair, won't it?'

Obediently, all three girls closed their eyes.

'Shortest straw wins . . . Oops, dropped one. There . . . got it. Eyes tight shut now until everyone has a straw. Verity?'

Verity drew a long straw.

'Millicent?'

Millicent drew a long straw.

'Hazel?'

Hazel reached out. And so deftly had Gloria Gilbert swapped her left hand for her right that even a cheat who had peeped (which neither Verity nor Millicent and certainly not Hazel had been tempted to do) might have questioned the evidence of her own two eyes.

Hazel drew a short straw.

'That just leaves me,' Gloria said. And quick as a whip she transferred the other short straw in her right hand deep into her jacket pocket, then pushed one of the two remaining long straws in her left hand up under the cuff.

'A long straw for me—oh well. Let's see then. Oh, Haze, it's you! You got the short straw! Well, I'm glad for you, honey. You deserve it.'

Hazel curled her fingers round the winning straw and beamed. Verity and Millicent were congratulating her so warmly anyone would think she had already, and single-handedly, got women of England The Vote.

*I won!* she thought to herself. *I've finally won something!*

Gloria leaned back and smiled, benevolently.

'You'll never forget this action, girls,' she said. 'You'll remember it always, for the rest of your lives. Trust me. Oh, and wear the suffragette colours under your coats, then you'll really feel the part. Shall we ring for tea?'

# CHAPTER 14

Our action will be carried out on Saturday. We are all very excited and hoping for a crowd. I won the shortest straw so will be responsible for the most important part. Gloria should do it really, as the whole thing was her idea, but as my father always says, some you win, some you lose. It's all even-stevens in the end.

What we are going to do on Saturday is top secret so cannot be discussed, not even on this page, but it has something to do with Loyd George, the Chancellor of the Ex-Checker. Gloria says our action is not dangerous, or against the law—like Miss Davison throwing stones and other suffra-gettes setting fire to things—but it will give spectators a huge shock and make them all sit up and think hard about the rights of girls and women.

My aunt Alison is still here. I am sup-posed to return to Scotland with her as soon as school finishes but may not do so after all because Gloria has invited me to Italy. I do not think Aunt Alison will mind very much about this change of plan, for Gloria's mother is an heiress, and very popular in Society, and she doubtless knows a great many very wealthy people, both in London and in Italy, whose sons might not mind marrying down one day.

According to Miss Christabel Pankhurst (an important leader of the suffragettes) marriage is a great risk, however, because of men sowing wild oats with fallen women and catching awful diseases which they then pass on to their innocent, unsuspecting wives.

The sooner we have The Vote the better because then we will be able to make laws that will stop men sowing their wild oats here, there, and everywhere, with such nasty consequences. Even Verity and Millicent are glad, now, to be part of the KDG and involved in Saturday's action. None of us want to marry a diseased man, however kind and wealthy he may be.

At school the mornings dragged. With the summer holiday about to start not a single daughter of a gentleman cared two hoots about French conversation, or for Miss Amelia's latest project—painting buttercups and violets around the edges of old dinner plates. As for *King Lear* . . . how sick and tired they were of droning their way through that endless tome. How their hearts sank whenever the books came out of the cupboard. How they wished William Shakespeare had never been born, or had grown up to be a potter, or a crusher of herbs.

*'Where have I been? Where am I? Fair daylight? I am mightily abused. I should e'en die with pity to see another thus . . . '* King Lear was going mad. He thought his daughter didn't love him. Was this what a breakdown was like? Hazel wondered. And she found herself glaring at the words on the page—at the lovely, impenetrable poetry of it all which she couldn't properly understand and which Miss Amelia was making no effort whatsoever to explain.

On Friday, with less than an hour to go before lunch, the front doorbell jangled. Almost immediately the Whineys' old housekeeper came bustling into the Yellow Room to call Miss Amelia away.

'Finish decorating your plates, girls. We are running low on yellow, so be sparing, if you will, with your buttercups. Lots of pretty violets—that's the ticket. Won't be long. Toodle-oo.'

'I've got the stuff,' Millicent whispered to Hazel as soon as the door closed. 'At least, I will have it by Saturday. Daddy is going to show me precisely what to do. It isn't difficult, he says, but we must be careful not to mix things that might explode or produce a poisonous vapour.'

*'What are you whispering about?'*

*'Tell! Tell!'*

*'Is it to do with Gloria's bruises?'*

*'Have the police or anyone been asking questions?'*

152

'Are the police here now? Is that why Miss Amelia's been called away?'

Hazel nudged Millicent, to get her to be quiet.

'It's got nothing to do with Gloria's bruises, or with Miss Amelia,' she replied, truthfully. 'And you had all better be quiet or Miss Eunice will come in and make us look at dead things.'

'Spoilsport,' muttered Jennifer.

But: 'She's right,' said Marjorie. 'And I do so *hate* Miss Eunice's dead things.'

Everyone hated Miss Eunice's dead things. The very thought of having to prise something out of a jar to study the sheen on its wings or count its tiny bones was enough to put them off lunch. Without another word, they got up to fetch their painting things.

Hazel waited until everyone was occupied, sorting out colours and brushes, filling jam jars with water from the sink, trying to remember whose half-decorated plate was whose. Then she drew Millicent to one side.

'Your father—he doesn't suspect anything, does he?'

Millicent shook her head. 'Not a thing,' she whispered back. 'I told him exactly what Gloria said to tell him—that Miss Amelia wants us older girls to do a scientific experiment. Just the one, I said, so that we'll understand a little bit about the great world of science.'

'And what you said just now, about explosions and poisonous gases . . . '

'Don't worry,' Millicent told her. 'My daddy knows all there is to know about chemicals and will explain everything to me very patiently, and probably more than once. He offered to come in to school next week, to conduct

153

the experiment himself, but I told him Miss Amelia is perfectly capable of handling strange and foreign substances and might even be offended by the offer.'

'That was sharp of you,' said Hazel. 'Well done, Millicent.'

The yellow had run out, and so had most of the purple, when the gong sounded for lunch.

Miss Amelia had not returned.

'It's the police,' said Jennifer. 'I'll bet you anything you like the police have come and taken Miss Amelia away.'

'But we would have heard something,' said Hazel. 'She would have screamed.'

'Let's check the hall,' said Phyllis.

'Good idea,' agreed Jane, for Miss Amelia, as they all knew, would never go two steps out of doors without her hat and gloves on, not even to go to prison.

The hall smelt of boiled greens and gravy. Miss Amelia's hat was on its peg and her white kid gloves in an udder-like scrunch on top of the hallstand.

'She's still here,' whispered Jane. 'Who's she talking to, then? It's been ages.'

'Look,' said Octavia. 'Over there—a man's hat and umbrella.'

They all looked.

'I've seen those somewhere before,' said Phyllis. 'I'm certain I have. I just can't remember where.'

Hazel stared very hard and for a long time at the hat and the umbrella. They were ordinary enough in shape and size; it was the colour that was distinctive—a turquoisey-green with a sheen to it, like the flash of a mallard's chest or a swirl of oil in water. They were too gaudy to be the property of a gentleman. Mrs Sawyer would have called them vulgar.

'I believe . . . ' she began, but then the door to the Green Room swung open and out strode Miss Eunice, followed by a stream of younger pupils all eager to get lunch over with so that they could go home.

'Chop, chop, senior class,' Miss Eunice growled. 'What *are* you all doing, hanging about the hall? Go straight to luncheon *now*. And in *silence*, if you please. The first girl to speak will stay behind and clean out the tadpole tank.'

The tadpole tank was vile. There were things mouldering in it which may or may not have been amphibious once, and the water was the colour and consistency of pea soup. No frogs had ever reached maturity in that tank, so far as anyone knew, and it hadn't been cleaned since Christmas.

In total silence, the girls filed into the dining room and took their seats at the table. In total silence they ate their greens, their steak and kidney pudding, and their pink blancmange.

'School dismissed,' barked Miss Eunice as the clock struck two.

'Tomorrow . . . ' Hazel murmured to Verity and Millicent. 'We'll meet tomorrow on the steps of . . . '

'Miss Mull-Dare—you will stay behind.'

'But . . . '

'You will stay behind for talking, Miss Mull-Dare, and you will clean the tadpole tank until it gleams. The rest of you—on your way.'

'But . . . '

'I will tell your servant to come back for you at three.

No arguing, dear girl. Rules are rules. Just strain the tank over the sink, throw the contents in the slop bucket and you'll be done in no time. You know where the pinnies are. Off you trot.'

The others left as fast as they could. Through the window of the Green Room Hazel watched them go, relief written all over their faces. She saw Florence cross the road, looking peeved.

*Sorry*, she mouthed, against the glass, before turning to face the tank.

She was dipping a stick, searching carefully through slime for any signs of life, when a door above her slammed and footsteps—two sets—came thudding down the stairs.

*'Get out of my home. Out! Out! And don't you dare come back. Coming here under false pretences . . . I will not be threatened, sir, do you hear me? Do you understand?'*

Throwing down her stick, Hazel ran out into the hall, just in time to witness Miss Amelia, all flailing limbs and shaking fists, jump the last two stairs and land, with a small skid, on a rug.

The man being chased—the visitor—had wrestled the front door open and was on the verge of getting away. His hand was on the latch but that was all Hazel could see of him as he moved, quick sharp, around the door. It was enough, for she had seen that hand before—seen, and hated, every finger, knuckle, and pore as it had pressed into the small of Gloria Gilbert's back and bent her, like a doll.

*'Yours, I believe,'* Miss Amelia shrieked, flinging his hat after him. 'And, pray, do not leave without your brolly.'

It was a good throw. Excellent. And if ever a furled

umbrella could be said to resemble a spear it was at that precise instant, as it sped from Miss Amelia's grip and struck the fleeing man in some soft and penetrable spot just above his collar.

*'Hah! That'll teach you!'*

Thinking only that the brolly might have bounced, causing anger more than injury, Hazel stepped back into the Green Room.

It seemed to take an awfully long time before the umbrella clattered onto the steps and, by then, its target had wheeled round and come stumbling back into the hall; a look of utter disbelief on his face.

Valentine . . . Val . . . not smirking now, or tangoing either, just swaying like a drunk on the 'Welcome' mat and turning a peculiar shade of blue around the mouth.

He didn't spot Hazel straightaway. In fact he appeared to be having trouble focusing at all, and in deciding which way to walk.

'Get out, you little worm!' Miss Amelia hissed. 'Out! Out!'

*If he falls backwards and down the steps,* Hazel fretted, silently, *he really will hurt himself.* But before she could make any move to help him, or to shut the front door, Val crumpled at the knees and then toppled slowly forward—already so hurt by the exceptionally long, sharp point of his vulgar green umbrella, that a tumble onto the pavement and a crack or two on the head would have made no odds.

He looked faintly ridiculous, sprawled over like that with his bottom in the air and an ear to the floor—like a man eavesdropping on the basement, or checking a garden for moles.

Aghast, Hazel waited for him to get up. To give Miss Amelia what for. To strike her, perhaps, even though she was a woman. But Valentine didn't move. He didn't even blink. He just lay right there on the parquet floor, his head twisted towards Hazel so she could see his astonished face but not the hole in the back of his neck.

*'What are you doing here?'* his eyes seemed to say to her. *'You're supposed to have gone home by now. And why are you wearing such a ghastly pinny? And what has this madwoman done to my . . . ?'*

Quickly, Miss Amelia jumped over his body and scanned the empty street. Then she banged the front door on the outside world, got down on her knees and began frisking his coat pockets. She hadn't spotted Hazel—yet. And she was moving so fast, and muttering so intently, that it took a while before Hazel realized that her rummagings beneath Valentine's ribs had nothing to do with First Aid.

'A-*ha*!' With a look of triumph Miss Amelia pulled something free and held it up. 'Got it . . . *got it.*'

'Oh . . . ' Hazel breathed.

Miss Amelia spun round.

'Miss Mull-Dare,' she squeaked, her throat turning as red as a turkey's wattle. 'Why are *you* still here? Not to worry. Don't be frightened. We've had an intruder, as you can see, but I caught him—I caught him good and proper.'

She had tucked the photograph from Val's pocket hastily into the folds of her own skirt, but not before Hazel had recognized the person in it—and the bruises round her neck.

158

Val was making no attempt to stand, or to reclaim his property—or rather, Gloria Gilbert's property. Miss Amelia gave him a sharp prod. '*Get up,*' she roared. '*Stop shamming and get up. Get up! Get up! Get up!*'

Then, in a flurry of running feet and sharp exclamations, Miss Eunice and the housekeeper were there, and Hazel was being hustled into the Yellow Room.

'Stay!' growled Miss Eunice, slamming the door in her face.

Hazel stayed. There were jam jars of paint water to be emptied so she tipped them into the sink, listening out, as swirls of yellow and purple gurgled down the plughole, for the sound of an ambulance bell.

'Is he all right?' she asked at once, when Miss Eunice reappeared.

'He will be,' Miss Eunice grunted. 'The nasty little streak. He was a chancer, Miss Mull-Dare; a wicked young man intent on taking our money and destroying the good name of our school. All dealt with now, though. All done and dusted. And I will thank *you* to say nothing whatsoever about it. Not to your parents, not to the other young ladies—not a single word to anyone, do you understand?'

Hazel nodded, meaning yes, she understood. Miss Eunice's face was set very hard, like Rascal's when you tried to take away his pig's ear. 'Good girl,' she said, but in a tone that suggested quite the opposite.

'You have another year with us, don't you?' she added, in the same oddly menacing tone. 'For which your dear father has already paid? There are no refunds, you know, and it would be such a shame for us to have to let

159

you go, particularly with your father's health the way it is. How is he, by the way? Do we know?'

'No,' Hazel said. 'We don't.'

'Ah—well. Early days, I suppose.'

'Have you called for the police?'

'I beg your pardon?'

'The police. Are you going to tell the police about V— that man? About what he was doing here?'

Miss Eunice grunted.

'No need to involve the Law, Miss Mull-Dare,' she said. 'That nasty little specimen won't bother us again. He'll be halfway across London by now, I shouldn't wonder— running away with his tail between his legs and a bit of a sore head.'

The jangle of the doorbell made both of them jump.

'That will be Florence,' Hazel said. 'My servant. Only I haven't done the tank yet.'

Miss Eunice looked blankly back at her.

'The tadpole tank,' Hazel reminded her. 'I haven't even emptied it out.' Could they expel her, she fretted, for not cleaning a tank out? Or for talking at luncheon? She hoped not, but, with Miss Eunice, you could never tell.

'Please don't worry,' Miss Eunice replied, baring her teeth in a terrible smile. 'Please don't give the tadpole tank another thought.'

# CHAPTER 15

'Gloria! Thank goodness you've called. Have you seen Val today—since this afternoon I mean?'

'Val? No. Why?'

'He came to the school. To see Miss Amelia. It was about you, I'm quite certain it was; about what she did to your neck. He—'

'Whoah. Stop. Are you sure it was Val? How do you know he was at the school? Who saw him?'

'Only me. And Miss Eunice. And Miss Amelia, of course. Oh, and their housekeeper. It was after school, when all the other girls had gone. I wouldn't have seen him either, only I was doing the tadpole tank. Miss Amelia threw his umbrella at him and hurt him rather a lot. Then she took a photograph out of his pocket, while he was lying on the floor, and it was a photograph of you, with all your bruises showing. Miss Eunice told me not to say anything but she doesn't know I know who he is. And she doesn't know, either, that I know about your neck, or about your father taking Miss Amelia to court or—'

'Who else knows? About Val being at the school? Who else have you told?'

'No one, Gloria. Only you. But—'

'Then don't breathe a word. Not to Millicent, not to Verity, not to anyone. Let me deal with it.'

'Can you, Gloria? Are you sure? I'm so sorry about Val

*turning out to be so low. Miss Eunice said he was trying to get money out of them. That's terrible, isn't it? And your photograph—he must have stolen it from your house while no one was looking.'*

*'Yes. He must have.'*

*'And now Miss Amelia has it, so you don't have any evidence.'*

*'True.'*

*'Oh dear . . . oh dear, Gloria. What can we do?'*

*'Not much, for the moment . . .'*

*'Gloria . . . are you still there? Gloria?'*

*'What? Yes. Now listen, Hazel; listen to me. Let's think about the action. Nothing must distract us from that—it's too important. You will be ready, won't you? Tomorrow at two? You're sure you can get away?'*

*'Yes. Quite sure.'*

*'Good. I'll see you tomorrow then.'*

*'Wait—Gloria?'*

*'What?'*

*'I was just wondering . . .'*

*'What?'*

*'About going to Ita—oh, nothing. It doesn't matter. Although . . . there is just one other thing. When you see Val—if you see him—will you forgive him for what he's done?'*

*'Nope. Not in a million years. Not until Hell freezes over. You can bet your sweet life on that.'*

It was hard to sleep. Impossible. Three times Hazel threw back her coverlet, got up and paced around. She would have liked to sit down and type something but the clatter

162

of the keys, in the still of the night, might have woken her aunt or her mother.

Around midnight it began to rain—a light shower but enough, Hazel hoped, to chill the air and keep it that way. She thought of Emily Wilding Davison, and wondered whether she, too, had lain awake the night before her action, hoping for inclement weather so that going out in a long heavy coat would not arouse suspicion.

But then, Miss Davison's action had been dangerous, so dangerous it had killed her, so she had probably had more than the weather on her mind the night before the Derby. Spiritual things, perhaps, or memories of being young.

It had not been difficult, after all, to fashion a banner in the suffragette colours. Her green silk scarf had done nicely for one long, broad stripe, and cutting up a white petticoat, to make the middle swathe, had felt deliciously bad. Finding something mauve had been more of a challenge, until she'd remembered a piece of brocade, the exact colour of wisteria flowers, that had covered the sideboard one Easter and was currently doing service as extra padding in Pipkin's basket.

Normally, Hazel hated sewing. It was her least favourite activity at the Kensington School for the Daughters of Gentlemen and she had vowed to give it up just as soon as her father let her (it was a tradition—their tradition—that she always gave him a handkerchief on his birthday, with his initials and a lucky horseshoe stitched, crookedly, in one corner). Sewing the suffragette colours, however, had been a joy. Like typing. Even pricking her finger, twice, had been worth the sting—had made her feel, in some small way, like a martyr for the cause.

The banner was in her wardrobe now, safely hidden until morning. She had attempted to sleep with it wrapped around her shoulders, wanting the closeness of the colours as action-day dawned, but the mauve bit had smelt so badly of dog that her nose and eyes had watered.

*I should have washed it, and hung it out of the window to dry,* she thought. *Only then Mrs Sawyer might have seen it and told Aunt Alison . . .*

Drifting, at last, towards sleep, she thought briefly of Val and about what Gloria might have to say to him if he ever dared to show his face again. She didn't mind betting, though, that they had all seen the last of that chancer now that his wicked plan to blackmail Miss Amelia had been thwarted.

And she couldn't help but wish (*knock on wood, fingers crossed*) that he had gone somewhere far, far away; to a place where Gloria wouldn't ever find him, even if she looked, and where women and girls would be way too smart to fall for his ferrety good-looks and easy charm.

And in all of these respects—since he was as dead as a doornail and already under the earth—she was very much in luck.

The rain had stopped before dawn and it looked like being a warm day. With all morning to kill, Hazel began to feel anxious.

*What if it all goes horribly wrong? What if Millicent doesn't mix the chemicals properly, or her father decides we can't have them after all? What if the Chancellor of the Ex-Checker isn't there, or I don't recognize him among all the others? What if . . . ?*

Expecting her mother to be at work, and Aunt Alison to be out shopping, it surprised Hazel greatly, and did little to calm her nerves, when she found both women sitting down for breakfast and waiting, quite clearly, for her.

Trying—and failing—to look aimless and sleepy she helped herself to scrambled egg and sat down to eat.

'We have a surprise for you,' her mother said. 'A nice one.'

Hazel glanced up, warily.

'Have you? What is it?'

Her mother and Aunt Alison exchanged glances. *Shall we tell her?* those glances said, *or shall we keep it to ourselves a bit longer?* Hazel hated it when grown-ups did that. Still, it was proof, she supposed, that her mother and her aunt were getting along all right, for once.

'Your father has turned a corner,' Aunt Alison said. 'He's on the mend.'

Hazel imagined her father turning, quite literally, into their street. In her mind's eye he was just as she remembered him: bright-haired and cheerful, with minty sweets in his pockets and a grin on his face as he hurried towards his own front door and the familiar life behind it.

The thing she couldn't quite imagine—not so precisely, anyway—was herself, running to greet him.

'That's a relief,' she said. 'Will he be home soon?'

Her mother and her aunt both shook their heads.

'Not yet,' her aunt told her. 'But we're hoping he'll be well enough to join us in Scotland, before the end of the summer. We can look after him nicely there, can't we, and the fresh air will be a tonic.'

Happily, assuming that was all, Hazel went back to eating her breakfast.

'He's longing to see you,' her aunt continued. 'And since he's so much better your mother and I have agreed that you may visit him. With us. This afternoon.'

Hazel swallowed a mouthful of egg. Swallowed it carefully, aware of how close she had come to choking on it.

'I can't,' she said.

She didn't have to look up to know the two women were stunned.

'What do you mean you *can't*?' Her aunt's tone, after a moment's silence, was not very ladylike. 'Did you actually *hear* what I just said? Were you *listening*?'

'Shhhhhhh . . . ' Mrs Mull-Dare's shushing was soft, but insistent, as if her sister-in-law's voice might wake a baby, or bother a dog. 'Hazel?' she said, gently. 'Don't you want to see your father?'

Scarlet-faced, and close to tears, Hazel dared to look her mother in the eye.

*Did she want to see her father?*

'No,' she whispered and, to her shame, it was the honest truth.

'*Well!*'

Aunt Alison threw down her napkin. 'I can see we're going to have our work cut out with you, young lady. For if you can't or won't visit your own sick father, what earthly chance will a husband ever have of—'

'Shhhhhhh.'

Mrs Mull-Dare had to stand up and lean across the table in order to reach, and clumsily pat, her daughter's hand.

'It's all right, pet,' she said. 'You don't have to come with us if you don't want to. You can come another time. Next week perhaps.'

Swallowing hard, Hazel allowed her fingers to flutter, gratefully, beneath her mother's hand.

'Will you tell him,' she managed to say, 'that I'm happy he's on the mend?'

'Yes, of course.'

'And . . . and that I missed him on my birthday? That it wasn't the same?'

'I can do that, certainly. Although why don't you write him a letter? Or type it even, on your new machine?'

Aunt Alison snorted.

'She's his *daughter*,' she sniffed. 'Not his secretary. A hand-written note on a pretty sheet of paper would be far more appropriate. And, Ivy, dear, excuse me for mentioning it, but your hair is trailing in the butter.'

```
Dear Daddy,
   I hope you will forgive me for not vis-
iting you today. I promise on my life I
will come soon and when I do I will bring
all your favourite sweets.
   I am writing this on the typewriter my
friend Gloria gave me for my birthday. It is
not as precious as the charm bracelet you
and mother gave me, but I like the funny
sound it makes when you hit the keys hard.
   School finishes next week. The
Shakespeare play we are reading is 'King
Lear'. Do you know it?
```

We are also decorating plates to bring home and although we have been told to just do violets and buttercups I am going to sneak some green and do a four-leafed clover on mine. Then, when you come home, you will be able to eat your breakfast off a lucky plate.

I look forward, very much, to seeing you in Scotland. What's the betting it will rain most days?!!

Your affectionate daughter,
    Hazel Louise Mull-Dare

With her aunt and her mother gone it should have been the easiest thing in the world for Hazel to slip out of the house unnoticed. She might have guessed, however, that Dottie would choose the moments before her departure to do her business in the hall.

'Goodness me, Miss Hazel,' exclaimed Florence, looking up from doing the scrubbing, 'what are you doing in that coat? It's the middle of summer. You'll melt.'

'I'll be fine,' Hazel told her, skirting round the bucket. 'Really.'

'Are you going out with your American friend, miss? Is the car calling for you?'

'I'll be fine,' Hazel repeated, heading quickly for the door. 'I'm meeting some girls from school outside the sweet shop. Then we're catching the bus to Baker Street for . . . for a special project, to do with science.'

Her fingers were on the door handle.

'Wait, miss. Just a tick.' Florence's knees cracked as she rose to her feet. 'Give me a minute to empty this bucket and then I'll come with you.'

'No! I mean, no thank you, Florence, there's no need.'

Florence lifted the bucket and threw in the scrubbing brush. 'There's every need, miss, if you'll pardon my saying so. Your father would send me packing if he knew I'd watched you walk out of this house without a chaperone. So you just wait there like a good girl while I tip this mucky water away.'

*No! No! Gloria will be furious. She and the others—they'll think I've blabbed. And Millicent and Verity are allowed to cross a few streets unchaperoned. I'll look like a baby with you tagging along. And what if you insist on catching the bus to Baker Street with us? Then what will we do?*

'Oh, will you look at that daft dog . . . ' Florence had paused, halfway across the hall, to shake her head at Diggy Bert. 'I don't think he's been walked. Drat . . . as if I didn't have enough to do already.'

Hazel looked at Diggy Bert's big, shaggy head poking round the door that led down to the kitchen. Then she reached for the red and brown lead.

'I'll take him,' she said. 'Then you won't have to walk him, or chaperone me either.'

Florence hesitated.

'It's the perfect solution,' Hazel added. 'Come along, Diggy. Walkies.'

'I . . . I don't know, miss.' Florence looked from the dog, to the lead in Hazel's hand, and then back at the dog. 'I'm not sure you'll be able to manage him. As for taking him on a bus . . . '

169

But Hazel was already clipping on the lead, hanging on tight as Diggy Bert strained to be outside, his whole body wagging in anticipation.

'We'll be fine,' she said, and opened the door.

'Well, only if you're . . . '

*Wooomph* . . . It was like being dragged down the steps by a runaway horse.

*'Slow down, boy! Stop! Sit!'*

Only by digging in her heels and keeping the lead short did Hazel manage to avoid being pulled right over.

*'Diggy Bert, slow down. And we're not going to the Gardens— no! This way, THIS way, Diggy . . . '*

The others were waiting, outside the sweet shop.

Gloria, Verity, and Millicent.

Verity and Millicent had their coats on, buttoned all the way up to conceal their suffragette colours, and Millicent was carrying a holdall. Gloria was wearing a neat little jacket over a blue summer dress and, so far as Hazel could tell, had nothing remotely green, white, or mauve about her person.

Holding tight to Diggy Bert she began to cross the road.

'Oh, Lord,' she heard Gloria exclaim. 'She's only gone and brought the wolf.'

# CHAPTER 16

'I'm . . . sorry . . . I . . . didn't have . . . much . . . choice.'

It wasn't easy bringing Diggy Bert to a halt. He wanted to jump up and lick faces. He wanted to drag Hazel into the place where chocolate lived. He wanted to do an about turn and go back towards Kensington Gardens. He wanted—*oooh, look at that one*—to chase cars.

'Mind the bag! Mind the bag!' squealed Millicent as he half leapt and half twizzled, almost choking with the joy of it all.

'Are you out of your tiny mind, Hazel?' said Gloria. 'Bringing your damned wolf on an action? There's no way they'll let him in—you do know that, don't you? I doubt he'll be allowed on the bus, even.'

Hazel yanked, hard, at Diggy Bert's leash, persuading him, finally, to sit.

'He's been on buses before,' she said. 'With my mother. The conductors don't mind, so long as she pays for him and he keeps off the seats. And we can leave him tied up, while we do our action. I'm sorry, Gloria. It was either him or one of the servants. They treat me as though I'm nine years old, still, and won't let me out alone. I hate it.'

'O . . . K,' said Gloria, slowly. 'OK, I guess we can cope. And here's the bus. Just keep him away from Millicent's bag, and don't let him slobber on my boots.'

The bus, luckily, was almost empty and the conductor a sucker for pets.

'What kind of dog would this be then?' he asked Hazel as she counted out pennies for the fare.

'Wolf . . . ' muttered Gloria.

'Irish wolfhound,' Hazel corrected her. 'Crossed with something else—I forget what.'

'A large rug, by the look of him,' chuckled the conductor. 'Or a bale of hay.'

Other passengers were turning to stare and smile. Hazel wished they wouldn't. A man with a thick moustache was looking, not at Diggy, but at them; his eyes flicking from Verity, to Millicent, and then to Hazel before coming to rest on Gloria's chest.

Did he think it strange, Hazel wondered, that three out of the four of them were wearing their winter coats? Had he noticed the way Millicent was guarding the holdall, gripping it close as if she feared it might grow feet and run away?

What if he, or one of the other passengers, put two and two together and guessed what they were up to?

Anxiously, Hazel tightened her grasp on Diggy Bert's lead and tried to look pleasant and normal. With every minute that passed she was feeling less like a suffragette and more like an ordinary thirteen-year-old girl who just wanted to go home and read a book.

She wished the bus would get a move on, but it appeared to be stuck in traffic.

172

Gloria, who had taken the seat in front of her rather than risk getting dog-drool on her boots, looked anxiously at her wristwatch and tutted.

Hazel leaned forward, to whisper in her ear: 'Have you heard from Val?'

'No,' Gloria snapped, jerking her head away. 'I haven't.'

'So, do you think he's left London then? For good?'

'I don't know. And I don't care. Now shush.'

Rebuffed, Hazel swivelled round in her seat and smiled, weakly, at Millicent and Verity. They hadn't heard. They weren't listening. Their faces were flushed; their hairlines beaded with sweat from the heat of their coats, and they were gazing out at the dresses in shop windows as if they wished, more than anything, that that was where they were going—out shopping for pretty clothes.

The bus began to move, but at a snail's pace.

'Perhaps there's a big parade happening up ahead,' said Hazel. 'Or . . . ' she lowered her voice, 'another *action*.'

Gloria scowled.

'Gloria? Are you all right?'

'I'm *fine*. I just want us to get there, preferably before Christmas.' She checked her watch for the umpteenth time and muttered something, under her breath. Diggy Bert, sprawled in the aisle and half asleep, raised one ear.

Lowering her voice, but keeping her distance this time, Hazel said: 'The Chancellor will definitely be there, won't he, Gloria? I mean, it's not as if he's going to be sent anywhere else, all of a sudden, is it? So it won't really matter if we're a little bit late, will it? Gloria?'

Diggy Bert raised his other ear and shifted, uneasily,

as Gloria spun round; her expression so unkind, so . . . *unfriendly* that Hazel felt the pit of her stomach lurch, as if the bus was going over a humpity bridge.

'Just pipe down, Hazel, will you,' she hissed. 'No more talking, all right?' And she turned her back, in its thin blue jacket, before Hazel could so much as nod in pained agreement.

'It'll be fine, honey,' she added, then, in what was clearly an effort to sound a bit more pleasant. 'Once we finally get there, it'll all be fine.'

Quietly, sadly, Hazel reached down until her fingers touched the stubble of Diggy Bert's head. He was wide awake now, and tensed to spring, bark, or even bite, should the human with the mean voice continue to threaten one of his people.

Sensing his mood, Hazel kept the contact; gently stroking his head, scritching behind his ears and smoothing down the hackles on his neck. After a while, as the bus continued its slow crawl towards Baker Street, she began to feel better and so, she sensed, did Diggy Bert.

'Good boy,' she murmured, wishing she had brought him a pig's ear. 'Good boy, Diggy . . . '

At last, at long last, the conductor rang the bell for their stop.

'Right,' said Gloria, as they stood on a corner and got their bearings. 'This is it! Hazel, I'm sorry I snapped at you, honey. I was feeling mighty queasy in that damned bus, if you want the truth.'

'Oh . . . Well . . . are you all right now?'

'Not really. In fact, I tell you what: you girls go on in and I'll wait here with the hound.'

'*Gloria!*'

'*We can't! We can't possibly do this without you!*'

'*We should all stick together. The KDG is a team—your team. You thought of it.*'

'I know . . . I know . . . ' Gloria pressed a hand to her forehead, as if to ease a jagged pain. 'But let's think practically, shall we? We can't take the hound—'

'Diggy Bert,' said Hazel.

'We can't take Hazel's dog in there, so one of us is going to have to stay outside with it. It can't be you, Hazel, because you drew the lucky straw, it can't be Millicent because she's mixing the chemicals, and if it's a toss-up between Verity and me, well—you're not the one who feels like spewing her guts up, are you, Verity?'

'We could tie Diggy to those railings over there,' Hazel said. 'He wouldn't mind.'

Gloria wrinkled her nose.

'That seems a little cruel to me,' she said. 'What if he got loose?'

'He wouldn't,' Hazel said.

'All right, all right . . . What if somebody stole him, then? The anti-suffrage people would have a field day over that, wouldn't they: "The Kensington Daughters of Gentlemen Take Action for Women's Rights but Neglect a Helpless Animal". I can see the headlines now . . . '

*Headlines?*

Hazel hadn't thought about headlines. She hadn't thought about anything much beyond the thrill of doing an action—of being a proper suffragette.

'Do you really think we'll get into the newspapers?' she said, excitement rising in her voice. 'Because if we do,

175

maybe Emmeline and Christabel Pankhurst will read about us.'

'Sure they will,' said Gloria. 'And they'll be as proud as punch. This time next week, the KDG will be the toast of the Women's Social and Political Union. Of the whole of *London* even! We'll be everybody's darlings; as famous as Emily Wilding Davison, only alive and kicking and able to make the most of it.'

'Gracious . . . '

'So . . . leave the hound with me, Hazel, and off you go. Good luck and don't waver. Only weaklings waver, and suffragettes aren't weak, are they? Think of Miss Davison. She didn't waver, did she, not for half a second. And who knows, she could be looking down on you, right this very minute, willing you on.'

Without another word, her mind full of headlines and dizzy, already, with the prospect of success, Hazel handed over Diggy Bert's lead. He was snuffling at something nasty on the pavement so didn't notice straight away.

'*Arrivederci!*' Gloria called merrily, as the three dark-coated figures mounted a broad flight of stone steps. 'I'll be thinking of you.'

Hazel didn't even turn around. Later, she would regret that:

```
I didn't even turn round. I just left
Diggy Bert with her, and kept on going. I
thought he would be all right. I thought
everything would be all right. But I was
wrong. And Gloria lied.
```

The layout and feel of the building, once they got in, was just as Gloria had described it—a vast entrance hall,

176

with a marble staircase sweeping impressively to the upper floors. Other visitors were consulting guidebooks and wondering where to go first. Children clutched the hands of parents, or nannies. 'Who will we see?' they wanted to know; and: 'Is the King of England up those stairs?'

'Have you been here before?' Hazel asked Verity and Millicent, keeping her voice low even though it was a perfectly innocent question.

No, they replied. Have you?

'No.'

'You'd think at least one of us would have,' said Verity. 'Perhaps our parents never wanted us to be brought here.' She too lowered her voice: 'Not the right kind of place for young ladies to be seen in.'

For a moment Millicent and Verity stood very still, both thinking about their parents and about how their fathers, in particular, were likely to react if what they were about to do got reported in *The Times*.

'Oh dear,' said Verity after a while. 'I do hope Gloria's right and we're not going to get arrested or anything.'

'She was absolutely certain,' Hazel reassured her. ' "Beyond the Jurisdiction of the Law"; that's what she said this place is, remember?'

'Yes. You're right. I'm just being silly. So . . . Come on, then, let's hurry and find Lloyd George. Where did Gloria say he would be?'

'Up here,' said Millicent. 'Follow me.' And she unbuckled the top of her holdall, in a brave show of readiness, before leading the way across the hall, to the marble staircase.

'In here?'

'No . . . in here.'

'Is that him? Sitting at the desk and signing a paper?'

'No . . . It isn't. Oh crikey, they all look the same to me, these important men . . .'

'Here. He's in here. I've found him. Quickly, you two . . . Verity . . . Millicent, get ready with the stuff . . . I'll get closer. As close as I can . . .'

'Shhhh. Not so loud.'

'It's all right. It's . . . Oh!'

For some reason Hazel hadn't expected to get this close to Lloyd George—so close that she could see the whites of his eyes and all the pores on his skin. He had a kind face, she decided. A very kind face, for a man who wouldn't let women have The Vote. And although his hair was brown, not foxy red, and he didn't have a single freckle, there was something about him, the air of kindness perhaps, that reminded her so much of her father that it almost broke her heart.

'Throw the stuff right in his face,' Gloria had said. 'And make sure everyone around you knows why.'

Despite herself, Hazel's legs began to shake. She wasn't sure she could do it—throw chemicals at this man's features and watch them slowly dissolve. She wasn't sure she had the nerve, or the stomach, to stand firm and shout for women's rights while his mouth got eaten away and his nose bubbled and popped, like something in a pan—even though he was only a waxwork.

But Gloria . . . Gloria would never forgive her for losing her nerve. She had drawn the short straw—the lucky straw—and it was too late, now, to back down.

'*Millicent,*' she hissed, reaching out, without turning around, for the jar of acid. '*What are you doing? Hurry up.*'

Millicent's voice seemed unnecessarily loud as she answered: 'But there's nobody here.'

'What?'

'*There's nobody here.*'

Confused, Hazel turned around.

'See—not a soul,' said Verity, with evident relief. 'There were two old men, when we came in, and a lady with a limp, but they've left. The people we saw downstairs must have gone straight to the Hall of Kings or to look for the scary stuff. They've got a waxwork somewhere here of Mary Queen of Scots having her head chopped off—our parlourmaid told me—and another of Lord Nelson, dying in Hardy's arms.'

Hazel saw that Millicent and Verity were right. Nobody, it seemed, was interested right now in looking at Lloyd George. And why would they be, she told herself, if there were other wax figures here at Madame Tussaud's doing something far more interesting than simply looking kind.

'We could wait a while,' she suggested. 'Until people start coming in here. They're bound to come eventually, aren't they, if they want their money's worth.'

She didn't sound convinced.

Millicent shook her head. 'We need a crowd,' she said. 'An action's not worth doing without a crowd.'

'How many's a crowd?' Verity wondered. 'Ten people? Twenty?'

'More than none,' said Millicent, glumly. 'More than zero, that's for sure. Shall we just leave? It's not our fault nobody's here.'

'No.'

Hazel's head was beginning to ache. She was so hot, in her coat, it was like brewing a fever and the wisteria-coloured brocade, that still smelt of Pipkin, had bunched itself into a bothersome lump beneath her left armpit.

But this wasn't like snipping the heads off fake flowers, in the privacy of your own bedroom, or making a rocking horse rear while you pinned colours to its bridle. This was real life. Her first chance—her only one, perhaps—of doing a proper action, in a public place, instead of simply playing at it, like a child.

'No,' she repeated,. 'If we can't do it here, we'll have to go to where there's more people and do it there. Come on!'

So off they trooped:

Through the Hall of Kings, where the waxwork of Queen Victoria had drawn quite a crowd.

'How about her?' whispered Verity.

But the way Hazel saw it, throwing chemicals all over a female figure, particularly one as much-loved as the late Queen, might not do a lot for women's rights.

Into the Hall of Tableaux where 'The Arrest of Guy Fawkes' looked promising until Millicent pointed out that, since Mister Fawkes had wanted to blow up the Houses of Parliament, he'd had more than a little in common with some of the more militant suffragettes.

On to the Grand Hall where they stood for a moment in front of the armoured waxwork of Joan of Arc—not, for one moment, to consider throwing acid in her face, but in genuine awe.

'She's like the girl who led Miss Davison's funeral parade,' said Verity. 'Isn't she?'

180

'Yes,' breathed Hazel. 'Exactly like.'

'Come on,' said Millicent. 'There's a lot of people over there. Let's see who they're looking at.'

The crowd in question parted, automatically, for the three girls in dark coats—they looked so determined to see the figure.

'He's good, isn't he?' a gentleman in tweeds murmured to Verity. 'Wonderfully lifelike.'

'Excuse *me*.'

A tall, thin woman clutching a guidebook glared, fiercely, at Hazel, Millicent, and Verity and began tapping her foot on the floor. 'Excuse *me*, girls, but this is a private tour, organized by the Stratford-upon-Avon Historical Society. Would you mind waiting until we've moved to the next exhibit?'

'Oh, let them stay and listen,' said the man who had spoken to Verity. 'Three more tagging along won't hurt.'

The woman continued to glare. 'It's highly irregular,' she snapped. 'They don't belong. And they haven't paid.'

'Oh . . . just get on with it, Dorothy,' someone else piped up. 'We'll be here all day at this rate, and I'm longing for a cup of tea and a nice sit down.'

With great reluctance, the tall, thin woman lowered her glare to her guidebook, adjusted her spectacles and continued with her speech:

*'The great man we see before us allegedly died on his birthday, April 23rd 1616, leaving a body of work behind him that may never be equalled . . .'*

Hazel, Millicent, and Verity gazed, along with the others, at the waxwork in front of them. And all three felt a ripple of dislike for this small, dome-headed man as they recalled the many long and tedious hours they had spent poring over the body of his work at the Kensington School for the Daughters of Gentlemen.

'*And we, of the Stratford-upon-Avon Historical Society, can be immensely proud that he lived and worked in our town and was laid to rest among us, at Holy Trinity Church.*'

'Now!'

Millicent didn't need telling twice. Down on one knee she went, shielding the holdall from view as she unscrewed the lids of two glass jars and, with surprisingly steady hands, transferred half the contents of one very neatly into the other.

Quickly, as the fullest jar began to fizz, she clamped its lid back on and began counting, silently, to ten.

Luckily, most people were staring fixedly at the waxwork or attending to what Dorothy was saying. The few who did look down, to see what the little girl with the big bag was up to, assumed she was getting herself a drink.

'No eating or drinking allowed, dear,' one woman bent to whisper. 'Didn't you read the notices?'

Millicent, still counting, nodded, smiled widely, and kept her hands very still around the jar of acids until the woman turned round again. *Six . . . seven . . .*

'*Standing here we can quite clearly see that our illustrious fellow-citizen was a fine-looking fellow, of average weight, with dark hair and a noble forehead . . .*'

Millicent stood up, shielding the jar as best she could against her coat. The contents were still fizzing and the jar itself was getting warmer and warmer, like a pan on the boil.

Hazel kept her eyes fixed on the waxwork's brocade-covered chest as she waited for what she guessed was long enough. Then very slowly and without, she hoped, being too obvious, she reached out her right hand.

*Ouch!*

The shock of the hot glass against her palm made her wince.

*Please don't let me drop this. Please don't . . .*

She had already undone the buttons of her coat and just knowing that the suffragette colours were there, albeit bunched awkwardly under her armpit, helped strengthen her resolve as she clamped her fingers, bravely, around the very hot top of the jar and turned away from prying eyes to open it.

*Do it quickly*, Gloria had said. *In one big whoosh. Like throwing paint water down the sink.*

She was glad that William Shakespeare looked neither kind nor like her father.

The lid of the jar was loose enough to come away easily but its underside was hot enough to burn, and sticky, too, as if the jar had once contained marmalade and hadn't been properly rinsed.

Quickly—*ye-ouch, ye-ouch, ye-ouch*—she slipped the lid into her coat pocket.

*Now. Do it now.*

It wasn't as if he was real, was it? It wasn't as if this figure in front of her was going to scream, or writhe in agony, the instant a slosh of acid hit his bald patch. The flesh and blood William Shakespeare had been dead for donkey's years. He would be nothing but dust by now, in his tomb at Stratford-upon-Avon, and way beyond caring what the KDG was about to do to his image, in the name of women's rights.

*Miss Davison didn't waver did she?*

It was easy—a comfort and a spur—to imagine Miss Davison hovering close by, willing her on, but not so palatable to think of the great William Shakespeare glaring down at her, like a bald avenging angel.

*Now! What are you waiting for?*

The Stratford-upon-Avon Historical Society was about to move away. Dorothy had turned a page in her guide-book and the others were shuffling their feet or talking, quietly, among themselves, as they waited to be led towards the next exhibit.

*Quick!*

The dig in her back, Hazel realized, was either Verity or Millicent, prodding her to hurry up and do it. To throw the acid while there was still time . . . before the crowd dispersed.

And even as she faltered, her fingers throbbing around the jar, the troubling idea of William Shakespeare's spirit waving its fist and mouthing beautiful angry words, faded beside the grander thought of Emily Wilding Davison smiling and nodding encouragement. And then there was Gloria, waiting outside.

Emily and Gloria. Gloria and Emily.

She couldn't let them down. Not at this, the final hurdle.

'VOTES FOR WOMEN!'

Her aim was good, for she had been practising at home, flinging jars of tap water against the tiled bath-room wall.

Her aim was true, for the acid struck Shakespeare full

184

in the face before dripping onto his shoulders and eating holes in his jacket.

Her aim was so perfect that, luckily for her, only a couple of tiny splatters flew back and hit her coat. She had dropped the jar, instinctively, before any trickles or drips touched her fingers, but it would be many hours before she found the damage to her coat and realized, in belated horror, what the consequences would have been for her, personally, had even one drop of those chemicals splashed onto her skin.

'JUSTICE FOR WOMEN!'

'GIVE WOMEN THE VOTE.'

'DOWN WITH LLOYD GEORGE. EMILY WILDING DAVISON IS A SAINT IN HEAVEN . . . '

That was Verity, calling out about Lloyd George and Miss Davison . . . little cry-baby Verity who wouldn't normally say boo to a goose.

Hazel wanted to turn right round and hug her friend, but her legs wouldn't function. She couldn't even turn her head, to smile a smile of triumph, for her neck didn't want to work either. Feebly, she plucked at the suffragette banner beneath her coat—at the white bit, which had been her petticoat, and which was all she could reach since the mauve and green bits had shifted down her arm.

It was too much. Too difficult. And already it felt as if the moment for waving those colours had passed.

'VOTES FOR WOMEN!' she called again, for her voice was still working, just about. And her eyes, which were working fine, gazed in horrified fascination at what was happening to what was left of William Shakespeare's face. And her ears . . . her ears began to tingle, and then to

185

burn, as somewhere behind her, amidst all the hoo-ha, a little girl began to cry.

'Right, miss—you're coming with me. Nice and quiet now. No trouble.'

The grip on her upper arm was so tight it hurt, and the policeman's face, looming high above her own, looked as nasty as it was possible for man's face to look—next to Shakespeare's.

'I'm not,' Hazel managed to say. 'I've got my friend waiting outside, with my dog. And you can't arrest me in here, or the others either. We haven't harmed a real person. We are Beyond the Jurisdiction of the Law.'

The policeman gave her arm a little shake. It appalled her, that shake. It took her breath away that he could do something like that to her, as if he owned her and could treat her exactly as he pleased.

'You're coming with me,' he repeated. 'And forget all your fancy talk. You're in trouble, young lady. Big trouble.'

'But my dog . . . ?'

He was pulling her away, tugging her by the arm so she had no choice but to follow. To the right and to the left, members of the Stratford-upon-Avon Historical Society stepped back to let them through, their faces twisted in shock and by some grim satisfaction that she, Hazel, was being dealt with.

*Don't they care?* Hazel wondered, wildly. *Aren't they for us after all?*

She thought—believed—some of the women would come leaping to her defence, for she had acted in their best interests, as they surely understood. But, if anything, the women looked more unforgiving than the men and she was reminded, suddenly, of the crowd at the Epsom Derby . . . of how the women had looked with particular contempt upon the suffragette being yelled at and hit, as if it was no more than she had deserved.

Had Miss Davison's death achieved nothing then? Nothing at all? The general public, according to Gloria, was all for the suffragettes now that Miss Davison had given her life for the cause. It was only the Government, she'd said, that needed winning round.

The KDG would be the toast of London, Gloria had said, once news of their action got around. The talk of the town. Everyone's little darlings.

*How could she have got that so wrong?*

'Millicent!' Hazel called, feeling suddenly, horribly, alone. 'Millicent! Verity! Where are you?'

And then she saw them. Just as she reached the door, and seconds before being dragged through it and away. Across the other side of the room she saw them, standing shoulder to shoulder with their heads bowed and the suffragette colours trailing limply from their hands, like broken kites.

They had their own policeman with them, but he hadn't grabbed their arms. He was towering above their bowed and sorry heads, talking fast and wagging his finger. He was clearly extremely angry but not enough to make arrests.

*It's just me*, Hazel realized. *It's just me they're taking.*

*Because I threw the acid.*

*I drew the short straw.*

# Chapter 17

'What did I tell you?' Cook said to Mrs Sawyer. 'What did I say? There'll be consequences, that's what I said. Reaper-cush-ons. Our little lady would never have gone to the bad if Mister Mull-Dare had been at home; if he hadn't gone and done what he did without a thought for anyone else.'

'That's enough,' snapped Mrs Sawyer. 'And hurry up with Lady Mac's cocoa, will you, so we can all get to our beds. It's been a long night. Florence? Stop snuffling. Stop it this instant before I lose my temper.'

'I . . . *sniff* . . . can't help it, Mrs Sawyer. I should've stopped her. I should've realized . . . *sniff* . . . that she was up to summat. And now it's too . . . *sniff* . . . late.'

'Maybe it is,' the housekeeper replied, reaching for the sugar bowl. 'And maybe it isn't. Either way, Miss Mull-Dare has only got herself to blame—although that American piece will have a lot to answer for, I'll be bound. Her and her fancy man.'

'Lady Mac's cocoa,' said Cook, setting a steaming mug on a tray. 'And that's me done for the night.'

'She'll have three sugars in it,' ordered Mrs Sawyer. 'And a dash of brandy. For the shock. Wash your face and blow your nose, if you please, Florence, before carrying it through.'

'What about . . . *sniff* . . . Miss Hazel? Shall I take her up some warm milk?'

'You'll take her nothing,' said Mrs Sawyer sharply. 'She's in disgrace.'

Mrs Emmeline Pankhurst, when asked what
she thought about the KDG's action said:
'I am very proud. Hazel Louise Mull-Dare
has done a great service for the women of
England. When we finally get The Vote it
will be largely thanks to her.'
The policeman who manhandled Miss Mull-
Dare is said to be full of remorse.
'There was no need for him to be such a
bully,' said a woman called Dorothy from
the Stratford-upon-Avon Historical
Society. 'Miss Mull-Dare is the toast of
the town and everybody's darling. And in
any case, who cares about a mouldy old
waxwork? The rights of women are a million
times more important and—

Stifling a sob, Hazel ripped the sheet of paper up and out, scrunched it into a ball, and aimed it at her bedroom wall. Who was she trying to fool? What was the point of pretending? Of making things up? Without bothering to cover the typewriter she threw herself onto her bed and yanked up the pink silk coverlet.

She had neglected to turn her light off but had neither

the heart nor the energy to get up and do it even though a servant, or her aunt Alison, might see the glow beneath her door and come knocking.

Her mother might see the glow too, when she finally came home.

*Please let her find him*, Hazel silently begged. *Please don't let him be totally lost or . . . or worse.*

She hadn't—wouldn't—cry over Gloria Gilbert, nor had she shed a single tear over the dismal failure of the KDG's action. But the thought of Diggy Bert, lost somewhere in the dark, brought an ache to her throat that wouldn't go away.

He would be hungry by now, and thirsty too. And what if he had tried to chase a car? With no one to stop him, or call him back, he might have had an accident. A really bad one.

*Please, please keep Diggy safe. I don't care what happens to me. I don't care about The Law, or a scandal, or about wrecking my chances of marrying up. Aunt Alison can rant and rave at me all she wants. I'll even go to prison if The Law decides I ought to. Just let my mother find our dog and bring him home by morning. Please . . .*

She didn't expect to get much rest, so when a loud knocking woke her up shortly before 9 a.m., she assumed it was because of her light.

'Mother?'

'It's me, miss. It's Florence. You're wanted on the telephone.'

Kicking back the coverlet, and squinting through sore eyes at the strange combination of sunshine and lamplight in the room, Hazel's first feeling was one of guilt for having slept so deeply and for so long. Then a mixture of hope and doubt, every bit as disorientating as the two kinds of light, got her out of bed and across the room.

'It's not . . . ?'

'Your American friend? No, miss. It's one of the other young ladies. Miss Millicent.'

Hurrying downstairs and across the hallway, Hazel dared to glance up at the pegs where the dogs' leads were kept.

Diggy Bert's still wasn't there.

Miserably, she picked up the telephone's receiver. It smelt very strongly of lily-of-the-valley.

'Millicent?'

'Hazel? Thank goodness. I was scared they might have taken you to prison.'

'No,' Hazel told her. 'Only to a police station. My aunt came and got me. I'm at home now, but still in a lot of trouble. Tell me, quickly, have you heard from Gloria?'

'Italy.'

'*What?*'

'It-a-ly,' Millicent repeated the word very slowly. 'She's gone to Italy. I can't talk any louder, Hazel, I don't want Daddy to hear. He doesn't know anything about our action, thank goodness, and I don't want him finding out. Gloria and her parents went to Italy yesterday for the whole summer—maybe longer. That's what their house-keeper told me, anyway, when I telephoned last night.'

'*Yest*erday? They went yesterday? But . . .'

'In the afternoon, just after four. Apparently it was all arranged. That's why she didn't wait for us, and why she left your dog tied to the railings.'

191

Hazel narrowed her eyes.

'She didn't tie Diggy up,' she said, coldly. 'Only the lead. She tied the lead to the railings and let Diggy go.'

'Are you sure? I mean, I know he wasn't there either but . . .'

'Diggy would never slip his lead. His head's too big. It would be quite impossible.'

'Is he . . . ?'

'Still missing? Yes. Alive? I don't know. My mother went out looking for him. I don't think she's back. She's been gone all night.'

There was silence then; a bleak, dejected silence that said all there was to say, for now, about Diggy being missing, and about Hazel's mother searching up and down streets, behind every dustbin and in and out of alleys. Alone. In the dark. Without a chaperone.

'Do you think,' said Millicent, after a while, 'that Gloria did this on purpose? Got you into trouble, I mean? Do you think she knew, all along, that harming one of Madame Tussaud's waxworks was a criminal offence?'

Hazel had twirled the telephone's flex, like a bracelet, around her right wrist. It tightened, uncomfortably, as she moved the telephone trumpet from her ear to her mouth.

'I don't want to talk about Gloria Gilbert any more,' she said. 'Not now or ever again.' Her hands were trembling as she hung up and all she wanted to do was crawl back under the pink silk bedspread and, hopefully, sleep some more.

And so she did.

When someone came in and sat down she knew, straight away, that it was her mother. Aunt Alison would

192

have started ranting the second she entered the room. A servant would have knocked, and waited for a reply.

'Have you found him?' Her voice shook as she came fully awake.

'Not yet.'

'Not yet' was better than 'no'. 'Not yet' suggested there was a chance, still, that Diggy Bert might come home. 'Not yet', Hazel realized, was probably what her mother had been saying for years and years to every man, woman, and child who came, distraught, to the Battersea Dog's Home in search of lost, loved creatures.

'I am so, so, sorry.'

'I know you are, pet. And it wasn't your fault—or your friend's, necessarily. Diggy's a big dog. If he felt like bolting she might not have been able to hold him.'

Hazel clenched her fists, twisting two handfuls of pink satin until her nails dug into her palms. That person, that ex-friend of hers, who was never again to be mentioned, could have held on to Diggy for hours if she'd wanted to. She could have stuck to him like grim death if she hadn't had a holiday to go on—or an action to desert.

'I should never have got involved,' she said aloud. 'I should have said no, right from the start . . . '

At the police station, they had taken her name and address and written it in an enormous ledger. They had wanted to know who had 'set the thing up' (meaning the action) and whether she had ever met Emmeline Pankhurst or any other 'big names' in the Women's Social and Political Union.

She had answered them truthfully, but they hadn't seemed interested in the KDG or the short straw or the fact that a girl called Gloria Gilbert had sworn blind that throwing acid at a waxwork was not an illegal act.

'You say you went to the Wilding Davison funeral,' the policeman had said, looking sternly down his nose at her from behind the enormous ledger. 'Did anyone speak to you there? A grown-up? Did they give you any pamphlets? Or invite you to a meeting? Did anyone offer you sweeties?'

No, Hazel had said. And no, and no, and no.

'Where did you get the chemicals? Did a grown-up give them to you?'

'Yes.'

'Aha.' The policeman had sat up straighter, then, and written more words, very fast. 'Did she tell you her name?'

Hazel had leaned back, not liking his eagerness, or the way he was leaping to conclusions.

'It wasn't a her,' she had told him. 'It was a he. We tricked him, I'm afraid, because he's In Chemicals and could tell us what to do. He thought the acid was for an experiment at my school and that my teacher would be in charge of it.'

The policeman had put his pen down at that point and sighed, very deeply, as if he—or Hazel—had just failed an important test.

'So . . . you've never had any direct communication with any member of the Women's Social and Political Union?'

'No.'

'Or with any other society, or adult individual, sympathetic to the suffragette movement?'

'No. Only the Stratford-upon-Avon Historical Society,

194

and I think they are all far fonder of William Shakespeare than they will ever be of suffragettes.'

She had taken the white, mauve, and green banner out of her coat and was holding it, partly-folded, on her lap.

A policeman passing by to get to his desk had recognized the colours and sniffed.

'They're recruiting kids now, are they?' he had sneered, his lip curling. 'Not the smartest move.'

Then her aunt Alison had shown up . . .

'There won't be a scandal, will there?' Hazel's voice was tiny, half-muffled against her pillow. She was too ashamed, now, and too anxious about Diggy Bert, to look her mother in the eye. 'It won't get reported in *The Times* or anything?'

'I don't know. I hope not.'

Hazel heard the chair creak. 'I have to go to work,' her mother said. 'Someone might bring Diggy there. Will you be all right?'

'Yes.' For once in her life Hazel didn't mind coming second to a stray.

'Aunt Alison will want to speak to you again, I'm afraid.'

'All right.'

'She thinks you ought to go away for a while, until we can be sure that this will all blow over.'

Hazel frowned into her pillow.

'I thought I was going to Scotland,' she said. 'As soon as school finishes.'

'Well . . . Aunt Alison and Uncle Douglas aren't sure that's possible now.'

'You mean they don't want me there any more.'

The chair creaked again as her mother stood up. 'Let's leave it to your aunt, shall we? She's much better than me at sorting things, and she really has had a lovely idea about where you might go for a nice visit. Somewhere special. She'll talk to you. I'm sorry, pet, but I really do have to get to work.'

For a long while after her bedroom door clicked shut, Hazel remained exactly where she was: cocooned in her bedspread with her face turned to the wall. She didn't feel hungry, she didn't feel thirsty, she didn't want the lavatory and she didn't want to think. She just lay there, like something hibernating or waiting to be transformed, and if a thought tried to enter her head she squashed it.

Maybe she slept again and maybe she didn't, but the first she knew of anyone else's presence was the rattle of a teacup being set down a few inches from her head.

'Florence?'

'I've brought you some tea and toast, miss. And I'm running you a bath.'

'Florence?'

'Yes, miss?'

'Do you know where they're thinking of sending me?'

She had rolled herself over, the better to judge, from Florence's face, precisely how much the servants had found out, either from listening at doors or being told. One quick glance let her know it was a lot.

'It's not my place, miss . . . ' Florence began and then faltered, as if wondering—and not for the first time— what her place actually was in this big ill-fated house.

'Please tell me,' said Hazel.

Florence eyed the bedding.

'You've made a right scrunch of your covers, miss,' she said. 'Just look at them, all twisted up.' She picked up a spoon and began stirring the tea.

'You're making a right slop of that,' Hazel told her. 'Just look at it, spilling into the saucer.'

Not grinning, but almost, they allowed their eyes to meet.

'Get away with you,' said Florence. And then: 'Across the sea, miss, to your grandaddy Mull-Dare's. To the island where the sugar comes from.'

# CHAPTER 18

Everything happened very fast after that.

'I've put an advertisement in *The Lady*,' Aunt Alison announced less than forty-eight hours after escorting her niece from the police station. 'With luck we'll have a chaperone for you by the end of next week, then we can book you your passage.'

'What kind of a chaperone?'

Aunt Alison threw her a sour look.

'A strict one,' she said. 'As strict as I can find, at such short notice.'

They were sitting in Mrs Mull-Dare's parlour, just the two of them. Diggy Bert was still missing and Hazel had not been allowed back to school. The parlour, to her, felt exactly like a prison, and her aunt like the worst kind of jailer.

She had seriously considered going on hunger strike, which was what any suffragette worth her salt would have done, upon being deprived of her liberty. But since she wouldn't have put it past either her aunt or Mrs Sawyer to try force-feeding her porridge, through a funnel and a piece of old pipe, she had thought better of it.

Her education, Aunt Alison was telling her now, had been put on hold. But whoever was found to act as chaperone would also be her teacher, once they got to her grandaddy's plantation.

'But it's almost holiday time,' Hazel dared to complain. 'Why must I study during the holidays? Nobody else does.'

Her aunt's mouth sprang open like a trap: 'We're not talking about ordinary lessons, my girl,' she snapped. 'What you need—and the sooner the better, it transpires—is some intensive, immediate instruction on how to conduct yourself like a lady.'

There was no answer to that. None at all. And already, it seemed, this 'serious instruction' had begun, for Hazel had been put to work sewing lavender bags. She would need at least a dozen, her aunt said, to sweeten her clothes during the long voyage out, and to keep them that way in the Caribbean heat.

'I cannot tell you,' she said, for the umpteenth time, 'how fearsome the heat is over there, and how difficult it is for a lady to remain *fresh*.'

*Then stop trying to*, Hazel silently begged. *Stop telling me altogether, for you're making it sound as if I am being sent to Hell.*

'Aunt,' she said, 'how long will I be away?'

'That depends.'

'On what?'

Her aunt rose out of her chair and smoothed her skirt.

'My goodness, Hazel Louise. Questions, questions. You really do have a great deal to learn when it comes to good manners. Now—I must go and talk to Cook. Tiny stitches, remember, when you join your squares, or the lavender flowers will leak. And tomorrow we must go shopping.

199

You will need at least two parasols, a modest suit for sea bathing, and a *very* broad-brimmed hat.'

Left alone, Hazel picked up a small square of white cotton and jabbed it, rebelliously, with her needle. She was to embroider it with leaves and flowers before turning it into a little bag and stuffing it with bits of lavender.

*'It depends', does it? On what? The weather? The price of fish?*

The green thread trailed like a stalk between her fingers.

White cotton.

Green thread.

Purple lavender flowers.

That was funny. Hadn't Aunt Alison realized how funny that was?

She wished she could tell someone—anyone—that her oh-so-proper aunt (a woman who thought the Pankhursts were evil and swore she would never want or use The Vote, not even if it came to her gift-wrapped through the post) had got her trapped in the parlour, making dainty little bags in suffragette colours.

She wished she could talk to Millicent or Verity but there was little chance of that for she didn't have their telephone numbers and, anyway, they would be at school.

There was, she knew, only the rest of this week to go before the Kensington School for the Daughters of Gentlemen closed for the summer holiday. The girls in the Yellow Room—her friends—would be looking forward to going to Scarborough . . . or Margate . . . or Eastbourne or, if they were lucky, and their parents adventurous, to the southern coast of France (she wouldn't think 'Italy', not now or ever).

200

'I've rather outgrown Scotland,' she imagined herself saying to a circle of their envious faces. 'So I'm off to the Caribbean instead, to finally meet my grandparents, Gideon and Louise Mull-Dare. They run the family sugar plantation, you know . . . '

The square of white cotton was starting to warp between her fingers, as she jabbed it with green stitches.

The girls in the Yellow Room would no doubt be putting the final touches to their painted plates. She had promised her father a lucky four-leaved clover on his and it bothered her, suddenly, that she would not be able to keep that promise.

Perhaps, though, the plates were still in a cupboard, and the girls were reading the last few pages of *King Lear*.

Thinking about Shakespeare made her feel worse— and not just because of what she had done to his face.

*I am being banished,* she told herself, laying down her sewing as this thought, suppressed for several days now, came at her in a rush. *Banished, like Cordelia. I am a thankless child, so they are sending me away. A long, long way from England and far from my father's house.*

Her father . . .

*If he ever finds out, what I did at Madame Tussaud's . . . what I know about marriage and men's wild oats . . . how I danced the tango at my party . . . how I went out without a chaperone and lost Diggy Bert . . . my father would be horrified. He might even break down again, from the worry and the shock . . . Aunt Alison knows this and so does mother . . .*

*My father would be ashamed . . .*

That was it; the one hard nugget of truth beneath all

the talk of sea-bathing, lavender bags, and a nice little holiday on the island where the sugar cane grew.

That was the rub of it, as Shakespeare would have said.

She was being banished because of what she had become. Quickly and expediently, before her father found out. And although she would never speak of it . . . never type it on a page or write it in a book . . . all the pride she had felt, over becoming a suffragette, got mixed with so much remorse, because of what her father would think of her, that all she had recently learned, and seen, and felt, and done seemed vulgar all of a sudden . . . flashy and foolish and altogether wrong, like Valentine's hat and umbrella.

*I will be good*, she promised her absent father, silently. *I will be sweet to my grandaddy and grandma Mull-Dare, and kind to my new teacher. I will wear a broad-brimmed hat religiously, so I do not catch the sun, and will learn all there is to know about good manners and correct behaviour. When I come home you will be proud of me. And then I will marry up.*

The lavender bag she'd been working on had slipped from her knees onto the floor. She picked it up and examined the stitches. The leaves were all right, only a little bit crooked, and if she hurried, there would be time to embroider a flower or two before the gong sounded for lunch.

The threads Aunt Alison had picked out were on a small tray in front of her, along with a tiny pair of scissors and a thimble. The sewing basket lay open at her feet; a jumble of buttons and pins and rainbow colours.

For a second or two, after unslotting the green from the eye of her needle, Hazel's fingers hovered over the skein of mauve.

Then she swapped it for a pink.

How exciting! My aunt has found me a chaperone—
a spinster lady with a thirst for travel—
and we leave for the Caribbean next
Thursday. Her name is Miss Fritillary and,
according to Aunt Alison, she will very
soon have me versed in all the ways and
graces of young ladyhood. The fact that
Miss F. possesses the very latest edition
of Cassell's Dictionary of Etiquette is
probably what got her the job—although it
has to be said that only one other person
applied, and she wanted to take her crippled
mother along with us on the voyage.

My trunk is half packed and I am looking
forward, very much, to this great adventure.

*'You're not taking that with you,' Aunt Alison exclaimed.
'For Heaven's sake, child, it weighs a ton. And what use will it
be? None. Your grandma Louise will have plenty of writing
paper and Miss Fritillary will supply pen and ink. Such an ugly,
clattery machine. Why anyone would want to use one, ever, is
beyond my understanding . . .'*

The weekend passed in a flurry of sorting and checking
and packing and shopping and by Monday evening it was
all done. Neither Millicent nor Verity had telephoned,
and Hazel was trying not to mind.

'Your uncle Douglas arrives tomorrow,' Aunt Alison

informed her over supper on the Tuesday. 'He'll drive you to the docks on Thursday and see you safely introduced to Miss Fritillary before you board the ship. You'll be sharing a cabin with Miss Fritillary but it's a good one—first class. And you're not to be nervous about this journey. What happened to the *Titanic* was a fluke.'

'You aren't nervous, are you, pet?' Mrs Mull-Dare asked.

Hazel kept her eyes on her plate and shook her head. 'No,' she said. 'Not at all.'

'It will be wonderful,' her mother said, cheerily. 'An amazing experience for you.'

Hazel did not reply. Not being nervous was one thing; being expected to show gratitude, or excitement, was quite another.

There was strawberry ice cream for pudding with almond biscuits and chocolate sauce.

'I must go and thank Cook later,' Hazel said. 'She's making all my favourite things. And Florence has given me a ship-shaped tin to keep pencils and things in, so they don't roll around at sea—wasn't that sweet of her?'

Aunt Alison dabbed her mouth. 'You'll find everything very different at the plantation, Hazel,' she said. 'There'll be no being familiar with the servants there.'

Hazel didn't understand.

'Don't grandaddy and grandma have servants, then?' she asked.

'They have *workers*,' Aunt Alison said. 'Some in the house, some in the fields. But they aren't at all the kind of people a young lady would want to befriend. In fact to chatter away to *those* people, the way you do with Florence, would be very strictly frowned upon.'

'Why?'

'Because . . . ' Aunt Alison's mouth went into a pucker, 'they are *different* from us, that's why.'

'In what way?'

'In every way.'

Hazel opened her mouth to ask more, but closed it again as some kind of bustle and commotion downstairs claimed everyone's full attention.

'Oh, my goodness gracious!' they heard Mrs Sawyer exclaim, with uncharacteristic delight. 'How wonderful! I can't believe it!'

'What . . . ?' Mrs Mull-Dare rose to her feet, her eyes wide as she threw down her napkin. Dottie, Pipkin, and Rascal had surged, already, from beneath the table and were heading through the open door, yapping and barking and piddling for joy.

'That can't be Douglas, surely?' clucked Aunt Alison. 'He's a day early. He would have telephoned.'

'*Yoo-hoo! Look who's here!*'

'It's not Uncle Douglas,' said Hazel, pushing back her chair. 'I think . . . I do believe . . . ' She didn't dare say what she believed as she hurried after her mother and ran helter-skelter down the stairs. But the dogs knew. The dogs had known at once. And so, too, had Ivy Mull-Dare, for she began calling, well before she reached the hall: '*Diggy! Diggy! Where are you?*'

Hazel felt her stomach lurch. What if it *was* her uncle Douglas after all, calling 'yoo-hoo' in a silly high-pitched voice, to make them all laugh. He might mistakenly

imagine he was the one being greeted with such rapture—
'*Dougy . . . Dougy . . .* '—and by his wife's sister-in-law of
all people!

But no . . . oh, thank the stars . . .

'There you are,' her mother cried. 'Oh, *there*. Good boy,
Diggy Bert. Good boy . . . Oh, Rosa, where was he? Who
brought him in?'

Quietly, Hazel sat herself down on the third from
bottom stair. It was suspiciously damp, that stair, but
she didn't care. Her mother was crying and laughing all
at once, and Diggy Bert was lick-slobbering her hands
and her face (*chocolate sauce . . . yum*) while the other
dogs leapt and yapped and the woman called Rosa,
who had worked for many, many years at the
Battersea Dogs' Home, looked happily on and said: 'A
young couple found him roaming the streets near
Paddington.'

Hazel's mother threw back her head, protesting happily as Diggy Bert almost knocked her flat. 'But he looks
so *well*,' she said.

'He *is* well,' Rosa agreed. 'We've checked him over and
he's absolutely fine. The couple took him in over a week
ago so he can't have been a stray for long. They wanted
to keep him but the woman felt so guilty about whoever
might have lost him that her husband finally brought him
in to us this afternoon.'

'Thank Heavens,' cried Hazel's mother. 'And thank *you*,
dear Rosa, for bringing him straight home.'

'My pleasure,' said Rosa. 'I had a feeling he was going
to turn up. There were two magpies in the hedge this
morning—a good omen, you know. Oh . . . ' The sight of

someone sitting so very still and small on the stairs had clearly startled her, 'Hello, young Hazel.'

'Hello.'

They were all staring at her now. Her mother. Rosa. Even the dogs. It should have made her feel part of things but it didn't. Her mother, she couldn't help noticing, was looking surprised, as if she hadn't realized, or had clean forgotten, that Hazel had followed her down the stairs.

*This time next week, I won't be here at all,* Hazel thought, bitterly. *I'll be in the middle of the ocean somewhere. And I bet you won't miss me anywhere near as much as you've missed that smelly old dog.*

That smelly old dog pricked up his ears then, as if Hazel had spoken aloud, and over he lolloped, all trust and drool, to lick her hands and say hello.

'There now,' Ivy Mull-Dare said, smiling fondly as her daughter held out her arms. 'There, now. Diggy's home and everything's fine.'

*No it's not,* thought Hazel. *NO . . . IT'S . . . NOT.*

# CHAPTER 19

A nd then it was Wednesday and Uncle Douglas was there, filling the house with authority and the bonfire-smell of cigars.

'Well now, lassie,' he boomed at Hazel. 'All packed and ready, are we?'

'There's a typing machine in her trunk,' Aunt Alison chipped in, before Hazel could reply. 'Can you believe it? She's taken half her clothes out for a typing machine. I pity the poor black who has to carry *that* all the way up to the house.'

Hazel looked at her aunt and frowned. *Did she say 'black' or 'back'?*

And then her mother arrived home (early, for once, as it was Hazel's Last Night) and the strange business of eating dinner, as if everything was normal, began.

Uncle Douglas sat at the head of the table—Hazel's father's place usually or, in recent weeks, her mother's—and Hazel found herself wondering in which book of etiquette it was written that a man, unrelated except by marriage, had the right to take over like that.

There were more of her favourite things to eat, but she couldn't manage much.

'You'll dine well on the ship, lassie,' Uncle Douglas boomed. 'You and this Miss Frippery.'

'Fritillary,' Aunt Alison corrected him.

'You and Miss Fri*tillary*. I've made sure of that. It's all covered.'

*He's paying*, Hazel realized. *He's footing the bill for my banishment.*

After dinner she had a bath and went straight to bed. A good night's sleep was what she needed, her uncle and aunt had said. A good night's sleep, ready for an early start.

She couldn't sleep though. The sky beyond her curtains was too pale, still, and her uncle Douglas had wound the gramophone, for a spot of entertainment. He liked his music loud, Uncle Douglas did, so the sound of the record he had chosen drifted clearly through the floors and the walls and into Hazel's ears.

It was one of her and her father's favourite songs—the one he always used to play just for them. And the beat and the ache of it, this night of all nights, would have reduced her to tears if it hadn't started jumping about all over the place.

> *See you at two, my bibbety-boo,*
> *See you at two my hon-eee.*
> *(jump)*
> *See you at two, you'll (jump) see if I do,*
> *My bibbety-boo*
> *My onl-eee . . .*

The door opened quietly, and her mother came in and sat down.

'That record's jumping,' Hazel said. 'It sounds terrible.'

'I know,' her mother replied. 'I think there's something wrong with the gramophone.'

Even as she said it, the song abruptly stopped, and all they heard after that was the boom of Uncle Douglas, chastising the ruddy thing, and then silence.

*Valentine . . . Valentine damaged father's gramophone, and on purpose, too, I'll bet. That chancer! If I ever set eyes on him again I'll . . . I'll . . .*

'I have something for you,' her mother was saying. 'It's not valuable, and most of the stones are missing, but I'd like you to have it.'

Mildly curious, Hazel sat herself up and leaned back against her pillows.

'Here. . .' her mother said, 'hold out your hand.'

Obediently, Hazel held out her right hand, fingers curled so that she wouldn't drop this gift, whatever it was.

'Oh,' she said, as a cheap little brooch hit her palm. 'Thank you. Did . . . did father give you this?'

It was her mother's initial: the letter 'I' set in a circlet of ivy leaves. Most of the stones had, indeed fallen out—the 'I' was no more than a stick of bare metal, with indentations where the sparkles had once been—but Hazel doubted they had ever been worth more than tuppence.

Her father, she knew, bought only the best jewels for her mother. Emeralds . . . rubies . . . diamonds as big as hailstones. Even her own new bracelet, which she guessed he must have chosen before his breakdown, was clearly expensive with its jangling weight of charms.

'It was given to me years ago,' her mother was saying. 'Long before I met your father.'

'By a man?' Hazel wondered.

210

'Yes,' her mother said. 'By a man. Anyway . . . I know it's the wrong initial for you, so you probably won't want to wear it, but I'd like you to take it with you.'

Hazel touched the circlet of ivy leaves with the tip of a finger.

'It's pretty,' she said, kindly. 'I *might* wear it. It could be "I" for something else, in my case, couldn't it? Like . . . I don't know . . . "I" for "Idiot" since that's what I've been.'

For a few strange moments she thought her mother was going to hug her; and not just a brief squeeze either but a vast, clinging embrace that might even involve tears.

*Don't*, she willed her, leaning away.

Her mother patted her leg.

'It will be all right, pet,' she said. 'You'll see. Your father has only ever spoken with fondness of Gideon and Louise, so they are bound to treat you kindly. And it won't be for long. Not long . . . '

'You said that about father being at a rest home,' Hazel reminded her, mournfully. 'That it wouldn't be for long.'

'I know,' her mother answered. 'And it won't be.'

'Does father know I'm going away?'

'Yes, pet. But not about why. He agrees that it's for the best. Just until he's properly well again, and everything's sorted out financially.'

'And he's all right? He's not worrying too much? About money or. . . '

Her mother smiled and patted her leg again.

'He's worried you might get sunburn,' she said. 'He's worried you'll go on a nature walk with this Miss Fritillary and get scratched by a poisonous twig. He's worried you'll

211

go sea-bathing too soon after luncheon and get a cramp. He's worried you'll see chickens being killed at the market, and it will be too much for your Delicate Senses.'

Hazel had forgotten all about her Delicate Senses. She wasn't sure she had any left. Carefully, she reached across to her bedside table and put down the 'I' for 'Ivy' brooch, wondering as she did so what kind of man had given it to her mother so many years ago. She guessed he must have been poor but, then, her mother had been poor too before marrying into sugar.

'Get some sleep, pet,' her mother said. 'I'll come with you tomorrow if you like. To the docks. It's up to you. I didn't think you'd want a fuss.'

'I don't,' Hazel answered quickly. 'It's all right. I'll be all right with just Uncle Douglas.'

Hunching her shoulders she wriggled back down under the bedclothes, closing her eyes and composing her face, like a sleepy girl's, as soon as her head touched the pillow.

*If the gramophone plays again she'll kiss me . . . if it doesn't she won't . . . and if the record jumps within five seconds of starting . . .*

The gramophone remained silent.

'Goodnight, pet. I'll see you in the morning. Before you go.'

'Goodnight.'

And somehow, she slept. And then it was the morning and there was toast to force down, along with last-minute advice from Aunt Alison, while Diggy Bert flopped heavily on to both of her feet as if he meant to stop her leaving. And then Florence came in and hugged her, just as she was

212

chewing a crust, which made her choke so badly that she had to have her back thumped and she and Florence ended up laughing hysterically while Aunt Alison looked on, disapproving.

And then it was time for Uncle Douglas to fetch the car, and all the servants started congregating in the hallway as if royalty was coming or going, and all of the dogs, not just Diggy, were following her everywhere, even to the lavatory; and it seemed important, all of a sudden, for her to be completely alone, just for a minute, before she went from the house.

Up in her bedroom the curtains had been drawn and the window opened an inch, but her bed was as she had left it: dishevelled and unmade. She was glad no one had come in yet, to strip off the sheets and pillow cases and maybe fold the pink silk coverlet into a neat square, ready to be put away with mothballs. Glad, too, that her clothes from yesterday had remained over the chair where she had dropped them.

*I will never see this room again. Never sleep in that bed. Never sit over there, in front of the mirror. Never hear the magnolia tip-tapping at the window.*

It was melodramatic, she knew, to be thinking like that but she couldn't help it; it felt true. She looked at her dolls, high up on their shelf, and at Spearmint who hadn't been ridden for weeks.

*Go on*, these things seemed to be telling her. *Off you trot.*

And then Uncle Douglas's voice came booming up the stairs: 'Come along, lassie, time to go!' and Pipkin was piddling dangerously close to her boots as she hurried down the stairs, and the servants were farewelling her, all in a row, passing her closer and closer to the front door with every hug and handshake . . . And then it was her aunt Alison kissing both her cheeks and telling her to behave herself and learn her lessons well and then . . .

'Oh! Wait! I've forgotten something . . . '

*'Hazel—the car. You'll be late . . . '*

Back up the stairs she bolted, the dogs yapping at her heels (*Is she staying? Is she staying?*); back into her bedroom where the air, it seemed, still tingled from her leaving; over to her bedside table where—yes—her mother's brooch still lay where she had put it.

Down the stairs again ('Dottie—out of the *way*.'), past the servants and Aunt Alison, and 'I . . . forgot . . . something,' she panted as Uncle Douglas parped the horn and Diggy Bert leapt, hard, against the front door, wanting to be let out.

'Quick, pet,' her mother said. 'Don't let Diggy through or he'll chase the car.'

Obediently, Hazel reached for the latch. Her mother couldn't do it, for she needed both hands to keep hold of Diggy's collar. She was right by the door though, not dragging the dog away, and was that a kiss, Hazel wondered, aimed clumsily at her cheek? Or an involuntary stumble as Diggy heard the latch click and made another leap?

And then the door was open, just enough to let her out, and then she was out and it was shut.

*Parp, parp.*

It was the Old Girl, waiting in the road with Hazel's trunk strapped tightly on the back. 'She needs a good run,'

Uncle Douglas was saying from the front seat. 'Otherwise her engine'll seize.'

Without a word Hazel walked down the steps and around the car, opened the passenger door and slid into her seat. She had been so involved, up until now, in the bustle and stress of leaving that any tears she might have shed hadn't had time to form. She had thought she would be all right, once she was in the car, but not this car, no. Not the Old Girl with her familiar smells of humbugs and leather and—yes—her father's driving gloves right there, still, on the dashboard.

Uncle Douglas revved the engine and, seconds later, they were passing Kensington Gardens. The balloon woman was there, in her usual place, giving Hazel the excuse she needed to turn sharply and wave, while she blinked and blinked her tears away.

'That reminds me,' her uncle said, as the sweet shop came into view. 'I got you something to take with you. There, on the shelf in front of you. Careful—there's a lot of them.'

Still blinking, Hazel reached forward. She still had her mother's brooch, growing warm in one hand, but managed, nonetheless, to ease the bulging paper bag out onto her lap and peep inside.

Granny Sookers. Dozens of them.

'Thank you, Uncle,' Hazel said. 'Do you want one?'

'Nay, lassie,' he replied, affably. 'They're all yours.'

Unable to resist, Hazel probed a Sooker out of the bag and popped it in her mouth. The sour taste made her shudder, just like it always had and 'Hah!' her uncle laughed as her face went like an old granny's. 'See? It gets you every time.'

After that they didn't speak much. Hazel even dozed a little, the brooch and the bag of sweets held tightly in both her hands. The Old Girl's engine settled into a steady rhythm once they were out of London and the sound of it was soothing to Hazel, as if the car was singing to her the way her father used to do.

'We're here,' Uncle Douglas said, eventually, and at that Hazel pinned the brooch on to her blouse, put the sweets away in her pocket, and sat up straight.

The docks were bustling—heaving—with people; all of them in such a hurry, criss-crossing in front of the car, that Uncle Douglas had to keep parping the horn so that nobody got run over.

'How will we recognize Miss Fritillary?' Hazel wondered, as the Old Girl inched closer to the harbour's edge.

'A tall plain woman, your aunt said. Tall and plain and wearing a hairnet. She'll be waiting for us outside the ship's office. Now—can I park here a wee while, I wonder? Aye, why not. Aha—there is she is!'

Thinking that he meant her chaperone, Hazel peered from the car into the passing crowds and said 'Where? Which one? I can't see her?'

'Right in front of your nose, lassie. That hulking great white thing, as big as a palace.'

He was talking about a ship, Hazel realized. Her ship. The one she was to sail away on.

'Oh my . . . '

Her uncle had opened his door and was booming up at someone:

'What? Aye. Thank you. Wait here, lass, just a tick,

while I organize your luggage. Then we'll get you sorted out, all right?'

Hazel nodded. She was gazing up, still, at the immense vessel with the buff-coloured funnels that was to carry her, and hundreds of other passengers, through sunsets and storms, around icebergs and coastlines, all the way to the Caribbean.

She was watching seagulls as they flew like hurled objects over the ship, away and then back again, and she was wondering whether it was all right to feel just a tiny bit excited, as well as sorry and ashamed, when you were about to be banished from your native land.

A scuffling and a jolt, at the back of the Old Girl, let her know that her trunk was being taken down. She thought of her typewriter, stashed away among petticoats, night-gowns, and lavender bags, and hoped that the porter would be careful.

'Where's your other bag, lass? Pass it here, that's right. Got your sweets? Let's go then.'

The air outside the car smelt of sea salt and tar and Hazel breathed it gladly.

'This way,' said Uncle Douglas. 'Don't lose me now. The ship's office is right over here. Now—is that her? The woman waving? Aye, it must be. Well, she looks decent enough, although trust me to get it wrong about the net. That'll teach me, won't it, lass, to listen to your auntie Ally with just the one ear and half a mind.'

Hazel barely heard him. She had stopped dead in her tracks. There were people bumping into her . . . veering round her . . . tutting as they hurried to board the big white ship. And the seagulls overhead were wailing, now,

217

as if something unseen by the humans on the dock had threatened some terrible harm.

Her uncle swivelled round. 'Hurry up, lassie,' he boomed. 'And where are your manners? You look as if you're crunching on a big Granny Sooker.'

Obediently, Hazel began to move. On towards the ship . . . towards the great unknown of the Caribbean . . . towards the person hired to take her. *What were the odds?* she marvelled to herself, as her chaperone grinned and beckoned her on. *What kind of a million-to-one chance is this?*

And 'Come along, Miss Mull-Dare,' her chaperone twittered, lifting and waving her specimen net. 'Quick sticks!'

# CHAPTER 20

'*T*ime was, some of our people could fly. I'm tellin' you,
child, it's so. High over Africa they flew, free as birds
and equal sassy. Then many of them people got captured
for Slavery; taken on ships far, far to this here place and that.
Them folks were full of anguish then. And no more flying. No,
sir. Not in front of white folks cracking a cut-you-open whip and
hollerin' "Git on board!" Not tied fast to this earth by the Slave
Man's chains. The flying ones, they left their wings in Africa.
Shucked 'em off before goin'. Kept the power, though. Brought it
with them across the water and kept it hid.*

'*One such was an old man. Another such a young gal. We'll
call them Abel and Jenny for these were the bad-fit names they
got given, along with plenty more anguish, and plenty hard
labour in the fields where the sugar cane grows . . . '*

'Hey, Jeremiah. Hey, old man. What time they gettin'
here, the Moulder girl and her teacher? They comin' before
dark, you reckon?'

The man called Jeremiah placed a hushing hand on
the head of the child at his side and gazed away over the
veranda rail, across to where the sugar fields met the hot
blue of the sky, on the very edge of the island.

'Have patience, Tommy John,' he said. 'And listen to the
story . . .

'From sun-up to sundown Jenny and old man Abel did labour, and Jenny with a pickney tied to her back, a-sleepin' mostly, while his mumma did stoop and plant, stoop and plant, stoop and plant all the day long till her body an' spirit be broken-sick. No rest for Jenny at plantin' time, nor old man Abel, nor all them other slaves. No, sir.

'Now the massa he was some flinty-eyed fella. Orange hair, of course, like Massa Giddy, and same bad-fit skin that go red-to-blister in the Caribbean sun. He stay home most days, to keep that skin of his from cookin', but he tell his man—his Over-see-er—to stand for no trouble from them slaves of his. And by trouble he mean no goin' slow with the stoop and plant, even though them slave-folks was fit to fall on the earth from hunger and worse.

'Now young Jenny she a strong-enough gal. But her pickney, he just a babe, tied to her back and not knowin' a crab from a mango, nor a good man from a bad. And say he got fretful and started bawlin'. And say poor Jenny couldn't stop her stoopin' and plantin'; not to soothe her pickney and quiet it down; not for any reason in this world . . .'

'You reckon Hazel Moulder have orange hair?' said Tommy John. 'You reckon she'll have the nose blobs too, like Massa Giddy and her dadda and all them other Moulders? You reckon she'll go red to blister in the sun?'

'I don't know, child. Let's wait and see . . .

'And say the massa chose that time to come ridin' by, to check up on his sugar and reckon himself a top fella, and he hear this pickney bawlin' and he say to his Over-see-er, in a big lordly manner: "Keep that thing quiet."

'And say the Over-see-er felt mighty picked-upon, like he bin told he no good at keepin' those slaves in order. Why, he so vex-mad *he licked that whip of his right across the babe—cracked it good and hard so the babe began hollerin' like any hurt child and Jenny, she fell to the earth. Had to. No choice.'*

'No choice . . . ' murmured Tommy John, pressing his face to the veranda rail, as he watched and listened out for Massa Giddy's buggy. 'Poor slave-girl Jenny . . . poor babe . . . But this happen a long time ago now, right?'

'It HAPPEN,' Jeremiah told him, sternly. 'Never mind the year or the day. It happen, boy, so you listen with both ears . . .

*'Straightaway, old man Abel he hurry down the row and help Jenny to her feet.*

*'Straightaway Jenny sat back down. She too weak and sick-hearted to stand. The sun burn hot, hot on her face and her pickney cried and cried.*

*'"Get up, you black bitch!" called the Over-see-er, an' that whip of his snarled again, right round Jenny's legs. Her dress tore down to strips. Her legs bled into the soil. She couldn't get up, no, sir.*

*'Old Abel he look to Master Moulder, sittin' high, high on his horse, but saw no mercy in that red-to-blister face.*

*'Then he look back down at Jenny.*

*'"Go," he said to her. "Go as you know how to go. Before it's too late."*

*'Young Jenny she lift her head. Nothing but misery in them eyes of hers.*

*'"I forget how," she answered him, all slow and sad. "The magic gone."*

*'That Over-see-er he cracked his whip again, wrapping that girl's ankles in one big lick of pain.*

*'"It ain't gone," old Abel told her. "And you ain't forgot."*

'And he raised her up, her and the pickney—raised them all of a stagger, and held firm to Jenny's arm while she found some kind of a way to stand.

'"Go," he repeated, willin' her on.

'So Jenny, she lifted one foot on the air. Lifted one cut-about foot like she was climbin' on a gate. Then she looked up into the sky. Looked up at all that blue, as her pickney cried and cried, and lifted the other foot.

'She flew clumsy at first. So clumsy and slow that the Master could have caught her if he hadn't gone fallen off his horse in a big thud of surprise. And the Over-see-er, once his mouth stopped catchin' flies, he might have grabbed her, easy.

'Then the magic filled her. The African mystery. And she rose, with her pickney in her arms, as free as any bird.

'Tall trees couldn't snag her and nor-neither could the Over-see-er. High over the sugar fields she flew until . . . '

'Jeremiah? *Jeremiah!* I see you, nigger, leaning on that broom. Well, you'll get your black hide down the steps right now and do the sweeping later. Miss Mull-Dare has arrived and there are trunks and bags to carry. And you—Tommy John—what did we say to you, boy? Get home NOW. And don't you come nowhere near this place again until Massa Giddy and I say you can. *No-where near*, you understand? Now git. Not this way, idiot-child—round the back. Go on. Shoo.'

Slowly, and in his own good time, Jeremiah propped the broom against the side of the house. He had known for a while that this was the Big Important Day but had not been let in on the timing of things.

Peering down through the oleander trees, beyond the stout, hurrying-away figure of Missis Louise he could see

222

Massa Giddy's horse and buggy coming up the drive, weighed down with luggage-stuff and raising great clatters of dust. The girl and the teacher-woman he couldn't see at all, but there were two enormous hats jouncing around among the luggage-stuff, so he guessed they were somewhere under those; hanging tight to their seats and fretting some.

'Wish I knew-could fly, like Jenny and old Abel,' Tommy John muttered, close by his side. 'Wish I could, for goin' bayside now.'

Jeremiah smiled and patted the boy's head.

'Well, best you just pick up those heels of yours for now, boy, and git like you've been told,' he said. 'Otherwise, it's your mumma will feel the trouble. You know how and why. Now go.'

'Jeremiah? *Jeremiah?*'

'Me go.'

'All-rightey now.'

'Me gone.'

But Tommy John couldn't resist staying; just long enough to bob up over the veranda rail to see Massa Giddy's grand-daughter for himself.

'You better keep that head of yours down, boy.'

'I is. That her, you think? The long one. Why, she uglier than an old potater. And why she swayin' around like that?'

'She ain't found her legs yet after long time at sea. And no, that ain't her. She way too old . . . '

Down below, the voice of Louise Mull-Dare switched from shrill ('*JE-RE-MI-AH! Get your lazy black hide down here.*') to honey-sweet: 'My darling girl! We are so, so

223

happy to meet you at last. Come and give your old granny a hug.'

And Hazel, stepping dizzily from the buggy, had no time to register anything more than the hardness of the ground and the lurch of her shadow upon it before she was clasped in a hot bosomy embrace that took her breath and tipped her hat clean off her head.

'That her for sure,' murmured Tommy John. 'That's surely her. I go tell my mumma.'

Left alone, Jeremiah scanned the unswept veranda. There was a dead-looking cockroach under the table. Moving in, he nudged it with his big toe—nudged it good and hard right out into the open, where it would be seen, for certain sure, if it didn't revive itself and crawl away.

Then he flexed his big hands; flexed them good and proper until the knuckles cracked. They were old, old hands now. Old hands; old spine; old shoulder bones . . . all of him too old, now, to be humping luggage-stuff.

They were coming up to the house. He could hear their shoes on the wooden steps: Massa Giddy, Missis Louise, the long tall teacher-woman, and the girl.

Massa Giddy's grand-daughter.

The good-for-nothing's child.

At long last I have arrived at my grandparents' sugar plantation. It is all very
strange, like a dream that is both beautiful and odd, and as I am very, very tired
and very, very HOT I do not think I will
type much tonight. The voyage out seemed
to take for ever and even though my

224

chaperone and I travelled first class it was not the same as having a cabin all to myself. Really, I felt very cramped.

Also, to my complete astonishment, my chaperone has turned out to be none other than my schoolteacher, Miss Amelia Gumm. She tells me she has always wanted to visit the Caribbean because it is populated by rare and wonderful butterflies, and birds with bright green throats. She has her specimen net with her, of course, and is keen for us to go on all kinds of rambles, despite the sweltering heat.

When I asked why she saw fit to change her name, before applying to be my chaperone, she said, 'Fritillary is so much prettier than Gumm, don't you think?' and as someone who would have been a Moulder, had my rat-scally ancestor not altered it, I could not argue with that.

When I asked about school—for it will be impossible, I now realize, to get back to Kensington for the beginning of term—she said Miss Eunice will cope admirably without her and keep everyone under strict control. I could not argue with that either.

Anyway, we are here now, and better the devil you know, as Florence would say.

I am going to miss Florence. Aunt Alison was right, the servants here are not the

same and I find them rather frightening.
The night-time is frightening too. It is
very black outside, even though it is neither
winter nor late, and there is a loud noise
out there, part ringing and part buzz, which
my grandfather told me is made by insects
rubbing bits of their bodies together.
Miss Amelia was all for going out and netting
one which made my grandfather roar with
laughter as these insects are the tiniest
things.

Tomorrow we are to have a tour of the
plantation and a drive around the island.
Now I must try and sleep. I would like to
leave my lamp burning but have been told
not to do so because it will attract insects
into the room—not the singing ones but
another sort, which bite.

I must tell myself that the dark, in
this part of the world, is nothing to be
afraid of; that it is really no different
from at home—it just seems that way.

Goodnight.

# CHAPTER 21

In the morning one of the servants came and opened Hazel's shutters—opened them fast and loudly, so that they deepened a couple of dents in the faded English wallpaper. Blinking like a mole in the sudden, glittering light, Hazel sat up in bed and yawned.

Through the gauzy net that was supposed to keep insects from biting her she saw the servant move away from the window. 'Good morning,' she said, lifting great clumps of the net with both hands and peering out. 'We haven't met yet, have we? My things haven't been unpacked either, although I managed to get my typewriter out.'

The servant did not reply, only regarded Hazel, coolly, before picking up a petticoat and dropping it on a chair. *I don't care about your things*, the look on her face said. *And I don't care about you.*

'Do you speak English?' Hazel asked her, more puzzled than intimidated. There had been foreign-tongued people on board the ship—members of the crew who scoured the deck and dealt with the cargo—but they had spoken only among themselves.

'Hah! What else you expect me to speak, girl?'

'Oh. Well . . . good. We can talk then. What's your name?'

'You get to call me Winsome.'

'Winsome?' It put Hazel in mind of horse racing—of winning something—until she remembered that it meant 'charming'.

'Winsome . . . ' she repeated. 'That's a pretty name.'

The servant shrugged. Hazel couldn't take her eyes off her.

'I can't take my eyes off you,' she said. 'I've never seen a person with such black skin before. And I love your dress. It's like a poppy. I can't wear red—or orange or yellow or any of those bright colours. They make me look washed out. You're lucky.'

Winsome clucked and raised her eyes to the ceiling.

'You finished?' she said. 'You done for now?'

Hazel felt herself blushing.

'Yes,' she said. 'Sorry.'

After Winsome had gone, Hazel got herself washed and dressed. She wanted to explore. Now that it was light and she had slept, for the first time in weeks, in a bed that didn't pitch and roll with the ocean, she wanted to look around.

This bedroom of hers had once been her aunt Alison's. It reminded her of home with its flowery wallpaper and ornate four-poster bed. There was an oil-painting on one wall of a bluebell wood, and the big china bowl she had washed her face in was as English as a maypole with its pattern of ribbons and posies. If it hadn't been for the enormous net around the bed and—*oh*—the view from the window, she might have imagined herself at a very nice guest house in Margate.

The view though . . .

The house had been built on top of a hill, so that the landscape unravelled downwards. Had Hazel been alive two centuries earlier, and standing at this very window, she would have seen her family's sugar crop rippling to the very edge and limit of her vision and mistaken it, perhaps, for the sea.

Things were different now, though, and so was the view.

'Miss Mull-Dare? Are you up? Good bananas. Shall we go in search of breakfast?'

In strode Miss Amelia and Hazel almost laughed. In the past—in London—Miss Amelia had dressed exactly as one would expect a spinster teacher to dress: like a mouse. Even on the ship she had worn only sombre shades of grey and brown (although Hazel had been quick to notice a lower neckline, when they dined at the captain's table). Today, however, she was wearing yellow. Canary yellow. And pinned to her front was the largest, deadest, brightest, bluest butterfly Hazel had ever seen. Her hair, too, looked different; pulled back in its usual bun but with strands of it left loose to twirl around her face and neck like the tendrils of some fast-growing plant.

'Look,' Hazel said, to cover her amusement. 'Look out there. Isn't it wonderful?'

Miss Amelia looked.

'Where are the mangrove swamps?' she fretted. 'Where is the rainforest? There are specimens there I want to go after. The whistling duck . . . the many-banded daggertail . . . the pearly-eyed thrasher . . . '

'They must be further away,' Hazel told her. 'On the other side of the island. My grandfather will know. The

229

land around here was cleared long ago, for our sugar. Look. Look at that thing way down there, like a big stone sandcastle. That's our mill.'

'Humph.' Miss Amelia reached up to adjust the pins in her bun. There were wet stains, already, under her armpits. 'Looks more like a ruin to me. An old dwelling, perhaps, or a lock-up—somewhere to keep the savages.'

Hazel frowned.

'You mean the workers?' she said.

'Of course.'

'But they're not savages. How can they be? My grand-father would never employ, or keep, anyone wild or dangerous. That would be stupid.'

Miss Amelia smoothed her yellow frock. 'Could be they've tamed 'em, over the years,' she said. 'Made 'em more civilized. I hear there are schools for the little ones, now, and some are growing up to be teachers themselves. Nurses too. And Men of the Lord. Best not to trust 'em, anyway, that's my advice. Don't trust 'em and keep your door locked fast at night.'

Hazel looked back down the hill. The harvest was in, her grandfather had told her that, and the remains of the old cane had sprouted fresh shoots called 'ratoons' which would produce a new crop soon without the need, or expense, of more planting.

Times were hard, he had told her—all this yesterday, when she had only just arrived and they were rattling along in the buggy. Times were very hard indeed, thanks to a big new factory which now owned most of the island's cane and was turning out cheap sugar faster than a man could piddle.

'All the old families, they've sold up and gone,' he'd explained, while the horses swerved round a dizzying bend. Miss Amelia had held silently fast to her specimen net, the sun beating down on her hat. 'But not us. Not the Mull-Dares. We've come through droughts, hurricanes, red rot, emancipation, and the Devil alone knows how much dysentery . . . so no jumped-up blighter with new-fangled machines is going to see us off. No, sir!'

He had said nothing, himself, on the subject of savages or about keeping doors locked at night. Miss Amelia, Hazel decided, was just being silly. Perhaps the heat was getting to her.

'Come on,' she said. 'Let's go and see what's for breakfast.'

She had expected her grandfather to be out in the cane fields, doing whatever needed doing at this time of year to keep times from getting harder. It was a surprise, therefore, to find him in a rocking chair on the veranda, watching the sky and not wearing very much.

'Put some trousers on, Giddy,' his wife scolded. 'I'm sorry, Miss Fritillary . . . Hazel . . . we've grown unused to company.'

Gideon Mull-Dare went plodding cheerfully away, winking at Hazel as he passed and—oh, goodness—leering like a gargoyle at Miss Amelia who jumped back in disgust.

Hazel giggled. She already liked this grandfather of hers. His freckles were so dense you couldn't have put a pin between them and although his hair was white as snow it was still tufty, like his son's. He looked like a story-book teddy, or a naughty little boy, going off in his pants to do as he'd been told.

231

'Sit down, dear,' her grandmother said. 'And help yourself to fruit and bread. You too, Miss Fritillary.'

Winsome brought coffee. Hazel watched her hover.

'Black or white?' her grandmother asked Miss Amelia.

'White.'

Stepping forward, Winsome began to pour.

Hazel's grandmother was talking about her garden; about the sheer impossibility of growing delphiniums and sweet peas although roses did all right, so long as you tended them like babies and didn't take it personally if they straggled.

Miss Amelia wasn't listening. She was sitting bolt upright in her chair—bolt upright and leaning so far away from the edge of the table that she looked in danger of falling backwards. Her whole face, not just her throat, had turned such a livid red that Hazel feared, momentarily, that she had suffered some kind of a seizure. She looked terrible, all tight-lipped and affronted, as if someone had just insulted her or broken wind an inch from her nose.

Perhaps, Hazel thought, she was still traumatized by the sight of Gideon Mull-Dare all paunchy and freckled in his baggy old pants. This was, after all, a woman who wouldn't even look at a word in a book if it offended her Delicate Senses. But no . . . Miss Amelia was staring, fixedly, at her coffee cup . . . watching the hot liquid streaming into it as if she imagined it might poison her.

When the cup was almost full Winsome set the pot down.

'You want sugar?' she asked.

'Yes,' squeaked Miss Amelia, as if it pained her to reply.

'White or brown?'

'White.'

The bowl of white lumps was within easy reach but the sugar tongs were a stretch away, where Gideon Mull-Dare had set them down after using them to pull a small splinter from his foot.

Slowly, in her own good time, Winsome leaned across the table. Miss Amelia's intake of breath, as the younger woman's arm passed inches from her face, was loud enough to be heard. And the further forward Winsome leaned, the further away from her Miss Amelia cringed until—thwack—her knees hit the underside of the table, her chair tipped, and she would have crash-landed on her spine had not Winsome, with admirable speed and dexterity, turned and grabbed her by the shoulder.

*Well done, Winsome,* Hazel thought.

But 'Aaaargh!' shrieked Miss Amelia, flailing like something on the end of a hook and beating at Winsome's fingers with her own right fist. 'Get your filthy hands off me! Let go of me, you black devil!'

'All rightey then. No skin off my heels . . . '

And Winsome let go of Miss Amelia like a bag of dirty washing, casting her off so suddenly that Miss Amelia staggered backwards, clouting her thighs and jarring her buttocks against the overturned chair.

Without a word, Winsome picked up the coffee pot and carried it round to Hazel's grandmother. Without a word she served the old lady, while Miss Amelia bang-slammed her chair upright and sat down, furious.

Hazel could hardly bear to look at her teacher . . . at the flushed and fuming face . . . at the ridiculous hairstyle . . . at the awful dead butterfly quivering on her chest. Instead she looked at Winsome, meaning to catch that woman's eye and let her know by a nod or a smile that not everyone from England was as mean, or as mad, as Miss Amelia.

Winsome, however, just carried on pouring, as dignified as royalty compared to the red-necked woman who had just insulted her. And as she sat wordless in her place, waiting to be served in her turn, Hazel felt ashamed.

*Why?* she wondered. *Why should I feel guilty when I haven't done anything wrong?* But the sense of shame stayed with her.

'You want coffee, child?'

Hazel had never drunk coffee in her life. It wasn't the Done Thing at home. But Winsome had spoken so nicely—the word 'child' sounding cosy, somehow—that Hazel wanted to please her; to be normal and kind; to make up, as best she could, for Miss Amelia's appalling lack of grace.

'Yes, please,' she said. 'Black.'

There was silence for a while after Winsome returned to the house. A small bird with a bright lemon breast landed on the veranda rail and fluttered there, hoping for crumbs. It crossed Hazel's mind to ask Miss Amelia if she knew what kind of a bird it was but she bit the words back. Miss Amelia didn't deserve to be spoken to in a civilized manner.

Then Hazel's grandmother cleared her throat and said:

'I do sympathize, Miss Fritillary, with your aversion to the blacks. But you have to understand: the good old days are long gone. Giddy and I, we tread a very fine line between keeping them in their place and trying not to push them too far. Do you get my meaning?'

234

'Pshaw!' snorted Miss Amelia, which could have meant anything.

Hazel's grandmother picked up a strange-looking fruit and began to peel it.

'If they were to do a bunk,' she mused, as juice dribbled onto her plate, 'it would leave us in a dreadful pickle. It's *doubtful* they would find other work on the island—at least none that pays so well—but some of 'em are so cussed that, had they a mind to, they would sleep all day, drink all night, and die of starvation rather than lift a finger to serve us ever again.'

Miss Amelia blinked, crossly.

'It sounds to me, Mrs Mull-Dare, as if the darkies have got you and your husband over a barrel,' she said. 'Bring back the good old days, is all I can say.'

'Amen to that,' Hazel's grandmother sighed, before sinking her teeth into the flesh of her fruit. 'A . . . *dribble* . . . men . . . *dribble* . . . to that . . . '

When Gideon Mull-Dare reappeared—fully dressed this time in a white drill suit, buttoned stiffly to the neck—Hazel was glad to see him. And when Miss Amelia said she had lessons to prepare, so would forgo a tour of the plantation, she was relieved.

Her grandfather shrugged and scratched his belly. He was squinting at Miss Amelia's butterfly brooch as if trying to decide if it really was a brooch, or had landed on her front, by mistake, and become petrified.

'Swimming later then,' he said, jovially. 'A nice dip in the ocean. Pick up a few shells. See a turtle, perhaps. No lessons today surely? Go on, Miss Frit. Be a devil.'

Trying not to snigger at the thought of Miss Amelia in

235

a bathing suit, Hazel excused herself from the table and went to fetch her hat.

Her bedroom smelt sweet, although her stash of lavender bags, along with most of her clothes and all of her books, were still waiting to be removed from her open trunk and put away in cupboards and drawers.

*Florence would have seen to that immediately,* she thought. *And without being asked. She would have made my bed by now as well, and taken away my washing water.*

One thing, though, was different—and strangely so. For there, in her typewriter, was a sheet of paper with what looked like a line of typing on it. Had she left it there last night? No. She would never leave a part of her diary on display. Not in London, not here, not anywhere in the world.

Indignant, yet curious, she went over to the table where the typewriter stood and looked down at the words on the paper. There weren't many, but whoever had typed them had rolled the page up, just enough to make them immediately and clearly visible.

LOOK OUT FOR TOMMY JOHN

# CHAPTER 22

I t was hard to see very much in the curing house, after stepping from the dazzle of daylight, but Hazel's
grandfather was used to the transition.

'Yo-ho-ho and a barrel of rum!' he sang out, slapping
a big indistinct shape as if it was a favourite mare, or a
woman's bottom. 'That's the beauty of sugar cane, young
Hazel. Nothing wasted. Ever been allowed a tot of rum?
Never? Well, you'll try a drop tonight perhaps, with a
slosh of pineapple juice so your granny won't nag. We'll
give your Miss Frit a drop or two as well, shall we? But
without the juice. Loosen the old stick up a bit, eh? Put
some fire in her veins.'

Hazel's eyes were adjusting to the gloom. She could
make out the barrels now, up on a timber framework, and
the stone troughs set underneath to catch drips of molasses and channel the thick trickle away to the stillhouse.

Rum made her think of pirates. Of Captain Hook in
*Peter Pan*. Of her rat-scally ancestor who had won all of
this—the land, the house, the fields, the sugar, the rum—
in a game. It made her feel proud, part of an unbroken
chain, to be standing here now with her grandfather
while he explained the distillation process and patted his
barrels.

Then she saw the whip up on the wall.

'A relic,' her grandfather announced, seeing where her attention had wandered and noting, perhaps, the question on her face.

'Of the Good Old Days,' she murmured.

'Well, yes. Exactly.' He sounded surprised and rather pleased, the way Miss Amelia did if a girl at the Kensington School for the Daughters of Gentlemen answered a difficult question correctly and well.

Hazel looked back at the whip, curling like a beast's tail against dark, damp bricks. From handle to tip it was taller than her, and the leather thong had a knot in the end. Anyone lashed with that, she calculated, would have been cut to agony.

'I'd assumed you young 'uns over in England were all wishy-washy Liberals,' her grandfather was saying. 'I know young John is. Alison's boy. Well, well, well . . . ' He clapped Hazel on the back. She flinched. 'Come on,' he added, merrily. 'I'll show you the fields.'

Back outside Hazel adjusted her hat and tried not to think any more about the whip on the curing house wall. This was nothing like any hot day she had ever known in England. The very air was oppressive, weighing her down and making her sweat as she strode diligently up a slope.

Her grandfather was telling her some more about the cane: 'See those shoots? Twenty feet high they'll get to be if we're lucky; if rats don't munch the lot. Seen a mongoose yet? Brown blighter with a bushy tail? Well, you will. Island's swarming with 'em. Brought here centuries ago they were, to kill off the rats. Trouble is, the mongoose feeds by day and doesn't climb trees. So what does the rat do? Eats cane by night and climbs trees to stay alive. Cunning blighters, rats . . . '

They stopped on a ridge, to survey the land—waves of brown and green stretching away to where the sea met the sky in identical swathes of turquoise. Hazel's grandfather produced a bottle which he uncorked and then drank from, in long, loud gulps, before passing it to Hazel. She drank too, in smaller gulps, then wiped the top of the bottle, just as he had, before passing it back. She had half hoped there would be rum in there, but water, she supposed, was more refreshing when you were out in the heat, surveying your land.

Down below, she could see workers moving slowly along the rows of sprouting cane. Some were hoeing, by the look of it, others bending to pull things from the earth. The ones who were bending looked very small and very young.

'Grandfather,' Hazel said. 'Who is Tommy John?'

He didn't answer straight away. Instead, he took another swig from the bottle, screwing up his eyes against the sun as he tipped back his head. He didn't offer Hazel any more, and took his time replacing the cork.

Then: 'Who's been talking to you?' he said. 'Which one?'

His voice wasn't loud, or particularly harsh, but there was something about it that put Hazel on her guard. If it had been his usual tone she would not have liked him at all. She might even have been afraid.

'N-no one,' she replied. 'It's just a name I came across earlier. I don't know any more. No one's said a word. It just came to my attention, that's all.'

'Don't you go listening to any nigger-talk, you hear me? Any of those lying blighters start telling you tales you tell me or your grandma so we can put you straight. All right?'

'All right.'

Down in the cane fields one of the workers began to cry. The sound of it, drifting through the claggy air, made Hazel's skin prickle.

*That can't possibly be a grown-up.*

'Time to head back,' her grandfather said. 'For a spot of lunch. Then we'll go and dunk Miss Frit in the sea, eh? Find out if she sinks or swims.'

He cackled then, back to his teasing self, and Hazel allowed herself to feel better.

Lunch was already on the table by the time they reached the house, and Hazel's grandmother and Miss Amelia were halfway through theirs. They were talking so loudly that their voices came fluttering down through the oleander trees as Hazel and her grandfather approached the veranda steps.

'Frightful things, jellyfish,' Hazel heard her grandmother say. 'You'll find them in the mangrove swamps, Miss Fritillary, lying upside down—*upside down, I ask you*—to soak up as much as they can of the light.'

'Like Cassiopeia,' twittered Miss Amelia. 'The mythical queen turned into a constellation of stars, only the wrong way up, all topsy-turvy, as a punishment for her vanity.'

'*Is* that so? Well I never . . . '

Hazel ate quickly and then escaped to her room. She could tell, as soon as she opened the door, that someone had been in there. Not just because the bed had been made and her things put away, at last, but because a fresh sheet of paper had appeared in her typewriter.

```
The past no go away for longtime. Things
buried come up soon to do haunting.
```

The bathing costume Aunt Alison had bought for her in London had been laid out on the bed, along with a large towel and a flimsy-looking pair of sandals made from plaited straw. Hazel moved to fetch them, then hesitated . . .

The typewriter's paper-feeding mechanism grated, like teeth, as she rolled it up a notch.

```
What do you mean? she typed. I don't under-
stand what you're trying to say to me.
```

Then she scooped up her swimming things and left the room. She knew she ought to tell her grandparents that someone—one of the servants most likely—had been using her typewriter. Perhaps it was Winsome, although where Winsome had learned how to spell, never mind type, was a thing she couldn't guess at.

The trouble was, there was bound to be a fuss if she told. The person responsible might be dismissed as a troublemaker and then what would he or she do? Sleep and drink and starve going by what her grandmother had told Miss Amelia at breakfast.

No, she decided. She wouldn't tell. Not yet. No harm had been done, after all.

Miss Amelia was hovering on the veranda, wondering aloud whether there would be bathing huts on this beach, and a donkey to pull her and Hazel and Mrs Mull-Dare down to the water's edge.

Hazel's grandfather was finding all of this most amusing. 'If we're very, very quick,' he said, with a wink, 'we might catch a Punch and Judy show on the pier, or a brass band playing "Rule Britannia".'

'Giddy,' his wife scolded. 'Don't tease. There are no bathing huts, Miss Fritillary, but the sea-grape bushes provide screening enough for changing and this beach, unlike the ones in England, will be completely deserted.'

Only slightly mollified, Miss Amelia reached for her specimen net. Hazel averted her eyes. Even now, even here, she couldn't catch sight of that net without being reminded of a certain person's trapped head . . . a certain person's humiliation . . . a certain person's furious voice spilling though the mesh: 'Let me out! I'm warning you!'

*The past no go away for longtime . . .*

The road to the beach was as curved and as scary as a snake.

'Slow down, Giddy!' begged Hazel's grandmother as the buggy hit a pothole and they all rose up in their seats. 'Poor Ivy would have a fit if she could see her daughter now.'

It was the first time either grandparent had mentioned Hazel's mother. They had never even met her, so far as Hazel knew. Not once in—what—thirty years? Hearing her name like that, right out of the blue, felt as odd as seeing a daffodil among the oleanders or having a snowball hit the back of her head.

'Do you miss your mother, Hazel?'

'No. I miss my father most. Although grandfather is so like him that it's sort of as if he's here.'

242

Her father and his breakdown had been touched on sympathetically, but briefly, as if he was a stranger; which considering how long he had lived away from this island he practically was.

'Yes . . . ' Her grandmother's arm pressed, warm as a loaf, against her own skin as the buggy swerved round a bend, and her 'yes' could only just be heard above the clatter of hooves and the bounce of rusty springs. 'Yes . . . Maurice always was a chip off the old block. And you're his spit and image, dear, although a lot more sensible, I'm sure. Giddy, will you *please* slow down.'

Hazel's grandfather turned, and leered.

'Hang on to your hats, ladies!' he yelled, thwacking the reins. 'And watch out for the Greenaway jumbies!'

'The Greenaway what's—*whooooaaa*!'

Hazel had never been canoeing, or sledging, or even on a slide, so the feeling that her stomach had risen to her chest and that she was moving . . . falling . . . whizzing downwards as fast as a fish or a bird was a new and, yes, *exhilarating* experience.

'For the love of . . . ' Her grandmother clamped a hand on her thigh as if to anchor her fast to the seat. Miss Amelia, sitting diagonally opposite, with her back to the cantering horse, let out a shriek like a boiling kettle. Both women had closed their eyes; Hazel kept hers open. Her grandfather was half-standing, urging his old black horse on down the hill and using the reins as a whip. And the hill was steep, with a dizzying drop a mere topple to the left . . . a sheer almost perpendicular drop, through strange bushes and trees, to rocks that would smash you to pulp if you went toppling over, and a turquoise sea that would swallow you whole.

'YAAAAAAAAR!' yelled Giddy Mull-Dare, bending at the knees like a praying mantis and punching the air in glee.

'YAAAAAAAAR!' yelled Hazel, excitement thrilling her veins as her hat fell off, and 'YAR-YAR-YAAAAAAAAAR!' as her own fist punched the air.

But: 'NOOOOOOO!' shrieked a ghost-faced Miss Amelia, followed by *'Forgive-me-my-trespasses-as-I-forgive-those-who-have-trespassed-against-me-and-deliver-me-from . . .'*

And then, just when toppling seemed inevitable, the road levelled out and the horse slowed down and everybody's stomachs settled back into their middles.

Hazel's grandmother was the first to speak.

'Gideon Mull-Dare,' she said, sternly, 'one of these days you will meet something coming up that hill and then your luck will run out, YOU STUPID OLD MAN.'

Miss Amelia, trembling all over, clutched her specimen net to her breast, like a close and personal friend, and moaned: 'I thought my time had come. I did! I did! I thought I was off to meet my maker, with no time to repent.'

'Repent, eh?' Giddy Mull-Dare bent sideways and gave Miss Amelia a dig in the ribs, making her leap far higher than careering down the hill at breakneck speed had done. 'And what grievous sin, or wicked crime, might a respectable teacher-lady like yourself be guilty of, eh?'

'I . . . I . . .'

'Giddy, that's enough! Pay no attention, Miss Fritillary. He's teasing you. How about a little game, now that the scenery is no longer a blur? First person to spot a mongoose gets a peppermint . . .'

The beach, when they finally reached it, really was deserted and as close to perfection as anywhere ever gets. Hazel, used to hobbling over rocks and slime to brave crashing British breakers, gazed across pure white sand to the silky blue drag of the water and was enchanted. Miss Amelia, however, took one look at the only-just-waist-high bushes she was expected to undress behind and declared herself unimpressed.

'Sit on the rug with me, Miss Fritillary dear, if you don't want to swim,' Hazel's grandmother called to her. 'Here in the shade. We can play Snap or Happy Families—I've brought the cards—and I can tell you more about my roses.'

Miss Amelia threw the sea-grape bushes a desperate look, as if willing them to grow three feet in two seconds so that she might opt for a swim after all. Then, with a reluctant pout, she resigned herself to the rug and the shade.

Gideon Mull-Dare, having stripped down to a pair of loose pyjama bottoms, was already heading for the waves so Hazel took herself off behind the bushes to change. There was no one to see her. Looking up there was only the slope and tangle of rocks and trees. Looking back there was only her grandfather, churning his way out to sea like some tufty-headed walrus, and the two women settling themselves beneath the scritchy fronds of a coconut palm.

There was no one and nothing to see her, except perhaps a mongoose or a Greenaway jumby (whatever that was) and yet . . .

'I felt as if I was being watched,' she told her grandmother, on her way down to the water's edge. 'From up there somewhere.'

Her grandmother was counting out the playing cards—Mister Bun the Baker, Mister Dose the Doctor, Mister Soot the Sweep . . . while Miss Amelia sat and scanned the shoreline, her specimen net within grabbing distance, half on, half off the rug.

'I didn't actually see anyone,' Hazel added. 'But it felt as if they were out there, looking down.'

Her grandmother picked up the cards and began shuffling them. 'Nelson's sailors,' she said, nodding towards the distant tree-smothered hills, 'are out there somewhere, dear, but way past being able to spy on young girls in their petticoats. They died of fever—oh, a very long time ago—and up there is where they got buried. Yes, Miss Fritillary, Lord Nelson stayed quite a while on this island, although he was just a young captain then. He visited our house—there's a record of it somewhere, along with the evening's supper menu—and moaned, non-stop, about mosquitoes biting his ankles. A very odd bod by all accounts. Walked a mile every night, even in hurricane season, and liked six pails of water poured over his head at dawn . . . '

The sand was uncomfortably hot under the soles of Hazel's feet. Quickly she continued her way down to the nibbly little waves and began wading out. It was like slipping into silk. It was bliss. Her grandfather was a long way off, floating on his back, and she found she was glad about that. Her father would have been swimming right there next to her, or watching anxiously from the tideline in case she got a cramp or a big wave knocked her down. Her father would never have allowed her to change into her bathing suit behind a shrub, however deserted the beach and however dead the sailors up in the hills. Her father would have been fretting, a lot, and she could not imagine him here.

Something touched her leg, making her jump. But it was only a fish—a tiny black and yellow thing, striped like a bee. There were lots of them, she noticed, flicking in shoals in the clear, clean water, and they were curious about her, that was all.

Wallowing contentedly, just out of her depth, she looked up at the hills . . . at the trees she couldn't name . . . at the heavenly blue of the sky, and wondered where the graves were. With the sun on her shoulders and the sea rocking gently against her back, it suddenly felt very good to be alive. She had never felt like that in Margate, or Scarborough, or in any of the other places she had spent summers with her parents.

*I'm free*, she realized. *Even with my grandparents around, and Miss Amelia here to teach me etiquette; even in a strange and foreign place which I don't know properly yet, I am freer now than I have ever been in my life.*

# CHAPTER 23

I t was shortly after her second glass of rum and pineapple juice that Hazel remembered to ask her grandfather about the Greenaway jumbies. There had been no message on her typewriter when they got back from the beach . . . no answer to her questions . . . no more words about hauntings or 'Tommy John' . . . so when her grandfather replied that jumbies were ghosts, not birds or beasts as she'd assumed, she was in the right kind of mood to know more.

'Ghosts? Really? Who were the Greenaways then? And how did they die?'

Darkness had fallen, as quick as a mudslide, and candles that smelt both medicinal and lemony had been lit at the table, and all along the veranda rail, to keep biting insects away. Mosquitoes, that's what those insects were called. Hazel knew that now. Moss-key-toes. Like English gnats, only nastier.

'Never mind about the Greenaways, and forget about jumbies. Superstitious load of twaddle . . . '

Gideon Mull-Dare was drinking rum the way he drank water—quickly and in gulps. Miss Amelia was sipping hers slowly, as if trying to decide whether she liked it or not. So far she had sipped three and a half tots that way and her eyes, in the candlelight, were starting to boggle.

Hazel's grandmother was sticking to juice. Later on she would have cocoa, like any true Englishwoman.

'Giddy, keep your voice down,' she scolded before turning to Hazel and saying: 'The blacks believe the dead come back as jumbies, to cause trouble to folk who wronged them. They say that if you call a jumby's name and it answers, you'll be dead by sunset. All nonsense of course.'

*Smack!*

Miss Amelia hit the table so hard, with the flat of her hand, that the rum bottle jumped. Then she raised the hand, like a child in a classroom, to reveal a tiny splatter of blood in the centre of her palm.

'A mosquito, eh? And you got the blighter, too—well done!'

'I'm being bitten,' Miss Amelia said, haughtily. 'Like Nelson. I think I will retire to my room.' Her voice was slurred and she appeared to be having trouble moving her chair so that she could stand up.

'Me too,' said Hazel. 'Come on, we'll go in together.'

Miss Amelia's room was close to Hazel's, along a landing that ran the length of the first floor. The landing was high-ceilinged but narrow, with rooms and stairways leading off it in a pattern as complex as honeycomb. Because lights attract mosquitoes, Gideon and Louise Mull-Dare preferred to let the upstairs grow dark after sunset while keeping windows and doors wide open, as late as possible, for any breeze to blow through. They knew the house so well they could have gone to bed blindfold. Hazel and Miss Amelia, however, were allowed candles so they wouldn't come a cropper.

'*Rule Britannia!*' Miss Amelia began to sing, holding her candle like a sceptre in one hand and thumping her heart, patriotically, with the other. '*Britannia rule the waves! Britons never, never* **neeever** . . . '

'Shhhhh,' begged Hazel, as they lurched towards the stairs.

'*Shall . . . beeee . . . slaves. Oops-a-daisy. Oh . . . shhhh . . . don't tell Eunice. Oh deary me, no; not a word to Eunice or she'll know where I . . . HIC . . . am!*'

'I think you're a little bit tipsy, Miss Gumm. But that's all right. I'm a bit unsteady myself I think. From the rum. Mind your candle. It's tilting.'

'*Yo-ho-hooooo and bottle of* . . . Miss *Fritillary,* dear heart, if you please. No more a Gumm, *nay neveeeeer no more.* I've cast it off! Left it behind with poor old Eunice and . . . and . . . oh dear, let's have another song. Take our minds off the past, eh?'

'*Mind* that candle. You nearly set your hair alight . . . '

'Dear Eunice. She was a big help to me. Knows all my secrets; all the worst things. Strong too. Did the digging. I couldn't face that . . . Couldn't . . . even . . . look while . . . '

'This is my room now.' Hazel let go of Miss Amelia's arm, but had to clutch it again as they both began to sway.

'It's all . . . *hic* . . . right, you know,' Miss Amelia said, half patting, half missing, the door handle. 'You can go in. Just remember to *lock up* after you. I will. *Hic.* I have a vivid imag-ina-shion, Miss Mull-Dare, and will have bad dreams to—*hic*—night, for shure. About jumblies.'

Hazel began to giggle. 'Jumbies,' she corrected her teacher. 'Not jumblies. You're thinking of the poem.'

'*Hic!* So I am. *They went to sea in a sieve they did! In a sieve they went to sea . . .* '

'Shhhh.'

Hazel had managed to get her door open. Her window, and the shutters, had been closed tight and there was a lamp burning on her writing table, just like the night before. Even from the doorway; even through her tipsiness, she could tell that a message had been left.

'I've got a message,' she announced, without thinking. 'Goodnight.'

But Miss Amelia would not let go of her arm.

'*Far and few, far and few, are the lands where the jumblies live . . .* A message, Miss Mull-Dare? Where? Who from?'

Impatiently, Hazel shook her off.

'Don't know yet,' she said. 'Could be a jumby. Or a jumblie even.'

'Don't say that, dear heart . . . don't even think it . . . '

Crossing the room was a slow and lurchy process. Somewhere in a rum-fuddled corner of her mind Hazel knew she ought to send Miss Amelia away, but the woman was right behind, stumbling over her own toes. And anyway, part of her was tempted to tell, and Miss Amelia was, after all, a responsible adult—most of the time.

No need you be scared. I got no bones to pick with you. Others yes. Persons close to you got plenty to be shamed about. Those

251

persons think they run and hide from
wickedness, long ways across the sea. But
trouble never set like the sun. Trouble
follow.

Hazel read the message twice and still didn't understand it. Over her shoulder, Miss Amelia read it once and
felt her blood turn cold.

'Who . . . ?' she whimpered. 'Who . . . ?'

Hazel frowned as she read the message again.

'I don't know,' she said. 'I don't know who typed this
and I don't know who they're talking about. I'll have to
think.'

Miss Amelia sat down, heavily, on the bed.

'The other messages made no sense either,' Hazel told
her. 'The first said "Look out for Tommy John"—whoever
he is. The second said something about a buried thing
coming up to do some haunting. That certainly sounds
like a jumby, doesn't it? Miss Amelia, are you all right?
You've gone a funny colour. Do you need a glass of water?'

'N-no, no, no. Not to worry. I must . . . Goodnight.'

Miss Amelia looked completely sober all of a sudden as
she went to leave the room. Sober but ghastly, as if she
had just been reminded of some terrible thing.

'*You* don't, by any chance, know who Tommy John is,
do you?' asked Hazel, suspiciously.

Miss Amelia shivered, one hand on the door frame.
'Why should I?' she snapped back. 'Why should *I* know?
Well, I don't. All right? I can tell you nothing. Nothing at
all.' And nor could she; for the nasty little specimen who
had tried to extort money from her . . . the man she had

252

accidentally done for when she hurled that wretched umbrella . . . had introduced himself only as Mister Price (and that, more than likely, had been his idea of a joke). His Christian name could have been anything: Bob, Dick, Arthur . . . It could have been Rumpelstiltskin for all she knew. It could even . . . oh dear, yes it could . . . have been Thomas John.

'Lessons tomorrow,' Miss Amelia squeaked. 'Back to normal, that's the ticket . . . ' And then she was gone, scuttling along the hall towards her own room, her own netted bed, and the dreams—the very grim dreams—that would claim her when she finally fell asleep.

Left alone, Hazel lay down, fully-clothed, and tried to think things through.

*Persons think they run and hide long ways across the sea.*

Who could that be, if not Miss Amelia? Who else did she know who might have run away from trouble? Someone close, it had to be. Someone with good reason to be ashamed.

Aha.

Rolling off the bed made her head spin, and the ratchets of the typewriter sounded unnaturally loud as she wound the paper up.

```
Do you mean Gloria Gilbert? she typed. I
don't see how you, or anyone else on this
island, could know about her, but what you
say all seems to fit. She has only gone to
Italy, which isn't far across the sea
(from England anyway) but she certainly
did a wicked thing, abandoning Diggy Bert,
```

and I hope she is riddled with guilt and remorse.

I still don't know who Tommy John is so have no way of looking out for him. And who were the Greenaways? I'm just curious to know.

I'm not scared, thank you.

When she woke Winsome had already opened the shutters and left a jug of water. She must have crept in quietly this time but, even so, Hazel was amazed that the light hadn't roused her. The clothes she had flung off, before collapsing into bed, were still strewn all over the floor, so she picked them up herself and put them on a chair.

Then she checked the typewriter. It was spooky to think someone might have crept in while she was fast asleep (she hadn't locked the door, after all) and managed to leave a message without her knowing. It was one thing opening a door quietly, but typing in silence was surely impossible.

*If there is a message,* she told herself, *then it's almost certainly from Winsome, and I am most definitely the heaviest sleeper in the world.*

But there was no message.

Gideon and Louise Mull-Dare had already breakfasted and taken the buggy into town. Miss Amelia, too, was up and dressed and waiting for Hazel in the room set aside for lessons.

'I take you there,' Winsome said. 'But you eat something first. Food before learnin' otherwise your head get all in a spin.'

'Did you go to school, Winsome?' Hazel enquired, doing her best to sound innocent. 'If you don't mind me asking. Were you ever taught how to read and write?'

'Hah!' Winsome picked up a tray loaded with crockery, fruit peel, and crusts and turned towards the house . . . 'What for I need schoolin', child? I's a lucky woman, don't forget, shimmyin' around all day in me red dress . . . You eat that pancake now before I come back.'

Hazel helped herself to syrup. She could, she knew, have asked Winsome outright if she had been typing messages. 'Winsome,' she could have said. 'I'm pretty sure it's you and I want you to stop.' The thing was though, she was wary, still, of Winsome—wary of offending her, with a false accusation, and afraid, too, of her scorn. Also, she wasn't sure she wanted the messages to stop. There was something intriguing about them; something tantalizing and mysterious, like the instalments of a story.

It was pleasant sitting by herself on the veranda. There was a breeze today, taking the edge off the heat, and the flowering trees that grew all around the house sounded glad as they rustled and rasped. The bird with the lemon breast flew down, skittered a moment on the veranda rail, and then half flew, half hopped to the edge of the table.

*You cheeky thing*, Hazel murmured under her breath. *Good job Miss Amelia isn't out here with her net.*

Slowly, slowly, so as not to frighten it away she broke off a tiny piece of pancake. It did fly away, but not very far, and when she tossed the piece of pancake a few inches from her plate it came straight back and got it.

It was a small pleasure, but enough to make Hazel smile as the bird flew heavily back over the veranda rail,

255

weighed down by batter. The sound of sweeping broke the moment and she looked round to find one of the workers nudging a broom up and along the veranda steps.

'Good morning,' she said to him.

He didn't look at her, only nodded and carried on sweeping.

'I've been feeding the birds,' Hazel told him. 'I hope that's all right.'

He nodded again, without raising his head or breaking his rhythm. He was an old man, Hazel realized. As old as the hills. Older, certainly, than her grandfather and nowhere near as sprightly.

She finished her pancake and sipped her coffee. It was very strong without milk but she sort of liked it that way. The old man was on the veranda now, sweeping close to the table.

'Do you want me to move?' Hazel asked. 'I'm waiting for Winsome, but I can move if you like.'

The lifting of his shoulders could have been a shrug or just a reflex of his tired old muscles as he manipulated the broom. *Perhaps he's going deaf*, Hazel thought to herself. *Or perhaps he didn't understand what I just said.*

There was sugar all round her mouth, from the pancake. She licked some of it off and let the sweetness dissolve before saying:

'Who is Tommy John?'

The old man stopped sweeping then and looked straight at her.

Startled, she put down her spoon, her sugary mouth an 'O' of surprise.

'Tommy John a good boy,' the old man said, his voice deep and low. 'He around here someplace. You see him maybe one of these days.'

The lemon-breasted bird had returned—straight to the table this time. Hazel ignored it.

'How will I recognize him?' she said. 'How will I know Tommy John?'

'By his black skin,' the old man told her. 'And by his orange hair.'

# CHAPTER 24

Miss Amelia had a headache. A really bad one. As a concession to this being a teaching day she had put on a dark skirt. Her blouse, however, was striped pink and white, like a candy cane, and she had pinned a flower to it—a strange silk flower, shaped like a trumpet, with all its stamens sticking out. Shielding her eyes with one hand she flipped open *Cassell's Dictionary of Etiquette* with the other and made a big effort to focus on the first page. 'I suggest we begin with the As,' she said to Hazel, 'and work through.'

'All right,' Hazel replied.

'So that covers . . . let's see now . . . "acceptance of invitations", "accidents at table", and "addressing persons of rank in conversation". That will be enough for today, don't you think? And then, after luncheon, we can go for a nice little ramble, can't we? Keep our eyes peeled for daggertails and the pearly-eyed thrasher.'

'All right,' Hazel said again.

'Good bananas. The As then. Let's make a start . . . '

They were in a smallish room, at a vast mahogany table upon which *Cassell's Dictionary of Etiquette* looked as lost and insignificant as a petal on a road. The table was rectangular and Miss Amelia had placed Hazel's chair on one side, with its slatted back to the window, and her own directly opposite so that she herself could see the sky.

There were paper, pens, ink, and a blotter on Hazel's side. It would be a good idea, Miss Amelia said, if she dictated everything slowly and Hazel copied it down. Then Hazel could study what she had written until she knew it backwards, forwards, and inside out and could recite the lot from memory.

'Wouldn't it save time,' Hazel said to her, 'if I just read the whole book for myself?'

'No quibbling!' Miss Amelia retorted. 'Just do as you're told and we'll be at "Weddings", "Whispering", and "Wine" before you know it.'

Hazel assumed, from this, that there was nothing under 'X', 'Y' or 'Z' that she was required to learn in order to marry up. Nothing about how to play the xylophone politely, or stifle a yell or a yawn. Nothing about how a young lady should conduct herself at a zoo, or in Zanzibar, should she ever go there.

Stifling a groan, she picked up her pen.

*Black skin and orange hair*, she thought to herself. *It seems a strange combination to me, like Miss Amelia's blouse with that big red flower.*

The morning dragged slowly; too slowly for Hazel, who found herself longing to be outdoors—at the beach, collecting seashells, or swimming in the silky water among the stripy fish. And then, as her pen scratched out instructions for deferring, politely, to a duke, she pictured her empty bedroom . . . imagined the door opening and someone tiptoeing across the wooden floor. Was it Winsome? She couldn't tell. In her mind's eye it was a shadow-person, neither male nor female, black nor white . . . a harmless and rather interesting someone with a tale or a lesson to share.

As she struggled to memorize the As of good behaviour, Hazel became aware that Miss Amelia's head was drooping. By the time she was ready to recite, little snores were whistling across the table.

'Shall I start?'

'*What*? Ar-hem. Start? Of course, of course! Off you go. Act four scene . . . where were we? Where did we get to?'

Hazel shook her head, despairingly.

'You were asleep, weren't you?' she accused.

Miss Amelia sat up straight and blinked. Her eyes had dark smudges underneath them and her whole face looked haunted.

'I'm feeling fragile,' she admitted. 'And I had the most terrible dreams last night. I told you I would.' She bent forward, crushing the red silk flower against the table top as she leaned as near to Hazel as possible and mouthed, '*Any more messages*?'

'No,' Hazel replied.

'Well then . . . ' Miss Amelia sat back again, her flower all twisted. 'Never mind about reciting. I suggest we stop for luncheon.'

'All right,' Hazel agreed at once. 'I don't expect I'll ever need to address a duke in conversation anyway . . . '

I know of no such Gloria. She sound like
bad trouble so good riddance to her I guess.
The persons I speak of, they closer to you for
sure and to this island also. And they forget,

260

it seem to me, that where you throw water it run but where you throw blood it settle.

Them Greenaways were no good peoples, like most planter families. Them slaves of theirs work day and night in the sugar fields with no rest or sitting time, not even on a Sunday. They live on horse beans and bad-rot herring and get whipped for any small thing, like smilin' up at the Heavens or lookin' slantways at the massa's chickens.

Young William Greenaway he marry himself another planter's daughter. Could have been a Moulder girl, I don't know. Big celebrations then among the two families. Night of the wedding, young William he forget himself coming down Fig Tree Hill. He think himself so fine, in his fancy carriage with his sweet girl-bride at his side that he forget every blessed thing of use in this life.

That hill steep, steep. That hill a danger to Greenaways and other fools. Them old-day planters, they git their slaves to set wild fig all along the edge of that hill, thinking to form some good obstruction. But them trees too weak to catch strong roots. Them trees gave false assurance. Young William Greenaway and his bride, they go fast, fast down that hill, not a care about anythin' in this world. And they tip over good and proper, right through they figs, and messy-smash on

the rocks like any poor slave jumpin' clear
off the point, hopin' for better things in
the Kingdom-to-come.

Folk say those smashed-up Greenaways come
back often times as jumbies, for they too
proud and white and young to believe they
dead like that. They hang about them cliffs
making big mischief for other white folks,
specially those ones growing old with
plenty years of marriage pilin' up behind.

Your gran-dadda better watch out going
lickety-split down that hill. Only reason
those Greenaways not get him, I reckon, is
other jumby got bigger score to settle.

I tell you about that some other time.

Very carefully, Hazel unspooled the page and hid it
away in her trunk. Then she fetched another piece of
paper and fed it in.

Thank you for the warning about my
grandfather. I will tell him to slow down.
I don't think he is a bad man though,
just abrupt in his ways.

She paused then, before typing the question that was
nagging like toothache:

By slaves, do you mean workers?

She thought of the whip, hanging up in the curing
house, and felt a goose walk over her grave.

'Yoo-hoo. Miss Mull-Dare, are you ready?'

'Yes. I'm just getting my hat.'

Miss Amelia wanted to come in, Hazel could tell. She was itching to know if there had been another message.

'Psssst. Any messages?'

'Just a minute.'

Hazel picked up her hat and opened the door.

'Well?' Miss Amelia said at once. 'Spill the beans.' She was trying to be flippant, but her face was in agony from her need to know, and the look in her eyes reminded Hazel of Diggy Bert when her mother held up a pig's ear but told him to sit first, and beg.

*I can't lie to her,* Hazel thought, wildly.

'There was a message,' she admitted. 'But I don't think it has anything to do with you, really I don't.'

Miss Amelia reached out and clutched Hazel's wrists.

'What did it say?'

'Well . . . ' Hazel didn't like being gripped like that. Gently, but firmly, she tugged herself free. 'It was telling me, mostly, about the Greenaway jumbies. About how they were young people who went over the edge of the cliff on their wedding night a long time ago. I'm going to tell my grandfather not to go so fast down that hill from now on. It's dangerous.'

Miss Amelia's eyes were like magnifying glasses, scanning her face.

'What else?' she said.

'It said not to worry about the Greenaways haunting my grandfather because there's another jumby out there with a much bigger score to settle.'

Miss Amelia flinched.

263

'Tommy John?' she whispered.

'It didn't say who.'

Miss Amelia nodded, her face ashen beneath the brim of her straw hat.

'Anything else?' she said.

Hazel felt herself turning pink.

'Not much,' she mumbled.

'Liar!'

'I am not. I never lie.'

'So tell me.'

Hazel took a deep breath.

'It said about slaves,' she said. 'About slaves being treated unkindly, *very* unkindly, on the plantations. It said planters—all planters—were cruel people. Do you think my grandparents—'

'Never mind about that. I'm not interested in that. What else about the jumby? And about the person who has . . . who is supposed . . . to have gone overseas to hide from trouble?'

Hazel shrugged. 'I thought that was Gloria,' she said, sadly. 'But it isn't. It's somebody else.' She was struggling now, to remember precisely what the last message had said. Her grandfather, she knew, had been told to watch out for the jumby. But he couldn't be the one who had run away from trouble because, as far as she knew, he hadn't left this island for more than thirty years.

Miss Amelia stifled a whimper.

'Well, it can't be you anyway,' Hazel said, impatiently. 'Why would it be you?'

She was confused now. Confused and cross.

'It's probably one of the servants playing tricks,' she

264

said. 'Getting you and me all worked up over nothing. Maybe one of them has a grudge against my family, over wages or something. *I* don't know. Anyway—can we forget about the messages now, please, and go for our walk?'

It took almost twenty minutes just to amble down the driveway and out through the gates of the Mull-Dare property. With every step she took Hazel saw something to wonder at—a fountain run dry, with rust flaking from its spout; a bed of straggling roses; a shed with only three sides and no door, inside which a worker-woman was sitting on an upturned bucket, eating melon.

'Hello,' Hazel said to her, in passing.

The woman nodded, her face impassive above the grin-shaped slice of fruit.

Outside the gates, a track led down through the sugar fields to the places Hazel had already visited: the mills where cane was pressed; the boiling house with its cauldrons and furnaces, ladles and scummers; and the curing house where molasses dripped and the whip hung.

Hazel did not recall seeing much down there to excite Miss Amelia. No whistling ducks; nothing with stripes, or a green throat. Miss Amelia, though, appeared too caught up in her own anxieties to be interested in anything that might flutter or scurry by; and her specimen net—usually cocked, like a gun, when there were bushes and trees around—was trailing, limply.

'Which way shall we go?' Hazel asked.

Miss Amelia gave a little jump, as if Hazel had just prodded her.

'Up,' she replied, but not as if she cared. 'Yes, why not? Up will do . . . '

There was a small path disappearing into a dense thicket of trees. It was impossible to tell how far it led, or whether there would be anything worth seeing along the way, but Miss Amelia stepped on to it anyway and Hazel followed.

At first the going was easy, and interesting too with the trees so very different from the ones in Kensington Gardens—skinny and twisted, with vines hanging from them and the leaves so high up that they couldn't be touched. This was surely part of the rainforest that Miss Amelia had so wanted to explore, but she didn't seem all that thrilled to be walking through it at last.

'Quick—look!' Hazel called out, as something flashed blue-green overhead, on the very edge of her vision.

'A humming bird,' Miss Amelia said, without breaking her stride. 'Two a penny in this neck of the woods.' She was holding her net like a walking stick and beginning to pant as the path steepened and forked to the left. They were moving away from her grandparents' house, Hazel guessed, and up into the hills that stretched behind and beyond the plantation until they presumably met the edge of the island, and the Caribbean sea.

The path grew stonier underfoot and soon there were biggish boulders to go around, or scramble over, and prickly shrubs or fallen, vine-choked branches to contend with. Then the path divided into two forks, one going higher and the other levelling out. Without a word Miss Amelia took the easier route—only it didn't stay easy for long.

'Shall we go back?' grumbled Hazel as a twig lashed her hat and she stumbled a little on loose rocks and stones. 'The path's disappeared and I'm getting thirsty.'

Miss Amelia's dark skirt had red dust all round the hem. Her own hat had slipped off, to rest like a hump on her back, and her bun had straggled loose so that her hair hung in limp twizzling strands, brown-grey like the vines.

'Well? Shall we?' Hazel repeated. 'I really am very thirsty.'

Miss Amelia stopped then, shaded her eyes and squinted off to her right where, she noticed, the light was brighter and there appeared to be some kind of a clearing.

'All right,' she said. 'We'll head back. But we'll rest awhile first. No point overdoing it in this heat. It'll be bad bananas if one of us faints. I've a bottle of tea in my bag. Biscuits too. Just the ticket!'

Hazel had noticed the leather satchel bumping against her teacher's side but had assumed it contained her specimen jars. Following on, away from the path, she found herself in a definite clearing, with a circle of stumps where some trees had once stood and the charred and flaking remains of a fire.

'Look,' she said. 'Someone's been here.' Her voice sounded shrill, like the call of a parrot, but she didn't feel at home in this clearing the way a bird might have done. She felt like a trespasser. She felt as if she had walked right into somebody's house and was snooping around their parlour, looking in vain for portraits or slippers or some other clue as to what kind of person had been sitting here, watching logs burn.

'I'm not bothered about a drink after all,' she said, lowering her voice. 'I think we should go.'

'Nonsense.'

Miss Amelia had found herself a large slab of rock, long enough and flat enough for two people to sit upon while they sipped their tea and nibbled a piece of shortbread. It was shaded by all the foliage tangled way above it but hotter, still, than most of the radiators she had ever tried to warm her hands on back in England.

'Lovely,' she declared, placing her bottle of tea on the rock and diving back into her satchel for cups. 'Just right. And when we've had our refreshments, Miss Mull-Dare, I'm going to set you a task.'

Quickly, reluctantly, Hazel drank her tea. She didn't want a biscuit though, nor was she looking forward to this task, whatever it was. Even in a clearing, the forest felt oppressive and when the undergrowth rustled, just a couple of feet from her boots, she slopped her tea and gasped.

Miss Amelia, though, was up in a trice, net raised; eyes glowing, at last, with the thrill of possible chase.

'Mongoose,' she said, as something brown and fast plunged away through the scrub. 'Too quick for me, though. Too big as well. He'd've chewed right through the netting. We'd've had to bash his head.'

Hazel shuddered.

'What's this task you're setting me?' she asked.

'Ah yes . . . the task.' Miss Amelia had turned a little bit green, as if that sudden leap with the net had been too much for her. 'Nothing arduous. Nothing tricky. Just find yourself three objects, three very *different* objects, for tomorrow's drawing lesson. Different sizes, different textures . . . you know the drill. And take your time, dear heart, because I'm going to stretch out here and have a little snooze. Off you go now. Happy hunting.'

So saying, Miss Amelia cleared the rocky slab of teacups and biscuit crumbs and lay down upon it like a sacrifice. 'Very nice,' she mumbled, slipping her satchel beneath her head and closing her eyes. 'Surprisingly comfy, in fact.'

Hazel could not believe that anyone, let alone a bony creature like old Whiney Gumm, could get comfy on a rock—not enough for a snooze anyway. But it took less than a minute for the little snores to start.

*Well . . .*

Three objects. Just three. All different—but how different? Would three different-shaped stones do? Or three leaves of varying sizes?

With Miss Amelia asleep Hazel felt very much alone. She could hear her own breathing; even her thoughts seemed loud, and that other feeling was back again—the one of being watched.

Above her, where the trees rose and leaned across the clearing, something snapped. *Just a twig*, she told herself, without looking up. *Just a dry twig being stepped on by a mongoose or a pearly-eyed thrasher.* And she bent down to pick up a stone. A biggish, reddish stone, with lots of bumpy edges. Just right for the next day's drawing lesson.

'*Hey, Moulder girl! Don't throw that thing. I ain't meanin' no harm.*'

She looked up then; so fast she felt her neck crick.

And there he was, leaning down between the trunks of two spindly trees. A little boy wearing too-big trousers, held up round his skinny waist by knotted string. A little boy with black skin and a shock of orange hair.

Tommy John.

# CHAPTER 25

Miss Amelia didn't stir as Hazel crept from the clearing. She was dreaming of butterflies, her face twitching like a sleeping dog's.

'She hurt or what?' mouthed Tommy John, looking down, still, from the ridge.

'No,' Hazel whispered back, beginning to climb. 'She's just asleep.'

The ridge was crumbly with dry earth and small stones but it was possible to climb, Hazel realized, as long as she got a good foothold, and grasped tight to a root or a tree trunk, before taking another step up.

'You an OK climber,' said Tommy John. 'For a no-good white girl.'

'It's got . . . nothing . . . to do with being . . . white or . . . a girl,' Hazel panted. 'It's my skirt . . . I keep treading on it.'

And then she was level with him, on top of the ridge.

'I'm Hazel Louise Mull-Dare,' she said, holding out her hand. 'And you're Tommy John, aren't you?'

She had pictured him as being older . . . a grown man . . . someone to be politely wary of when they eventually crossed paths. She had expected to be repulsed, frightened even, of a man with black skin and orange hair, but this was a child—a little boy—so she felt completely safe.

Solemnly, Tommy John looked at her outstretched fingers and then up at her face.

'You want we hold hands?' he asked.

'Well, it's manners to shake,' she replied. 'But you don't have to if you don't want to. What are you doing here anyway? Where do you live?'

He pointed through the forest with the hand she hadn't shaken. 'That ways,' he said. 'You want to meet my mumma?'

Hazel looked where he had pointed, but saw only trees. 'Is it far to walk?' she asked. 'I can't go if it is; in case Miss Amelia—that's the woman down there—wakes up and calls for me.'

Tommy John was already striding ahead. He had nothing on his feet, Hazel realized, yet the ground wasn't hurting him, or making him wince, any more than a carpet would have done or a soft, English lawn.

'We hear her yellin' for certain,' he said, without turning round. 'All teacher women yell like old devils. You come and meet my mumma now. She glad to pass a bit of time with you, I reckon.'

Hazel smiled and began to follow. *Bless him*, she thought to herself, as he stomped on ahead. *He's like a little chocolate soldier, marching through the forest. A little chocolate soldier with his hair on fire!*

They were on a proper path again, and the trees were thinning out.

And then: 'Oh,' Hazel breathed, for suddenly they were out of the forest and there, far below them, was the

271

sea. They were so high up that she couldn't hear the waves, only see them frothing, like good soap, against jagged piles of rock. The light was sapphire-bright after the muggy gloom of the forest. It hurt her eyes and made her wobble.

'Careful now,' warned Tommy John. 'Path narrow here.'

*Narrow?* It was a snail trail; a gritty ribbon; a single track for one very small mongoose at a time.

'Hang on to those trees,' Tommy John advised. 'And don't look down. That sea got some big swish on it today.'

The trees were spindly things, butting up against the path and scratching at Hazel's left side as she leaned away from the dizzying drop on her right. Obediently, she grabbed hold of the nearest trunk, took a step and then grabbed another. The bark was rough, and so warmed by the sun it was like clutching each tree by the throat. 'These aren't wild fig, are they?' she asked as her boots sent tiny pebbles rattling over the cliff edge.

'Me don't know. I not studied that. Look now—there's my mumma. *Hey, Mumma!*'

Tommy John was running now along the last bit of the narrow path. Humbly, Hazel inched after him, her hands still grabbing the trees. And as she watched him go she no longer thought, *Little chocolate soldier—how sweet*, for he seemed older and tougher than her now, for having helped her along so gravely.

Then she too was off the path, standing at the top of a slope with a breeze flattening her skirt against her legs. Tommy John had run quite a distance to reach the woman who was his mumma and was talking excitedly, pointing back at Hazel as she began walking down towards them.

The woman looked up, shading her eyes. She had been spreading clothes on bushes to dry and there was a basket at her feet half full, still, of brightly-coloured things. Hazel was watching her own two feet, so she wouldn't stub her toes or tread on anything living, but every time she raised her head and saw the woman tracking her progress she felt unaccountably shy.

'Miss Mull-Dare. MISS MULL-DAAAAAAARE. Where are you?!'

Tommy John had been right. They could hear Miss Amelia loud as a bell. The workers in the cane fields could probably hear Miss Amelia. The Greenaway jumbies, over on Fig Tree Hill, were no doubt covering their ears and swooping for cover, because they too could hear Miss Amelia.

For a moment Hazel stood where she was, looking down, vexed.

'Come again some other day,' Tommy John called up to her. 'Come tomorrow.'

His mother had her left arm around him, pressing him close to her side, and the sun had formed a red-gold halo round his hair. Whether hers was the same startling colour Hazel had no way of telling, for her head was covered by a cotton wrap, similar to the one Winsome wore.

'MISS MULL-DARE . . . HAZEL . . . *Answer me!*'

Hazel hesitated, her left boot scuffing the ground. She wanted, more than anything, to ignore that Whiney Gumm and carry on down the slope. She wanted to talk more with Tommy John, to say hello to his mother and go into their house for a cup of tea or something. Where was their house though? It couldn't be all that far from where they hung their washing. There was a wooden hut built up against the slope, with a roof like the lid of a sardine can. But that, she thought, was probably for the goat tethered next to it.

'HAZ-EEEEEEEEEEEEL!'

There was real panic now, in Miss Amelia's voice.

'Here! She's here!' shouted Tommy John but his voice was too little to carry far. He was agitated, Hazel could tell—sorry that some poor woman had woken up alone and in a panic.

Reluctantly, she took a long, deep breath.

'STAY THERE!' she yelled, the words so loud that they hurt her throat. 'I'M COMING BACK . . .'

Tommy John wriggled free from his mother to wave her goodbye. 'Tomorrow! Come tomorrow, Moulder girl. You know the way now.' His mother said nothing and nor did she wave. But it seemed to Hazel that she nodded, in solemn, silent assent, before bending to pick a small shirt from the laundry basket.

Retracing her steps along the edge of the cliff, Hazel grasped each tree in turn and kept on shouting: 'I'M NEARLY THERE . . . NOT FAR TO GO . . . DON'T MOVE . . . I'LL FIND YOU.' The shouting made her bolder, and the walk less of an ordeal.

And then she was back in the forest, leaping nimbly from rock to rock and boulder to boulder, until she could see the candy-stripes of Miss Amelia's blouse and the specimen net raised straight and high, like a giant swat.

'Here I am,' she said, loudly.

'Oh—tush! Oh, *bad* biscuits. I nearly had him then . . . '

Hazel stepped into the clearing. 'What was it?' she said, for she had seen nothing fly up, or go running for cover.

'Lizard,' said Miss Amelia, licking her lips. 'Black, but with a vivid green stripe. A *most* unusual specimen. Bit small, but we could have popped him in a jar and had a better look.' She eyed Hazel's empty hands. 'Where are your objects?' she scolded. 'For tomorrow's drawing lesson?'

Hazel told the truth: 'I didn't get any. But I did find where the forest comes out, and there's a beautiful view from there across the sea. Perhaps we could come back tomorrow and I could do a landscape. You could look for the lizard again, or have another snooze. I'd be perfectly safe, and I'd come when you called.'

'Hah—like a jumby.' Miss Amelia's face clouded as she remembered.

'Not a bit like a jumby,' Hazel said. 'I don't honestly think there are such things, you know. I think jumbies are like the bogeyman in England—made up to frighten children, and make them go to bed.'

Miss Amelia picked up her satchel and shouldered her specimen net. 'At least I had my forty winks,' she said. 'It was most pleasant, lying out here in the shade. No mosquitoes biting me. No darkies around. No silly old men in their undergarments. I'm sorry, dear heart, but your grandfather is a slob. I've known hogs with better manners.'

Hazel smiled and shook her head.

'Let's go, shall we?' she said. 'Let's get back on the path.'

You ask about slavery like it some chat-
about thing you never give no heed to

before. What they tell you of such matters over the sea in England? Not much, I reckon. Not enough. Maybe they ashamed of their bad-lot peoples and the way they gets to be so fine and rich all down the years. Maybe not.

That subject big, big like the sea. That subject too deep and wide, I reckon, for one piece of paper. It mess me head to go way into past times and bear witness to great suffer-ings for your better understanding, which can be no understanding at all. For you guilty by blood, girl. It passed down like pieces of silver or a dress for your wedding day.

Slavery done been abolished now. Long times since that happen. But you think that makes my peoples free? You seen any white folks yet, shining a black man's shoes or cooking up a pot of fungee for a black woman's table?

Hazel rolled the message up a notch and sat down to reply. For several minutes she sat there, in front of her typewriter, without touching the keys. Then she pushed back her chair, stood up and left the room.

At supper Miss Amelia drank neat rum again, match-ing Gideon Mull-Dare glass for glass. Hazel and her grandmother drank pineapple juice and water. The mos-quitoes drank everyone's blood and the insects that sang by rubbing bits of themselves together sounded especially loud and frenzied.

Hazel retired early and this time she locked her door.

276

There were no more messages for her, nor did she leave one herself before climbing into bed and drawing the folds of her net close round her.

She was exhausted. She was drained from too much thinking; from wanting to know and yet not wanting to know more about slavery and her family's connections to it. And when she slept she dreamt that she was back in London, sitting all by herself in the dining room eating a dish of porridge. It was salty porridge, like the kind she had in Scotland, and the milk was a funny colour—blue, like ink or the Caribbean sky.

Then her father came in and said, 'I've brought you some sugar, pet.' He looked perfectly well, not broken down at all, but he held out the sugar bowl bashfully—apologetically—as if he wasn't quite sure she would take it.

She did take it. Why wouldn't she? She liked a lot of sugar. They both did. In her dream she took the bowl from her father and picked up the spoon . . . the special spoon with holes in it that they always used for sprinkling. Only *no, oh no* . . . suddenly the room was filling with water . . . seawater swirling in through the open door; lapping around her ankles, as warm and as blue as the milk in her dish.

'Quick, pet!' her father shouted, leaping onto the dining table. 'Grab the cloth and hang on tight!'

'But that's my wedding dress!' Hazel cried out. 'Someone has covered our table with my wedding dress. And I can't . . . I won't . . . '

And she woke in a sweat, her eyes wet with tears and her hands clenched tightly in the folds of the fallen mosquito net.

# CHAPTER 26

'What for you lock your door?' chided Winsome in the morning. 'You think I walk straight through it? You think I got that ability? And look at your net, girl, all messed and flung about. Looks like you been out fishing with the thing.'

'Winsome,' said Hazel, as her shutters banged open.

'Yup?'

'How long have you been working here?'

Winsome bent down to pick up the mosquito net. 'Long enough it seems,' she muttered. 'Looong enough.'

'And have you always lived on this island? Is this where your family—your ancestors—are from?'

Winsome straightened up and tossed the mosquito net on the bed. And it seemed to Hazel that she stood extra tall, and that the lines of her face hardened, although her eyes grew soft as she looked away out through the opened shutters and replied: 'My ancestors from Africa.' Then her face grew even harder-looking, and so did her eyes as she turned her attention to Hazel.

'Did . . . did your ancestors work here?' Hazel stammered. 'On this plantation, I mean—in the fields, or in our house, like you?' She was blushing, she could feel it, but she met Winsome's gaze as well as she could and managed not to flinch when the answer came:

'My ancestors brought here in chains, girl. They sold like cattle to this planter or that. To your people maybe, or to others. They don't leave no marks no place and ain't no one rememberin' their born-given names, or knowin' where to lay flowers above their bones. They work like sorry beasts till they drop down dead, and that's all there is.'

Hazel nodded and lowered her gaze.

*Here*, she told herself, sadly. *Winsome's people may well have worked here. Men, women . . . children too. I bet there were children. And if they didn't work hard enough, out in the fields, they were whipped—or worse. Everyone knows it. Grandfather, grandmother . . . all the grown-ups. My father and Aunt Alison must know it, too, for they grew up on this island.*

*'Bring back the good old days,' Miss Amelia said, and my grandmother agreed with her. 'Amen to that,' she said.*

*They were talking about slavery.*

*They were wishing they could have slaves working here again, instead of people who might leave at any minute. Only . . . Winsome and the others can't leave because although they are free they have to earn their living. And they have to earn it right here, where their ancestors were slaves, because there's no other work to be had.*

'I'm sorry, Winsome,' she whispered, her eyes stinging. 'I didn't know. I'm so, so sorry.'

She should have left it at that—no more questions. But there was one other thing, just one, that she felt she needed to know.

'Were they all black-skinned people?' she asked 'The ones brought here from Africa? The ones sold as slaves?'

Winsome's laugh was like the mocking of a crow. 'Girl,' she said, 'you been living in a box or what these past years? What that long woman been teachin' you that you don't know the simplest things about the way life is?'

Hazel thought of *King Lear*; remembering the pages with 'bosom' and 'bastard' blanked out. She thought of *Cassell's Dictionary of Etiquette*, with its lessons on eating asparagus correctly, and the right way to address an earl. And then she remembered Christabel Pankhurst's pamphlet, and *The Suffragette* magazine.

'I know about men and their wild oats,' she said, defensively. 'I know about the diseases they catch and pass on to their innocent wives. And I know that women like us need to get The Vote, to be more equal with men and to have more of a say in how things are done in this world . . . In England, anyway . . . ' she finished, lamely.

And then Winsome gave her the strangest of looks— a mixture of pity and scorn. And Hazel realized, in a rush of remorse, that the concerns of Christabel Pankhurst, and all the other English suffragettes, did not reach this far across the world. And even if they did, the chances were they would not address the needs, far less stir the soul, of a black worker-woman descended from slaves.

As she struggled to find more words to say—the right words, if they existed—Winsome turned away.

'I fetch something to bang this net back up,' she said, briskly. 'Otherwise you get pinched bad tonight by mosquitoes. Ain't no locked door keeps *them* from gettin' in and they don't care what colour skin they bite.'

During morning lessons the sun shone hard on the

back of Hazel's head as she got to grips with a very long list of 'Bs'.

BALLS AND DANCES: *the floor of the ballroom should be polished with beeswax and then rubbed over with French chalk;*

BEVERAGES: *sherry with soup, hock with fish, burgundy, claret, champagne or port with dessert;*

BOOTS: *when visiting a private house, soiled boots and shoes should not be put outside the door at night but placed near the door inside the room.*

By the time she got to 'bread'—when to break rather than cut it, and how never to bite a roll—she was struggling.

'This room's too hot,' she complained. 'I need some air. We could take a picnic, couldn't we, up into the forest. I could make a start on my landscape.'

Miss Amelia was feeling fragile again, so had nothing against the idea of venturing back to the clearing where she could snooze, undisturbed, on that nice flat rock. This time, she decided, she would take a proper cushion for her head and maybe a tot of rum to have with her cup of tea.

'Any messages this morning?' she remembered to ask.

'No,' Hazel replied.

It wasn't easy, getting out of the house and away. The picnic wasn't a problem—a basket was very soon packed with sandwiches, cake, and a bottle of tea—but when her grandmother heard that they were off on a jaunt she surprised them by throwing a sulk.

'Stay here and have luncheon with me,' she wheedled, as they stepped on to the veranda, ready to go. 'Giddy has gone into town for the post so, as you can see, I am all by

281

myself, twiddling my thumbs. We can have a jolly meal, all three of us, and then Hazel can go and draw something in the garden while you and I, Miss Fritillary, have a nice little chat and a game of whist. How about that?'

Hazel held her breath. It was relatively cool on the veranda, and there was a long wicker chair set out so that a person could lie down and doze contentedly in the shade—all afternoon if she wanted to.

Miss Amelia looked at that chair and hesitated. It would be more comfortable than her rock and a heck of a lot easier to reach. Then she looked at the old woman sitting next to it, boredom and loneliness written all over her face, and realized that if she stayed she would be expected to entertain this person, with no chance of a doze this side of bedtime.

'I'm sorry, Mrs Mull-Dare,' she said, briskly. 'But your grand-daughter and I must stick to our timetable. Book learning in the morning, light exercise in the afternoon. See you later. Toodle-oo.'

She moved fast today, and so did Hazel. And when they reached the clearing among the trees Hazel scanned the ridge, hoping for a sight of Tommy John—a grin, a wave, a flash of orange hair. He wasn't there, but she wasn't unduly worried. He and his mother would be waiting for her at their house, she was sure about that.

'Can I take my share of the picnic away with me?' she asked.

'Go on then.' Miss Amelia unbuckled her satchel. 'Borrow this,' she said. 'It will hold your lunch, as well as your sketchbook, and you can carry your tea in one of my jars.'

So saying, she lifted two large specimen jars from the satchel, unscrewed the one that was empty and half filled it with milky tea. 'It's perfectly clean to drink from,' she said. 'You won't need a cup.'

Hazel was staring at the other jar.

*No.* Had Miss Amelia been *piddling* in it? Disgust puckered her face.

'Preserving fluid,' Miss Amelia fibbed, raising and swirling the jar so that its contents sloshed, pale gold in the light. 'For that little black lizard—when I catch him.'

'I see.' Hazel shouldered the satchel, then picked up the jar of tea by its string handle. 'Right then,' she said. 'I'll see you later.'

Miss Amelia grunted and waved her away. She was arranging her cushion on the flat rock, looking forward to her snooze and to a lovely splash of rum in her tea. And should the lizard reappear she would get him this time—get him and keep him and look him up in her books. He might be unique. He might be rare. He might even be *undiscovered* and if so she would have the honour and the privilege of naming him. That was certainly something to pin a hope on . . . something to take her mind off those eerie messages and the memories that came at her after dark.

Humming bravely, she poured herself a cup of tea, added a splash of rum from her specimen jar, took a sip and shuddered.

*Lovely. Just the ticket.*

Behind her, something rustled—the lizard perhaps? She took another sip of tea and waited.

Nothing.

Very slowly, she turned round.

No sight of it.

Oh, well . . .

'No getting sandwich grease on your sketchbook, dear heart!' she called up through the trees. 'And remember the laws of perspective!'

Hazel was already on the cliff path, hurrying from tree to tree as quickly as she dared with the satchel bumping and the jar of tea swinging, and her heart leaping with the same strange joy she had felt while swimming in the sea.

'ALL RIGHT!' she hollered back. 'DON'T WORRY!'

She hoped Tommy John and his mother had heard the shouts and would come out to greet her. More than anything, she wanted this child and this woman to see her as a sweet person. It hadn't mattered so much yesterday, but it did now.

*You guilty by blood, girl. It passed down . . .*

The message had made her feel bad, and so had the things Winsome had said. Bad about her rat-scally ancestor, bad about her grandparents and bad about herself. But she wasn't a horrible person; she knew she wasn't. Ignorant, perhaps, but not horrible. Tommy John had told her, yesterday, that his mother would be happy to meet her. 'Glad to pass a bit of the day with you,' that's what he had said.

Well, she would show these people that being white and a Moulder did not make her a tyrant, like the slave-owning Moulders of old. She would be gracious and friendly and treat them like equals. They were going to *love* her.

Meanwhile, back in the clearing, Miss Amelia lay fast asleep on her rock, her net close by and her discarded specimen jar attracting all kinds of insects to the one or two drops of alcohol left inside.

When a branch quivered, above her head, it triggered a dream . . . a strange, yearning dream . . .

*She sleeping like a long ugly baby*, thought Tommy John, peering down. *She sleeping sounder than the dead sailor boy buried beneath that stone she on.*

He shook the branch again, then pursed his lips and whistled. Not too loud—no louder, anyway, than the thrash of a lizard, or any noise he might make stealing into the clearing.

Miss Amelia did not stir.

Satisfied, Tommy John slid down from between the branches and began, slowly, to creep towards her.

# CHAPTER 27

C ould that really and truly be where they lived? That shed-like structure with the tin roof that she had taken, yesterday, for a barn? Hazel bit her lower lip. It had to be, for there was nowhere else.

The goat raised its head as she approached the door.

*Where do you live then?* Hazel wondered. *Don't you have a shelter?*

The door was so flimsy it was barely worth having. It was a good job, Hazel thought, that it never got freezing cold in this part of the world, but what about burglars? A burglar could break in here as easy as pie.

'Hello?' she called softly. 'Tommy John? Hello?'

No answer.

She pushed at the door with the flat of one hand, and it opened.

'Hello? Is anybody at home?'

No hallway, of course, and no steps either—just straight into a dim, square space with nothing but the ground for a carpet and the underside of the roof making do as a ceiling. A table and three chairs . . . a peculiar-looking stove . . . a few shelves for pots and pans . . . that was all that Hazel could make out as her eyes adjusted.

'Hello?' she called again.

Leaving the door wide open, to let in some light, she took one . . . two . . . paces into the room and examined its contents more closely. The smallest chair was probably Tommy John's. It had been painted bright blue but the seat had flaked, revealing splinters of pale wood. The biggest chair had solid arms and looked as if it might rock. Was that the father's? Tommy John hadn't mentioned his daddy. The third chair had a cushion on it—flame-red with yellow stitching—and a cotton shawl flung over its slatted back.

Hazel felt like Goldilocks as she hovered there, alone, but she didn't sit down for that would not have been polite. The floor of hard, red earth was beautifully clean but so *odd*. What if the roof were to leak? Surely the rain would sink into the soil and make it all slippy—a carpet of mud.

There was another room off this one, screened by a curtain. It . . .

'Hey? HEY? Who's in there? What you doin' snoopin' around my place?'

With a jolt and a gasp, Hazel swung round. A man . . . a big, black-skinned man was lumbering towards the house, anger in his face and something—oh goodness, a weapon—raised above his head.

Terrified, Hazel's first instinct was to hide . . . to dive under the table or behind the stove . . . anything rather than run . . . be chased . . .

*But if I stay I will be trapped!*

The man was far enough away, still, for her to reach the slope ahead of him, but close enough to catch her if he tried. He was peering intently, as he ran, shading his

287

eyes to see better, the sun striking the machete in his other hand. He couldn't tell, yet, who it was across the threshold—some harmless intruder or a thief with a weapon of his own—but Hazel wasn't to know that as, with a thin and helpless wail, she made a dash out into the open.

Past the goat she ran . . . along the side of the house . . . tripping, almost falling . . . not daring to look back. She had ditched the jar of tea—dropped it on the floor when she heard the man yell—but Miss Amelia's satchel was bumping against her spine, adding to the trouble she was having with the length of her skirt and the weight of her boots and the sheer, blind terror of knowing she could be caught, and felled, at any moment.

On she stumbled, gasps and sobs catching in her throat, and only when she reached the top of the slope did she dare to look back—one quick glance, before braving the path, just to see how close she was to being captured and hurt.

*If he's right behind me I'll jump*, she thought, wildly. *I'll jump off the cliff and into the sea rather than let him get me*.

But the man was nowhere near. He wasn't even following. He was standing by the house, at the bottom of the slope; just standing there watching her flee. He could have brandished the machete, to frighten her some more, or shouted an apology for having scared her in the first place but he did neither of those things; Hazel had no intention of waiting in case he had yet to decide.

Her hands, and her knees, were trembling as she moved out of his sight and on to the path. She wanted to hurry, to start running again, but that would have been lunacy for then she would have fallen for certain and the sea would have gulped her down.

*One step at a time . . . one step at a time . . .*

It helped to keep a chant going, in her head, as she clutched each tree in turn and pigeon-stepped closer to safety. He could still catch her. Even if she reached the clearing, where Miss Amelia was, he could still catch up and hurt both of them, if he wanted to.

*One step at a . . .*

She was so busy watching her feet that she didn't notice Tommy John; didn't see him coming towards her until they almost collided—would have collided if he hadn't spotted her first.

'Hey, Moulder girl.' He spoke softly, so as not to startle her so close to the edge of the cliff.

'Oh . . . ' Straight away she was glad to see him. Clinging tight to the nearest tree, she babbled out what had just happened to her—the man, the blade, the terror . . .

Tommy John shrugged. 'You just met Zebenjo,' he told her. 'He a good man—just guarding his place, I reckon. He wouldn't have done you no harm. You thieve anything from us?'

'Of course not!'

'Why you go into our place then, and not wait on the porch like manners say?'

Hazel glared at him.

'What porch?' she snapped. 'There was no porch.'

He shook his head, solemnly. 'There's a porch,' he said. 'You just missed seein' it, that's all. You want to come back there now? Say hello-and-sorry to Zebenjo?'

'No,' Hazel told him, indignantly. 'I don't.'

'My mumma back soon. She be sweet to you, make up for the fright.'

'No,' Hazel repeated, as strictly as she could. 'I haven't got time now. I've got a drawing to do. And what's that you're eating?'

Tommy John looked down, surprise on his face as if he had clean forgotten about the thing in his hand.

Then: 'Sand-witch,' he said, holding it up. 'A good one.'

The bread was white, shaped like a triangle, with the crusts cut off. Between the two pieces, Hazel knew, was fish paste and some very thin slices of what passed on this island for cucumber.

'Did Miss Amelia give you that?' she said. 'My teacher? The loud lady?'

'No,' he replied. 'I thieved it.'

And as Hazel gaped, lost for words, he took a huge bite.

'Miss Amelia,' she managed to say then. 'Did she see you? Did she wake up?'

'Nah,' he replied, through his big mouthful of food. 'She dead to this world, that one; flat out and sleepin' with the jumbies.'

'Well . . .' She felt she ought to scold him; order him back to the clearing, to confess and make amends, but his honesty had disarmed her, he'd been so matter-of-fact. And anyway, it was only a sandwich . . . nothing precious.

'I need to get past you,' she said. 'How are we going to do that?'

Tommy John rubbed his buttery fingers on the sides of his trousers.

'I turn round and go your way,' he said. 'Pass a bit of time with you while you draw something. You got paper? You got the kind of pencil that draws thick-dark or almost nothing, depending how you press?'

He was moving away. Hazel hesitated, looking back the way she had come.

'Zebenjo won't show up,' Tommy John called back. 'That man want to raise Hell with you he be here by now.'

Adjusting the satchel, Hazel reached for the next tree trunk and took one step after another until she caught up with Tommy John at the place where the path curved inland, away from the edge of the cliff. There was a flat, shrubby bit of ground here, before the forest began—a good place to stop and sit down if she was going to get any drawing done before Miss Amelia woke up.

'Here will do,' she said, lifting the satchel off her back and reaching into it for her sketchbook.

Tommy John craned to look. 'You got sand-witches in there,' he observed. 'And *cake*.'

'Help yourself,' Hazel told him, flipping open the sketchbook and sitting herself down. 'I don't want any. That man, that Zeb-whatever-he's-called, made me lose my appetite. Is he your father?'

'Nope,' Tommy John replied, his mouth full of Victoria sponge. 'He just Zebenjo. He look after me and my mumma. People get mean with me—throw stones or call names—he give them Hell all right.'

With the cake in his right hand and a sandwich in the other he plonked himself down on the seat of his trousers and squidged and shuffled forward, until his little body was companionably close to Hazel's side and the shock of his hair cast a shadow on her book.

'What you drawing, Moulder girl? You making it up or what?'

'I don't know,' Hazel told him. 'You're blocking my light. But . . . hang on, don't move away. I tell you what, Tommy John, sit very very still, right where you are, and I'll draw you.'

Immediately the shadow of Tommy John's head stopped wavering on the page. His mouth froze mid-chew and the hand, with the cake in it, fell stiffly to his side.

Hazel began to draw, sketching lightly around the shape on the page that was Tommy John's chin.

'Who's mean to you?' she asked him, after a few moments' silence. 'Other children?'

'Yuh,' he grunted, keeping his jaw as still as possible. 'And grown ones.'

'Because of your hair?' Hazel said.

'Yuh.'

Hazel stopped drawing and held the sketchbook out at arm's length.

'OK for me to swallow now?'

'Oh . . . yes, of *course*. Then you'll need to sit opposite me while I do your eyes, nose, and mouth. And it's all right, by the way, for you to talk while I draw.'

'And to eat stuff?'

'And to eat stuff, yes.'

They shuffled round and Hazel began to do the eyes. They were amber, she noticed, not black as she'd supposed. Gently and carefully she began to shade the curve of the eyelids.

Tommy John was asking about England.

'Is it cold?'

'It can be, in the winter. It's autumn there now so the days will be getting shorter. Soon the leaves on the trees will turn orangey-red . . . '

'Like our hair.'

'Well, yes. And . . . and then we might get snow.'

Snow.

Tommy John had heard about snow. It was like sugar, he said—white sugar, not brown—falling out of the sky in great big dots; so many dots that they piled up in the streets, and in all the English fields with pigs in them, until the streets and the fields and the pigs all disappeared under the whiteness and the cold.

Hazel had stopped listening to him.

*Our* hair?

Her own hair was in two plaits, the ends like paintbrushes tickling the sketchbook. She hadn't considered, up until now, how precisely the colour of it matched the marmalade-orange springiness on Tommy John's head.

'I go to England one day,' Tommy John was saying. 'With you maybe. I glad to know you, Moulder girl. Missis Louise say to keep away while you staying at the big house. She threaten me bad with this thing and that. She ashamed, my mumma says. She want to keep me a secret. Massa Giddy, too—he want to keep me secret most of all.'

'Why?'

She didn't stop drawing—the hand holding the pencil kept on moving—but her skin went to goosebumps, all down her neck and arms, and her empty stomach gurgled with the beginnings of alarm.

Tommy John had no trouble answering the question. He didn't even pause. And had Hazel found the nerve to look him in the face she would have recognized the expression on it—the quiet, wide-eyed candour of a child who never lies.

'We linked by blood,' he said, happily. 'You, me, and Massa Giddy. We're *family*.'

# CHAPTER 28

Rain. Torrents of it. Hitting the veranda roof like fists and drowning most of Louise Mull-Dare's roses. For some reason Hazel hadn't expected to see rain in the Caribbean—at least not the bucketing down kind that showed no signs of stopping.

Her grandfather was pacing the veranda, scowling out across his land through a curtain of falling water. He was fretting about the cane; predicting floods, rot, and other disasters. A bit of a sprinkling was essential, he told Hazel. Short regular cloudbursts led to decent crops—but not a godforsaken deluge. This kind of a downpour was sent to plague him, particularly as it was so often a sign of even worse weather to come.

'A hurricane,' he said, miserably. 'There's a hurricane on its way. I can sense the blighter getting ready to knock the stuffing out of us.'

'Put some trousers on, Giddy,' said Hazel's grandmother.

But Gideon Mull-Dare continued to glare at the sky, his face pugnacious, his fists clenching and unclenching as if he would punch and hit those big black clouds, if he could, just to show them who was boss down here and how angry he was they were over his plantation, messing things up.

295

Hazel considered his back view; hating it, hating all of him.

*How can my grandmother stand it?* she wondered. *Knowing that he's been sowing wild oats? Knowing that he fathered Tommy John? How can she bear to stay married to him? How?*

'Are you all right, dear?' her grandmother asked her. 'Don't listen to your grandfather. It's been years since a hurricane hit this island.'

Giddy Mull-Dare turned and scowled. 'Then we're due for another one, aren't we, you stupid old woman!'

*I want to go home*, Hazel silently cried. *I want to go back to England. Now. Immediately.*

Last night, as if she hadn't been given enough to fret over, her grandmother had given her two letters, one from her mother and one from her aunt Alison. Both said the same thing, more or less: that the house in London—her home, the place she had grown up in—was going to have to be sold, to pay off her father's debts.

*'I am so glad you are away from all the trubble and nuisense ,'* her mother wrote, *'and I hope you are happy and that your new teacher is not too strict .'*

*'I trust you are being good and applying yourself to your lessons,'* her aunt wrote, *'for it is more important than ever, now, that you marry up one day.'*

Her father, they both informed her, was in Scotland convalescing. Her aunt, who was with him, had no more to say about that than her mother, who had remained in

London with the dogs. He sent his fondest love, was all either of them said, and would write to her very soon.

She had read both letters twice over. How formal they seemed, in their different ways, and how carefully both women had chosen their words. 'Trubble and nuisense'? Even misspelt it was an understatement.

*Where will we end up living?* Hazel had wondered, laying both letters down in the light of her bedroom lamp, as if other, better, words, penned in invisible ink, might suddenly appear and tell her more. *And what will happen to Florence, and to Cook and Mrs Sawyer?*

She'd known she ought to reply at once but hadn't had the heart. And as she lay beneath her net, hearing the insects sing, the Kensington house, and everyone in it, had seemed so very far away that they might have existed in an earlier century, or on a different planet.

Now though, with the rain pelting down, and her grandmother fussing, and the very sight of her grandfather turning her stomach, she found that she longed, suddenly, for London, and, surprisingly, for her mother.

'You're not feeling poorly are you, dear? Don't drink that coffee, if you are. I'll get Winsome to mix you a tonic. Something fizzy to settle your tum.'

'No, I'm fine. Really. Only, I think I'd better go indoors now. Miss Amelia will be waiting for me.'

CALLS: *there are a great many occasions when calls should be paid. There are calls of congratulation, condolence, and courtesy. The hours of calling are between 3 and 6 p.m.*
CALLING: *when callers rise to take their leave the lady of the house rings the bell that the servant may be at hand to open the*

*outer door. If the gentleman of the house be present he escorts the lady to the hall door and sees her into her carriage.*

'It's stopped—look, the sun's coming out. Good bananas! We'll give it another hour. Have luncheon here, if we must. Then, if there are no floods, we'll have our constitutional. We can take an umbrella, in case of more rain. Now, where were we? "Carving", that's the ticket. *"When it is done at table the host usually carves and he must learn to do so adroitly."* Did you get that, Miss Mull-Dare? Pay attention, dear. The sooner we're through all the "Cs" the sooner we can head for the hills.'

There were no floods—at least none that Hazel could see from the veranda—and the sky was so blue again that had it not been for the dripping trees and the intense after-rain scent of a certain white flower you would never have known it had rained for so long.

'If I'm lucky,' twittered Miss Amelia, as they set off down the drive, 'I'll catch the cheeky specimen that stole my sandwich yesterday. What's the betting it was a mongoose? Or some kind of native squirrel? Um . . . any messages?'

'No,' said Hazel.

'Good bananas. Maybe they've stopped.'

'Maybe,' Hazel agreed.

It was hard-going, reaching the clearing, for the stones underfoot were slippery from the morning's downpour and every branch they grabbed tipped a shower on their hats. Hazel wondered about the floor of Tommy John's house, and hoped it had not turned to mire. She had made no promises about going back there today, allowing him to believe that she was scared of

Zebenjo. Because of the rain, he might not be expecting her anyway.

*If the cliff path is passable I'll go*, she decided. *If it's not I won't.*

The cliff path was fine.

*'There are a great many occasions when calls should be paid.'* This is a call of courtesy, Hazel told herself, treading carefully down the slope. And of condolence, I suppose. This time, she could tell, there was somebody at home. Smoke was rising from a tin pipe sticking, like a broken elbow, out of the roof and there was more washing laid out on the shrubs, dripping heavily, and steaming in the sun, as if it had only just been put out.

Approaching the door she noticed a few planks of wood, set flat on the ground, and the way the roof projected over them, providing a lozenge of shade.

The porch.

The door was open, but she knocked anyway, being mindful, this time, of her manners. Inside: the smell of cooking; a rich, spicy aroma that made her mouth water.

'It's me. Hazel Louise Mull-Dare,' she said, when Tommy John's mother finally appeared, wiping her hands on an apron and looking less than pleased. 'I thought . . . I hoped . . . Just say if you're busy and I'll go.'

'Tommy John not here,' the woman said. She sounded strange, as if that wasn't what she had intended, or wanted, to say to Hazel at all. And she was staring in a hard and peculiar way, as if the freckles on Hazel's nose, and the green of her eyes, were things she might easily spit upon, but then just as tenderly wipe.

'Tommy John away in the forest someplace,' she added. 'Looking for you, I guess.'

Hazel shuffled her boots, glanced away for a moment and then looked back. This was trickier than she had expected, with this woman appraising her so oddly . . . not inviting her in but not sending her packing either.

Then: 'Wait now,' the woman said, before turning and going back into the house.

Hazel waited. Behind her, the goat began to bleat although, when she spun round, there was nothing that could have startled it. No storm cloud. No jumby. No one heading their way with a raised machete.

'What's the matter with your goat?' she asked when Tommy John's mother reappeared with a chair—the small one, painted blue.

'Nothing—or it sniff the goat I got cooking, maybe, and get spooked. Here—sit.'

Obediently, Hazel sat upon the blue chair. It was too small for her and she hoped she wouldn't break it. There were chairs out here already—rickety contraptions that could have been flung against the house by the last hurricane for all the use they looked. Tommy John's mother hauled one of these across for herself.

'It smells very good, your dinner,' Hazel said, politely. 'We don't eat goat in England—at least, I never have. We don't eat a lot of meat at all. My mother's a vegetarian, which means she won't have anything on her plate that once had a face.'

Tommy John's mother had positioned her chair next to the blue one, so they were sitting side by side, looking out across the goat, and the washing, and the shrubs to where the hills and the trees rose up and away before plummeting down to the sugar fields.

'What's your name?' Hazel asked, after a while.

'You get to call me Abi.'

'That's pretty. Is it short for Abigail?'

The pause, although short, was enough to make Hazel uncomfortable. *I only asked about her name*, she fretted to herself. *What's wrong with that?*

'Abidemi,' came the eventual reply. 'Ah-bee-deh-mee.'

Hazel wanted to repeat it, to taste the sound on her tongue, but something told her that this would not be acceptable, here on this borrowed chair, in this small rectangle of shade, on land that may or may not have been owned by the Mull-Dares but upon which she felt she had no right to be.

'I was christened Hazel because my mother is called Ivy,' she said, to cover her discomfort. 'It was my father's idea, to carry the plant names on. He can be terribly sentimental sometimes.'

'Can he now,' said Abi. 'That's lucky for you, I guess.'

They were on awkward territory, Hazel realized, talking about fathers. And although she longed to tell this woman that she knew—about her grandfather being Tommy John's father—good manners prevented her from saying anything outright until they were better acquainted.

'Tommy John is a dear little boy,' she said, instead. 'I like him a lot.'

Abi's chair creaked beneath her, as if she had winced or made some gesture.

'Tommy John a clever child,' she said. 'Doing well at

school. Reading and writing. Wants to be a teacher someday.'

'That's good,' Hazel said. 'I'm sure he'll make a wonderful teacher.' It surprised her to hear that Tommy John went to school, but to say so, she knew, would sound terribly rude—as if she'd seen him as some kind of simpleton, roaming the forest until he was big enough to cut cane. In a way, that was precisely how she *had* seen him. It was a salutary lesson, learning otherwise, and she felt it humbly enough.

'Where is his school?' she asked. 'And shouldn't he be there now?'

Beside her Abi shook her head and sighed.

'His school away in the town,' she said. 'But he stop going for a while. Things not right for him there. He pulled all kinds of ways.'

'Because of—the way he looks?'

'That, mostly. You want some water to drink?'

Hazel turned her chair to a more companionable angle.

'No thank you,' she said. And then, because Abi suddenly smiled at her—a rueful but genuine smile—she carried on, in a big rush: 'I know about Tommy John. He told me. I should have guessed, really, because of his hair only . . . Well, I know now and I just think that my family . . . my grandfather . . . should be taking more responsibility for him. Buying him things, I mean. Making sure you and he have somewhere proper to live. Somewhere with a decent roof and more bedrooms. In town maybe, closer to Tommy John's school . . . '

Her voice was starting to shake.

'I'm sorry,' she said. 'It's come as a shock, that's all. I really am truly sorry—for you and for Tommy John.'

Abi sat up straighter in the rickety cane chair.

'What for you sorry?' she said quietly. 'Because we niggers? Because you got black sheep in your fold?'

'No!' Hazel felt as if she'd been slapped. 'That's not it at all . . . no . . . And anyway . . . ' She had been about to say, 'You're not black, you're more of a toffee-brown,' but realized in time that that was as ridiculous and by-the-by as saying, 'You're not white, you're freckled.'

'Damn it to hell, girl . . . you think your family be any different towards us—towards me—if Tommy John born paler? You think that make everything all right with them?'

Hazel's head was starting to whirl. She wasn't used to such anger, nor to the complicated feelings that were making it so difficult for her to answer truly.

'For him it might have done,' she blurted out. 'For Tommy John. Everything might have been easier for him if he only looked . . . '

'Hah!' Abi slapped one hand against the arm of her chair. 'Go on! Say the word, Miss Hazel Louise Mull-Dare. Say it!'

' . . . normal.'

There was silence then; a long, cool silence which Hazel did not know how to break.

Then: 'Don't you worry none about my Tommy John,' Abi muttered, almost to herself. 'Nor me neither. You and your gran-daddy want us to go and live in town, where you can't see us, that's your affair, but we just fine where we are, I reckon. You can go now. Visiting over.'

Shakily, Hazel rose to her feet. The goat lifted its head, its eyes baleful.

'I didn't mean to offend you,' Hazel said, in a final attempt to bridge the gap. 'It just seems to me that my grandfather should be doing more to help. That you have a right to it.'

Abi shrugged. 'Your gran-daddy just a sad old waste of skin,' she said, her voice slow and sour, 'and he don't owe us nothing.'

*She has never cared about my grandfather*, Hazel realized, backing away from the house. *She didn't love him and she can't have wanted to have a baby with him. Which means . . .*

'I should never have come here,' she said, raising her voice as she moved further and further away. 'It wasn't a good idea.'

'You said it, girl. You said it . . . '

The sky began clouding over as Hazel returned to the forest. More bad weather was coming, from over the sea. Hazel didn't care. Let it pour. Let it rain cats and dogs— rats and mongooses even. Let it soak her right through to her freckly white skin and give her a chill to last until Christmas.

She had tried to be kind back there—done her best to be friendly and polite—but what she had said had got all twisted up somehow. Her thoughts and feelings had come out all wrong—or been heard wrong, as if she and Abi had been speaking languages as different as their backgrounds and the colour of their skins. Could she blame Abi for rejecting her so bitterly? Not really, she supposed. Could she blame her grandfather?

Absolutely.

Stomping into the forest she began calling down to Miss Amelia.

'It's me! I'm back! Wake up!'

Her voice, she knew, sounded mean. But that was how she felt and Miss Amelia was going to have to bear the brunt of it—at least until they got back to the house.

'Wake up and let's go,' she yelled, stumbling and sliding down the path that led into the clearing; not caring if she scraped her boots or got mud on her skirt. Behind her, but still a good way out to sea: a rumble of thunder like a jumby's cough.

'I *said* . . . OH!'

Miss Amelia wasn't asleep. She wasn't even lying down. She was sitting bolt upright, clutching her specimen net, like a giant crucifix, to the front of her candy-striped blouse. And she was moaning—keening softly as she stared, wild-eyed, into the trees.

*'Whatever is it? What's the matter?'*

Slipping and sliding the last few feet into the clearing, Hazel ran to her teacher and touched her, lightly, on the shoulder.

'Miss Amelia? Has something bitten you? Talk to me.'

In growing alarm, she grasped the woman's shoulder and shook it.

The sound Miss Amelia made in her throat could have meant 'Yes—a snake,' or 'No, stop badgering me.' But something had clearly hurt her. Or scared her. Or both. And she had been drinking alcohol. Hazel could smell it on her breath.

'You have to stand up now,' she said, impatient for some response. 'We have to go. The weather's changing.'

At that, Miss Amelia snapped out of her trance.

'I saw him,' she hissed, wetting Hazel's face with rum-flavoured spittle. 'Leering at me through those trees. I swear, I woke up and I saw him.'

So she had slept after all, there on the damp slab of rock.

'Saw who?' said Hazel, tetchily.

Miss Amelia grabbed her sleeve, clinging tightly like a child being sent to a cellar.

'*Tommy John.*'

Hazel didn't want to talk about Tommy John. It was none of Miss Amelia's business. And how typical of this woman, she thought, to be so repulsed by a child with black skin and orange hair. It was pathetic. It was contemptible.

'Well, he's nowhere around here now,' she said, pulling away, 'or I would have seen him myself.'

Miss Amelia moaned, softly, and shook her head. 'He was singing an old sea shanty,' she insisted. ' "*Farewell and adieu to you, Spanish ladies . . . farewell and adieu to you, ladies of Spain . . .*" ' Her voice was quavery and out of tune. A drunk's slur. 'Just a glimpse of him I caught, before he disappeared . . . melted away, like they do. But I'm sure it was him . . . I'm certain . . . taunting me with his song.'

'Perhaps it was a dream,' Hazel told her. 'People imagine all kinds of things, don't they, when they're only half awake. And anyway, there's no need—*listen*!' She paused and turned her head towards the east. 'That's the thunder getting closer,' she said. 'We need to hurry. Where's the umbrella?'

For a moment she thought Miss Amelia was going to retch. Miss Amelia thought so too, and suffered a

moment's struggle. Then, not daring to look . . . only raising a trembling finger to point . . . she finally found her
voice: 'I hung it over there . . . from the branch of a tree.'

'Well, it's not there now. It's gone.'

'*Oh no, oh no* . . . ' Miss Amelia closed her eyes, her face
turning as grey as an old washcloth. 'Maybe it fell,' she
whispered, hopefully. 'Maybe the wind took it, although
it was furled, definitely furled . . . Maybe I'm mistaken
and I propped it behind my rock . . . ' Leaping to her feet,
she began swiping foliage aside with her net, searching
the ground . . . all around the rock . . . under the nearest
trees. '*Oh no, oh no, oh no* . . . '

She looked demented as she searched—demented and
genuinely terrified. Hazel didn't know what to say. It was
obvious to her that Tommy John had helped himself to
the umbrella, just like he'd helped himself to Miss
Amelia's lunch the day before. But there was no need,
surely, for hysterics. It was only a stupid umbrella.

'Please stop,' she begged. 'You'll tear your net. We'll
manage without an umbrella, even if it rains. It doesn't
matter.'

'Oh, but it does . . . it does . . . '

Miss Amelia was prodding the rim of her net beneath
and around the stone slab, just in case the furled umbrella
had rolled underneath. 'He's taken it,' she moaned. 'My
umbrella, of all things! It's a sign, Miss Mull-Dare. A clear
and terrible sign. That nasty little chancer . . . he's stalk-
ing me. He is! He is! He followed me here and he means
to get me. To stab me in the back with my own umbrella.
I know he does, I know . . . '

'Stop it! How can you even think such horrible things?'

307

The first drops of rain were falling now; fat splashes hitting the ground and bouncing off Miss Amelia's stone slab.

'If you don't come straight away,' Hazel continued, feeling each splash, like a nip through her blouse, 'I will write to my aunt Alison. I will tell her you drink rum all afternoon, instead of teaching me, and that it's giving you wild fancies. I mean it, Miss Gumm. I really do.'

That shocked the old Whiney. That gave her food for thought. Had she continued to prod, and tear vines away from her slab she would have spotted a date carved into the stone—1785—and the name of the sailor whose bones she had been sleeping over. But she stopped just short, shouldered her net, and moved away.

'Your sketchbook,' she mumbled, reaching for her satchel . . . 'where is it?' Her voice sounded odd, straining towards its usual briskness.

'I left it behind,' Hazel told her. She meant at Tommy John's house, beside his blue chair, but wasn't going to be specific unless asked straight out.

'Just as well,' said Miss Amelia, as the rain came faster, drenching their clothes and battering their hats. 'Or it would have been bad bananas for your landscape. How's it coming along by the way . . . ?'

And as they left the clearing for the relative shelter of the downward path, she swung her net at the rain—a dripping, leaping, unhinged woman, making out she could capture thin air if she wanted to . . . thin air and whatever it harboured.

Meanwhile, across the forest, along the path, and down the slope, Tommy John propped his unfinished portrait up against his dinner bowl and beamed.

'She a good drawer,' he said, against the drumming of rain on the tin of the roof. 'She got me about right, I reckon. I miss seeing her today. She come tomorrow, you think?'

Abidemi looked at Zebenjo and shook her head in gentle warning. *Don't say nothing to this boy. About her being here earlier and treating me cold. He'll discover soon enough that she's as bad as all the rest.*

From a hook above the stove Miss Amelia's umbrella dangled and dripped. Tommy John had taken that all right. Caught and questioned he would have owned up straight away and given it back. *Easy come-to-me, easy go.*

But the long one hadn't stirred; not when he'd lifted his find from the tree, nor as he'd tippy-toed away. Dead to the world she had been again, above the bones of Nelson's sailor.

And the singing?

Tommy John liked to sing. At school he sang 'Jerusalem' and 'God Save Our King' louder than anyone. Not sea shanties though—too vulgar, his teacher would have said.

He had never even heard of 'Spanish Ladies'.

# CHAPTER 29

I'm sorry if I offended you last time. I didn't mean to. I offended somebody else today — Tommy John's mother — and that wasn't deliberate either.

I know about Tommy John. I have met him and been to his house and I know that my grandfather is his father. This makes Tommy John my uncle, doesn't it, which feels very peculiar. (But not because he is black. It wouldn't matter to me if he was striped like a zebra or orange all over. I just want you to know that, in case you're about to take offence again.)

I intend to tackle my grandfather about what I have discovered. Tonight if I get a chance. It's really not the done thing for young ladies to discuss matters of a bodily nature but I cannot stand lies, or secrecy, and he has behaved shamefully in my opinion.

Once again, I apologize for annoying you. Can I say, though, that it wasn't strictly fair of you to suggest that I should carry the guilt for things that

happened a long time ago, before I was
even born.

I am bitterly ashamed that my ancestors
were slave owners. I would rather we had
never won this sugar plantation and
remained poor all down the generations,
and that is the honest truth.

It was almost time for supper. Miss Amelia was having
hers on a tray in her bedroom ('I feel a cold coming on,
dear heart, after that unexpected drenching') so it would
just be her and her grandparents sitting down to eat.

A bath and a hot lime-and-rum toddy had revitalized
Hazel, after her own unexpected drenching, and she was
ready to face her grandfather—to shame him with what
she knew.

*How do I say it, though? What are the words? It wasn't wild
oats. That makes it sound frivolous.*

From far away the memory came: Rascal chasing after
Dottie, pursuing her down the stairs, into the garden,
round and round the magnolia tree . . .

*My grandfather is like an animal*, she thought, heat rising
in her face. *Worse.*

Because of the rain, gusting now, across the veranda,
supper had been set in the dining room. Hazel, being
the first to arrive, sat down to wait for her grandparents.
It felt claustrophobic, being indoors to eat. Warm too,
despite the bad weather; as warm and as muggy as the
hothouse at Kew Gardens.

Unbidden, another memory slipped into her head:
Florence in her father's study, dusting under Isis, the

311

precious ebony goddess, and condemning 'doolally women' for destroying the orchids at Kew.

And as she sat there, all by herself, she suddenly understood the way those suffragettes had felt—the mixture of rage and helplessness that had driven them to do what they did. She hadn't grasped it before; not even in Madame Tussaud's when she was about to throw the acid at William Shakespeare. Back then, if she was honest, she had just wanted to please Gloria Gilbert.

Now though, as she prepared to confront her grandfather, she felt more than ready to smash a window, rip the throaty red flowers from the vase in front of her, or throw a toxic substance at the portraits on the wall (all Moulders, all white, all men) shouting 'Justice for Abi!' all the while.

It was exhilarating. It was scary. It made her feel part of something grander than just herself. Something women like Aunt Alison and Miss Amelia would never understand and *Cassell's Dictionary of Etiquette* had no words to describe.

Then her grandmother came in. Alone.

'Giddy's down in the fields,' she said, bustling across to her place at the table. 'The new shoots are waterlogged. He'll be there all night at this rate, trying to drain the furrows.'

Deflated, *cheated*, Hazel watched as her grandmother picked up a brass bell—a pretty thing from England, shaped like a girl in a crinoline—and shook it by the head. 'It's roast chicken tonight, after the soup,' she said. 'And just you and me to eat it. How about that? We can have a nice little chat, dear, just the two of us. I've been meaning to ask about your mother. Does she still breed racehounds?'

*Racehounds?*

With some effort Hazel fixed her thoughts upon her mother, and her mother's motley collection of mongrels and strays. Diggy Bert chased cars, but that was hardly in the same league as running a race, and Rascal's hot pursuits of poor Dottie certainly didn't count. And anyway, none of the dogs had been bred for their pedigree, not by her mother or by anyone else. Diggy, she knew, had been found in a dustbin, and Pipkin in a sack with two brothers and a sister already dead.

'My mother has *never* bred racehounds,' she said, 'so far as I know.' She smiled tentatively at Winsome who had come in to serve the soup. Winsome nodded back.

'But . . . according to your father she does—or did.'

*Then my father lied,* Hazel silently thought. *For whatever reason, he lied through his teeth.*

'Well . . . ' Clearly rattled, Hazel's grandmother shook out her napkin. 'That's rather a shame, for a good racing dog in England fetches a most respectable price. And Ivy's—your mother's—family. They are in the grocery trade, I understand. How is that doing? I trust they are exporting. How many shops do they own now, the Montague-Jacksons?'

'*An open mouth catch plenty flies,*' murmured Winsome, ladling clear soup into Hazel's dish.

'Thank you, Winsome,' Hazel's grandmother snapped. 'That will be all for now. I'll ring when we're ready for our chicken.'

Hazel had stopped gawping, but her face was bewildered.

'My mother doesn't have any family,' she said. 'She's

an orphan. There was a widowed cousin she used to visit—her cousin Cynthia—but she didn't own a shop, or anything else, and when she died father paid for her coffin.'

'I see.'

'I know the Montague-Jacksons sold cabbages and violets and things,' Hazel continued, 'but that was out in the streets. Mother's uncle wanted her to go out selling flowers but she became an artist's model instead. My mother was very beautiful, when she was young.'

'I see,' Louise Mull-Dare said again. 'Would you kindly pass me the bread?'

The chicken, when it arrived, was dry from being too long in the oven. Hazel ate it dutifully.

'Will the sugar crop be ruined?' she wondered.

Her grandmother was hacking at a drumstick. 'Oh, I'm sure your grandfather will save the day,' she replied, her tone as dry as her supper. 'And the rain's stopped, which is something, at least, to be grateful for.'

'And is it just grandfather down in the fields, trying to drain them?'

'Heavens no,' her grandmother said. 'It's all hands on deck at a time like this. They'll be working through the night I expect, every man jack of them.'

'And woman,' Hazel observed, quietly. 'And child.'

'Well, not the children,' her grandmother said, pushing the hacked-about chicken bone to the side of her plate. 'At least, not the smallies. They'd be more of a hindrance than a help.'

Hazel hadn't finished her food, but she set her knife and fork down anyway. Correctly. Politely. To show that she had had enough.

'I just hope Tommy John never ends up in our fields,' she said, 'slaving away in all weathers. He deserves better than that, don't you think?'

She hadn't intended for anyone but her grandmother to hear those choice words—couldn't have known that Winsome would pick that very moment to come in and clear the plates.

But Winsome kept her eyes lowered, stacked the plates and left.

Louise Mull-Dare sat in silence a moment or two longer. Then: 'So, you've met Tommy John,' she said. And to Hazel's immense surprise she didn't sound all that bothered, never mind ashamed.

'Yes,' she replied. 'I met him several days ago, in the forest.'

'Well,' her grandmother said. 'I suppose it was bound to happen. I warned Giddy it would. "Hazel and Miss Fritillary," I told him, "they go walking every afternoon— out of our gates and up into the hills. They'll bump into that little lad sooner or later and *then* the fat will be in the fire." If I told him once I told him a dozen times, and do you know what he said to me?'

'No,' Hazel replied. 'What?'

'He said "Lou-Lou, I'm starting to think that wouldn't be such a bad thing."'

Hazel blinked. This was not how she had expected the conversation to go.

'So—how much do you know?' her grandmother asked her. 'What did Tommy John tell you?'

'Everything,' Hazel said. 'I know everything. And I met Abi yesterday as well.'

Louise Mull-Dare took a very deep breath, then nodded as if this too was inevitable and all for the best.

'Well, you're being very calm about it, dear, is all I can say,' she said.

*No I'm not*, Hazel thought. *I'm just biding my time*.

'And Miss Fritillary?' her grandmother said, sounding dismayed for the very first time. 'Does she know about any of this? Is that why she's refusing to dine with us? I do hope she isn't too appalled. It would be a terrible shame if she left on the next boat.'

'She doesn't know anything,' Hazel told her. 'Not a thing.'

'Good. Let's try and keep it that way, shall we? These spinster teachers—they can be terribly prissy and unforgiving. And of course she cannot relate to the blacks on *any* level. They are totally foreign to her. I'm afraid she would see Giddy and me in a very poor light, even though what's done is done and we have simply tried to make the best of a bad job.'

Hazel's mouth was in danger of catching flies again.

*What's done is done? The best of a bad job?*

Her grandmother Mull-Dare, she decided, had to be saintly, stupid, or both. Or was she so completely dependent on her husband for everything from the roof over her head to a sense of who she was, that she was prepared to forgive him anything?

'When women have The Vote, Grandma,' she said, 'things will be very different.'

Louise Mull-Dare looked askance at her grand-daughter before reaching for the bell.

'Yes, well, that's as maybe,' she said. 'I think we'll have pudding now, shall we?'

She rang the bell abruptly, three sharp sounds.

'And in case you hadn't realized,' she added, quickly, 'your father has no idea that Abi and Tommy John exist. We thought it best, Giddy and I, to keep it from him. I know that may seem harsh to you, but we believed it to be for the best. Alison doesn't know either.' She smiled, ruefully. 'Had she done so, she would have thought twice, I'm sure, about sending you out to stay with us.'

She rang the bell again, impatiently.

'Whether you can keep our secret is something only you can decide,' she added. 'We'll discuss it further another time—with your grandfather, once his crisis in the fields has passed. All right?'

Hazel could only nod, as Winsome swept in with the sorbet.


What crazy notions you harbouring, girl?
The sun mess with your head or what?
Your gran-dadda done put you right by
now I reckon. Some shock to him you
hauling him over hot rocks with your big
accusations. Hah! His bodily nature go
all of a spin over that I do suspect.

He guilty of wickedness all right but
not the kind you thinking of. He's not the
father of Tommy John.

You never do a jig-saw when you a
smaller child? Never fit them odd-cut
pieces together to see the picture

whole? Your dadda and Miss Ally-son had
jig-saws. Big one of the world, with the
Queen of England's empire all coloured
pink. Lots of pink on that jig-saw I
recall; half the world that shade, like
the skin of a pig.

Seems like you been seeing things all
wrong, girl, fitting pieces together any
old how. And maybe it suit your gran-
dadda, still, for you to have bits missing from the whole sorry tale.

Tommy John's dadda ten times the worth
of any Moulder man. Just never got a
chance to prove it is all. When his child
born with hair orange like the midday sun
he feel it like some mighty blow to his
pride. He do his best but one day he go
off on his boat and he don't never come
back. Gone to some other island, folk
reckon. Fathered himself more pickneys,
perhaps, with black hair to pat and a
look that don't say 'white devil' to him
whenever he look in the crib.

Tommy John born easy—that why he an
easy-going child, maybe. His mumma's
birthing, though, a thing of complications.
Sad like no other sadness.

YOU ASK YOUR GRANDADDA ABOUT THAT. YOU
ASK THAT OLD MAN ABOUT THE NIGHT TOMMY
JOHN'S MOTHER GOT BORN AND THE LIFE THAT
WAS LOST IN THE BEARING OF HER.

There it is now. The piece you got
missing. The bit kept secret more than
thirty long years. A birthing woman bled to
death, right here in this house, because
your people wanted her gone. Gideon
Mull-Dare stand over her and watch her die,
while she call out for mercy and for the
doctor to come that had never even been
sent for. Then, when she call out no more,
your gran-dadda give her pickney to another
black woman to raise and he wash his hands
of the whole sorry business.

Abidemi.

That the name the mother give her new-
born baby girl with the last breath in
her mouth. And only reason that babe left
to live, I reckon, is she more black than
white. No orange hair, no specks on her
nose like the good-for-nothing Moulder who
helped himself to her mumma then disappeared for ever, across the sea to
England, to live in London town.

Ah-bee-deh-mee.

Meaning 'born during her father's
absence'.

There.

You get the whole picture now. You a
wiser girl.

# CHAPTER 30

Winsome opened the shutters quietly.

'Sun shining,' she said. 'But no birdsong today. No wild cats around the kitchen neither while Massa Giddy's bacon cookin'. They done head for the hills these past hours. Bad storm comin' our way.'

Hazel turned her wide-awake eyes from the light. They felt as if they had been open for ever. And the things they had seen, in the black of the night—the images that had formed as she thought of her father and what he had done—were still scalding them. 'Winsome,' she said, 'may I please ask you something?'

'You wantin' my permission first? This an upside-down day for sure . . . '

Hazel tried to smile but couldn't.

'What is it, child? This about Tommy John?'

Hazel nodded, then shook her head. 'Yes. No. Sort of . . . '

Winsome came across to the bed and began looping the mosquito net up and out of the way.

'Both me ears waitin',' she said. 'Though I'm thinking you know most of it. And what you don't know, it's Missis Louise and Massa Giddy should be doin' the telling.'

Hazel closed her eyes. She hadn't slept. The light was hurting. She thought she might cry.

'It's just one small thing,' she said. 'Nothing at all really. I just wondered . . . Abidemi's mother. Tommy John's grandmother. What was her name?'

The net trailed briefly across her face as Winsome adjusted it. Had she not known what it was she would have thought it was some ghostly thing—the brush of a wing, or a sleeve. Her eyes were still shut, deliberately so, as Winsome replied:

'Isis. You would have got to call her Isis.'

DEATH: *the coffin should be ordered without delay. It should be made of plain elm or oak and the handles should be of oxidized iron or brass. The expense of a grave depends on whether a vault has been made . . .*

'I've had enough of this nonsense.'

Hazel looked up, her pen poised.

'I beg your pardon?' she said.

'This!' Miss Amelia waved *Cassell's Dictionary of Etiquette* high above her head then slammed it down on the table, like a winning card. 'I can't bear to read another word. Not about death today, or escorts tomorrow, or forks and gloves and handshakes and handkerchiefs in the days and weeks to come. It's all nonsense, dear heart! Tedious biscuits and boring bananas. And anyway, I have more important things to do today. Other fish to fry.'

'Like what?' Hazel asked, thinking, *Rum. She's having it for breakfast now, poured on a mango or added to her coffee.*

'Like facing my demons, Miss Mull-Dare. No more running scared. No more cowering in my bed at night, afraid of my own shadow or the zizz of an insect. I am going back to the forest. Now. This very minute. *You* may do as you please.'

Hazel put down her pen. Her own demons were swarming, making learning the Ds impossible. Her father . . . She couldn't hate him for what he had done, or blame him for all that had followed. More than anything, it felt odd knowing everything while he knew nothing at all, as if she was the grown-up and he was the child. He didn't know that he had a grown-up daughter, living here on the island—Louise Mull-Dare had made that quite clear last night. Nor did he know about his grandson, Tommy John. He had been kept in the dark, all this time. For most of his life, if you counted back the years.

Long ago . . . It had all happened years and years ago; before Hazel was thought of; before her father had even met the red-haired girl who was to become his wife. If he had known about Abidemi, Hazel pondered to herself, he would surely have wanted to meet her, to spoil her like a little princess and see that she wanted for nothing. For he was a good man, really. A gentleman. Was Abidemi aware of that? Had anyone bothered to tell her? Or had *she* been kept in the dark as well?

'I'm coming too,' she said to Amelia Gumm. 'I'm coming with you to the forest.'

Only one person saw them go.

'Bad weather coming, ladies,' he said, looking up from his sweeping. 'A hurricane, I'm thinking.'

'Get back to work!' Miss Amelia hollered. 'Insolent nigger.'

Jeremiah shrugged.

'You hear the wind start to sing,' he said directly to Hazel. 'You come home fast. Never mind what she say.'

'Quiet!' Shaking her net, as if keeping a tiger at bay, Miss Amelia chivvied Hazel ahead of her, down the veranda steps.

'Not enough discipline in this household,' she muttered, her boots thudding down the steps, then mashing the gravel as she strode off down the drive. 'A darkie should speak only when spoken to in the presence of his superiors.'

Hazel threw her a look.

'Where exactly does it say that white people are superior beings?' she said. 'In the Bible? In *The Times*? In *Cassell's Dictionary of Etiquette*?'

Miss Amelia ignored her.

'A hurricane, my foot,' she scoffed. 'He was just trying to frighten us. Look at that sky! Not a cloud in sight and not a breath of air to be felt either.'

'It *is* very still,' Hazel agreed. 'Too still maybe. The calm before the storm.'

'Nonsense! Did you bring your sketchbook? No? Well, when we get to the clearing I suggest you make yourself scarce. Go for a walk. Find some leaves to press, or a big fat flower. I'm going to face that Tommy John. I saw him off once and I'll see him off again—straight back to Hell where he belongs.'

*Not if I warn him first*, Hazel thought to herself. *Which I've every intention of doing.*

For a while they walked in silence; a silence made eerie by the complete absence of birdsong and the peculiar stillness of the air. Then: 'Your blouse looks odd,'

Hazel said, as Miss Amelia led the way into the forest. 'I've only just noticed. Didn't you realize when you put it on this morning? The stripes have run, all down your back. It must have happened yesterday, in the rain.'

Miss Amelia said she didn't care tuppence about the stripes on her back; that all that mattered to her right now was showing that thieving chancer that she wasn't frightened of him any more. That she was ready to take him on.

Hazel thought anxiously about Tommy John. Would he be waiting today, hidden among the trees? There was so much she wanted to say to him. And to Abidemi. She wasn't sure where she was going to start. It was all still sinking in.

The last thing she needed right now, she thought, crossly, was Miss Amelia getting all hot under the collar about her stolen umbrella, and threatening all sorts.

'If Tommy John *is* there,' she said, 'let me talk to him first. I'm sure I can persuade him to give you your umbrella back, and then you must leave him alone. Live and let live.'

'Hah!' snorted Miss Amelia, thrashing aside a vine. 'Too late for that, I'd say.'

Hazel stopped walking.

'What . . . what do you mean "too late"?'

Appalled, she reached out for some support; clutched a tree and held it tight. 'Miss Amelia, *what have you done to Tommy John*?'

Miss Amelia swung round. 'Nothing,' she twittered. 'Not to worry!' But her throat was as pink as the stains on her blouse and she was blinking nineteen to the dozen.

'But you're talking as if . . . as if he was *dead*.'

Guilt, followed by confusion, followed by even more guilt, flickered in Miss Amelia's face as she blinked and blinked and blinked. Then 'Am I?' she said, carefully. 'Did *I* say he was dead or was it those messages? Surely it was the messages. I've never said anything to you about a Tommy John being dead . . . I'm quite certain I haven't. It was your messages that gave us that idea. Not me. Never me.'

Hazel shook her head.

*She's lying. She's confused about the messages, but it's more than that. She's covering up for something. I can tell.*

'Miss Amelia,' she said, her voice as clear as a bird's in the stillness of the forest, 'if you've done something— hurt someone . . . if . . . if it's weighing on your conscience then you really ought to confess. Telling the truth . . . it might make you feel better, in the long run.'

Amelia Gumm rested her net on the ground and leaned against it, exhausted, suddenly, by the weight of her conscience.

'All right,' she said. 'I confess. I killed him. He died.'

Hazel gasped and clung tighter to the tree. *Tommy John*, she wailed silently inside her head. *Little boy. My nephew.* 'Where,' she heard herself say, 'have you left him?'

'Oh, Eunice buried the body. Mucky old job. I couldn't face it. She'll have planted something on him by now. A buddleia perhaps. Attracts butterflies, the buddleia— great clouds of them. Red Admirals in particular. And Tortoiseshells . . . You know what, Miss Mull-Dare, you're right. I *do* feel better. Anything else you want to know about that unfortunate chancer, you just ask away. Go on. Now's the time.'

Hazel stared at her, blankly. *Miss Eunice? Red Admirals? What did they have to do with anything?*

'He was *blackmailing* me,' Miss Amelia continued, wanting it all off her chest now; babbling it up like bile. 'All charm, he was, while we drank our tea, but then nasty, nasty . . . demanding money, a very *large* sum of money, to keep quiet about the bruises on that awful girl's neck. I told Eunice it was all a fraud. Trick photography. A con. For I netted that girl carefully, *most* carefully, the way I've always netted my specimens, so as not to mark the skin. So yes, I killed him. Accidentally, mind, and under the greatest provocation. But then, you were there, dear heart. You heard how upset I was. You saw him trying to escape. All I did was throw his wretched umbrella. Didn't mean to puncture him . . . to spear him like a fish.'

Hazel nodded, as if she understood, as if it was all right. Spooling back, she remembered the way Val had remained slumped on the floor in the Whineys' hall, with his bottom in the air—not temporarily stunned, as she had foolishly assumed, but . . . but . . .

Poor Val. What a terrible thing . . . and not all right at all, however vile a person he had been. Appalled to think she had witnessed his death, without even realizing it, Hazel sent him a thought . . . a prayer . . . a sorry . . . which she fervently hoped would flutter, like the butterflies, above the place where he lay, and that he would know.

Then she looked straight at her teacher and said:

'Is he the only one?'

Miss Amelia looked perplexed.

'The only one what, dear heart?'

326

'The only . . . person . . . you've hurt. Badly, I mean. Has there been anybody else? Here on the island . . . in the forest? A child, perhaps?' Her heart was thumping, for she dreaded the answer.

Miss Amelia, however, adjusted her net, straightened her spine and replied, with the greatest indignation: 'Good gracious me, Miss Mull-Dare, whatever do you take me for?'

Slowly, Hazel let go of the tree. It was important, she told herself, to carry on walking now. To pretend everything was all right even though she still feared the worst. It was important to keep Miss Amelia from losing her temper, from exploding.

'All right,' she said. 'If you say so.'

'I most definitely do say so. Of all the blessed cheek . . . '

'But . . . if . . . Tommy John appears again, will you promise not to hurt him?'

'Hah!' Miss Amelia shouldered her net and turned away. 'That chancer! I'll send him packing all right. I've got my nerve up now.'

'But no more . . . bloodshed. Promise?'

'Oh no. No more of that, dear heart. I've already told you.'

A breeze had sprung up. Only a light one, no more than a whisper. And because it was barely cooling the sweat on Hazel's face, she paid it no mind.

'Did you bring a bottle of tea?' she asked, determined to keep things normal as they continued up the path.

Miss Amelia was way beyond *that* piece of pretence.

'Just the rum,' she snapped back. 'A full jar. For courage.'

By the time they reached the clearing the breeze was

whispering loud enough to make itself heard and the sky, now that they could see it better, looked different—still blue but ribbed by a succession of long, thin clouds, each one more ragged than the last.

'I've never seen clouds moving so fast,' observed Hazel. 'Perhaps Jeremiah was right. Perhaps we ought to go back.' She spoke reluctantly, unwilling to return to her grandparents' house until she knew for sure that Tommy John was unharmed.

'Turncoat!' Miss Amelia hissed. 'Traitor! I'll have no mutineers aboard. Leave me to it. Go on.'

She propped her net against the stone slab. Straight away it blew over.

She propped it again.

This time it blew away.

'Nothing wrong with a good stiff breeze,' she declared, scampering across the clearing. 'Stirs the blood. Shakes up the senses. A bit of a squall will flush that chancer out— and this time I'll be ready for him.'

So saying she retrieved the net, jammed it upright between two rocks, and set about unbuckling her satchel.

'I'll go for my walk then,' Hazel said to her. 'All right?' She was already moving away, desperate to get to Tommy John's house, to find out if he was safe.

'Yes, yes. Toodle-oo.'

The breeze, more of a light wind now, lifted the brim of Hazel's hat, making it flap as she scrambled out of the clearing. At the top of the ridge she paused and looked back. Miss Amelia was perched, majestically, on her slab, oblivious to the flapping of her own hat or the darkening of the clouds above her head. She was muttering to herself, the words blowing clean away before Hazel could catch them. And every few seconds—so frequently it was hardly worth lowering her arm in between times—she raised her specimen jar to her lips and took a hearty swig.

*Tommy John*, Hazel willed him. *If you're out here, give me a sign*.

Nothing.

Just the wind in the trees. Singing now, definitely singing, as the clouds began rolling like barrels right over the sun.

'COME ON, YOU VILE LITTLE MAN!' Miss Amelia hollered, raising her jar and drumming her heels on the side of the stone slab. 'GHOST . . . JUMBY . . . WHAT-EVER IT IS YOU'VE BECOME . . . FRIGHTENED OF ME NOW, ARE YOU? OR IS IT THE WHINING OF THE WIND KEEPING YOU AWAY? SHOW YOURSELF, YOU COW-ARD! YOU PATHETIC . . . KNOCK-KNEED . . . MEWLING LITTLE SPECIMEN . . . '

Somewhere out to sea—but still scarily close—lightning forked, filling the sky with an eerie light.

'COWAAAAAARD!' Miss Amelia yelled again, her head tipped back, her face gleeful, as the wind took her hat and bowled it away.

She was in her element, Hazel realized. As drunk as a fish and oblivious to any danger posed by the strengthening wind or the altering sky.

'MISS AMELIA,' she called down. 'WE NEED TO TAKE SHELTER. THERE'S A HURRICANE COMING. I KNOW SOMEWHERE WE CAN GET TO IN TIME, BUT WE'LL HAVE TO HURRY.'

Miss Amelia whipped round, her eyes blazing.

'GET LOST!' she shrieked. 'GO ON—SCRAM!' And she flung out both arms, embracing the wind as it filled her sleeves; willing it to blow, boys, blow; to swell the mainsail and set a course for dear old England.

'FAREWELL AND ADIEU TO YOU, SPANISH LADIES . . . FAREWELL AND ADIEU TO YOU, LADIES OF SPAIN . . . '

Hazel turned away.

*Oh, you mad, crazy woman . . . Well, I tried . . . I did my best . . . You'll just have to stay there . . . baying at nothing . . . singing at the sky . . . until this storm passes.*

Then she was walking against the wind, bending into it, feeling the pressure of it on the crown of her hat like the hand of a bully intent on pushing her back. And all around: the sighing of trees, as the song of the wind grew louder still, and the sky turned a violent purple.

*Hurry . . .* Hazel told herself. *Hurry, hurry, hurry . . . You can still manage the cliff path, so long as this wind doesn't get any worse.*

She had no idea, really, how bad a hurricane could get. Didn't know (for she had never been told or taught) that this was just a prelude to the main event; that the hurricane was miles out to sea still, gathering strength and speed.

Vines lashed at her head and her arms, flailing across her path like a cat-o'-nine-tails. She couldn't hear Miss Amelia any more. Didn't notice when her sailor-song ended and she began calling, once again . . . calling for Tommy John to come out, come out, wherever he was; come out and be a man.

Had Hazel stopped, then, and listened hard, she might have heard the call cut short—reduced to a terrified gurgle by the reply that came floating back through the shrieking of the weather.

'I'M HERE! TOMMY JOHN COMING TO GET YOU!'

*'They say that if you call a jumby's name and it answers, you'll be dead by sunset.'* If Miss Amelia remembered Louise Mull-Dare's words she didn't show it; only lifted her jar in one jittery hand and drank what was left in it. For courage.

'FOLLOW ME, TEACHER WOMAN. HERE I AM! FOLLOW ME!'

Had Hazel heard any of it, and hurried back to the clearing, she might have seen Miss Amelia spring from her rock and grab her net . . . tussling to keep a tight hold of it . . . needing both hands to do so as it caught the wind. And her heart would have leapt, in sheer relief, as Tommy John came bounding into view intent, out of the kindness of his heart, on leading Miss Amelia out of the forest before lightning could fry her, or a tree fall on her head.

She would have kept on thinking *'Thank goodness . . . thank goodness,'* as Tommy John began climbing the ridge towards her, his hair a shock of brilliance in the purple-blue light. And she would have hollered out a warning— a frantic, necessary warning—as Miss Amelia, after a moment's fascinated, rum-fuddled hesitation, raised her net high, against the buffeting of the wind, and went after him.

# CHAPTER 31

The hurricane struck when Hazel was three trees in, along the cliff-top path, and already calling herself a fool. It struck so hard she thought something solid must have hit her—a giant bird, the side of a house, a wave rearing up from the ocean.

Seconds later came the rain, battering her hat . . . drenching her clothes . . . running in icy rivulets up her nose and into her ears so that she thought it would swamp what little breath she had left in her after being knocked sideways, off her feet, by the hurricane's violent punch.

*I'm going to die . . . no, I'm not . . . I'm going to die . . . no, I'm not.*

Sprawled like a corpse but clinging with one hand, still, to the bent-over spine of a tree, she waited, her eyes sealed shut, her breath gurgling in her nose and throat, for the hurricane to do whatever hurricanes did to finish people off.

She assumed it would be quick. She believed she would be lifted up, like a rag or a twist of paper, and hurled through the air until she smashed against a rock or was dropped, like unwanted carrion, into a field of drowning cane.

She was sure that she herself—her will to live, her desperate hold on the tree—could be no match, in the end, against the power of this storm. It was awesome. It would show no mercy. And the thunder, and the lightning, were like the wrath of some god, calling her bad names and illuminating her final moments.

Hazel Louise Mull-Dare. Guilty by blood. Condemned to die for the sins of her fathers . . . pinned to the earth, like a butterfly on a board, before the hurricane took her away.

She began to cry, and then to scream.

*It's not fair. It's not fair.*

But *why isn't it fair?* shrieked the wind. *Because you're white and your name is Mull-Dare? Oh . . . this is fair, all right. As fair as anything ever gets. And your name, by the way, is Moulder . . .*

For seconds . . . minutes . . . she lay there, waiting for the inevitable. Numbed by shock and javelins of rain she gradually became aware of a throbbing in her left wrist—a dull ache, getting worse and worse the longer she strained to hold on to the tree. It only had to flip upright again, that tree, and she would go arching over the cliff like an arrow from a bow. And if the tree got uprooted she and it would go together, joined in the air like a witch and her broom.

'HEY! HEY! . . . YOU ALIVE? . . . YOU HANG ON . . . HANG ON, HAZEL MOULDER. I'LL HELP YOU . . . '

It was too dark for Hazel to see, nor could she summon the strength to speak as Tommy John came crawling towards her, his body flat to the ground so the hurricane couldn't knock him down and hurt him some more.

When his wet hair reached her face she turned against it, beyond tears.

'YOU ALIVE?' he bellowed in her ear.

'Yes,' she whimpered back.

'GOOD. YOU GOT TO MOVE. NOT SAFE HERE. THINGS FLYIN' AROUND.'

And then he was past her, inching painfully over and under the wind-bent limbs of the trees, hanging on where he could, bracing himself against whatever there was to cling to—a root, a branch, a tussock of flailing grass.

Realizing that it was possible . . . just possible . . . to move without getting whirled away, Hazel dared to let go of the tree; just for a second—two seconds—while she edged onto her stomach, the better to crawl. The wind caught her, rolled her . . . almost took her. But she grabbed the tree again, with both hands this time, and prepared to haul herself after Tommy John.

Her skirt . . . her skirt was a liability, sodden and twisted and catching on things. And her hat . . . how on earth had that stayed put on her head? How very well-mannered she must look. . . how ladylike . . .

'FOLLOW ME,' Tommy John yelled back at her. 'ONLY WAIT TILL THE LIGHTNING COMES, SO YOU KNOW WHERE I AM.'

She'd thought she *had* known where he was—which direction she should go in—but it was too dark . . . too dangerous . . . and she couldn't tell any more whether forward led to safety or the very edge of the cliff.

She thought, wildly, of Miss Amelia. Would she be safe, back there in the clearing?

Then the island lit up like a stage and she scrambled for her life.

The house was shaking. The house was trembling fit to bust apart.

Zebenjo stopped his pacing. 'Enough!' he said. 'I go look for him.'

Abidemi stretched out her hand. 'No,' she said. 'Don't.'

He shook his head, bashed a fist into the flat of his other hand. 'I can't stay here all useless,' he told her, 'cooped up like the goat while the boy out there someplace.'

Outside something heavy struck the tin roof, bounced off and flew away.

'You go out there,' Abidemi said, 'you be killed for certain. Tommy John in God's keeping now. God decide what happen to that child.'

*And the one my mumma named after,* she thought without saying it . . . *The goddess Isis will watch over Tommy John.*

Closing her eyes, blocking her ears to the shriek of the wind . . . the bleating of the goat . . . the helpless rage of her man . . . Abidemi began to pray:

*Isis, queen of the heavens, mother of all things . . . be with my son now and for ever . . . Isis, dark goddess of magic and motherhood, look after Tommy John . . . Isis whose symbols are hair braids and knots, buckles and stars, wings and milk and the empty throne . . .*

'Mumma! Mumma!'

Hazel couldn't believe the little house was still standing.

Logic told her it should have been one of the first things to go: huffed and puffed to splinters by the hurricane's first breath.

Tommy John had her by the hand. He had tugged her all the way down the slope, hauling her up when the wind threw them down, knowing his way by instinct through the mayhem and the dark.

'*Mumma!*'

The door blew in. Fell in. Caved in. Hazel never knew. But somehow they were through it and somehow it blew or fell or got shoved back shut and they were standing, at last, in a space that wasn't whirling round their ears or tearing at their clothes or beating them with rain.

And the lightning that rent the sky at that moment—directly overhead and so loud it hurt—lit the little room like Christmas. Just for a moment, for the briefest flash of time, but long enough for Hazel to see the gouts of blood all over her clothes, and in Tommy John's hair, before she crumpled at the knees and fainted.


'You been calling out for someone.'

'Have I?'

'A Miss Gun or somesuch. Told us she was still out there, alone in the forest. Lie still now. Storm passing. Worst is over, I reckon.'

'Tommy John. Is he all right?'

'His head got bashed but it looked worse than it is. He sleeping now.'

'And Miss Amelia . . . Miss Gumm, my teacher . . . She's not . . . ?'

'Zebenjo gone looking. We'll know what's what with her soon enough, I reckon.'

Hazel closed her eyes. She was lying on a bed of cushions, wrapped in an eiderdown, and every bit of her was beginning to ache. She'd thought, when she came to, that her hat was still on but it was just the mark under her chin she could feel, where the wet elastic had rubbed and chafed.

'And you're all right, in case you're wonderin',' Abidemi added. 'Just dizzied around some. A few scratches. One or two bruises later maybe.'

Hazel managed a nod.

'We've been lucky, haven't we?' she said. 'Me and Tommy John. We could have been killed out there.'

She was starting to shiver; her teeth rattling in her head.

The cup Abidemi held to her lips had rum in it, and some kind of herb that stuck to her teeth like spinach.

'Abidemi?' she said, eyes wide open now, her mouth and throat tingling.

'Yes now?'

'I got things wrong before. There were things I didn't know.'

Abidemi tutted, softly.

'That day done and gone,' she said. 'I was harsh on you. It takes big trouble, sometimes, to push little troubles out the door. That hurricane done a bit of good maybe. And hey—our house still standing. Zebenjo right. This dip of land the right place to be when the wind blow so hard it scatter the days of the week.'

The rum and the eiderdown were warming Hazel up.

Before long she would be able to move. Shyly, she studied the contours of Abidemi's face . . . searching . . . wondering.

'Is it really true that you are my sister?' she said after a while. 'My half-sister, I mean? My father Maurice's child?'

'So they tell me,' Abi replied, evenly. 'Though I miss out on those ugly nose blobs, I'm glad to say. Tommy John too.'

Laughing hurt. Laughing made hurricane-bruised ribs twinge like you wouldn't believe. But Hazel couldn't help it. She laughed so loudly that the goat began to bleat in alarm and Tommy John stirred and opened his eyes.

'Hey, heart-string,' his mother murmured to him. 'You back with us now? You want some soup?'

Tommy John touched the back of his head, found it had stopped bleeding so left it alone. That long teacher woman had wanted his hide for sure. Twice she had cracked that net of hers smack-down on his skull. Third time she would have got him for certain, netted him like a butterfly-boy if he hadn't run her right to the very edge of the cliff, then dodged.

'What so funny, Moulder girl?' he said. 'Why you laughing like a crazy person?'

Hazel wiped her eyes.

'I don't know,' she said. 'I honestly do not know.'

*Farewell and adieu to you, Spanish ladies . . . farewell and . . . adieu . . . to you, ladies . . . of . . . Spain.*

*The decks of warships, in Nelson's day, were painted red to disguise the gore of battle . . . If you swore, or used mutinous language, Nelson had you flogged and when the coffee ran out you scraped burnt toast into a mug of water . . . Nelson loathed the Caribbean; kept a barrel of rum aboard his frigate, to preserve his body and deliver it home, should the fever take him . . . He saw off biting insects by igniting gunpowder in an iron pan and sprinkling vinegar over it . . . A man of the arts though . . . Encouraged amateur theatricals during the hurricane season when it was prudent to stay indoors (ha!ha!). Was particularly fond of Shakespeare . . .*

Amelia Gumm didn't know how she knew all of this, but she did.

Worse, it seemed to her she could smell the gunpowder, hear the bad language and—oh dear, yes, she might have known that a coarse sea-faring specimen like Horatio Nelson would favour *King Lear* . . .

When she came to her senses—or what were left of them—on the bit of a ledge that had broken her fall when she tumbled over the cliff in pursuit of Tommy John, she thought, at first, she had been napping on her slab, so tried her best to get up. Had her legs worked, she would have swung herself into a straight, sheer drop.

Confused . . . unable to move . . . not in agony yet, but about to be . . . she squinted up at the sky. The storm had passed (she had been out cold for most of it) and the clouds were thinning to let in a watery light.

She could hear the sea—a furious boiling way below—and as she lay there, still wondering why, a great wodge of cliff-dirt, loosened by the wind, came sliding down and hit her smack in the face.

It was bad bananas for Miss Amelia Gumm.

It was very grim biscuits indeed.

Whimpering, and spitting grit, she scrabbled weakly

around for her net. It wasn't there. Scrabbling further, as far as she could reach, her fingers encountered the rim of the ledge and the great big nothing beyond.

Then she remembered. Then she realized where she was. And closing her eyes, and opening her mouth, she began to scream.


Zebenjo had been about to give up when he heard the noise. He had found big trees flattened, seen the cane fields under lakes of mud, heard birds commence to sing as if nothing much had happened. No sign of any white woman though, dead or alive.

He was about to head for the Mull-Dare house, knowing the old ones there would be worrying sick about their girl, and in need of reassurance. After that he would go to the places all around where, he knew, the hurricane would have taken a terrible toll. He would do what he could, for the people affected and so, he hoped, would Massa Giddy.

When he reached the cliff edge and looked down he had to close his disbelieving eyes for a moment and then open them again, in case what he saw turned out to be a mirage—or a jumby come to lure him to his doom.

But the woman on the ledge was real all right. As real as Sunday morning and cursing like a pirate. How to fetch her up from there though? That was going to be a tricky thing. She was too far down to be got unless . . .

He could have gone to the Mull-Dares for the necessary rope but did not want to waste precious time. The woman might need hospital attention. And if she didn't, there were sure to be others, trapped in flattened houses on the other side of the cane fields, who would; so the sooner he dealt with this the better.

Peering back over the cliff he saw that the ledge the woman was sprawled along was not a thing of permanence. It was shedding itself in stops and starts; bits of stone and slips of earth falling and rattling straight down to where the ocean frothed on killer rocks.

That was it then. No choice.

The belt holding his trousers up went four times round his waist, with a good loop at one end. It was made from thick strands of plaited goatskin and had done service in its time as a clothes line, or a means of securing baskets to a donkey. It was as strong as any rope and just about long enough, he reckoned, for what he needed to do.

The closest tree, he was glad to discover, was not a fig. But whether it would bear the weight of two people, or had been weakened by the hurricane enough to pop its roots, he supposed he would very soon find out.

Throwing his fallen-down trousers under the nearest bush he looped the all-purpose belt around the tree, pulled hard to test its security, and then lowered himself hand over hand down over the edge of the cliff.

So hysterically was Amelia Gumm shrieking, and so tightly shut were her eyes, that she neither saw nor heard Zebenjo until he was angled directly above her, bracing his weight against the face of the cliff and twisting his head round to speak.

'You got to grab my hand,' he called, relieved that she had stopped screaming and that he had her full attention.

341

'You got to heave yourself up and then hang on to me tight. I step on that bit of cliff you're on it could break clean away then we both go fallin'—and that sea ain't got no back door. You hear what I'm sayin'?'

He could feel the strain on his rope. Please Lord it wasn't frayed any place, or cuttin' through that skinny tree like a wire through cheese. This woman could have snapped some bones or done bad damage to her head. But the will to live, he knew, was a mighty powerful thing and could blot out the worst pain. If her neck was broke she was doomed. If not, she had a chance.

'You got ten seconds, teacher-lady,' he said, sweat popping on his forehead. 'Otherwise I'm done here.'

Amelia Gumm . . . murderess, teacher of etiquette, despiser of 'darkies' . . . stared boggle-eyed at what she could see of Zebenjo, which was plenty.

*Devil!* she thought, wildly. *I am caught between the devil and the deep dark sea!*

Beside her head, just inches from her left ear, a sizeable chunk of the ledge broke, like pie crust, and fell away. A bird—a big one—circled over her head. Vulture? No. A pelican.

'For pity's sake, lady,' Zebenjo called down. 'Do what you got to do. Come on now.'

His fingers were straining to reach her; his face ugly from the effort of hanging on. But no man could have looked less devilish, or so oblivious of his naked state as he willed her to take his hand. He was risking his life, Miss Amelia realized. And he was her only hope.

Her neck (unbroken) moved to order. So did her shoulders, her arms, and her spine. Her legs, however,

342

being smashed in several places, were nowhere near as co-operative.

'*Too late!*' Zebenjo cried, as the ledge cracked, audibly. '*May God have mercy on you . . .*'

And then, as the whole ledge shifted beneath her, and began to tear away, Miss Amelia stood. With a movement so agonizing that she almost passed out, and a cry so awful it scared every flying, crawling creature within earshot she grasped hold of that helping hand and rose to her feet.

'*High on me back . . . Jump! Jump! You got about three seconds . . . one second!*'

And oh, if standing had been agony, scrambling up the torso of another human being, with its slippy-soft skin, and sad lack of footholds, was pure torture. But she did it. Like many a trapped creature given just seconds to live and only one way out, she leapt for her life and she made it.

'*Good . . . job . . . you not . . . fat . . . as well as . . . long . . .*' huffed Zebenjo, before saving his breath for a short but treacherous climb up a belt that might not hold and a cliff that was crumbling faster than sugar-cake.

'*Heave* away,' he chanted in his head, to keep himself focused as he carried his burden upwards. '*Haul* away . . .'

And as the remains of the ledge hit the rocks and the sea, Amelia Gumm pressed her pain-racked face against the black of his neck and knew herself unworthy.

343

# CHAPTER 32

Everything is all right. Everything is fine. And I want you to know about my family's side of things which, I hope you will agree, puts us all in a better light.

After the hurricane we sat down and talked—me, my grandparents, my sister Abidemi, and my nephew Tommy John.

And the most important thing I learned is that my father did not run across the sea to hide from trouble, as you said he did. He loved Isis and she loved him. It just wasn't a match that could ever end in marriage because of all the prejudice in the world, and because my father had a duty, the same as my aunt Alison, to return to our family's roots in England and marry up (in actual fact he married down, but that is another story).

My father never knew that Isis was going to have his baby because he left this island before she found out that she was pregnant. Nor was my father ever told about her death or about anything to do with

Abidemi or Tommy John because my grandparents thought it was for the best.

My grandfather swore to me, on my
grandmother's life, that he DID send for a
doctor for Isis. It was the doctor's choice
not to come because he was a white man
who would not treat black people.

My grandparents are very fond of Abi and
dote on Tommy John. It upset them to have to
tell Tommy John to stay away from this house
for as long as I was here, but they did not
know what else to do. They have tried to help
Abi with money and things but, as she herself
admits, she has been too proud a lot of the
time to accept anything from them. She says
now that she will let them help a bit more.

My grandparents told me they are very
sorry for having kept Abi and Tommy John a
secret for so long but they genuinely believed it was in everybody's best interests.


The reply came several days later. Just one line, the letters hard to make out, as if the typewriter's ribbon was
fading:

They would say that wouldn't they.

Miss Amelia Gumm was to spend many weeks at the
hospital in the town, waiting for her bones to heal and
her mind to settle. Louise Mull-Dare visited often, not

minding that her stream of chatter appeared to be falling on deaf ears.

'No more gadding about the rainforest for *you*, my dear Miss Fritillary,' she announced, some six weeks after the hurricane. 'The doctors say you will be confined to a wheelchair for quite some time to come and in need of round-the-clock care when you finally leave this hospital. Well, you're not to worry. I've spoken to Giddy and he agrees: you are to stay on with us and *I* will look after you. How about that?'

Miss Amelia's smile was like rigor mortis.

'And you're not to fret about Hazel,' Louise Mull-Dare continued, happily. 'She is a bright girl and perfectly capable of absorbing the lessons in that little book of yours all by herself. And when the time comes for her to return to England we can easily find her a chaperone among other passengers on the list. You must concentrate on getting well, Miss Fritillary—or may I call you Amelia? No . . . don't thank me, dear. Just concentrate, as I said, on regaining a little strength; enough, at least, for a nice game of whist when we finally get you home. The roses have perked up, I'm delighted to say, and I'm thinking of ordering new curtains for the dining room. The old ones are terribly faded, as I'm sure you've noticed, but that's hardly surprising, is it, since they've been up now for . . . oh . . . at least twenty years. Giddy says we can't really afford new curtains until we know for sure that the sugar has survived. But I'll talk him round. I always do. I was thinking a nice blue. Or turquoise maybe. I have some swatches of material right here in my bag. Look, I'll hold them up and you can blink to say which you prefer. Two blinks for the blue, three for the turquoise. What fun! And, oh—I see you are blinking already, in anticipation . . . '

HANDKERCHIEF: *a handkerchief when borrowed must never be returned to the owner soiled. It should be sent to the laundry and returned with a note of thanks.*

HANDSHAKING: *heartiness and cordiality should be expressed without the slightest approach to boisterousness.*

HERALDRY: *when a man marries he impales his wife's paternal arms by placing them upright on the left side of his own in the same escutcheon. The arms of a widow are composed of her husband's and her father's impaled within a lozenge. Those of a maiden lady are her father's only, or quartered with those of her mother, if she were an heiress. Ladies may place their arms in a lozenge, but not in a shield.*

Enough.

Enough, enough, enough.

'Grandma,' Hazel said, 'if you don't mind, I would like to take my typewriter into the room where I've been doing my lessons. I'll learn faster, I think, by typing things out.'

'If you say so, dear,' her grandmother replied. 'I'll get someone to carry it for you. Jeremiah! *Jeremiah!*'

Winsome had been in and tidied Hazel's bedroom, so everything was in its place and looking neat as Jeremiah crossed over to the table where the typewriter stood. Hazel hopped and hovered anxiously behind him, wanting to help but aware that any offer to do so might cause offence.

The whole room was bathed in sunlight; the mosquito net hanging motionless, the picture of the bluebell wood baking on the wall. There was no reason for Jeremiah to shiver as he passed beside the bed, but he did.

'Oh—are you all right?' exclaimed Hazel. 'If you think the typewriter's too heavy for just one person to lift I'll . . . '

'Someone die in this room,' he said.

Hazel gazed at him, not frightened, just surprised.

'This was my aunt Alison's room,' she told him. 'Before she left the island. Since then it's been a guest room—only, since I'm the first guest practically in living memory, whoever died in here must have done it a very long time ago.'

Jeremiah was staring at the bed in sadness and wonder, as if the mosquito net surrounding it was a veil between two worlds. 'Maybe,' he murmured, heavily. 'Maybe not.'

Then he picked up the typewriter as if it was a clattery child, and carried it easily away.

Louise Mull-Dare was fussing with mats and cloths, trying to decide which one would look best beneath the typewriter, while protecting her good table from scratches. 'There's at least another hour before luncheon,' she said, as Jeremiah and Hazel came in. 'So I suggest you carry on with your studies, Hazel dear. Goodness me, that's quite a contraption, isn't it? Whoever invented such a thing? Call me old-fashioned, but pen and ink have served mankind perfectly well down the centuries and will continue to do so, I'm sure, long after these monstrosities have had their day.'

Left alone, Hazel lifted the lid from her typewriter, wound in a fresh sheet of paper and wondered what to put. Her diary seemed an obvious and neglected project but where would she start? And what would she say?

What truths would she commit to paper and what would she leave out?

She ought, she knew, to write to her mother and father. But again, saying what?

For a long time she sat there, staring out of the window into perfect, cloudless blue; hearing laughter from the kitchen and the chink of plates.

Then:

WHO ARE YOU? she typed, in bold, black capitals before leaving the room, to wash her hands for luncheon.

She did not, in all honesty, expect a reply so was neither offended or surprised when none came. For several weeks she attended to her lessons ('introductions', 'invitations', 'jewellery', 'knives and forks', 'luncheons', 'menus', 'monograms', and 'neatness') winding the WHO ARE YOU? out of the typewriter first thing, and putting it back again after her morning's work was done.

It crossed her mind that she was more likely to get a reply if the typewriter went back into her bedroom, but she told herself it would be too much trouble, now, to have it moved again.

In the afternoons, Tommy John came to meet her, striding up the drive to the house as if he already owned the place and bursting with ideas as to how he and his aunt Hazel Moulder would spend a bit of time. One afternoon Zebenjo took them fishing—rocking out to sea in a small wooden boat—and Hazel surprised herself by hating the whole experience.

You are right, she wrote in a long-overdue letter to her mother, fish really do have faces. I hadn't paid much attention before, when they were on my plate with peas and things, but when I caught one, and it went flapping around the bottom of the boat, trying its best to stay alive, it looked straight at me and I felt terrible.

'Tell me about your mumma,' Abidemi asked her one day, as they sat on her porch sipping lime juice and watching the goat.

'My mother,' Hazel replied, 'is . . . I don't know . . . she's hard to describe. Sometimes I think she would have been happier—or just as happy anyway—if she had never got married or had me. I was born when she and Daddy were already quite old, you know—over forty. Daddy says I was an unexpected gift. I think he thought he would never have . . . oh, I'm sorry, Abi, what a stupid thing to say.'

Abi smiled, lazily. She had asked very little about Hazel's . . . her . . . their . . . father and whenever Hazel talked specifically about him she listened more from politeness, it seemed, than genuine interest.

'It don't matter,' she said now. 'Things are how they are. I got my son. I got my man. I'm happy in my skin.'

Hazel nodded gravely.

'You going to tell him?' Abidemi asked her. 'About me and Tommy John?'

'Yes . . . I suppose so . . . when I get home. I just can't imagine what he'll say . . . how he'll react . . . '

Abidemi laid a sisterly hand on her arm. 'No need to go tellin' him on my account,' she said. 'Or Tommy John's either. What we never had we don't miss. And last thing we need is Maurice Moulder coming back to this island with his face full of guilt, wishing we had no existence but pretending to us, and to you, that we got some importance in his fine life.'

'His life isn't all that fine,' Hazel told her. 'Believe me it isn't. And anyway, Tommy John wants to come to England one day. He told me so.'

'Hah!' Abidemi tipped back her head and gazed up at the sky, narrowing her eyes against the glare. 'You see Tommy John fitting in over there?' she said. 'You think white folk get to see beyond the look of him? He get his spirit broke for sure, that boy. He end up hating every bit of himself and goin' bad inside. No. Tommy John better off stayin' here.'

Aware that she was probably right, and having no reason to believe that one day, when Tommy John was grown, attitudes might have changed, Hazel fished a slice of lime from her empty glass and began, very slowly, to eat it. The taste made her face pucker worse than a Granny Sooker. Without sugar, it was unpalatable.

'I wish . . . ' she began, then paused before continuing: 'I wish your mother hadn't died. I wish you could have known her, at least.'

Abidemi smiled. 'Sometimes,' she said, 'I get the feelin' she's around. Watchin' out for me and Tommy John. But she gets all muddled up, in this head of mine, with the goddess she was named for, so I end up thinkin' she was more than she was. More powerful, I mean. It's just wishfulness, I reckon—just me tryin' to keep her alive in my heart.'

And then Hazel told her about the ebony statue of Isis that their father kept on his desk; about the softness that came into his eyes whenever he looked at it and how it was so precious to him that servants had never been allowed to dust it, in case it fell and broke.

And not only did Abidemi look interested, at last, but her own eyes got that exact-same softness, just from listening and imagining, and Hazel was glad. 'Here,' she said. 'Why don't you have this? I think you should—I'd like you to.' Impulsively, she undid the brooch on her blouse (the letter 'I' with most of its stones missing) and held it out to Abidemi on the palm of her hand.

'Your mother and my mother,' she said, as Abi looked questioningly down. 'Their initial is the same. "I" for Ivy and "I" for Isis. You could wear this, couldn't you . . . ?' Her voice faltered suddenly. Not in case she had offended her sister but because . . .

Abidemi reached out, then, took hold of Hazel's hand, and gently curved the fingers around Ivy Mull-Dare's brooch until it was hidden from them both, like the kernel of a nut.

'You keep it, sweet girl,' she said, quietly. 'It a gift to you from your mumma, and you lucky to have her on this earth, I reckon, for however long a time. I got plenty gifts from my mumma already. They just not the kind you can see is all.'

Back at her grandparents' house, while supper was being served, Hazel thought about asking Gideon and Louise which room Abidemi's mother had died in. But it seemed there was no way to phrase such a question without sounding crude and ill-mannered. And anyway, she decided, what would knowing prove?

WHO ARE YOU?

The question nagged less and less as Christmas

approached. On some mornings, after getting through yet another solitary lesson in etiquette ('opera', 'postponements', 'receptions', 'receiving royalty', 'servants', 'soup', 'surnames', 'slang', 'tips', and 'toothpicks' . . . ) she forgot to wind the piece of paper with the question on it back into the typewriter.

By the time she finally reached 'weddings', 'whispering', and 'wine', and could look forward to closing *Cassell's Dictionary of Etiquette* for ever, the paper had fallen to the floor and she had forgotten about it completely.

# CHAPTER 33

The letter came four days before Christmas, along with a card that had a drawing on the front of a bulldog dressed as Santa Claus. Louise Mull-Dare read the card first, before unfolding the letter, and said it was from Maurice and Ivy.

'Not Maurice's usual thing at all,' she sniffed. 'He usually sends us a nice Nativity scene, doesn't he, Giddy? And this isn't his writing.' She looked across the table at Hazel, who had her own card from home, and presents too, but was planning to save them for Christmas morning.

Hazel looked back calmly.

'Maybe Daddy wasn't up to writing cards this year,' she said. 'He's still convalescing after all.'

'I'm sure you're right,' her grandmother replied. 'Christmas is bound to seem tawdry when you're fighting your way back to health. And then there's all the worry he has over losing the house, the poor dear.'

Gideon Mull-Dare, still hot and bothered after his trip into town to collect the post and deliver a rum-sodden fruit cake to poor old Miss Frit, slurped his soup and grunted. He would barely have time to digest this spot of lunch before heading back to the cane fields where the new crop was so sparse and storm-damaged they would be lucky to break even with it, never mind make a profit.

'Douglas will take 'em in,' he said. 'The blighter's wealthy enough, and there's bound to be a turret or two going spare in that castle of his. How would you feel about living in Scotland, young Hazel, eh? A bit chilly and grim it'll be, after living here.'

Hazel hadn't given much thought to her parents'—or her own—prospects back in Britain. With so much to get used to in the here and now, her past and her future seemed distant and misty. A lot like Scotland, in fact. She and Tommy John were about to decorate the dining room with poinsettias from the garden—big red flowers that made her think of robins, and children's mittens, and would add a traditional touch to what was otherwise going to be a very unconventional Christmas indeed.

*Scotland* . . .

On Boxing Day she, Abidemi, Zebenjo, and Tommy John were going into town for the annual carnival procession: painted acrobats and whirling tumblers . . . white-cloaked 'Long Ghosts' and 'Moko-jumbies' striding about on stilts . . . drums and shakers, ching-a-chings and boompipes . . . folk wearing animal horns and witch-doctor masks . . .

She was planning to let her hair down.

*Scotland* . . .

Aunt Alison might, even now, be making a list of all the eligible bachelors in the Highlands. Soon she would be dropping hints to their mamas about her sweet young niece, currently completing her education abroad, but soon to return to the fold. Hazel Louise Mull-Dare. A perfect English rose with a pedigree as pure as the driven snow.

Just thinking about what life would be like for her in Scotland, with Aunt Alison plotting her future and all those eligible bachelors lined up, like tartan skittles, made her feel bleak. And would she ever see London again? Or any of the girls from school?

Gloria Gilbert would have returned weeks ago from her holiday in Italy. Thinking about her was like probing a bad tooth and finding it strangely better. Had Gloria ever tried to trace Val? Hazel wondered. Well, she herself would never tell her—or indeed anyone else—about that chancer's death. What would be the point? It had been an accident, after all, and Miss Amelia was in no fit state to return to England, or to ever face a trial. No . . . Miss Amelia would remain on this island for the rest of her days. Trapped in a chair and haunted. You had to feel just a little bit sorry, Hazel thought, for that old Whiney Gumm.

Then: 'Oh my goodness,' Louise Mull-Dare exclaimed. 'Well . . . I . . . never . . . '

'What? *What is it*?'

It wasn't bad news, Hazel could tell. But from the tone of her grandmother's voice it was definitely something unexpected. A real turn up for the books.

'Come on, Lou,' said Giddy Mull-Dare, gruffly. 'Spit it out.'

Louise Mull-Dare read the letter again, mouthing each word silently. Then: 'It's *Ivy*,' she said. 'She has inherited a house—two houses—and a substantial sum of money from an artist she used to model for. She says here—her spelling is quite dreadful—she says she hadn't seen this artist, this Oscar Aretino Frosdick, for almost forty years. But it seems he died a bachelor, with no dependants and no one left alive who might have contested the will. He left everything to her. To Ivy. *Every*thing. All his worldly goods . . . '

*Well . . .*

Hazel listened, amazed, as her grandmother read the final few lines of the letter aloud:

'*There are two houses. The first is in London, close by the river in Chelsea. The other is a manor*—spelt m-a-n-n-e-r, but never mind—*in the countryside near Oxford. The one in Chelsea is where we are going to go and live, starting in January. The dogs will be very happy there and so, I hope, will Hazel.*'

*Well, well, well . . .*

Gideon Mull-Dare grunted and pushed away his soup dish. In a flash the bird with the yellow breast flew straight to the table and snatched up a piece of leftover bread. It was a hefty morsel for such a dainty little bird. But it took it with surprising ease, flying away over the veranda rail and up into a tree to enjoy its treat in safety.

'So,' said Giddy Mull-Dare. 'Our son married himself an artist's model, did he? First I've heard of it. I thought Ivy's people were In Groceries.'

Hazel was watching for the bird, wondering if it had a nest out there somewhere with chicks and a mate to feed. 'At least they weren't In Slavery,' she said, icily. Then, while both her grandparents trawled their minds for something worth saying, she opened her own card from home.

The pencil sketch on the front of the card showed two

dogs, of indeterminate breed, snout to snout and beaming, soppily, beneath a sprig of mistletoe.

Inside the message was short and simple: *'Now you can marry up or down or not at all and love whoever you will.'*

It was the first and only lesson Hazel ever took to heart.

*'What we get to do today, Moulder girl? Your last day. Got to do something special, I reckon.'*

*'I'd like to go swimming, with you and Massa—with your great-grandfather. Then, this evening, I want us all to eat at the big house, just like we did on Christmas Day.'*

*'Zebenjo too?'*

*'Zebenjo too. The whole family.'*

*'And you'll come back soon, to spend a bit of time with me and my mumma? Next Christmas maybe?'*

*'I don't know, Tommy John. I'd like to, but I can't promise.'*

*'One day I come to England for Christmas. Meet my grandfather Moulder. See the white snow covering all of London town. You get to have acrobats over there at Christmas, and Long Ghosts playing ching-a-chings?'*

*'No, Tommy John. Everything's very different in England.'*

*'At Christmas time you mean?'*

*'I mean all of the time.'*

*'Maybe I do some acrobatics when I come to England. Tell English peoples about the Long Ghosts and the Moko-jumbies and teach them to play the ching-a-chings and so on. Then Santa Claus and me and you, and my grandfather*

*Moulder, get to dance with the Moko-jumbies and we all have a good party through the snow. That sound like a good idea to you?'*

*'It sounds like a beautiful idea to me.'*

*'Then that's what will happen I reckon when Tommy John come to England, to spend a bit of time.'*


'This is it, Miss Mull-Dare. Cheyne Walk. And there's the house. Expect you'll be glad to see inside the old place again after all these months. No place like home, as they say.'

'Yes,' Hazel replied, too exhausted to explain as the hired chauffeur brought the hired car to a halt. 'Thank you.'

She stumbled a little on her sea legs as she stepped from the car to the pavement. It was warm, for March, but still she shivered. And the colours—everything looked so pale and prissy . . . pale primroses edging a path; pale buds, prissily furled; a haze of palest green on pale English trees.

Leaving the chauffeur to sort out her luggage Hazel started walking towards a freshly-painted front door. Halfway up the path she stopped, smiled, and stepped over something. As if on cue, the dogs began to bark. Pipkin's yap, Diggy Bert's gruffer woof, Dottie's and Rascal's excited yelps . . . she recognized each one, and braced herself for the onslaught—her first proper welcome since leaving the ship.

At the steps to the door she hesitated. Would her parents know, just by looking at her, that something had happened? That she had learned far more, during her time away, than the A to Z of etiquette?

During the long voyage home, and increasingly often as the ship edged closer to Southampton, she had asked herself: *Should I tell my father what I know?* And the further they had sailed, away from the island, the bigger the knowledge had swollen until it seemed she must either shriek it to the heavens or burst like a fruit from the pressure.

She missed Tommy John and Abidemi very much. She missed her grandparents, for all their faults and flaws. She even missed mad old Miss Amelia Gumm twittering 'quick sticks!' and bawling out a song.

She wasn't really seeing the door when it opened. Hadn't even realized that the dogs had quietened down. In her mind she was back in the Caribbean . . . seeing it, hearing it . . . smelling it . . .

*Will I tell my father what I've learned?* Back in England, on the steps of her mother's house, she really did not know.

'Hazel . . . '

Instinctively she flinched away, expecting any second to be knocked flying by Diggy Bert or drooled on by Dottie and Pipkin.

But: 'I've shut them in the drawing room, pet,' her mother said. 'Just until you're in and we've had a chance to welcome you home.' Then she held out her arms for a hug.

Florence . . . Cook . . . Mrs Sawyer . . . there they were, all three of them, waiting at a respectful distance just along the hall. The same women, yet different somehow in Hazel's eyes as she beamed shyly over her mother's shoulder, wrapped up still in her hug.

Then she was walking down another hall, with pictures on the walls. Big, gilt-framed pictures which she had never seen in Kensington. The first one showed a red-headed girl perched in a tree, playing some kind of harp. The second showed the same girl holding an apple. There was a snake coiling round her legs—at least Hazel assumed it was meant to be a snake although it looked to her more like a piece of rope. In the third frame the girl was floating in a river, her arms outflung, flowers caught in her hair and the lavender brocade of her dress.

'That's you, isn't it?' Hazel said to her mother.

'Yes,' Ivy Mull-Dare replied. 'That's me. The young me, anyway—or, rather, the me that poor Oscar Frosdick wanted, and chose, to see.'

Hazel nodded. She understood.

Her mother touched her arm. 'Your father's in the garden,' she said. 'And he's longing to see you.'

And then her mother slipped away, and the servants too went back about their business, and Hazel was alone, stepping into and through a glass conservatory and from there into the garden.

She saw her father before he saw her.

*Smaller*, she thought. *He looks smaller than I remember*.

He was sitting in a chair, with a rug over his knees, staring up at the sky through the blossom-tipped branches of an old plum tree.

'Hello, Daddy,' Hazel said, tears stinging her eyes as she stepped closer to his chair . . . saw the lines in his face, and the white in his hair, that had not been there before.

He flinched. She had startled him. A copy of *The Times* slid from his lap and landed all anyhow on the grass, its pages flapping like tongues.

'Hello, pet,' he said, his voice cracking.

And it was all there, right there in his face, as she hurried the rest of the way across the lawn. *Have I failed her? Does she despise me? Is she still my little girl? What's the betting she's ashamed of me now, for being such a failure. What are the odds?*

The Caribbean, Hazel realized, and everything to do with it, were the last things on her father's mind. He was stuck in the here and now, a fragile foolish man with a wife who appeared, after all, to have married a long way down and a daughter he might no longer be able to charm.

Isis—the real Isis—meant nothing to him any more. And he did not deserve, Hazel saw it straight away, to know about Abidemi and Tommy John. Not because it would break him but because they were better than he was and he would never see it. Never value them—treasure them—as he should.

And so Hazel hugged her father, crying for loss and for love, in forgiveness and disappointment, for the times that were gone and the different times to come.

'Well then,' he said, trying hard, through his own tears, to be jovial; to restore the old balance between them. 'Anything exciting happen on that island? I'll bet a quarter of humbugs it didn't.'

'You win, Daddy,' Hazel lied. 'You win.'

Julie Hearn was born in Abingdon, near Oxford, and has been writing all her life. After training as a journalist she went to Australia where she worked on a daily tabloid newspaper. She then lived in Spain for a while before returning to England where she worked as a features editor on a chain of weekly newspapers as well as writing freelance for magazines and the national press. After her daughter was born she went back to her studies and obtained a BA in English and an MSt in women's studies. She is now a full time writer. Her first novel, *Follow Me Down*, was published to much critical acclaim in 2003. *Hazel* is her fourth novel for Oxford University Press.

# Other books by Julie Hearn

'a beautifully crafted, spine-tingling story'
*Daily Telegraph*

'a corker of a novel, original and
rambunctious.'
*Observer*

'[a] roller-coaster read that's full of drama.'
Mizz

'Hearn has the skill of a conjuror and her
novel casts a spell'
*Sunday Times*

'This truly superb novel will have your
heart racing, your hands sweating and
your brain whirring. You must read it.'
*Guardian*

'a joy to read, this fast-paced story
deserves to be a best-seller'
*Bookseller*

'Ivy is yet another spellbinding turn from
Julie Hearn . . . a colourful and
lyrical novel'
*Becky Stradwick, Bookseller*